Rave reviews for J.A. JANCE, *New York Times* and *USA Today* bestselling author

DEADLY STAKES

"Jance melds elements of the thriller and police procedural with a touch of romance to carry readers swiftly to an unexpected conclusion."

—*Kirkus Reviews*

"Jance's story is well-crafted and keeps one's interest to its final word. . . . The rapidly moving story makes it a fascinating mystery, full of multiple suspects and numerous possibilities."

—*Bookreporter*

"Jance does her usual skillful job setting several story lines in motion and then tying them up neatly at the end."

—*Woman Around Town*

"It is easy to get carried along by a Jance story, and this one is no exception."

—*Mystery Maven Blog*

"Jance gets the action flowing from the beginning of the book and it continues throughout with plot twists and turns that leave you on the edge of your seat."

—*Fiction Addict*

LEFT FOR DEAD

"Jance at her best . . . engaging, exciting, and fast-paced."

—*Tucson Citizen*

"A truly thrilling case with red herrings, characters coming out of the woodwork, backstories that will make you gasp, and a conclusion that you will not see coming!"

—*Suspense Magazine*

CRUEL INTENT

"Compelling . . . satisfying."

—USA Today

"A fast-paced read with as many twists and turns as a county fair roller coaster."

—Seattle Post-Intelligencer

"Jance has honed her talent for writing entertaining, accessible mysteries that readers can zip through."

—Booklist

"An enjoyable and easy read . . . perfect for a weekend in front of the fireplace."

—Sacramento Book Review

HAND OF EVIL

"Entertaining. . . . Jance fits together the many pieces of this literary jigsaw puzzle into a coherent and satisfying whole."

—The Tennessean

"Jance at her best, weaving a masterful story of suspense."

—The Sierra Vista Herald

"A suspenseful climax."

—Daily Camera

WEB OF EVIL

"Gripping. . . . Jance's skills will keep the reader riveted. . . . Ali couldn't be better company."

—South Florida Sun-Sentinel

"Jance keeps the entertainment value at a steady level."

—The Augusta Chronicle

ALSO BY J.A. JANCE

J.A. JANCE

DEADLY STAKES

Pocket Books

New York   London   Toronto   Sydney   New Delhi

Pocket Books
A Division of Simon & Schuster, Inc.
1230 Avenue of the Americas
New York, NY 10020

This book is a work of fiction. Names, characters, places, and incidents either are products of the author's imagination or are used fictitiously. Any resemblance to actual events or locales or persons, living or dead, is entirely coincidental.

First Pocket Books paperback edition December 2013

POCKET and colophon are registered trademarks of Simon & Schuster, Inc.

For information about special discounts for bulk purchases, please contact Simon & Schuster Special Sales at 1-866-506-1949 or business@simonandschuster.com.

The Simon & Schuster Speakers Bureau can bring authors to your live event. For more information or to book an event, contact the Simon & Schuster Speakers Bureau at 1-866-248-3049 or visit our website at www.simonspeakers.com.

Manufactured in the United States of America

10 9 8 7 6 5 4 3 2 1

ISBN: 978-1-4516-2869-2
ISBN: 978-1-4516-2870-8 (ebook)

For Cindy B. It's about time!

DEADLY STAKES

Prologue

Even for June, it was ungodly hot as Gemma Ralston pulled into a nearly deserted parking lot and slid her Mercedes SLK into a spot just in front of the brick-and-mortar offices of Video-Glam. Despite the name, Video-Glam appeared to be anything but glamorous. The office was located in a mostly dead and partly repurposed strip mall at Indian School and Forty-third Avenue. Video-Glam occupied a single storefront at one end of the complex. At the other end, two units had been combined to serve as a Spanish-language Baptist church. In between were three empty units, their boarded-up windows a colorful catalog of three-foot-high graffiti.

For a moment, Gemma sat in her car with the engine running, wondering if she wanted to bother going inside. From the outside, it didn't look the least bit promising, even though the membership consultant at Hearts Afire, a dating site for "mature singles," had assured her that Video-Glam was the only place in Phoenix that they would recommend as a source for uploadable videos.

"It's like Glamour Shots," the young woman

had told her, "only with, like you know, videos instead of just pictures."

That comment had told Gemma a lot about the age and general qualifications of her membership consultant without engendering a whole lot of confidence in the process itself.

She was considering putting the SLK in reverse and backing out of the lot when a car pulled in beside her. It was a dusty green Subaru months beyond needing a complete detailing. A collection of doggy nose prints on the inside of the back side window obscured the interior of the car but let the world know that a large dog of some kind was often a backseat passenger.

The woman who hopped out of the driver's seat, a bedraggled thirtysomething, matched the car in every way. She looked harried and overworked and, from the way she hotfooted it inside, most likely late for an appointment. She was dressed in a pair of faded black sweats topped by a worn football jersey from Glendale High School. The whole woebegone outfit was underscored by a pair of blue rubber flip-flops. Stringy dishwater-blond hair was pulled back with a scrunchy. As far as Gemma was concerned, the woman looked like crap.

Gemma's first thought was that this was someone desperately in need of a little glamour. Her second thought was along the lines of "If that's the competition, I'm home free."

Based on that, Gemma couldn't help being a little curious if anyone at Video-Glam would be able to wave a magic wand at the poor unfortunate creature who was standing in front of the reception desk just inside the front door. Without really thinking about it, Gemma switched off the ignition, grabbed a small suitcase with her changes of wardrobe off the passenger-side floor as well as her out-of-season mink from its place of honor on the passenger seat.

Once inside, Gemma saw that the woman from the dusty Subaru was still ahead of her at the reception counter and in a full-scale case of hysterics. "I know I have to move on," she sobbed, dabbing at her tears. "But I just don't know how to do it. I've been out of the dating scene for so long that the whole idea scares me to death."

"You'll be fine," the much-pierced young woman behind the counter reassured her, passing along a box of tissues. This was evidently a situation she had dealt with on more than one occasion. As the weeping woman blew into one of the offered tissues, Gemma noticed the pale spot on the skin of the woman's ring finger from which, most likely, a wedding band had been recently removed.

Gemma felt a tiny stirring of irritation. It made no sense that she'd be in remotely the same boat as this unfortunate creature. If Charles had simply manned up and done what she had expected him to do—which was live up to his potential—things never would have come to this pass. He had told her that he would one day be a surgeon, and that was what she had expected. Had he done so, Gemma would have gotten a reasonable return on her investment, and she wouldn't have had to dump him. Instead, after one stupid mistake—and one lost patient who probably wouldn't have survived anyway—he had backed away from surgery and become a raving do-gooder. The money he made looking after Alzheimer's patients was far less than she had planned on. And since all these patients were going to die, too, what was the point?

Gemma had decided to cut her losses and look for greener pastures while she could. Fortunately, she was starting over with a lot more going for her than Ms. Flip-flops, standing as if frozen in front of the receptionist, who slid a credit card and a receipt across the counter. The woman signed it and stuffed her copy in her purse. At that moment, another young woman, this one dressed entirely in black, stepped through an interior door into the reception area.

"Oh, hi, Noelle," the receptionist said. "Here's your stylist, Rachel. She's the one who'll be helping you today. Just go with her and don't worry about a thing."

Looking more than a little lost, Rachel allowed herself to be led away while Gemma stepped up to the receptionist and tossed her fur on the counter in front of her.

"Is she here for Hearts Afire?" Gemma asked, nodding toward the door where Rachel and her stylist had disappeared.

"Oh, no." The receptionist's smile was one step short of a purr. "We do videos for several different sites. If you're with Hearts Afire, you must be Gemma."

Gemma had to beat back her first inclination, which was to say, "Ms. Ralston to you." She nodded. "I'm here for my ten o'clock," she said, pulling out her AmEx card.

"You're aware of our charges?" the receptionist asked. "You're paying for the shoot only, as well as your initial upload. We keep the videos on file, and you're charged a nominal fee each time you ask to have them uploaded on another site."

"Yes, yes," Gemma agreed impatiently. "That's fine."

Now that she was here, what she wanted more than anything was to get the process over and done with, sort of like going to the dentist for a root canal. She already knew it was going to be bad. The only question was how long it would take.

The receptionist ran Gemma's card, then passed back the card and receipt as the interior door opened again and yet another black-clad young woman appeared.

"This is Roxanne," the receptionist announced to Gemma. "She'll be your stylist today."

Roxanne was young—probably not over twenty-five—but as Gemma examined the young woman's hair and makeup, she could find nothing to complain about. Roxanne was naturally good-looking to begin with, and her carefully applied makeup and precision-cut bob added to her appeal. So maybe, Gemma thought hopefully, with any kind of luck, with someone like that doing the styling, it wouldn't be all that bad.

Gemma picked up her coat and suitcase and allowed herself to be led into the next section of the building, which turned out to be a tiny but exceedingly well-equipped beauty salon. There were four stations in all, two for hair and two for makeup. Off to the side was a walled-off section with a door marked WARDROBE.

"Most people stop here first and choose their outfits. That way we can be sure we have the right makeup," Roxanne explained, pointing toward the door. "Once you choose what to wear, we'll select which of our backdrops you'll want once we get to the studio."

"I don't need any of that stuff," Gemma told her stylist. "I brought my own."

As they walked by the wardrobe door, Gemma noticed that Rachel, the dishwater blonde, was inside trying on a Harley-Davidson jacket. A discarded stack of obviously fake furs lay on the floor beside her.

At a table outside the wardrobe, Gemma opened her valise and laid out her three different outfits. Eventually, they settled on her favorite, a chartreuse silk sheath that came complete with a pair of high-heeled strappy sandals.

Roxanne nodded approvingly and then brought up a series of photos on a laptop. One showed a summery garden through the rail of what was evidently a front porch. "We have a porch swing that we use with this one," she said. "That will be perfect with the dress."

"What should we use for the mink?" Gemma asked, wanting to be certain Roxanne understood that her coat was the real thing, not some rip-off fake.

Roxanne clicked through a series of photos. "What about this one?" she said, pausing on what looked like a snow-covered Swiss chalet. "I think this one will do it justice. Believe it or not, we have some perfectly wonderful faux snow back in the studio that looks just like the real thing."

By the time they finished background-shopping, Rachel had emerged from wardrobe, and the change was nothing short of miraculous. Noelle had evidently persuaded her to skip the Harley-Davidson jacket in favor of a sapphire wraparound dress with a plunging neckline and simple, flowing lines that evidently could be adjusted to fit almost any figure. The flip-flops had disappeared, replaced by a pair of classy pumps dyed to match the dress. The wardrobe department at Video-Glam apparently had a whole selection of shoes in all kinds of sizes to go with the very adjustable dress.

Roxanne went to work shampooing Gemma's hair. When she was finished, Gemma noticed that Rachel's formerly drab locks had been lightened by some kind of rinse and were trimmed swiftly but deftly. Once the new cut had been blow-dried, combed, and sprayed, Rachel looked like a different person entirely. The revised hairdo was followed by the meticulous application of makeup that took a full ten years off her face. Watching from the sidelines while her own hair was being shampooed and styled, Gemma couldn't help but be impressed. The sophisticated look made Rachel a different person, smiling and laughing and maybe enjoying herself for the first time in a long time. But the change in appearance didn't change the fact that Rachel had arrived for her shoot in a filthy Subaru with dog snot all over the windows.

"Noelle's really great," Roxanne commented. "She's especially good with the broken birds. She makes them look good, but she also makes them feel good."

"What about me?" Gemma asked.

Roxanne stopped and gave Gemma an appraising look. "I don't think you've ever been a broken bird," the stylist said with a laugh. "By the time I'm finished with you, though, you'll be spectacular."

Which turned out to be the case. Roxanne made no effort to adjust Gemma's already perfect haircut, but she did put just the right amount of curl and body into it, and the skillfully applied makeup left Gemma smiling and nodding at her reflection.

"You like?" Roxanne asked.

"Very much," Gemma answered.

When Gemma's makeover was complete, Roxanne led her into the greenroom, where it was time to hurry up and wait. Rachel had disappeared into the studio before Gemma's makeup was finished. While she waited, Gemma pulled out a hard copy of the script she intended to use. It was supposed to be three to five minutes long and would be transferred to a teleprompter before the actual filming. She had struggled with what to say. She wanted to hit all the right notes—breezy, fun, lighthearted. She didn't want people to think she took herself too seriously. Guys who were interested in fun and games weren't looking for serious.

"I'm Gemma," the script read. "With a name like that, it's only natural that I have a soft spot for gems, two in particular: emeralds because they match my eyes, and diamonds because diamonds really are a girl's best friend."

It seemed to her that simple introduction made it clear she was looking for someone with dollars in his wallet that he'd be willing to spend on her. Cubic zirconia? Thanks but no thanks! Not her type.

The script continued, "I'm looking for companionship, but I have no interest in getting married again." (Lose out on her hard-earned alimony? Not on your life!) "And I'm definitely not interested in kids. If I had wanted kids, I would have had my own. If you've got kids, I'm sure they have mothers who don't need any competition in the motherhood department. I'll be glad to meet your kids, but I don't want to raise them or take them away from their real moms.

"Without kids or marriage on the table, my age is none of your business. I believe in being open-minded as far as age is concerned, in both directions, up and down. If you're looking at this video and thinking I'm probably too old for you or too young, then you're probably right. So let's not even go there.

"By now you're probably wondering, *So what does she really want?*

"In a word—fun! I've spent enough of my life knowing that tomorrow would be a repeat of today. I want to be able to expect the unexpected. I want adventure. A white-water rafting trip down the Colorado? I'm there. An African safari? Yes; have passport, will travel. A sunset walk along a sandy beach, yes. A quiet evening of reading books in a snowbound cabin? Yes to that, too. Maybe you're into long-distance bicycling and would like to help me train. I'd also like to try my hand at ballroom dancing and bowling.

"In other words, the boring day-to-day stuff is fine for me to do by myself, but when I'm with you—whoever you are—nothing that sounds like fun is off the table, and the sooner we get started, the better."

Noelle emerged from the studio looking perplexed. "Sorry for the delay," she said. "Rachel looks great, but she keeps freezing up the moment the camera starts recording. It shouldn't be long, but the director was wondering if you brought along a copy of your script. If so, he wants me to start loading it into the teleprompter."

"No problem," Gemma said, smiling and handing it over. "I'll be ready when you are."

With that, she settled in to wait. She knew she looked good. She knew that before long, she'd have men groveling at her feet, but she also knew who to thank for it—her grandmother Natalie Hooper.

Gemma didn't remember the roach-infested hovel from which her grandparents had rescued her as a two-year-old, although her grandmother, also known as Nana, had told her about it so many times that she could see it in her mind's eye. Two days after Gemma's second birthday, Nana and Papa had gone to war with their drug-addicted daughter, Caroline.

Born with what should have been a silver spoon in her mouth, Caroline Hooper was the daughter of a small-town physician and a stay-at-home mom. Money was never an issue in their Lake Havasu home. In grade school and junior high, things were fine. Caroline got good grades and was considered an exemplary student, but once she got into high school, that all went south. By the time she turned fifteen, she was a pot-smoking dropout. By the time she was eighteen, she had an out-of-wedlock baby and a serious drug problem. For a time, Natalie and Daniel Hooper had done what they could to care for both their struggling daughter and her baby girl—paying rent and utility bills; sending money and gift certificates for groceries.

Caroline had told them that she was having a birthday party on Gemma's birthday, and it would be too complicated to try to include her parents. Two days later, Natalie and Daniel had turned up unannounced, expecting to deliver a stack of tardy birthday presents. They knocked, but no one answered, even though they could hear Gemma crying from somewhere inside. Finding the door unlocked, they let themselves into a nightmare. The apartment was filthy. The place was littered with empty pizza boxes. Cockroaches scurried out of sight as the door opened. There were flies circling a garbage can overrun with dirty diapers. Natalie went straight to the wailing baby and found Gemma dirty and hungry and inconsolable in a crib. Daniel found Caroline on a bare mattress on the floor in the second bedroom. She was passed out cold with a syringe lying on the floor next to her.

Natalie stayed with the baby while Daniel went looking for a police officer. Natalie wanted to change Gemma's diaper, but Daniel told her to wait. He wanted to be sure the authorities knew how bad it was, and he was right. The cops came, and so did social services. Child Protective Services was only too happy to turn the child over to a pair of responsible grandparents. A grant of temporary custody was soon made permanent.

Gemma stepped out of that filthy crib and into what previously was her mother's life. Caroline's room became Gemma's room. The playhouse that once was Caroline's was now Gemma's. Caroline's piano teacher became Gemma's piano teacher. Most important, Caroline's parents became Gemma's parents—Natalie her caring but disciplining mother and Daniel her doting father.

Soon after Gemma's arrival, the household's economic situation took a hit when Parkinson's forced Daniel into early retirement and he had to give up his medical practice. It was essentially the same stable home with the same two loving parents, but the results with Gemma were very different. She was bright and beautiful but cooperative, whereas her mother had fought her parents and teachers every step of the way. As far as Natalie and Daniel were concerned, raising Caroline had been a nightmare; raising Gemma was a piece of cake.

Unlike her mother, Gemma breezed through high school and graduated near the head of her class. When it came time for her to leave for her freshman year at Arizona State University, Natalie Hooper offered Gemma her own road map to success.

"When your mother was your age, Caroline was out smoking dope, protesting the war, and burning her bra. You can see how well that worked out for her," Natalie counseled Gemma. "So do what I did. Find yourself some dependable young man, preferably a premed student, and marry him. You can see that worked for your grandfather and me. Daniel was only a GP. You'd be better off finding yourself a surgeon. Those are the guys who make the big bucks."

Unlike her mother, Gemma listened to every one of her grandmother's words and took them to heart. Unfortunately, because she really was Caroline Hooper's daughter, she put her own particular spin on Natalie Hooper's heartfelt advice. Daniel Hooper's pet name for Gemma may have been Sugar, but she knew that when it came to sugar and spice and everything nice, she didn't come close. She also understood that it was entirely possible to *act* nice without actually *being* nice, though it was the best way to get what you wanted.

Growing up, Gemma had understood her mother's mistakes, and she had no intention of repeating them. As she packed her possessions to head to Tempe, Gemma instinctively accepted the idea that her grandmother had laid out an excellent game plan.

It was left up to Gemma to work that plan to the best of her ability, and she had done a masterful job. Now, after years of making the best of what she had come to consider a useful starter marriage, she was ready to reap some of the rewards.

Yes, she thought, sitting back and waiting her turn at Video-Glam. *It's about time.*

1

Several miles across town, Ali Reynolds sighed and looked at her watch. She had known when she had agreed to do the shoot at the Phoenix FOX affiliate that it would be the same day and time that her mother, Edie Larson, would be speaking before a luncheon meeting of local Sedona Rotarians as part of her run for mayor. Edie had done a number of informal coffee-hour appearances, but this would be her first major speaking engagement, one in which she would be going head to head with her thirtysomething opponent. As Edie's campaign manager, Ali felt she needed to be there to handle the background issues and put out any fires that cropped up. Unfortunately, the scheduled shoot for FOX's new *Scene of the Crime* news magazine had been chiseled in granite.

"You go do the shoot and don't worry about me," Edie had assured her daughter earlier that morning. "Brenda Riley is counting on you."

"But so are you," Ali had objected.

"You can't afford to miss the taping," Edie said

firmly. "Besides, with Brenda's book due to come out the same week the show is scheduled to broadcast nationally, she has a lot more riding on this than I do. I'll be speaking to that bunch of Rotarians, most of whom I know on a first-name basis. How bad can that be? Don't worry. I'll be fine."

Ali shook her head in resignation. What her mother wasn't saying was that both candidates had been invited to speak at the luncheon, and this was the first time Edie would be trading campaign rhetoric with an opponent socked with a supply of well-rehearsed replies.

"Why do I always end up with people counting on me?" Ali asked.

Edie smiled. "Because that's the way your father and I raised you," she said, "and we love you for it."

As a consequence, Ali had left her house on Sedona's Manzanita Hills Road a little before noon on that Tuesday morning to drive down into the sunbaked oven known as the Valley of the Sun. Since it was already pushing the nineties in Sedona, she knew Phoenix would be a scorcher. She didn't even attempt to put on camera-ready makeup for the drive down. Instead she took along the traveling makeup kit she had used back in the old days, when she was an on-air reporter and later a television news anchor.

For the better part of two years, she had known that her friend Brenda Riley, also a former newscaster, had been working on a book about a cyberstalker named Richard Lowensdale who, operating under any number of aliases, had victimized dozens of lonely women from all over the country, romancing them with digital sweet nothings that had promised the world and delivered only humiliation and heartache.

Richard's preferred victims were vulnerable women considered high-profile in their various communities. Ali had first met Brenda Riley when they were working as news anchors, with Ali at a news desk in L.A. while Brenda was at a sister station in Sacramento. Brenda had been drawn into Richard's clutches in the aftermath of a difficult divorce, along with a sudden sidelining from her newscasting job when she outlived her on-camera shelf life. For Brenda, those two major losses had resulted in a booze- and drug-fueled midlife crisis. Ali had been dragged into the fray when Brenda asked for help in doing a simple background check on the new man in Brenda's life. Unfortunately, that supposedly simple check had uncovered the existence of Richard Lowensdale's full contingent of fiancées, all of whom, like Brenda, had been wooed through cyberspace.

That revelation, coupled with all the other losses, had been enough to send Brenda off on an almost fatal series of benders. When Brenda finally sobered up and wised up, she set out to expose the man for what he was. Before she could do so, however, someone else beat her to the punch. Unfortunately for Richard, one of his erstwhile victims, Ermina Vlasic Cunningham Blaylock, happened to be a serial murderer in her own right. She had lured him into doing an illicit engineering job with the promise of a large payday when in fact she had every intention of taking him out once he was no longer useful.

Ermina had carried out the cold-blooded killing with utter ruthlessness, leaving evidence that should

have put the blame for Lowensdale's murder at
Brenda Riley's door. All of that might have gone
according to plan had it not been for the timely
arrival of Ali and a Grass Valley homicide detective
named Gilbert Morris. Brenda's mother had alerted
Ali to the fact that her daughter had gone missing.
Between Ali and Detective Morris, they not only
managed to capture Ermina, they also rescued
Brenda, who was found, close to death, locked in
the trunk of Ermina's rented Cadillac.

Their timely rescue had been good for Brenda
but not so good for an FBI surveillance team also
on the scene, intent on bringing down both Ermina
and the drug cartel movers and shakers who were
the intended end customers of her illegal stock
of supposedly dismantled drones. When offered
a possible plea deal, Ermina arrogantly refused.
Rather than walking away with what would have
been a hand slap on three separate charges of
homicide, she chose to go to trial. As a result,
juries in two different California jurisdictions and
one in Missouri all returned guilty verdicts.

Two years later, some legal maneuverings continued, but with Ermina sentenced to life without
parole in two different states, Brenda Riley, now
married to the retired detective Morris, was free to
publish the whole story. *Scene of the Crime,* a new
televised true-crime weekly magazine, was prepared to give the story full-court-press treatment
for its premiere show, and Ali had agreed to go on
camera to tell her part of the story.

It wasn't until she arrived at the television studio in Phoenix that Ali discovered one of Richard
Lowensdale's cyberstalking victims, Lynn Martinson, formerly of Iowa City, Iowa, was now living in

the Phoenix area and would be filming her segment with the same crew in the course of the afternoon.

Lynn—in her mid-forties, at least, a bit on the frumpy side, and incredibly nervous—was already in the greenroom when Ali arrived. A receptionist had just given her the unwelcome news that the film crew and host were delayed, having missed a flight connection. If Ali had known about the delay earlier, she could have stayed for part of the luncheon meeting and driven to Phoenix immediately afterward. Now that she was here, there was nothing to do but wait. She went into the greenroom powder room to reapply her makeup, then settled in to wait.

Lynn, on the other hand, paced the floor and agonized over her hair, makeup, and clothing. "Your makeup is perfect," she said, examining Ali. "Do I look all right?"

Ali had spent years in front of a camera, and she was an expert in what to do and what not to do. She didn't have the heart to tell the poor woman the truth.

"You're fine," Ali assured her. "The crew will probably have someone along who can doctor your makeup should they decide it needs fixing. Sit down. Relax. It'll be okay."

With a resigned sigh, Lynn sank down on one of the room's several uncomfortable chairs. "I take it you're one of Richard's victims, too?" she asked.

"No," Ali said. "I'm from Sedona. Originally, I was a friend of Brenda's. I'm the one who ran the background check that started the whole unmasking of Richard Lowensdale."

"Oh," Lynn said. "You're the detective, the one who figured it all out, you and that guy from Grass Valley."

"Gil Morris is the detective," Ali said. "I was a concerned bystander."

"Luckily for Brenda," Lynn said. "I'm glad you're not one of us. Because of Richard, I ended up losing everything—my job; my self-respect. And then my son committed suicide . . ."

"I'm so sorry," Ali murmured.

Those three words of sympathy were enough to launch Lynn on a long, sad monologue, leaving Ali no choice but to listen.

"Thank you," Lynn said. "Lucas died just after I learned the truth about Richard. That's where I met him, by the way—in a tough-love chat room shortly after Lucas was picked up on drug charges. Here I was, the superintendent of schools, and my kid was in jail for dealing drugs. You can imagine how that went over in a place like Iowa City.

"When Lucas was arrested, my ex refused to take any responsibility. He blamed the whole thing on me, and that's why I fell so hard for Richard. He told me his name was Richard Lewis. It's no wonder I fell in love with the guy. Here was a caring man who was willing to listen to my troubles and who really seemed to understand what I was going through because he had a similar story. Richard claimed he had a daughter who had gone down the same druggie path Lucas was on— including spending time in juvie. Fortunately, his daughter had come out all right on the other side.

"Hearing that gave me a glimmer of hope that maybe someday Lucas would be all right, too. Then I found out Richard was a complete fraud, that everything he had told me was a lie—he didn't even have a daughter. That's when everything caught up with me, and I went to pieces. I couldn't go to work.

Couldn't get out of bed some days. It was then, while I was lying around feeling sorry for myself, that Lucas committed suicide. He left a note saying he was sorry but he couldn't live in prison and he'd rather be dead. That's my fault, too. If I had been there for him, maybe I could have saved him."

Listening and nodding, Ali didn't bother saying what she knew to be true—that kids from even the most loving of families could fall victim to suicide. Survivors were always too ready to accept blame and assume that something they might have done or said, or might not have done or said, would have made a difference.

"I'm sorry," Ali said again.

Lynn nodded and continued. "With Lucas gone, I just gave up. I ended up quitting my job. I also lost my house. My parents had retired and moved to Surprise. By then my father's Alzheimer's was getting worse and worse, so I came here to help my mom look after him. That's one good thing. Once I was without a job, I was able to lend a hand. I think the stress of looking after a man who was essentially an eighty-year-old toddler would have killed my mother without my help. Alzheimer's is hell," she added.

Ali nodded again. Lynn's tale of woe was appalling. "How's your dad doing?" Ali asked.

"He passed away a few months ago," Lynn replied. "I'm sorry he's gone, but he was gone a long time before he died. It's not easy, but my mother and I are starting to recover. It's hard not to feel guilty about feeling relieved. Not everyone gets that. You need to have lived it to really understand. My mother has started reconnecting with her bridge-playing friends, and she's taken up golf again. As for me? There's a wonderful new man in my life. A real one this time," she added with a shy laugh. "Without my coming out here to help my mom, I never would have met Chip."

The sudden glow on Lynn's face had nothing to do with makeup, and Ali found herself hoping that Chip was as nice a person as Lynn seemed to think he was.

Ali's phone rang. The readout showed her mother's number. A glance at the clock told her the luncheon was most likely over. "Sorry," she said to Lynn. "I need to take this." Into the phone, she added, "Hey, Mom, how did it go?"

"Harlan Masters is full of himself," Edie muttered.

Ali laughed. "That's hardly news," she said. "Tell me something we didn't already know."

Ali's longtime boyfriend, B. Simpson, owned High Noon Enterprises, now an internationally respected Internet security company, though the company still did what once was High Noon's bread-and-butter business—security checks. The one they'd done on Harlan Masters revealed that he was a trust-fund baby. He had moved to Sedona from Southern California some five years earlier and had set out to bring Sedona up to what he regarded as an acceptable level of Southern California sophistication by running for mayor. During his first four-year term, he set out on a program to transform Sedona as far as rules and regulations were concerned. Having never gotten his hands dirty in the world of business, he did so without giving much thought to how much it would cost local businesses to implement some of his bright ideas.

The one that had galvanized Edie into running

for office was a city-imposed requirement that restaurants inside the city limits post the calorie and fat content of each item on a menu. That might not have been much of a hardship for chain-type operations, but for struggling independents like the Sugarloaf Café, redoing the menus not once but twice—first for the calorie count and later for the fat content—had been a costly process. Naturally, Edie's signature sweet rolls had been off the charts in both categories.

Emboldened by passing his restaurant regulations through a city council that was completely in the mayor's pocket, Masters had set off on a campaign to outlaw contrails inside the city limits, thus forcing commercial airline traffic to detour around Sedona's airspace. Edie thought the whole contrail controversy was nothing short of ridiculous.

"How did the meeting go?" Ali asked.

"He must have worked the word 'old' into every other sentence," Edie grumbled. "As in 'Now is no time to return to old, timeworn ideas.' Or 'Let's not settle for old-fashioned thinking when what's needed are progressive youthful ideas to carry us forward in the twenty-first century.' Everything he said implied that I was old and decrepit, and it took every bit of restraint I could muster to keep from calling that little jerk a young whippersnapper."

"Now, Mom," Ali said. "Let's not resort to name-calling this early in the process. In fact, let's not resort to it at all. What were the reactions from the audience?"

"Three people came up to me afterward and offered to host coffee hours for me. I have their names and numbers."

"You gave those to Jessica?"

Jessica Townley, a recent graduate from Sedona High School, was this year's winner of the Amelia Dougherty Scholarship, a program Ali personally administered. In the fall, Jessica would be attending Arizona State University on a full-ride scholarship. Since her intention was to major in political science, she had volunteered to spend the summer working as an unpaid intern in Edie Larson's campaign.

"Yes, I did," Edie answered. "Do you want her to wait until you get back to schedule something?"

"That's not necessary," Ali said. "Jessica has access to your campaign schedule, and she's perfectly capable of setting up events. When people say yes to something like that, it's important to follow up with them right away. So have her call. If she has any problems, she knows she can always call me for backup. And now that you know Harlan is going to go after you on the age issue, we need to strategize on how to disarm that attack the next time you run into it. The best way to do it is turn it into a joke instead of getting all bent out of shape about it."

"All right," Edie agreed grudgingly. "I'll give it some thought."

"And give yourself the rest of the afternoon off," Ali suggested.

"Can't do that," Edie replied. "I have a whole afternoon's worth of doorbelling to do. Jessica said she'll ride along on that, too."

"Don't overdo," Ali advised.

"What?" Edie retorted. "Because I'm too old?"

"No," Ali said, "because it's a long campaign, and you need to pace yourself."

When Ali hung up, Lynn Martinson was looking at her questioningly.

"My mother," Ali explained. "She's running for office for the first time—mayor of Sedona. She was at an event this afternoon, and her opponent is a young guy who thinks he's the greatest thing since sliced bread."

"I hope she wins," Lynn said. "I've met a few guys like that in my time, and it's fun to see them get taken down a peg."

The door to the greenroom opened, and a tiny black-haired woman bounded through it. "All right," she said. "I'm Carol, *Scene of the Crime*'s producer. We're ready to rumble. Ms. Martinson, how about if we take you first?"

"Sure," Lynn said, rising to her feet. "Is my makeup all right?"

Carol gave Lynn an appraising look. "We'll do a few additions and corrections before we turn on the cameras, but you look all right to me."

As Carol led Lynn out of the room, Ali turned on her iPad and switched over to her downloaded copy of *A Tale of Two Cities*. It was the latest in her self-imposed task of reading some of the classics—all those books she had heard about in school over the years but had never read. It was either that or sit there and worry about her mother's political campaign.

Right that minute, reading seemed like a more productive use of her time—better than worrying. Either Edie would be tough enough to survive in the ego-bruising world of small-town politics, or she wouldn't. However it went, there wasn't much Ali could do about it.

2

Standing at the gas pumps at the 7-Eleven on Camelback, A. J. Sanders felt conspicuous as he pumped twenty bucks' worth of regular into his Camry. He kept waiting for someone to ask him why he wasn't in school. It seemed obvious to him that he was ditching school, and he waited for someone to notice, but the clerk took his money without so much as a raised eyebrow. There were two patrol cars sitting side by side at the far end of the parking lot, but the cops paid no attention to him as he pulled onto the street and merged into traffic.

He might have felt less self-conscious if he had done it before, but he hadn't. Halfway through the first semester of his senior year, this was the first time ever he had ditched school. He sincerely hoped he'd get away with it. Other kids did it all the time. Why not him?

A.J. already had a note from his mother—one he had carefully forged—folded up and waiting in his wallet for him to turn in to the office tomorrow morning when he returned to Phoenix's North High. As long as he was back in town this afternoon in time to make it to his four o'clock shift as a stocker at Walgreens, he'd be fine.

The school probably wouldn't call his mother to check on him, but the manager of the Walgreens, Madeline Wurth, was his mother's best friend from the time they were in grade school. If he missed a shift, Madeline would be on the phone to Sylvia, A.J.'s mother, before he could blink an eye. That was how he had gotten the job—Maddy and Sylvia were friends—but Madeline ran a tight ship. She didn't tolerate unexplained absences or tardiness. The one time A.J. had shown up fifteen minutes late because someone had a tire-slashing spree in the North High parking lot, Madeline had called his mom before he had a chance to change the tire, change his clothes, and get to work.

So, yes, he could most likely get away with missing school, but he wouldn't ever get away with missing work, because if Madeline called Sylvia, the jig would be up. His mother would find out he'd been lying to her for a very long time. That was the last thing he wanted—for his mother to find out about the lies. He didn't want her to know, because if she did, he was certain it would break her heart.

A.J. got onto the 51 and then drove north to the 101 and finally onto I-17 again heading north. His father had given him simple directions. Take I-17 north to General Crook Trail. Take that exit west for six tenths of a mile. Walk north approximately fifty yards. Find the boulder with the heart painted on it. Dig there, behind the boulder.

His father. That was the problem. A.J. had an ongoing relationship with his father, and his mother had no idea.

Until a little over a year ago, it had been just the two of them—A.J. and his mom. His mother's favorite song, the one she had played and sung to him for as long as he could remember, was Helen Reddy's "You and Me Against the World." She had played it when he was tiny and she was driving him back and forth to the babysitter's. Later, when he was old enough to learn the words, they both sang along. A.J. and his mommy—the two of them and nobody else.

When he was in first grade, A.J. noticed that other kids had both a mommy and a daddy, and he had started asking the big question: Where is *my* daddy? Sylvia never said anything particularly bad about A.J.'s father. The worst thing she ever said was that he was "unreliable." When A.J. was six, the closest he could come to sorting it out was that you couldn't count on his father to do what he said he would do or be where he said he would be. Still, that didn't seem like a good enough reason not to have a daddy.

In Sunday school he found out that the Virgin Mary was Baby Jesus' mother, but Joseph wasn't exactly His father. Somebody called the Holy Spirit was. For a while A.J. thought that might be the case with him, too. Maybe his father was some kind of ghost, and that's why no one could see him and why there weren't any pictures of him.

By then he had a friend, a kid named Andrew who lived down the street. He didn't have a daddy, either. Andrew said that was because his parents were divorced, but he had a picture of his father that he kept in the drawer of his bedside table. A.J. wished with all his heart that he had a picture in his drawer, too. Not that he didn't love his mommy, but he had this feeling that something important was missing from his life, and he wanted it with all his heart.

By the time A.J. was in third grade, he had sorted out that Santa Claus and the Tooth Fairy weren't real, and he was pretty sure there was no such thing as a Holy Ghost, either, at least not as far as he was concerned. Besides, he was almost nine and other possibilities had arisen that were both more interesting and more ominous.

Andrew maintained that A.J.'s father was dead, while Domingo, who lived down the block and was a year older than A.J. and Andrew, suggested that perhaps A.J.'s father, like Domingo's uncle, had been shipped off to prison.

"When Uncle Joaquin went to prison," Dommy explained, "my grandmother took his picture off the wall in the living room, threw it in the garbage, and said he was no longer her son."

That simple statement had caused a knot of worry to grow in the pit of A.J.'s stomach. Maybe something similar had happened to his father. Maybe A.J. had done something wrong and his father had decided that he no longer wanted a son.

By fourth grade, A.J. was a genuine latchkey kid with his own house key and two hours to fill after he got home from school and before his mom came home from work. Some kids might have gotten into trouble. A.J. didn't because he didn't have time. He was far too busy. His mother made sure he went out for tee ball and Little League, for soccer and Pop Warner football. When it came to football, A.J.'s mother was the only mother who knew enough about the game to be one of the coaches rather than just sitting in the bleachers on the sidelines.

For most of his after-school activities, A.J. was able to make it to practices on his bicycle. For games that were farther away, his mother managed to organize complicated car-pool arrangements. On weekends when the dental office where Sylvia worked as a receptionist was closed, she did a lot of the driving to make up for what she couldn't do during the week. During the summers, there were day camps and swimming lessons at the YMCA, along with two weeks of camp with the Boy Scouts, usually somewhere in the White Mountains.

So most of the time, A.J. was too busy with sports and school to spend much time getting into trouble or thinking about what he was missing. By the time he hit high school, he'd come face-to-face with the reality that, although he had participated in any number of sports, he wasn't outstanding at any of them. He would never be big enough or strong enough to make a name for himself as a football player. He wasn't tall enough for basketball or fast enough for soccer. As for swimming? Forget it.

With only a high school diploma and a certificate from a business school, his mother had made enough to scrape by and keep a roof over their heads, but there wasn't much room in her budget for extras. From an early age, Sylvia Sanders made it clear to her son that he would need a college degree and that college didn't come cheap. Since an athletic scholarship was out of the question, an academic one was the only possibility. That made keeping his grades up essential. His mother also made it clear that while they were saving for college tuition, his having a car at his disposal was a no-brainer.

"It's not just the expense of buying a car," Sylvia had explained when he brought up the subject two weeks before his sixteenth birthday. "The cost of having an inexperienced driver would send my insurance premiums through the roof. Add to that gas and upkeep, and you have a major expense—more than what you're making stocking shelves for Madeline. Your legs work. Your bike works. Use 'em."

A.J. grumbled about it, but that was the end of the discussion until a week later. It was almost time for his shift to start. He had ridden from school to the store and was in the process of locking up his bike when a man who was standing nearby, smoking a cigarette, spoke to him. "Hey, kid," he said. "Aren't you a little old to be riding a bike?"

A.J. felt a hot flush of anger. He was tempted to lip off at the guy. What business was it of his what mode of transportation A.J. used? Then he noticed the plastic bag sitting on the sidewalk at the guy's feet. The Walgreens logo was clearly visible, and that meant he was a paying customer. Being rude to customers was something Madeline didn't tolerate in her employees—not at all.

"You gotta do what you gotta do," A.J. muttered.

He started to shoulder his way past the guy and go inside, but the man with the cigarette wasn't done with him. He dropped the still-smoking butt on the sidewalk and ground it out with the sole of his shoe.

A.J. wanted to say something to him about not using the sidewalk as an ashtray. After all, he'd be the one who would have to come out later with a broom to clean up the mess.

"Did anyone ever tell you that you look like your old man?" the man asked.

A.J. stopped in midstride. "You knew my father?" he demanded.

The guy grinned at him. "What's the matter? Do you think I'm dead? Is that what your mother told you?"

For a long moment, A.J. was too shocked to speak. He looked the man full in the face, and then he saw it. The resemblance to his own face was right there, especially in the eyes. All the things he had wondered about over the years— the questions he had long ago given up asking his mother—went roiling around in his head. He knew his father's name. One day while his mother was at work, he had gone searching through the strongbox she kept on the top shelf of her closet. There he had found his birth certificate. On it, A.J.'s father was listed as James Mason Sanders. A.J. had tried Googling the name several times, using Andrew's computer. He had found someone with that name who had gone to prison on charges of counterfeiting back in the mid-nineties, but he hadn't been able to ascertain if that James Sanders was his father or even if his father was still alive. Now, to A.J.'s amazement, the man was not only alive, he was standing right there, laughing at him.

"She didn't say you were dead," A.J. said when he found his voice. "She said you were unreliable."

Busy lighting another cigarette, James Sanders let loose in a burst of laughter that ended in a fit of coughing. "Unreliable," he said, grinning. "She got that right, didn't she!"

"What do you want?" A.J. asked.

"Wanted to see you, is all," James said. "Wanted to know a little about you. Have you worked here long?" He nodded toward the store entrance.

"Three months," A.J. said. "One of Mom's friends is the manager."

"That would be Bethany, maybe? Bethany Cole?"

A.J. shook his head. "Her name's Ms. Wurth."

"Oh," James said, nodding. "That would be Maddy. She and Bethany and your mother were always great pals. Called themselves the Three Musketeers."

A.J. glanced at his watch. "Look," he said, "I've got to clock in."

"Sure," James said. "Go ahead. It might be best if you didn't mention me to your mother—at least not yet. But about that bike. Shouldn't you be thinking about getting yourself something with four wheels? Do you even have a license?"

"I'm taking driver's ed, but Mom and I can't afford a car—not the car itself or the insurance," A.J. said bluntly. "I'm trying to save money for college."

"There you go, then," James said, blowing a cloud of smoke skyward. "Suit yourself, but don't work too hard."

A.J. hurried into the store. He made it to the time clock on time, but just barely. He was working on clearing out the back-to-school display and restocking the shelves with Halloween merchandise when Madeline stopped by to check on him.

"Who was that you were talking to outside?" Madeline Wurth asked. "I noticed that guy hanging around. I was about to tell him to move along when you turned up."

A.J. flushed. Anything he told Madeline would go straight to his mother. "Just a guy who was lost," A.J. mumbled. "He got Seventh Street confused with Seventh Avenue. I told him he needed to be on the other side of Central."

"Easy mistake to make," Madeline said.

Summoned by a page from the pharmacy, Madeline Wurth hurried away, leaving A.J. restocking the shelves and struggling with his conscience. Yes, he had lied to Madeline; with his mother, it wouldn't exactly be lying. He was just leaving something out—something she probably didn't want to know about in the first place. Besides, A.J. reasoned, if there were almost sixteen years between visits, it didn't seem likely that James Sanders would be showing up again anytime soon.

But that assessment was wrong. A.J.'s father had turned up again the very next week. A.J. came home from work on the day of his birthday, expecting that he and his mother would go out to have pizza, just the two of them. That was how they usually did it. As he rode his bike into the carport, he wondered about the strange car—a silver Camry—parked in the driveway behind his mother's Passat. On the window of the passenger side was one of those AS IS, NO WARRANTY stickers. Even before he opened the front door and smelled the cigarette smoke, he could hear the sound of raised voices. Quietly, he opened the door and slipped into the entryway, staying just out of sight of the living room, where his mother and James Sanders were arguing.

"After doing nothing for all this time, you've got no right to do this now," Sylvia declared hotly.

"Look," James was saying, sounding conciliatory. "That's what I'm trying to do here—make up for lost time."

"You think that will make up for sixteen years of being an absentee father? You don't raise a finger in all that time, but now you think you can walk in here and give him a car for his birthday? Just like that?"

"He's a good kid. He gets good grades. He works hard. He deserves to have a car."

"I don't know how you know about his grades or where he works, but A.J. and I have already discussed the car situation. Between insurance and gas, it would be more than we can afford."

"That's what this is for," James said.

A.J. heard the sound of something—an envelope, maybe—landing on the coffee table.

"What's this?" Sylvia asked.

"The title's in there, and so is the bill of sale," James answered. "It's all in order. I called an insurance guy and found out how much it'll cost to insure the Camry with an inexperienced driver. There's enough coin of the realm in there to pay the insurance costs for the next three years, as well as a hundred dollars a month for gas money."

"You can't do this," Sylvia objected. "It's not fair. Is this even real?"

"The money, you mean?" James replied. "Now who's not being fair?"

Afraid that his mother might be about to hand

the envelope back, A.J. decided it was time to stage an appearance. After quickly opening the door, he slammed it shut. "Hey, Mom," he shouted from the entryway. "I'm home." When he entered the living room, he stopped short. "Sorry. I didn't know we had company."

He was relieved to see that his mother, seated on the couch, was still holding the envelope. James, standing by the window, wasn't actively smoking a cigarette, but the room reeked of secondhand smoke.

He turned toward A.J., holding out his hand in greeting. "So this must be A.J.," he said with an easygoing grin. "Glad to meet you. I'm your dear old dad."

So that's how he's going to play it, A.J. thought— as though he and A.J. had never laid eyes on each other before; as though the conversation in front of Walgreens had never taken place.

A.J. glanced at his mother, staring at the envelope as if mesmerized. At last she raised her head and looked at A.J., giving an almost imperceptible nod. A.J.'s heart skipped a beat because he recognized the look of abject defeat lining Sylvia's face. The nod implied affirmative answers to both questions—yes, this was his father, and yes, she was going to let A.J. keep the car.

"It's true," she said. "A.J., this is your father, James Sanders. He's offering to give you a car."

A.J. took the proffered hand and shook it. "Glad to meet you, sir," he said.

That was the first real lie he ever told his mother, and he knew at once that it wouldn't be the last.

"I got my first car when I turned sixteen," James explained. "I thought you should have one, too. Did you see that Camry outside in the driveway? It's yours, if you want it."

A.J. turned to his mother. "Are you kidding?" he asked, trying to act as though he hadn't known it already. "A car of my own? Really?"

Sylvia nodded again. A.J. understood why. His mother was nothing if not practical. The car parked in the driveway and the contents of the envelope had wiped out all her objections to his having a car. The car was paid for; the insurance was paid for; the gas was paid for. End of story. Besides, if A.J. had access to his own transportation, his mother's life suddenly would be far less complicated.

"Happy birthday, son," James said with a grin. "Maybe you and your mom would like to take it for a spin." He tossed a set of keys in A.J.'s direction, and A.J. plucked them out of the air.

"Thank you," he said. "I can't believe it."

Sylvia sighed and got up. "I'll go get my purse," she said, heading for her bedroom.

While she was out of the room, A.J. and James stood in a conspiratorial silence. Between that first meeting and now, A.J. had come up with a million questions he wanted to ask his father, but there in the tiny living room, he didn't give voice to any of them. He didn't want to make a mistake and say something that would arouse his mother's suspicions.

"Nice car," he said. "I was looking at it as I came inside."

"Only two years old," James said. "Got a good deal on it. It's got a couple of dents in the trunk, like maybe somebody backed into a bollard, but other than that, it's in great shape."

Sylvia returned with her purse. "Can we drop you someplace?" she asked.

James took the unlit cigarette out of his mouth. "Sure," he said. "You can take me back up to Indian School. I'll catch a bus from there."

Since Indian School ran for miles, east and west, catching a bus there offered no clue about where he was going or where he was staying.

After dropping James off at the corner of Indian School and Seventh, right across the street from Madeline's drugstore, A.J. drove his mother as far as the nearest Pizza Hut. He was self-conscious about having his own car, and he felt guilty about it, too. It was as though he had helped trick his mother into accepting it.

"Why'd he show up now?" A.J. asked while they waited for their pizza. "Why after all this time?"

Sylvia shook her head. "I have no idea, but one thing you can count on."

"What's that?"

"You can't count on him. He paid for the insurance and gas three years in advance. That probably means you won't see him again for at least that long."

"But I thought I could get to know him," A.J. objected. "Find out about where he's been all this time; find out what he's been doing."

Sylvia shook her head. "I doubt that," she said sadly. "James isn't that kind of guy."

Her words proved prophetic. For over a year after that, A.J. saw and heard nothing from his father, not a single word. Then, the previous afternoon, when he got home from school, there had been a letter addressed to him, with no return address but postmarked Las Vegas, Nevada, waiting in the mailbox.

The address on the envelope and the letter inside had been written in a tiny but legible cursive.

Dear A.J.,

Please burn this letter as soon as you read it. I'll be leaving something for you. You'll need a shovel to dig it up. Go up I-17. Just south of Camp Verde, take the exit to General Crook Trail. Instead of going east, go west. Just before the dead end, take the first left. It'll be a dirt road, but the Camry should be fine. Follow that for six tenths of a mile. Exactly. Park there and then walk due north three hundred feet. You'll see a boulder with a heart painted on it. Dig there, on the back side of it. You should probably make sure no one is following you when you go there.

Because you're underage, you might need some help accessing the funds, but you're a smart kid. You'll figure it out. You deserve to spend time paying attention to your studies and having some fun instead of working at that crappy job at Walgreens. Don't tell Maddy I said that.

Don't thank me, and whatever you do, don't tell your mother. She'll try to make you give it back. If you're cagey about it and only use the funds in dribs and drabs, no one will be the wiser, including your mother.

Have a great life.

Your father,
James Sanders

A.J. stood with the letter in his hand for a long time, trying to figure out if it was real or if it was

James's idea of some kind of practical joke. And what about those last four words—"have a great life"? Did that mean A.J.'s father was out of his life forever, that he had seen James Sanders for the very last time?

Eventually, before his mother came home, A.J. did what he'd been told to do. After memorizing the instructions, he took the letter out into the alley behind the house, burned it, and then ground the ashes into the dirt. As the match flared and the paper caught fire, he remembered that old *Mission: Impossible* mantra: "This tape will self-destruct in five seconds."

Now, driving north as he'd been told to do, A.J. couldn't ditch the idea that he was doing something stupid, all because of a father who evidently wanted very little to do with him.

"Dumb and dumber," A.J. muttered to himself. "Like father, like son."

3

The persistent ringing of a cell phone was what roused Gemma Ralston from a cocoon of blessed unconsciousness. At first she thought it was the doorbell—that was the last thing she remembered, going to answer the door in the entryway of her spacious Paradise Valley town home. She tried to remember who had been there when she answered the door, but her mind seemed shrouded in cotton candy. As she came to her senses, she realized it wasn't her cell phone, it was someone else's—ringing nearby but with no one answering.

She turned her head, trying to locate the source of the sound. She was astonished to find herself lying flat on her back on the ground, staring up at a clear blue sky with no idea where she was or how she had come to be there. Next to her was an old burned-out couch, with tufts of scorched, charred batting and rusty springs spilling out of the back and arms. Beyond that was what looked like an old dishwasher. A wrecked fridge lay on its side, its doors permanently opened. The ground was littered with trash—beer cans and broken bottles and moldering fast-food containers.

The sun was bright overhead, but she knew it was cold because every time she breathed in or out she could see her breath. Somewhere in the far distance, beyond what looked like a scraggly clump of juniper trees, she could hear the rumble of heavy traffic—freeway traffic, most likely. Juniper trees meant she was miles from home, because juniper trees didn't thrive in the Valley of the Sun.

For a time she lay there, trying to clear her head and listening to the welcome sounds of civilization. Cars sped past, their tires whining on the pavement. Growling trucks, eighteen-wheelers probably, shifted gears up and down, but nothing in the passing traffic gave her any useful information. What the noisy traffic did tell her was that calling for help was useless. No one would be able to hear her voice.

The phone, silent for what must have been a matter of minutes or maybe longer, rang again. Moving her head, Gemma could see it lying on the ground just out of reach, but when she tried to turn her body so she could grab it, nothing happened. Her arms and hands refused to obey her brain's commands. They wouldn't move. That was a shock. She couldn't move—not at all. Not a finger; not a toe. Gritting her teeth, Gemma tried again, but again nothing happened. Tears of frustration spilled out of her eyes and rolled down her face. She could feel them slipping unchecked into her ears, but that was all she felt. The rest of her body told her nothing at all. She was alone, helpless, and trapped. For the first time it occurred to her that she might die. Once again she drifted into unconsciousness.

When she awakened, more time had passed. On the far side of the sound of traffic, the sun had risen higher in the sky. Gemma Ralston was all too aware of how direct sunlight could ravage her pale skin. In her adult life, she never set foot outdoors without a coating of sunscreen. This time the sun wasn't hot, but there was no shade from it, either—no protection. Already her bare arm—the little she could see of it—was turning bright pink.

The growing warmth brought with it far worse torments than the possibility of sunburn: flies, swarms of them. They landed on her body. Other than twisting her head back and forth to keep them from landing on her face, she could do nothing to shoo them away. Horrified, she looked at her bare arm and saw a line of ants scrambling across her reddening skin. She couldn't feel them, but she could see them and knew that soon they would be eating her alive. It was her worst nightmare, but at least she couldn't feel it. At least not yet. She drifted off once more.

The ringing phone awakened her again. Four rings this time, and then it quit. If only she could reach it and let someone know that she needed help—that she was badly hurt and maybe dying. She had enough of her wits about her to realize that if she were paralyzed, maybe dying was the best idea; better than spending the remainder of her life as a bedridden vegetable. She was terribly thirsty. Her tongue felt swollen. Even if she could have reached the phone, she doubted she'd be able to talk. With that, she drifted off.

When the phone rang yet again, she didn't bother

opening her eyes. There was no point. If she didn't look, she wouldn't see the ants and flies that she knew were there. But then a miracle happened. The fog in her head cleared a little. She remembered who had rung the doorbell. Then she heard the sound of something other than the thrum of traffic. It was a male voice, speaking to her.

"Hey, lady," he said. "Are you okay?"

She opened her eyes. A very tall young man was standing over her. Maybe he was an angel, but squinting up into the sun, which was now high overhead, she saw no sign of wings. He was batting at the flies milling around her and around him. That didn't make sense. Why would flies bother an angel? Still, the horrified look on his face as he stared down at her spoke volumes. He reached down and brushed something off her. An ant, maybe? She wasn't sure.

"Help me," she croaked, but the words came out more as a low moan, completely indecipherable. "Water. Please."

He backed away from her and disappeared momentarily from view. She was afraid he had abandoned her. "Don't leave me. Please."

"You're hurt," he said, reappearing above her. "Hold on. There's a phone here. I'm calling 911."

She closed her eyes, shutting out the blazing sunlight, but she heard the welcome sound of keys on a cell phone being punched. A moment later, he said, "Crap. No service. I wonder if a text would go through."

There was more key punching—lots of key punching. "Okay," he said. "I texted 911. They're coming. Can you hang on? I've got some water in the car. I'll go get it."

Gemma wanted to feel it in her throat, to taste it with her tongue; but more than water, more than anything, she didn't want to be left alone. Before her rescuer walked away, she tried her best to tell him what she remembered, but she could feel herself drifting away again. Maybe this time there would be no coming back.

4

Even without a hard copy in hand, A.J. followed his father's directions with no problem. Once he turned off the freeway, he had to cross a cattle guard, and before he could turn onto the nameless dirt track, he had to get out of the car, open a metal-framed gate, drive through, and then close it again. Once on the far side of the gate, he began measuring off the six tenths of a mile.

The road was narrow and rough in places but drivable, even in the Camry. Garbage tossed out on the shoulders—beer cans, mostly—testified that it was a party spot, the kind of place favored by kids A.J.'s age to do their illegal drinking and smoking, probably all kinds of smoking. Truth be known, now that he and most of his friends had cars at their disposal, A.J. had done a modest amount of desert-style partying himself, not enough to get in trouble, as long as they didn't get caught, but enough so that he recognized the landscape markers for what they were.

He had covered almost the entire six tenths of a mile when the narrow road widened out into a small clearing. Obviously, the area had long been used as an illegal dump, with abandoned rusting appliances and a collection of rotting furniture scattered here and there in the rocky dirt. Because this was the first wide spot in the road, A.J. decided to park and then walk the rest of the way. There might not be a place to pull off properly when he reached his destination.

He stopped next to the rusted hulk of what had once been a turquoise dishwasher. Remembering James's none too subtle warning about the possibility of being followed, A.J. got out of the car and stood for a while, listening and watching the road behind him. All he heard was the low grumble of traffic roaring down I-17 half a mile or so away. Between there and the turn-off, there was no telltale plume of dust that would have revealed a vehicle tailing him to the appointed place. Only when he was sure he was unobserved did he open the trunk and pull out the shovel he had stowed there. That was when he heard an unexpected noise—the shrill jangling of a cell phone, ringing somewhere nearby.

The hair prickled on the back of A.J.'s neck. With his heart hammering in his chest, he realized that whoever his father had been worried about most likely hadn't followed him here. They must have learned about the destination well in advance, and they were already here, waiting for him to show his hand. His first panicky thought was to ditch the shovel. He quickly pushed it out of sight under the back of the car, then straightened up and looked around. At first he saw nothing. There were no other vehicles, but if someone were watching him, he had no intention of walking closer to the original target and giving away the location of the critical boulder. Instead, shoving his shaking hands deep in his pockets, he sauntered as casually as he could manage in the opposite direction.

That was when he saw what looked like a lump of rags lying next to a burned-out hulk of a sofa with springs sticking out in every direction. At first he thought the pink he was seeing was a swath of material of some kind, like a long, thin scarf. It was only when he edged closer that he realized he was looking at a person, and the length of pink was actually a terrible sunburn on her long bare leg.

She lay so still, breathing so shallowly, that at first A.J. thought she was already dead. Dried blood from a wound on her chest had burned black in the sun, with flies and ants both feasting on the appalling mess.

"Hey, lady," he said. "Are you okay?"

To his surprise, a pair of green eyes fluttered open in the sun-blistered face. He reached down and brushed a single ant from her dried, cracked lip. Disturbed by his arrival, a cloud of frenzied flies swooped into the air. She made an awful sound of some kind, something he couldn't understand. Looking around, he noticed the cell phone lying just beyond the reach of her outstretched fingers. He grabbed it up. It was all he could do to make his fingers dial the emergency number. When he punched send, however, the NO SERVICE notice showed up on the screen. There was enough of a signal for the phone to ring, but not enough to place a call.

A.J. remembered someone telling him once that text messages sometimes went through when voice calls wouldn't. He tried texting 911. Almost immediately, a text response appeared on the screen: "911. What are you reporting?"

Typing with shaking fingers made for a slow,

cumbersome process. It took a lot longer than it would have taken to say where he was and describe the situation, but eventually, he made it work. Only when the operator told him that help was on its way did he turn his attention back to the stricken woman. He explained to her that an ambulance was coming. It worried him that she couldn't seem to move at all. The heartbreaking noises she made weren't words, but he realized that she had to be terribly thirsty.

"I've got some water in the car," he told her. "I'll go get it."

He was gone for only a matter of seconds—the time it took for him to race back to the Camry, retrieve the half-empty bottle of water he had left on the car seat, and make his way back. She needed water. Now wasn't the time to wonder if she'd object to drinking from a bottle with his germs on it. By the time he returned to her side, however, he could tell it was too late for water.

She tried to say something. "Dennis."

"Dennis," he repeated. "Who's that? Your boyfriend? Your husband?"

She didn't answer; she was gone. The light went out of the bright green eyes. Open and empty, they stared sightlessly into the blazing sun. For a moment, waiting to see if she would breathe again, A.J. found it hard to breathe himself. When she didn't, he dropped both the cell phone and the open water bottle and fell to his knees beside her, agonizing about what he should do. He wondered if he should try to revive her, but compressing her chest would have meant burying his hands in the bloody mess, and he couldn't bring himself to do that.

A.J. was a month and a half past his seventeenth birthday, but this was the first time he had ever seen a dead person. Sure, he'd seen pretend dead people in movies and on TV shows, but never like this. He knelt there, sick and dizzy, as the breakfast burrito he had eaten at a fast-food joint in Black Canyon City threatened to erupt from his gut and the spilled water disappeared into the parched earth.

A.J. stayed where he was, swaying on his knees, until he could breathe again; until he could quell his roiling stomach; until the sharp stones biting into his kneecaps got his attention. Then he staggered upright.

He needed to think, and he needed to put some distance between the dead woman and himself. When his head cleared, he had only one thought— to get away. Once the emergency responders got there, to say nothing of the cops, there would be all kinds of questions: Was A.J. the one who had placed the 911 text? Who was the woman, and who was he? If he didn't know her, what was he doing there? Why wasn't he in school? Eventually, the whole story would come out—the lame story about his father's fool's errand to find a buried treasure. If that emerged, so would all of A.J.'s other secrets—the ones he'd been carefully keeping from his mother.

Half sick to his stomach, he made it back to the car. Because he wasn't thinking straight, he did something incredibly stupid. He turned the key in the ignition, shifted into gear, swung the Camry into a tight U-turn, and drove away. He was opening the metal gate to let himself back onto the highway intersection when he realized he had left the shovel behind. He was tempted to go back and get it, but he didn't dare. Out here in the middle of nowhere, he had no idea how long it would take for emergency responders to arrive, but he was sure they were well on their way. If he went back for the shovel, they'd find him at the crime scene, and then he'd be stuck answering all those difficult questions. So he went through the gate, closed it behind him, got back in his car, and drove like a bat out of hell.

He hadn't gone over a mile on the freeway when he saw the flashing lights of an approaching state patrol car speeding north on I-17. As the cop car flew past, siren blaring, A.J. breathed a sigh of relief. He had made the right decision in not going back for the shovel. Had he done so, they would have caught him there for sure.

That was what he was thinking as he drove back to Phoenix with plenty of leeway for making it to work on time. No one had seen him come or go, and as long as he didn't tell anyone about it, no one was likely to find out. All he had to do was keep his mouth shut. As far as his mother knew, he was at school, and when he turned in his excuse tomorrow, school would think he had been at home with a sore throat.

It wouldn't take long, however, for A. J. Sanders to realize how wrong he had been. It turned out that leaving the scene of the crime was the worst possible thing a Good Samaritan could have done, and once the cops did come looking for him, his entire future would be hanging in the balance.

5

Edie Larson's election-night party in the rec room at Sedona Shadows should have been a disaster. After all, by the time the TV station in Flagstaff started scrolling election results across the bottom of the flat-screen TV on the wall, there was already a two-hundred-vote margin. As later results came in, that deficit narrowed, but not enough. The looming loss didn't seem to bother Edie, and it had zero effect on her high spirits. It looked to Ali Reynolds as though her mother were having the time of her life.

One of Bob Larson's new friends, a fellow resident from Sedona Shadows, was providing the music. Mike Baxter, a mostly retired DJ, played his music the old-fashioned way—on vinyl records. He had been widowed after fifty-three years of marriage, and his kids had suggested that taking care of the family home was probably too much for him. Mike correctly read the situation and realized that his kids weren't nearly so worried about upkeep on the old place as they were about seeing it turned into ready cash. They had wanted him to hand it off to an overeager residential developer who just happened to be his son's good pal. Resisting what he regarded as underhanded pressure, Mike had opted to sell the place to someone else, back when suburban Chicago property values were booming. He then departed the Midwest, taking with him a neat profit in real estate as well as his primo collection of vinyl records, gathered one by one over sixty-plus years. Once in Arizona, he settled happily into a new downsized life that included several years with a new wife.

For years Mike had supplemented his retirement income by spinning the old records at events for those he liked to call golden-agers. The music he brought had nothing to do with YMCA, rap, or disco and everything to do with crooners like Frank Sinatra, Patti Page, and Rosemary Clooney as well as the pioneers of rock and roll. Widowed a second time, he downsized yet again. This time he left the heat of Phoenix in favor of cooler Sedona. Even though he was on his own, he had taken a two-bedroom unit in Sedona Shadows. One bedroom was for sleeping, and the other was reserved for his record collection.

Once a week now, Mike did a Saturday-afternoon Sock Hop for the benefit of the facility's residents and any members of the public who cared to venture inside. His sidekick in the operation was Ali's dad, Bob Larson, who handled the electronics and the sound system while Mike handled the platters and the patter. Over the months the two of them had become good friends, and it had been Mike's idea that there should be music at the election-night party.

Ali had thought that was a good idea when she

hoped for a victory celebration. It had turned out to be an even better way to celebrate defeat. So were the several cookie sheets of Sugarloaf Café sweet rolls Edie had ordered from the new owners of the diner that once was the Larson family's livelihood. Edie herself cheerfully dished them out to everyone who showed up at the party, even though Ali suspected some of the attendees hadn't been among Edie's supporters.

The sweet rolls were gone, but the party was going strong. Bob and Edie had again taken to the dance floor when Ali's son, Christopher, stopped by to chat with his mother while his four-year-old son, Colin, snoozed on his shoulder.

"Grandma seems to be taking this all in stride," Chris observed. "How are you doing?"

Ali shrugged. "Losing by fewer than two hundred votes is a respectable loss," she said. "I think we'll be able to hold our heads up. It's not like we took a complete drubbing."

"You look tired, though," Chris said. He was a great son, but diplomacy had never been his strong suit.

Ali kissed the tip of Colin's nose and then smiled at Chris. "That's because I *am* tired," she said. "Running a political campaign is hard work. Truth be told, I think your grandmother had a lot more fun running for office than she would being in office, because then she would have to deal with all the various oddball factions out there."

"You mean like the anti-contrails folks?"

"That's one," Ali said.

Chris laughed. "Grandpa says he thinks they'll try outlawing gravity next."

Ali laughed, too. "Grandpa's opinions are part

of the reason it would be tough for your grandmother to hold office. She'd have to learn to deal
with one extreme out in public and the other
extreme at home. It probably would have driven
her nuts."

Just then Ali's daughter-in-law, Athena, showed
up with Colin's twin sister, Colleen, in hand. Colleen, the far more gregarious of the two, was going
strong at nine-thirty and had to be led from the
dance floor.

"Do we *have* to go home?" she demanded. "I'm
having fun."

"Yes, we have to go home," Athena said firmly.
"Preschool tomorrow."

Colleen made a face but didn't make a fuss. She
looked up at Ali. "Sorry Grandma didn't winned,"
she said.

Ali smiled at her granddaughter without trying
to straighten out that pesky irregular verb. "No, we
didn't, sweetie," she said, leaning down to collect
some night-night love. "Maybe next time."

As Chris and Athena left, Dave and Priscilla
Holman took their places. Dave, a Sedona native,
was the chief homicide detective for the Yavapai
County Sheriff's Department. Years earlier, when
Ali had come back home to Sedona after the collapse of her marriage, she and Dave had been an
item for a while, but the demands of his being a
single dad with sole custody of his kids had proved
too much for their budding romance. At a time
when kids and work were his two top priorities,
their love life had placed a very distant third.
Their breakup had been amicable, and they had
managed to remain friends. Ali had taken up with
B. Simpson, and when Dave's kids had gotten old

enough, he had hooked up with and eventually married Priscilla Morse, a savvy businesswoman who owned a local chain of nail salons.

Living in a small town meant there were very few secrets. From the beginning, Priscilla Morse Holman had known about Dave's previous relationship with Ali, but she had also been one of Edie Larson's staunchest supporters in the campaign for mayor. Initially, there were a few awkward moments between Ali and Priscilla, but the kinks had worked themselves out over the course of several months. Although the two women weren't exactly close friends, they weren't rivals, either.

"Sorry we're late," Priscilla said. "He was working," she said, sighing and sending a pointed look in Dave's direction. "Give this guy a murder case to work on, and he's like a dog with a bone—he just can't let it be." The sweet smile she sent in Dave's direction took some of the edge off what might have been considered bitchy criticism. "Now, where's that mother of yours?" Priscilla asked, looking around the room. "I assume she's got a handle on being a good loser?"

"See for yourself," Ali said, pointing to the dance floor, where Bob and Edie Larson were doing a credible job of rocking to Bill Haley and his Comets' iconic "Rock Around the Clock."

"I heard there were sweet rolls," Dave said, glancing hopefully in the direction of the refreshment table.

"Sorry," Ali said. "They're gone."

"All of them? Too bad!" Dave's disappointment was obvious. As a single guy, he had been a regular customer at the Sugarloaf Café and a devoted fan of Edie's sweet rolls, which the new owners still made according to Edie's recipe and specifications.

"You snooze, you lose," Ali said. "All that's left is coffee and punch and maybe a Girl Scout cookie or two. But what case?" she asked, leading him toward the coffee urns. "I've been so buried with election doings that I haven't paid attention to anything else."

"It just happened this morning," Dave said. "So you haven't missed much. Someone sent a text to 911 about an injured woman found off I-17 near General Crook Trail. By the time we could get to her, she was already dead, and whoever placed the call was long gone, too. No ID on the body, but we found a cell phone; we hoped it would lead us to the victim's name, but that turned out to be a dead end. The owner of the cell phone is alive and well and living down in Surprise. She claims that her cell phone disappeared overnight sometime last night, so that puts us back to square one on IDing our victim. The autopsy is scheduled for tomorrow morning in Prescott. I'd like to know who she is before the ME cuts into her, but I don't think that's going to happen."

"Maybe someone will file a missing persons report," Ali suggested.

Dave nodded. "Let's hope," he said.

At one time Ali had been on track to serve as a sworn officer with the Yavapai Sheriff's Department. After passing a challenging police academy course, she was disappointed when a budget shortfall had caused her to miss the cut. She was officially listed as a reserve officer with the department, although in the months leading up to the election, she had done no shifts. Had Ali been an ordinary civilian, Dave probably wouldn't have spoken so freely about the difficulties of the new investigation. In listening to him, Ali felt the tiniest twinge of regret—jealousy, almost. Dave Holman was working a case. Ali Reynolds wasn't.

At the table, Dave snagged the last remaining Thin Mint and a pair of Girl Scout badge–shaped shortbreads. "Missed dinner," he added, reaching for a coffee cup. "We were out working the crime scene until just before dark, then I had to go into the office."

Yavapai County covered over eight thousand square miles and was only slightly smaller than the state of New Jersey. The Investigations Unit worked out of the departmental office in Prescott, eighty miles away. That meant that between leaving the crime scene and arriving at the party, Dave had done about 160 miles' worth of driving. No wonder Dave and Priscilla had arrived at the party late.

"But Priscilla would have had my ears if we hadn't made it, so here we are." Dave reached for one of the last remaining shortbreads.

"If she hadn't, I'm sure my mother would have," Ali said with a laugh.

"Your mother would have what?" a beaming Edie Larson asked, arriving on the scene with Priscilla and Bob Larson trailing behind her.

Dave grinned at her. "You would have taken off my ears if we hadn't shown up for the party."

"That's right. You don't get off just stuffing envelopes and ringing doorbells."

"What are you going to do now?" Dave asked.

"I'm not sure," Edie said. "I'm exploring my options."

"What about taking another cruise?" Bob suggested. "What's that song Mike was playing a little while ago?"

"I suppose you mean 'If You've Got the Money, Honey, I've Got the Time'?" Edie responded.

"Exactly," Bob said, "and since we do have the money, I think we should have as much fun as we can while we can."

The idea that her father would become a cruise enthusiast was an unintended consequence of Ali's having sent them on a Caribbean cruise several years earlier. Since then they had chalked up a cruise to Alaska, but Bob had a whole list of cruise possibilities, and he was determined to cross off as many as he could.

With that Bob excused himself to help Mike disassemble his portable dance floor and pack that up, as well as all the DJ equipment. Dave's cell phone was ringing as he and Priscilla let themselves out. Leaving Edie to say good night to the rest of the departing guests, Ali busied herself helping a handful of campaign volunteers clean up. Chairs and tables had been relocated in order to create room for the dance floor. Those all needed to be returned to their customary positions. By the time Edie said goodbye to the last guest, Ali was carefully moving a half-completed fifteen-hundred-piece jigsaw puzzle back to its allotted place.

"Everyone keeps asking me what I'm going to do next," Edie said. "The problem is, I have no idea."

Ali gave her mother a sympathetic smile. "Welcome to my world," she said. "I've been grappling with that very question ever since the whole police academy thing blew up in my face. You handled yourself really well tonight, Mom. You did yourself proud under very difficult circumstances."

Edie nodded. "Thanks. I told myself this morning that win, lose, or draw, I was going to look like I was having fun no matter what. When the returns started coming in and I could see we were falling behind, I told myself, 'Stiff upper lip and all that.' The funny thing is, I started out pretending to have fun, but pretty soon I really was having fun. Besides," she added, "I know your father's relieved. Bobby's been a brick about all this, and he never would have voted against me in a million years, but I'm equally sure he would have hated it if I had won."

"He would have continued to be a brick," Ali assured her mother, "but I think he'll be glad to have you all to himself. From what you're saying, though, I take it you're not that disappointed that we lost?"

"I don't suppose I am," Edie agreed after a pause. "Not really. It was our first time out, and we came really close to unseating an incumbent. That counts for something. And I'm glad I ran. Doing that taught me that I can do anything I set my mind to. Now all I have to do is figure out what that is. Speaking of same, now that you're out of a job, too, what's your next step?"

"I'll have to start thinking about next year's scholarship nominees, and the symphony has been after me to take charge of next spring's author luncheon. I've been putting them off because I was too busy with the election."

Edie smiled. "You don't have that excuse anymore."

"No, I don't," Ali agreed. "I guess I'll give them a call and see if they've gotten someone else to handle it."

"When does B. get in?" Edie asked.

"He's due back from Hong Kong tomorrow afternoon."

"Does he know about the election?" Edie asked.

Ali nodded. "I sent him a text while you were giving your concession speech. He said you gave it the old college try and that he's proud of us both."

"We did give it a good try, didn't we?" Edie said. "We certainly did."

There was a hint of sorrow in her voice that belied her words, and Ali suspected that her mother was maintaining that stiff upper lip for her daughter's benefit.

"Get some rest, Mom," Ali advised. "I'll spend the morning pulling together the rest of the financial reports—paying the last few bills, that sort of thing."

"Is the campaign going to end up owing a lot of money?" Edie asked.

"No," Ali said. "No worries there. The outstanding bills amount to only a couple of hundred dollars."

Most of Edie's campaign had been done the old-fashioned way—expending shoe-leather and building yard signs—rather than buying television and radio airtime. "Edie for Mayor" campaign workers had done plenty of walking, but they hadn't spent much money, which was more than could be said for their opponent. According to federally mandated campaign finance reports, Ali had learned that the newly reelected mayor of Sedona had won that two-hundred-vote margin by spending almost two hundred thousand dollars in campaign funds, most of it his own money.

"That's a relief, then," Edie said. "I wouldn't want to be out busting my butt and asking for donations to retire campaign debt. People hate donating to lost causes. On that note, I think I'll head for the barn."

With that, her mother got up. Edie walked across the lobby with her shoulders back and her head held high. It was an impressive act, one that might have fooled someone else, but not her daughter. Ali saw right through it to the disappointment underneath, and it broke her heart that there wasn't a thing she could do about it—not a single thing.

6

Lynn Martinson was grateful that her mother was out of the house for most of the afternoon. Weather in the Valley of the Sun had cooled off enough that Beatrice Hart and some of her seventysomething pals had decided to play a round of golf, and for a daughter who had misplaced her cell phone once again, that was good news.

For as long as she could remember, Beatrice had poked fun at Lynn about being a scatterbrain, and that criticism wasn't entirely wrong, but what once was good-hearted teasing had taken a more serious turn. In the aftermath of Lynn's father's long struggle first with dementia and later with Alzheimer's, Beatrice was on full alert for signs that a set of missing car keys or an AWOL cell phone were harbingers of a first downhill slip that might signal the full-scale unstoppable slide that had taken her husband's life.

Lynn had noticed that the phone was missing much earlier that morning. When she had arrived home from Chip's place, the phone wasn't in its customary spot in a zippered pocket in her purse.

That she often spent the night at Chip's house was a bone of contention between Beatrice and her daughter. Lynn may have been in her forties, but Beatrice's opinions about "living in sin" weren't something she kept to herself. Lynn chafed under the criticism, but there wasn't much she could do about it. Economic necessity dictated that until she was able to find a job, living with her mother was her only real option.

There was the hope that Chip would pop the question, but in terms of living arrangements, he was in much the same boat. His high-priced divorce had left him in a financial bind that would take several years to unravel, and at age fifty, he was back home with his eightysomething recently widowed mother, living in a casita, a former maid's quarters, that had been built behind his parents' longtime Paradise Valley home. Chip's mother didn't like Lynn's sleepovers any more than her mother did.

To keep from rocking parental boats, Chip and Lynn, cast in the role of aging, lovestruck teenagers, had little choice but to sneak around. There was no privacy to be had in the small two-story tract home Lynn shared with her mother on West Willows Lane, so she usually went to Chip's place, arriving after his mother went to bed and leaving early the next morning. Lynn knew that if she left Chip's place by five-thirty, she could be back home before her own mother went out to the front yard to retrieve the morning newspaper.

It was after Lynn was upstairs in her room that she first discovered that her phone was gone. Lynn had put her keys in her purse and reached for her phone so she could call Chip and tell him she had arrived home safely, but the phone wasn't anywhere to be found. She had searched the entire bag, digging all the way to the bottom. In the process, she unearthed year-old gas receipts, lint from a clutch of deteriorating tissues, an almost empty compact, and several dead tubes of lipstick. When she turned the emptied carcass over and dumped it onto her bed, a few stray coins came out, but no phone.

Lynn's next thought—a perfectly logical one—was that in rushing around to come home, perhaps she had left the phone at Chip's place. When arriving there, she routinely deposited her purse, keys, and cell phone on the entryway table, a place where they'd be easy to find the next morning as she was leaving. She used her mother's landline to call her own number, thinking if it rang somewhere in his apartment, Chip would hear it and answer. When her phone switched over to voice mail, she dialed Chip's cell phone.

"It didn't ring here," Chip said once she had explained the situation. "Are you sure you had it with you last night?"

"I'm sure."

"Maybe it's not turned on," Chip suggested. "If you accidentally hit the off switch, or if the charge ran down, it wouldn't ring, and I wouldn't hear it."

"I took it off the charger last night when I was heading for your place," Lynn told him. "It should have had plenty of battery power, and I would have remembered turning it off."

"Probably fell out in the car somewhere," he concluded. "Maybe it slipped down between the seats or it's on the floorboard and slid under the car seat. Have you looked there?"

"Not yet. I called you first. I'll look there next."

"Sorry you lost your phone," he said, "but I'm glad to hear your voice. I miss you already."

The words made Lynn smile. "I miss you, too," she replied.

Beatrice emerged from the bedroom in time to hear the last comment. "Oh, for Pete's sake," she said. "Isn't it a little early for the lovebirds to be at it again? Don't you have something better to do than to stand around whispering sweet nothings?"

While her mother bustled around the kitchen making breakfast, Lynn went into her room and searched there, even though she was sure she'd had the phone in the car on her way to Chip's the night before. She tried calling her cell again, in case Chip was right. No dice. Then she remembered that she had stopped for gas on the way home. It was one of those places where you got a free wash with a fill-up.

The car had seemed dustier this morning than she remembered. She had opted for the free wash. It could be that the phone had fallen out while she was dealing with that, or else with the self-service gas pump, or maybe she had left it on the counter when she went inside to pay. Pulling the receipt out of her wallet, she located the gas station's phone number and called. The clerk reported that she hadn't seen an abandoned cell phone anywhere, not on the counter and not out by the pumps. If someone had found a lost cell phone, they hadn't bothered turning it in.

"Great," Lynn said with a sigh. "I guess I'd better plan on going out and getting a new one."

Lynn and her mother had fallen into a pattern where Beatrice did most of the cooking and Lynn did most of the cleaning up. Once the breakfast dishes had been cleared away, Lynn went out to the garage and performed a thorough search through her Ford Focus—to no avail. The rest of the morning, she dialed her own number periodically in hopes that, wherever the phone was, someone might hear it ringing and answer. Each time, however, when it switched over to voice mail, Lynn hung up. There was no point in leaving a message that she most likely would never be able to retrieve.

Once her mother left the house, Lynn searched everywhere again—in the house, in the car. She even went outside and pawed through the Dumpster. Finally, giving up, she forced herself to sit down at the computer. She was determined to find a job that would enable her to move out of her mother's house, and she devoted several hours each day, Saturdays and Sundays included, to diligent searching.

She had sent out dozens of résumés to dozens of school districts in hopes of finding an administrative position. Once, years ago, she had been a high school English teacher. She wasn't wild about going back to the classroom, but in this economy, even beginning-teachers' jobs were hard to come by. She also wasn't really comfortable with the idea that job searches were now conducted almost entirely online.

Her ill-fated online romance with Richard Lowensdale—he of the many interchangeable last names—had left her with the belief that everybody lied when they were on the Internet. She suspected that school districts overstated their needs as well as their pay scales, while applicants inflated their educational accomplishments as well as their job histories. Disheartening as the process had proved so far, Lynn refused to give up. Today she decided that at three o'clock she'd reward her diligence with a quick excursion to the mall to find a new phone. If she did that while her mother was off playing golf, she might never have to admit that she had misplaced the old one.

A few minutes before three, the doorbell rang. When Lynn looked out through the peephole, she was surprised to see a man in a suit and tie standing on the porch, holding up a law enforcement badge of some kind for her inspection.

Lynn's heart fell. Convinced that her mother had suffered some kind of health issue out on the golf course, she flung open the door in a blind panic. "Oh my God," she managed. "What is it? Has something happened to my mother? Is she okay?"

"I'm Detective Larry Cutter with the Maricopa County Sheriff's Department," the officer explained, handing her one of his cards.

Lynn studied it for a moment, then clutched at the doorframe in an effort to remain upright. "It says here that you're with homicide?" she demanded in a shaking voice. "Does that mean my mother has been murdered out on the golf course?"

Detective Cutter frowned. "May I come in?" he asked. "Does your mother's name happen to be Lynnette Martinson?"

Lynn stepped aside and allowed him to enter. "No," she told him. "That's my name. I'm Lynnette Martinson. My mother's name is Beatrice Hart. What's this all about? If my mother is all right, has someone else been murdered?"

Uninvited, the detective settled his lanky form on the sofa in the living room, where he studied Lynn with a kind of grim appraisal as she stumbled awkwardly into a nearby chair. His unreadable expression was nothing short of disquieting.

"What's this about?" Lynn's voice came out as a quaking squeak. She couldn't help it.

"When did you last see her?" Cutter asked.

"My mother? She went golfing with her friends. They left shortly before noon."

"Today?"

Lynn nodded.

"Then I'm sure your mother's fine," the detective said.

Relieved, Lynn let out a sigh. When she noticed that her hands were trembling, she gripped the armrests to steady them. "Tell me what's going on, then. Your card says you're homicide. That means someone has been murdered. Who? And why are you asking me about it?"

"The victim, a female, has not yet been identified," Cutter answered. "However, a telephone listed in your name and with an Iowa prefix was found at the scene. We were able to obtain this address from the cell phone provider because it's listed as the billing address. Does anyone else besides yourself have access to the phone?"

"No, no one else uses it—or," Lynn corrected, "let's say no one else is supposed to use it. The problem is, I lost the phone sometime overnight, either last night or early this morning. I've been looking for it everywhere and calling it, too, all morning long. I thought maybe I left it at the gas station when I filled up the tank on my way home, and I was hoping whoever found it would answer my call."

"On your way home from where?" Cutter asked.

"From my boyfriend's house in Paradise Valley," Lynn answered. "I spent the night there." She blushed when making that admission, though there was no reason to be embarrassed. After all, Lynn was a consenting adult, and so was Chip Ralston. Her love life was no one's business but her own; still, blush she did, and realizing that her face had reddened under Detective Cutter's un-smiling scrutiny made it that much worse.

"Do you remember the last time you used it?" he asked.

"Yesterday sometime. Late in the evening. I re-member calling Chip to let him know I was on my way to his place."

"After that, it disappeared?"

"As I said, I didn't notice it was gone until after I got home this morning."

"You have no idea who might have been using your phone? Is it possible that you lent it to some-one?"

"No," Lynn said firmly. "As I told you before, I lost it. In fact, I was about to go to the store to see about getting a replacement, but you still haven't told me who's dead."

"That's the problem," Detective Cutter said. "We don't know who the victim is. No identifica-tion was found on the body, and so far, no one matching the victim's description has been reported missing anywhere in the Phoenix metropolitan area. We initially thought that finding the owner of the phone would lead us to the victim."

"But I'm not dead," Lynn objected.

"I noticed," Cutter agreed, giving her a tight smile. "Let me ask you this. Do you have any friends or relations or acquaintances living in the Camp Verde/Sedona area?"

Lynn shook her head. "No one," she said definitively. "No one at all. I know about Sedona, of course. At least I've seen photos of it. I've heard that the red rocks are very beautiful, but I've never been there. I came to the Phoenix area a little over a year ago. My parents retired here, and my father's health was failing. When I lost my job, the only silver lining was that I was able to come here to help my mother. There wasn't any time or money for traveling while we were caring for him. Now that he's gone, maybe I'll be able to get around to some sightseeing." Realizing she was talking too much, Lynn paused and took a breath before asking, "Is that where the dead woman was found—in Sedona?"

"Near Sedona," Cutter corrected, "but closer to Camp Verde."

"We need to find whoever it was who took the phone," Lynn said.

"Yes, we do," Cutter said. "In the meantime, you say you were with your boyfriend last night?"

"Yes."

"All last night?"

"From ten-fifteen on." She didn't want to admit to the detective that she had timed her arrival for an hour when she could be confident Chip's mother had gone to bed.

"What time did you get back home?"

"I was here by six or so. I stopped for gas on the way and got a car wash while I was at it, so I must have left Paradise Valley around five-fifteen or so."

"Your boyfriend will verify that?"

"Of course."

"Good, then," Detective Cutter said. "Thank you for your help."

Lynn fully expected the detective to take his leave. Instead, Cutter reached into his jacket pocket and pulled out a notebook and a stubby pencil. He opened it to a blank page and then sat there with his pencil poised to write. "I'll need your boyfriend's name, then," he said, "and his number."

Lynn hated to think that her having stupidly lost her phone was about to drag Chip into some kind of unpleasantness, but there was no dodging it. "His name is Ralston," she answered. "Dr. Charles Ralston, although everyone calls him Chip."

That was a silly thing to say, Lynn thought self-consciously. *A cop wouldn't call him Chip. A cop would call him Dr. Ralston.*

"He's a psychiatrist specializing in Alzheimer's patients and their families," she added. "That's how we met. He was caring for my father—for both my parents, really."

"His phone number?"

Lynn was torn. She didn't want to reel off Chip's cell number to a visiting cop. That didn't seem right. "His office is just off Highway 60 in Sun City," she said. "I don't know the office phone number off the top of my head, but I'm sure you can find it."

"I'm sure I can, too," Detective Cutter said, pocketing the notebook and rising. "I can let myself out."

Lynn followed him to the door anyway. "I hope you find out who she was," she said. "More than that, I hope you find out who did it."

"That makes two of us," he said.

"What about my phone?" she asked.

"What about it?"

"When will I get it back?"

"It's evidence in a homicide, ma'am," Detective Cutter said. "It could take months or years for it to be released, if ever. I'd suggest that you do what you said you were planning to do earlier—go to the store and get yourself a new one."

Lynn stood in the doorway and watched Detective Cutter walk back to his unmarked car. As soon as he drove away, she returned to the house and sank down into the same chair in the living room where she'd been sitting during the interview. It was a little late for her to come to that conclusion, but she understood that was what it had been—a homicide interview, only without the two-way mirrors and the video camera that they were always showing on those true-crime cop shows.

She couldn't believe what had happened. How was it possible that her cell phone was considered evidence in a murder investigation? Moments later, she pulled herself together. Reaching for the landline, she dialed Chip's cell. She found herself holding her breath while the phone rang. When he answered and she heard the sound of his reassuring voice, she burst into tears.

"Lynn, what's the matter? Is something wrong? Are you all right?"

"You're not going to believe it," she said. "A cop just left here."

"A cop? Why? What's going on?"

"It's my phone," she blubbered. "Someone's been murdered up by Sedona, and they found my phone at the scene of the crime. I'm pretty sure the detective came here thinking I was the victim—the woman who's dead. Now he may think I had something to do with it."

"Did he come right out and say you were a suspect?"

"No, but he asked me where I was last night. I told him I was at your place, so he'll probably be calling you to verify that. What I can't figure out is how my phone got all the way up to Camp Verde."

"I can't, either," Chip said. "Camp Verde's got to be close to eighty miles from here. When's the last time you remember using it?"

"I called you last night to tell you I was coming over, remember?"

"Just a sec," Chip said. "Let me check." A moment later, he came back on the line. "Yes, I see in my call log that you called me on your cell around a quarter to ten. What time was the woman killed?"

"I don't know. Sometime overnight, I guess," Lynn said. "The detective didn't tell me that much, just that my phone was found at the scene. The only thing I can think is that I must have lost it when I stopped at the gas station on my way home this morning. Do you think I need an attorney?"

"Can you afford an attorney?"

It was an unnecessary question, because Chip already knew the answer.

"Not really."

"Well, then," he said reassuringly, "since we both know you weren't involved in anything, we'll just have to let things play out." Lynn heard a buzz in the background, followed by a woman's voice. "Gotta go," he said. "Tina tells me there's a detective Larry Cutter out in the waiting room."

Lynn sat with the phone in her hand for several

long moments after Chip hung up. She couldn't help but be grateful for the reassurance she had heard in his voice. After the whole ego-shattering mess with Richard Lowensdale, Lynn hadn't expected to fall in love again. For one thing, she hadn't expected to find a man she could trust, but she had, and Chip Ralston was it.

Lynn had come on the scene at a time when her father was so far gone that he had been beyond help. Her mother was the one who needed care and support, and Chip—Dr. Ralston to all of them then—had been sympathetic and supportive and incredibly understanding. Lynn had been more than a little attracted to him from the beginning, but she had never expected anything to come of it. After her father died, she was impressed when Dr. Ralston showed up for the memorial service. When he had called her a month or so later, asking how her mother was doing, she had thought it was just that—his being solicitous of her mother. It was only when he came courting that she was gratified to learn he had something else in mind.

Lynn was astonished to discover that what she'd thought was a one-sided attraction was reciprocated. Now this kind, caring, well-educated, and dependable man was part of her life—her scatterbrained life.

With that thought in mind, Lynn put down the landline phone and went looking for her purse. It was time to go to Verizon and get a new phone.

7

By the time the ten o'clock news came on that
night, A.J. was glued to the television set in his
bedroom. Somehow he had made it through
his two-hour shift at work and through dinner
without blowing apart. His mother had made *carne
asada* burritos. That was his favorite meal and usually he gobbled down several. That night he barely
managed to eat one.

"Since when did you stop liking *carne asada*?"
his mother asked.

"I'm just not hungry," he said.

"I made the amount I always make," she said.
"So we'll have the same thing for dinner again
tomorrow night."

A.J. helped with the dishes and then went
into his room, ostensibly to do homework, but the
words on the pages made no sense. What he kept
seeing in his mind's eye were those vivid green
eyes staring blankly up at the sun.

Who was she? A.J. wondered. *Who killed her
and why?*

He wasn't at all surprised when news about the

Camp Verde homicide was the lead story on the broadcast.

"The Yavapai County Sheriff's Department is investigating an apparent homicide near I-17, south of Camp Verde," the news host reported with a white-toothed smile that A.J. found completely inappropriate. "Our reporter Christy Lawler has been on the scene. What can you tell us, Christy?"

Another smiling face appeared on the screen. "Around noon today, officers responding to a 911 summons arrived at a location just off General Crook Trail, where they discovered the body of an unidentified woman. The death, which has been labeled a homicide, occurred inside Yavapai County, and the Yavapai County Sheriff's Department is investigating. Mike Sawyer, spokesman for the Sheriff's Department, told me earlier that officers are following up on clues found at the scene in hopes of identifying the victim."

A young man with a serious expression appeared in front of a bank of microphones. "Homicide investigators are actively seeking the identity of the person or persons who sent a text message to 911 operators, letting them know the location of a seriously injured person. By the time help arrived, the person who sent the message was no longer at the scene. That Good Samaritan, also unidentified at this time, is not considered a suspect in the case, but he or she is regarded as a person of interest. We are urging that person or anyone who knows who that person might be to do the right thing and contact the Yavapai County Sheriff's Department."

The broadcast quickly moved on to another story, that of a multicar pileup on I-10 just outside Casa Grande. A.J., staring at the screen, heard nothing about that story or the ones that followed it. The words "person of interest" kept running through his brain. That meant the cops were actually looking for him. He had sent the text for the best of all possible reasons—in hopes of getting help for the poor woman—and now he was part of it. He was involved.

They wanted to talk to him, but what good would "doing the right thing" do? A.J. had no idea who the woman was. He hadn't seen the killer. He had seen no other vehicles in the area, and he knew nothing that would help in the investigation. If he came forward, first the cops would learn that he had ditched school to be somewhere he shouldn't have been. Then they'd want to know why he was at that particular location at that particular time. Answering the question would mean letting the world and his mother know about his father's letter, as well as the buried-treasure story, which was sounding more stupid by the minute.

A.J. could imagine cops standing around and staring down at the shovel—at A.J.'s mother's shovel. It was easy enough to figure out what they'd think—that the person who had attacked the woman had come to the scene of the crime prepared to bury her. Once they examined the shovel, whose fingerprints would be on it? A.J.'s, of course, and maybe his mother's as well. It was an old shovel, but if they somehow traced it back to him, his fingerprints on that and on the telephone would place him at the scene of the crime. Suddenly, he'd be more than a person of interest—he'd be a prime suspect.

Panic rose in A.J.'s throat, fear mixed with shame. His mother knew nothing about the letter he had received from his father. He had kept quiet about the earlier meeting, too, the one that had led to the Camry. If he went to the cops and told them about his father's letter, everything would come out, and his mother would know that he had betrayed her not just once, not just twice, but several times. His mother had always been in A.J.'s corner. She had been the one person in his life he knew he could count on, no matter what, and he had let her down.

There was a tap on his bedroom door. Startled, A.J. jumped as if he'd been shot. A moment later, Sylvia poked her head into his room.

"What's going on?" she asked. "You never watch Jay Leno."

Jay Leno was already on? When had that happened? A.J. grabbed the remote from his bedside table and switched off the TV. "Sorry, Mom," he said quickly. "I must have dozed off."

"Glad I checked on you, then," she said. "Good night."

That night was not a good night for A. J. Sanders. After tossing and turning for what seemed like hours, he finally fell asleep. Instead of being lost in a waking nightmare, he found himself in the regular kind, with the same dream cycling endlessly through his fitful slumber. In each one, the light went out of those haunting green eyes as they stared emptily back at him. Each time they did, he jarred himself awake only to find his body drenched in sweat. When A.J. staggered out of bed the next morning, he felt as though he'd barely slept at all. He wondered if he'd ever be able to sleep again.

8

Ali slept late on Wednesday morning. For the first time in months, she had no schedule to keep. Yes, she was sorry her mother had lost, but she was glad to step off the campaign merry-go-round. B. would be home later in the day, and she was looking forward to a relatively uncomplicated week. Glad to be free to lounge around in her PJs, Ali spent all of Wednesday morning working on Edie's campaign financial reports. By the time she had paid most of the bills, there was a little over five hundred dollars in debt remaining, including a three-hundred-dollar bill for the sweet rolls from the party.

When she called her mother to discuss the situation, her father answered the phone. "Don't worry about that one," he said when she explained the reason for the call. "Your mother and I were just about to head over there to return their cookie sheets. We'll pay that one off ourselves while we're there. What else is there?"

"We still owe two hundred dollars for the last batch of yard signs."

"After that, we're square?" Bob Larson asked.

"Those are the only two bills that are outstanding. I paid everything else."

"If that's all, we're damned lucky," her father said. "I was afraid it would be a lot worse. Give me the amount of the sign bill, and tell me who's the vendor. I'll get that one paid today as well."

"I'll need to have the receipts so I can put them in the report."

"You'll have them either later today or tomorrow at the latest."

"I guess Mom was right about you, then," Ali said.

"Why?" Bob asked. "What did she say?"

"That you've been a brick, and you still are a brick."

"That's a compliment?"

Ali knew that the most recent usage of the word "brick"—Hardware Inoperable (thus turning a formerly useful electronics device into a brick)—was completely outside her mother's vocabulary, and the terminology wasn't part of her father's way of thinking, either.

"Definitely," Ali told him with a laugh. "Let me know when you have the receipts. I'll come by and pick them up."

By then the enticing aroma of baking bread was summoning Ali to the kitchen, where she knew she would find Leland Brooks, her eightysomething man of all work, in his element and bustling around an upscale kitchen that had been remodeled to his exact specifications.

When it came to the house on Manzanita Hills Road, Leland was the old-timer, and Ali was the relatively new arrival. He had served with the

British Marines during the Korean War and immigrated to the U.S. shortly thereafter. He had gone to work for Anne Marie Ashcroft, the original owner of the house. After Anne Marie's death, he continued to care for her troubled daughter, Arabella, until her eventual incarceration at a facility for the criminally insane.

By then, after years of deferred maintenance and willful neglect on Arabella's part, the house was a shadow of its former self. Even as a derelict, Leland knew that the place had good bones. When a developer threatened to buy it and bulldoze it, Leland had gone to Ali and convinced her to take on the project of buying the place and returning it to its former glory. They had assumed that he would hang around only long enough to see Ali through the renovation process, but by the time the first phase of construction was completed, Leland was perfectly content to stay on in the fifth-wheel mobile home that Ali had set up for him on the far side of the garage. By then he had set his sights on finishing the English garden that Anne Marie had envisioned for the front yard.

Leland hadn't participated in the digging and raking—Ali had made sure there were younger bodies to handle the heavy lifting—but he had personally overseen the entire project. Out of deference for his age, Ali encouraged him to hire people to come in and do the routine housecleaning, which was also done to his stringent standards, but there was no way she could boot him out of his kitchen. Cooking was something he loved to do, and they had agreed that he would continue to be in charge of it until he was ready to call it quits and not a moment before.

"What's on the menu for tonight?" Ali asked, seeing the mound of chopped vegetables that had accumulated on the island counter next to the stovetop.

"Beef stew," Leland answered. "When Mr. Simpson comes home from galavanting all around the world, he does like his comfort food. For that, freshly baked bread and steaming-hot stew are right at the top of the list."

That was true. B. Simpson's travels took him to plenty of exotic places with equally exotic food choices. It was no accident that when he was at home in Sedona, he gravitated to Ali's house and Leland Brooks's very capable cooking.

Ali helped herself to a new cup of coffee.

"Can I fix you something for lunch?" Leland asked.

Ali eyed the four loaves of freshly baked bread cooling on the counter. "What about a slice of one of those?" she asked. "Or is the bread still too warm to cut?"

"It's just right," Leland assured her. Moments later, he handed her a plate with a thick piece of crusty bread. Taking a seat at the kitchen table, Ali slathered butter on the warm bread, then found her eyes drawn to the television over the microwave, where the noontime edition of the local news was just starting.

"The Yavapai County Sheriff's Department just confirmed that a second body has been found south of Camp Verde, near where another homicide victim was found yesterday. That victim has been identified as a Phoenix-area woman. Her name has not been released while the authorities attempt to contact her next of kin. Reporter Christy Lawler is live on the scene. What can you tell us, Christy? Is there a serial killer stalking motorists driving the I-17 corridor?"

"So far the Sheriff's Department has made no mention of a serial killer, although that's on the minds of people traveling this roadway today," the reporter answered. "The second victim was found early this morning by investigators doing an extensive crime scene examination of the area. What we know so far is that the second victim is an unidentified male found with no identification.

"All authorities would say was that the victim died as the result of homicidal violence. Questions asked about the manner of death, and if it was similar to what happened to the previous victim, were met with an official reply of 'No comment.' However, authorities are cautioning motorists to beware of giving rides to strangers, and they are asking anyone who has seen anything unusual along this stretch of freeway to please come forward."

"Are motorists taking that bit of advice to heart?" the anchor asked.

"Absolutely," Christy replied. "Here's what one mother, Janie Brownward of Phoenix, had to say."

The camera panned to the driver's-side window of a minivan parked in what appeared to be the parking lot of a fast-food restaurant. "I'm scared to death," the woman said, speaking into the proffered microphone. "I drive this road all the time with my three kids, and to think that there might be a murderer lurking in every rest area is terrifying. We need people like this off the streets and off our highways and in prison, where they belong."

"What can you tell us about the woman who was found yesterday?" the anchor asked.

"Nothing more so far," Christy said. "All I can say right now is that there's a big Sheriff's Department response at the scene, and I'll let you know of any developments as the day moves along."

"All right, we'll look forward to hearing from you again on the five o'clock broadcast."

Leland took the remote from the counter and switched off the TV as Ali polished off the last bite of bread. "Delicious," she said, "and absolutely addictive. Shouldn't your bread be listed as a controlled substance?"

"Very kind of you to say so." He beamed. "It should go nicely with the stew."

"That's assuming there's still some left by the time dinner rolls around."

Leland took the hint and cut off another slice, which he buttered and handed over. "Have you heard anything from Sister Anselm?" he asked. "I hate to think of her out on the highway by herself when things like this are going on."

Ali's good friend Sister Anselm Becker was a Sister of Providence who worked out of St. Bernadette's, a convent for troubled nuns in nearby Jerome. When she was at home, she served as an in-house counselor for nuns dealing with any number of thorny issues from substance abuse to post-traumatic stress. She also spent a lot of time on the road, traveling from hospital to hospital, functioning as a special emissary from Bishop Francis Gillespie of the Phoenix archdiocese and as a patient advocate for people who had no one else to speak on their behalf.

"I'll give her a call and check," Ali said. "As far as I know, she's expected to be at the convent all week, but that could have changed."

"I know she's perfectly capable of looking after herself," Leland said, "but I worry about her all the same."

"That makes two of us," Ali agreed.

"Before you make that call, if you have time, there's something I'd like to discuss with you," Leland said. "It came up a few days ago, but you were so preoccupied with the election that I didn't want to bother you with it."

A frisson of concern passed through Ali's body. She knew exactly how old Leland Brooks was, and she worried that what was coming was some kind of announcement about a burgeoning health issue. She had known instinctively that forcing him to forsake his kitchen would be the end of him, but she also knew that the end would still have to come eventually.

"Of course," Ali said worriedly. "This sounds serious."

Wordlessly, Leland plucked an envelope out of his pocket and handed it over. The stamps, the return address, and the London postmark revealed that the letter had been sent from the UK. "It's from my grand-nephew," Leland explained. "My late brother's grandson. He's evidently developed an interest in genealogy and has seen fit to contact the black sheep of the family."

The words were spoken in an offhand way that belied the hurt behind them. Ali knew that after returning from Korea, rather than being welcomed as the hero he was, Leland had been shunned by his own family and sent packing. Compared to now, the early to mid-fifties had been the dark ages in terms of acceptance of gays in society. Fortunately for Leland, Anne Marie Ashcroft had reached out to him from across the ocean, offering him a job and agreeing to be his sponsor. Over the years, Leland had repaid Anne Marie's confidence in him many times over, and Ali Reynolds was reaping the benefit of his undying loyalty.

"It's all right," he said, nodding toward the letter. "Go ahead and read it."

Dear Uncle Leland,

I trust you won't think it too presumptuous of me to address you by that name, but that is indeed who you are, my great-uncle, being the younger brother of my late grandfather Langston. Having recently been bitten by the genealogy bug, I was doing a bit of family research with the help of my great-grandmother's letters which, upon her death, had been donated to the historical society in Cheltenham.

It was with these that I found letters from you to her, written presumably while you were serving overseas during the Korean War and after you emigrated to the U.S. Up to that moment, I had been under the impression that my late grandfather had but one brother, Leo, sadly, also deceased. It was only when I saw the signature on those letters—"Your loving son, Leland"— that I realized there had been a third brother, one whose existence, as far as I can remember, was never mentioned in family conversations.

Details of that time are notably lacking since, as I mentioned before, both my grandfather and Leo are now deceased. I'm forced to conclude that a family difficulty of some kind led to a serious falling-out that has lasted from that time to this. It is in the hope

*of overcoming whatever was the source of that
old enmity that I write to you today.*

*Through veterans' organizations, I was
able to learn of your honorable service in the
Royal Marines during the Korean War. They
were able to lead me to this address, the one
to which I'm sending this missive. At the time
of my writing, I have no idea if indeed you are
still there; nor do I know if, upon reading this,
you would be willing to consider reestablishing
any old family ties.*

*I am currently in the process of organizing
a family reunion that is scheduled to
take place in either Stow-on-the-Wold or
Cheltenham in May of next year. I am hoping
I can persuade you to consider attending.*

*Should you decide to come, you would
unfortunately be the last member of that
generation to be in attendance.*

*Again, whatever quarrel might have been
between you and your two brothers must have
been a serious one, but I'm hoping you'll be
willing to set that aside and join us. It would
be an honor to welcome you back into our fold.*

> *Sincerely,*
> *Jeffrey Alan Brooks,*
> *Esquire*

Ali carefully refolded the letter, returned it to
the envelope, and passed it back to Leland. "What
are you going to do?" she asked.

Leland shrugged and eased his spare frame
down onto a kitchen chair. "When I left there, I
vowed I'd never go back," he said. "That's what I
said, and that's what I meant."

"Things have changed for the better since then," Ali said. "The letter sounds welcoming, as though they really want you to come."

"All during the war, I was very circumspect in what I wrote to my mother. I doubt she had any idea of the real cause of the feud between my older brothers and me. It seems likely now that Leo and Langston died without telling anyone," Leland replied. "Jeffrey has no idea what happened—about them telling me there was no place in the family for someone like me. For all I know, he may share their opinion."

"Then again, he may not," Ali interjected. "And the truth is, how you've lived your life between then and now is none of the family's business." She paused and then added, "I hope you'll consider going."

"I'll give it some thought," Leland said grudgingly, returning the letter to his pocket. "I wouldn't have told you about it otherwise. The problem is, if I were to go larking off across the pond, who would look after you?"

"I'm sure I could manage," Ali said. She wanted to say that she wasn't exactly helpless, but she also didn't want to denigrate Leland's steadfast service in any way. "There's plenty of time. Maybe we could look around and find a temporary replacement."

"Perhaps," Leland said. "I'll take it under advisement."

Ali spent the afternoon getting ready to welcome B. home. She ducked into the nearest of Priscilla Holman's nail salons for a much needed mani-pedi, then settled into a chair in front of the library fireplace, where she returned to the world of Charles

Dickens. Losing herself in the intricacies of the French Revolution was a way to put aside the present for the time being, as well as keeping her from watching the clock.

By the time B. arrived, Leland had discreetly gone to his own digs in the fifth wheel, leaving them to enjoy B.'s homecoming dinner with some welcome privacy. They ate the savory stew, accompanied by slabs of freshly baked bread, in the cozy confines of Ali's spacious kitchen, which was far and away B.'s second favorite room in her house.

When they finished eating, B. leaned back in his chair and closed his eyes. "This is the best part of being away on business—coming home," he said. "I love what I do, but perpetually living out of a suitcase and being on no known time zone gets old after a while." He opened his eyes, looked at her, and grinned. "Don't worry," he said. "I'm not going to ask you to marry me again. A guy can only handle so much rejection. The problem is, Leland has always been my benchmark. As long as you kept him around, I figured I was safe, but if he's on a short leash . . ."

Just then Ali's phone rang. The caller ID said GATE. The security gate at the bottom of the drive closed automatically at sunset. From then on, anyone wanting access to Ali's home had to dial from the handset on the post.

Ali switched on the kitchen TV and activated the video monitor that allowed a clear view of visitors on the far side of the gate. An older woman stood there, holding the phone to her ear.

"Yes," Ali said, answering the phone. "May I help you?"

"My name is Beatrice Hart," the woman said. "My daughter, Lynn, is a friend of yours."

"Sorry," Ali said. "Are you sure you have the right person? I'm afraid I don't know anyone named Lynn Hart."

"You're the lady detective who helped catch Brenda Riley's cyber-stalker, aren't you?"

"I may have helped, but I'm not a detective—not officially," Ali responded.

"In that case, you probably know my daughter by her married name, Lynn Martinson. She was one of the women who got mixed up with that same guy years ago. I believe they filmed both you and Lynn at a TV station in Phoenix when Brenda's book was about to come out last summer and when they were doing that true-crime show for TV."

That was enough of a hint to trigger a vague memory. Yes, Ali did remember meeting a woman named Lynn in the greenroom for *Scene of the Crime* at the TV station in Phoenix when they were both there for a scheduled taping. At the time, Ali had been so preoccupied with her own issues—most notably her mother's election campaign—that she barely remembered anything about it.

"I follow Brenda on Twitter these days," Beatrice continued. "Did you know she's about to come out with another true-crime book? This one's about a serial killer who operated in Northern California and southern Oregon. When all of this came up this afternoon, I sent Brenda a tweet asking for her advice. She suggested I should get in touch with you."

"When all what came up?" Ali asked.

"Lynn's gone missing," Beatrice said, her voice

breaking. "She didn't come home this morning, and with this murder business all over the TV news, I'm terribly worried."

"This sounds like a police matter," Ali said. "I'm not sure how I can be of assistance."

"Please," Beatrice begged.

Of course, the use of the magic word—as Ali was forever telling the twins—was enough to tip the scales in Beatrice's favor.

"You'd better come on up," Ali said, relenting. "I'll buzz the gate open. It'll close automatically after you drive through. Drive to the turnaround at the top of the hill. I'll meet you at the front door."

"What's going on?" B. asked as Ali pocketed her cell phone and headed for the entryway. "Who's here?"

"Her name's Beatrice," Ali told him. "She's the mother of one of the women from Brenda Riley's book. Something about her daughter going missing. I couldn't just leave her standing in the cold, so I invited her up."

"If her daughter is missing," B. said, "what does she expect you to do about it?"

"Good question," Ali said. "I guess we'll find out when she gets here. Brenda Riley evidently suggested that the mother contact me."

"You go let her in," B. suggested. "In the meantime, how about if I clean up the kitchen and set out cups and saucers?"

"Good idea," Ali said. "From the sound of things, a hot beverage is just what the doctor ordered."

Leaving B. to do his voluntary KP duty, Ali went to the front door, turned on the porch light, and stood waiting while an older-model Chevy Lumina with a single occupant came up the drive and parked in the turnaround.

The white-haired woman who emerged from the vehicle and walked briskly up the drive looked to be somewhere in her late sixties or early seventies. She was wearing a red-and-white tracksuit and tennis shoes.

"Thank you for seeing me like this," she said, hurrying forward with her hand outstretched. "I can't tell you how grateful I am that you've agreed to help."

Ali had made no such agreement, but she let that pass. "You must be freezing," she said. "Come in." She led Beatrice into the house and through the living room before offering her a chair in front of the glowing gas-log fireplace in the library. "Would you care for something to drink? We can make coffee or tea, or perhaps I should offer you something stronger."

"Coffee would be welcome," Beatrice said. "Most welcome indeed. It's been a difficult day, and I'll need to drive back home once we're finished."

"So, tell me," Ali urged. "I understood you to say something about a murder. What's going on?"

Beatrice hesitated before she answered. "My daughter has always had terrible taste in men," she said. "First there was her ex-husband. Then came Richard Lewis—the guy with all the different last names. I'm sure you know all about him, because you were there when they found him. Now I'm afraid Lynn may be making the same kind of mistake with this new guy, Chip Ralston. On the surface, he looks nice enough, but now I'm not so sure. With all this murder business . . ."

"What murder business are you talking about?" Ali insisted.

"Chip's ex-wife has been murdered," Beatrice said. "Her name was Gemma Ralston. Someone found her body yesterday afternoon a few miles south of here, off I-17. They didn't release her name until early this afternoon."

Ali nodded. She and Leland had watched the noontime news broadcast. She didn't remember hearing the dead woman's name, although it wouldn't have meant anything to her at the time. The same broadcast had mentioned that a second body had been found in approximately the same location, or at least nearby. Given the fact that Camp Verde was inside Yavapai County, there was a good chance that Dave Holman was the lead investigator on both cases.

"Lynn routinely stays overnight at Chip's place," Beatrice continued, "but she usually comes home early in the morning. This morning she didn't. At first I didn't give it much thought. She's an adult, after all. It's not like she has to call me every time she and Chip have a change of plans. Still, it's not like her not to be in touch. I tried calling Lynn's cell phone any number of times, but there was no answer. The calls kept going straight to voice mail. I even tried calling Chip's office to see if his receptionist might know something—Chip's a doctor— but there was a recording saying the office was closed due to a family emergency. Then late this afternoon, when they mentioned Gemma's name on the news, I went into a complete panic.

"If Gemma's dead, maybe Lynn is, too. The killer always turns out to be the ex-husband or the ex-wife. What if Chip turns out to be a serial killer masquerading as a good-guy doctor? It wouldn't be the first time Lynn got involved with someone who wasn't what he professed to be. My first thought was that if Chip did it and Lynn found out about it, maybe he took her out, too."

"I believe the Yavapai County Sheriff's Department is investigating that homicide," Ali said. "If you have any pertinent information, you should be in touch with the local investigators. Did you try contacting them?"

Beatrice shook her head. "That's what Brenda said I should do, too, but I couldn't bring myself to do it. That's when she suggested I contact you. She said that with your connections to the Sheriff's Department here, maybe you could do that for me."

That was the moment when B. chose to make his entrance, carrying a tray loaded with coffee, as well as a collection of Ali's Royal Limoges china—cups and saucers, along with a matching sugar bowl and creamer. "Do what?" he asked.

"This is Beatrice Hart," Ali said quickly, "and this is B. Simpson, my partner."

The word "partner" was out of Ali's mouth before she had a chance to reconsider. In a discussion centering on Lynn Martinson's less than stellar choice of boyfriends, that word had been devalued enough that Ali was reluctant to use it in reference to B. She could tell by the small smile creasing the corners of his mouth as he set down the tray that her use of the word hadn't gone unnoticed.

Ali said to B., "Ms. Hart's daughter, Lynn, may be involved in some fashion with one of the cases Dave Holman is currently working on. Would you mind looking after her while I try to reach Dave?"

"Of course," B. said smoothly as Ali made her exit. "Cream and sugar?"

By the time Beatrice answered, Ali was already through the swinging doors into the kitchen and pulling her phone from her pocket. She found Dave Holman's cell phone number, still in her favorites file, and dialed it.

"Hey, Dave," she said when the call switched over to voice mail. "Give me a call when you have a minute. I have someone here at the house who would like to speak to you about the Gemma Ralston case."

Going back through the swinging doors, she crashed into B. coming the other way. "How'd it go?" he asked.

Ali shook her head. "Dave didn't answer. I left a message. What are you doing?"

"I think our guest needs food more than she needs coffee. Your 'partner' offered to heat up a bowl of stew, which she gratefully accepted. Thank you for that, by the way," he added. "I consider 'partner' to be a big step up."

"We'll see about your signing bonus later," Ali said with a smile. "Now I'll go entertain our guest while we wait to see how long it takes for Dave to call me back."

9

Back in the library, Ali found Beatrice Hart seated next to the fire, sipping coffee from one of Ali's delicate Beleme patterned cups. Beatrice glanced up worriedly as Ali resumed her seat.

"Sorry," Ali said. "My contact didn't answer. I left a message for him to call me back." She didn't mention that the contact was most likely the lead investigator on the Ralston case.

"Mr. Simpson offered me some stew, and I accepted. I hope you don't mind," Beatrice said.

"Not at all, but while we're waiting for that return call, why don't you tell me what you know about this Chip Ralston. Do you have any reason to make the leap from his being your daughter's beau to his being a possible murderer?"

"Lynn met him because he was my late husband's doctor—Horace's doctor," Beatrice explained. "Chip's specialty is Alzheimer's patients and their families, and I have to say, in that regard, he was a huge help to me and to Lynn. He helped us understand that Alzheimer's is a process that has a beginning, a middle, and an end, and that all those stages are longer or shorter depending on the individual. When your life is spinning out of control, it's reassuring to have someone telling you that what you're experiencing is within the parameters of some kind of normal. Dr. Ralston did that for our family and does it for a lot of other families, too."

"Sounds like a good guy rather than a bad guy," Ali suggested.

Beatrice nodded. "Except that where I come from, doctors don't become romantically involved with their patients or their patients' families. He waited a while, I'll give him that. He called me several times in the weeks after we lost Horace, ostensibly checking to see how I was doing, and he always asked about Lynn. Then one day he called when I wasn't home. Before you knew it, they were going out."

"I take it you don't approve?"

"For one thing, it's too soon. I know from asking around that Chip is still dealing with the aftereffects of divorce—a rancorous divorce—and Lynn is still in recovery mode, too. First there was her divorce, followed by that mess with Richard. Then her son, Lucas, my grandson, committed suicide. She lost her job and her house, and then Horace died. You put all that together, and it adds up to way too much. I told her she needed to give herself some time before she got involved in a serious relationship."

Before Ali could comment, B. returned with another tray, this one loaded with a bowl of steaming stew and several slices of buttered bread. He set the tray on the coffee table in front of Beatrice and then sat down on the love seat next to Ali. Beatrice gave him a questioning look.

"He knows all about this," Ali said, nodding in B.'s

direction. "It was due to a background check from his computer security company that Brenda Riley found out the truth about Richard Lowensdale."

"Oh," Beatrice said, nodding. "I remember. The High Noon guy. So I guess I have both of you to thank that Lynn wasn't hurt worse than she was."

The man who had helped Ali in the trenches had been B.'s second in command, Stuart Ramey, but neither Ali nor B. corrected Beatrice's understandable misapprehension.

Ali waited while Beatrice tasted a tiny spoonful of Leland's stew, then said, "Delicious. You're a wonderful cook."

Ali nodded her thanks and asked the next question without bothering to correct Beatrice's erroneous assumption about the stew. Sometimes it was simply better to let people be.

"You mentioned that Dr. Ralston was going through a rancorous divorce," Ali said. "How did you know about that?"

"Because Lynn told me," Beatrice answered. "The woman and her lawyers have taken the man to the cleaners. He ended up having to unload several properties in a disastrous real estate market. He also had to buy out her interest in his medical practice. That put him far enough behind financially that he had to go back home and live with his aging mother—not a good sign, if you ask me. According to Lynn, Chip's pet name for his ex is 'the green-eyed monster.'"

Ali managed to keep from smiling, and so did B. After B.'s own ego-damaging divorce, "green-eyed monster" was how he sometimes referred to his ex-wife, too.

"Did Lynn ever mention what caused the divorce? Was there any indication of domestic violence issues? For instance, did Chip ever voice any threats toward his ex?"

"Not as far as I know," Beatrice answered. "Still, it strikes me as a strange kind of divorce. According to Lynn, Gemma treated Chip like dirt, and yet she stayed in close contact with Chip's mother and his sister, Molly. I know a couple of times, when Lynn was staying over with Chip, Gemma dropped by to visit with either the former mother-in-law or the former sister-in-law. I don't know how most divorces work or even how they're supposed to work—Horace and I were married to each other for fifty-eight years—but you can bet that if I'd divorced him, I would have written his mother out of my life immediately. That's what Lynn did with her former mother-in-law, too."

"As far as you know, there was nothing unusual going on this week between Chip and his ex? No new crisis of any kind?"

"No new crisis," Beatrice allowed, "just the ongoing one. From what Lynn has told me, I'm sure Chip resents the neverending financial difficulties from the divorce settlement. He's a middle-aged man, and having to start over at that age is tough. Of course, there will be some money coming to him when his mother dies. I understand that his parents were very well-to-do. His father died relatively recently and suddenly. A stroke, I believe. Chip and his sister are their only kids. Not kids, of course. Their only heirs."

Ali noticed that all the while Beatrice Hart was answering questions, she was stowing away the bowl of stew. She finished it off by sopping up the last of the gravy with the remains of a thick slice of Leland's bread. She may have been worried about her daughter, but that hadn't affected her appetite. B. was offering her a second helping when Ali's phone rang. She excused herself and went as far as the dining room so she could answer with some assurance of privacy.

"Hey," Dave Holman said. "I saw that you called, but I've been knee-deep in two different homicide investigations all day long. It turns out the county attorney has put a deal on the table for one of them, so it's up to the lawyers to do their stuff. That means I'm on my way home and returning calls as I go. I trust you'll forgive me for calling back without listening to your message. What's up?"

Ali was sure she knew which investigations had kept him occupied all day, but she wasn't at all sure how he would react to hearing the identity of the visitor sitting in her library and savoring Leland's beef stew. "I was actually calling on behalf of someone, a woman named Beatrice Hart."

"Lynn Martinson's mother?" Dave demanded after a moment of stark silence. "How the hell did that happen?"

Although the name was one Dave clearly recognized, Ali thought it best to recount the whole story.

"Wait, wait, wait," Dave said when Ali finished. "Who's this Brenda Riley?"

"A friend of mine from back in my old news-broadcasting days. She's originally from Sacramento. Now she and her new husband live in Ashland. She's the one who got mixed up with the cyberstalker in California a couple of years ago. The guy's name was Richard Lowensdale/Lattimore/Loomis/Lewis. He had any number of aliases, and Mrs. Hart's daughter, Lynn, was one of his many victims. Given what Mrs. Hart describes as Lynn's unfortunate track record with men, Beatrice seems to think her daughter might be in danger right along with the new boyfriend's ex-wife. For some reason, she was reluctant to call you directly."

"I wish she had," Dave grumbled, "but it's too late for that now. I'm about twenty minutes out. If you can keep her there, I'll stop by your place before I head home."

"She'll wait," Ali assured him. "B.'s plying her with Leland's beef stew."

"If there's any left, I may ask for some, too," Dave said. "Priscilla's bent out of shape that I'm missing dinner again, but that's what she gets for marrying a cop."

"What should I tell Beatrice?" Ali asked.

"That I'm on my way," Dave said.

"How bad is it?" Ali asked, more than half expecting to hear that Lynn, like Gemma, had come to grief.

"About as bad as it can get," Dave answered. "Lynn Martinson is in jail and in a jumpsuit. So is her boyfriend, Mr. Ralston, or should I say Dr. Ralston? Cap Horning, the county attorney, is waiting to charge them, but he just made both of their attorneys the same offer. Whoever talks first gets charged with a lesser offense that takes the death penalty off the table. The plea deal expires at the end of twenty-four hours. If neither of them takes it, they both get charged with murder in the first degree, and all bets are off."

"You said 'both' attorneys?" Ali asked. "Does that mean Lynn has one and Chip has another?"

"That's correct. Dr. Ralston's attorney arrived from Phoenix wearing a five-thousand-dollar suit and driving a silver Porsche Carrera. Ms. Martinson is evidently in a somewhat different economic league. She has a court-appointed defense attorney named Paula Urban. Paula isn't exactly a greenhorn. She's done a boatload of drug charges, domestic violence cases, and grand theft autos. As far as I know, this is her first homicide case."

Ali knew those were words that Beatrice Hart wouldn't find the least bit reassuring.

"So what are you going to tell her?" Dave asked.

"That the lead investigator from the Gemma Ralston case is on his way from Prescott and that he'd like to speak to her."

"Fair enough," Dave said. "See you in a couple."

Pocketing the phone, Ali returned to the library.

Beatrice looked up at her anxiously. "Well?" she asked.

"I spoke to someone from the Yavapai County Sheriff's Department," she said. "I didn't mention it before, but Dave Holman is the county's lead investigator in the Gemma Ralston case and he's on his way here from Prescott. I asked them to have him stop by the house to talk to you. He should be here in the next fifteen minutes or so."

"What about Lynn?" Beatrice insisted. "Does he know if she's all right?"

Having already embarked on a little white lie, Ali didn't have much choice but to stay the course. "I didn't speak to Detective Holman directly," she said. "I was being patched back and forth. You'll need to ask him that when he gets here."

"He didn't tell you that something had happened to her, did he?"

"I'm sure she's fine," Ali replied. *In a manner of speaking.*

"She'll probably be upset when she finds out I've been interfering in her private life," Beatrice said wistfully, taking a sip of coffee from a recently refilled cup.

Ali said nothing. There was no point in giving Beatrice the bad news. *It most likely won't be private for long.*

When Ali's phone rang again a few minutes later, Dave was calling from the gate at the bottom of the drive. She buzzed him in and then went to the door to meet him. "Don't rat me out," she warned. "I claimed I hadn't spoken to you directly."

He nodded. "Thanks," he said.

Ali led him into the library and made the introductions. "I've been given to understand you're Lynn Martinson's mother," Dave said, settling down on a polished mesquite-wood armchair.

"You know her?" Beatrice asked hopefully.

Dave nodded. "So what's going on?"

"I haven't heard from her all day long," Beatrice answered. "That's so unlike her, and given what else has happened, I've been terribly worried."

"What do you mean by 'what else'?" Dave asked.

"Gemma Ralston's murder," Beatrice said quickly. "As soon as they announced the name of the victim, I was scared to death—afraid that if Lynn's boyfriend had done something to harm his ex-wife, he might have done something to Lynn as well."

"You're saying that once you knew Gemma Ralston had been murdered, your immediate assumption was that her former husband might have had something to do with it?"

"That's often the case, isn't it?" Beatrice replied. "Husbands kill their former wives; wives kill their former husbands. It happens all the time, at least on TV."

"Are you aware of any specific threat Dr. Ralston might have made in that regard?"

"Not really. Lynn and I don't talk about him much. She knows I don't necessarily approve."

"Of her relationship with Dr. Ralston?"

Beatrice nodded.

"Why not?"

"Because he was my deceased husband's doctor, for one thing," Beatrice said. "I think there's something suspect about doctors who become romantically involved with their patients or their patients' family members. I'm under the impression that Chip's family doesn't approve of Lynn, either, probably for the same reason."

"What makes you say that?" Dave asked.

"All the sneaking around, for one thing," Beatrice said. "Lynn goes to his house late in the evening, after Chip's mother has gone to bed, and she comes home early most mornings for the same reason—to be out of his place before Chip's mother is up and around. That's a sad commentary. Here they are, middle-aged people sneaking around like a pair of moony teenagers. But all you've been doing is asking questions. Do you know anything about my daughter, about where she is and if she's okay?"

"Unfortunately, I do, Ms. Hart," Dave said. "Your daughter and Dr. Ralston have both been arrested."

Beatrice blanched and held her hand to her

mouth while Dave continued. "They're being held on suspicion of murdering his former wife. That's why she hasn't been answering her phone. They were taken into custody early this morning. Your daughter was picked up shortly after leaving Dr. Ralston's place in Paradise Valley. He was taken into custody after he arrived at his office in Surprise. They have yet to be officially charged, which is why we haven't made their names public."

Once Dave stopped talking, Beatrice stared at him slack-jawed before she managed to speak. "Lynn—my daughter—has been arrested for murder? Is that what you're saying?"

Dave nodded. "We obtained a warrant to search your daughter's vehicle. We found blood evidence both inside and outside the car that we've been able to match to Gemma Ralston. We don't know where the initial attack took place. It's likely that the victim had already been wounded when she was placed in the trunk and then transported to the site south of Camp Verde, where she was left to die."

"This can't be happening," Beatrice objected. "It simply isn't possible. My daughter could never do something like that. She wouldn't. You're making a terrible mistake."

Dave pulled out a notebook. "Tell me about yesterday," he said. "Was there anything unusual about yesterday?"

"I played golf."

"Was Lynn home before you left for your golf game?"

"Yes, she was there—at our house."

"How did she seem to you?"

"Seem?" Beatrice asked, frowning.

"Did she seem upset about anything? Nervous? Out of sorts?"

"Not that I can remember."

"What about her phone?"

"What about it?"

"Did she mention that her cell phone had gone missing?"

"It wouldn't be the first time she's lost a cell phone," Beatrice answered, "and if she did lose it, it's completely in character for her not to mention it to me. My husband died of Alzheimer's. When we misplace something like car keys or a purse, or if we can't remember something, believe me, we take it seriously."

"Would it surprise you if I told you that your daughter's cell phone turned up at the crime scene?"

"Just because her phone was there doesn't mean Lynn was there," Beatrice insisted.

"We checked your daughter's credit trans-actions," Dave said. "Did she often stop off to have her car washed coming and going from Dr. Ralston's place?"

"She loves that car. She handles it with kid gloves, and she has it washed about as often as she fills it with gas. I understand there's a combination car wash/service station just off the 101. I'm pretty sure that's where she takes it."

"But she didn't mention having her car washed yesterday morning?"

"No. She wouldn't. How she looks after her car is none of my business."

"Has she said anything to you in the past about Gemma Ralston?"

"She's mentioned the woman now and then.

She thought Gemma treated Chip badly, and she certainly disapproved of the idea that Gemma was chummy with Chip's family. I mean, you don't see me hanging out with Lynn's ex-husband, do you?"

"What do you mean when you say Gemma treated him badly?"

"How else? Financially, of course," Beatrice responded. "According to Lynn, when Gemma decided to get a divorce, her lawyers were utterly ruthless. They took everything that wasn't nailed down. Lynn told me things were going to be tough financially for the next several years. Chip managed to avoid bankruptcy, but only barely."

"Dr. Ralston resented that?" Dave asked.

"I should think so," Beatrice replied. "Wouldn't you?"

Ali knew Beatrice had hit Dave where he lived, because he'd gone through a similar financial knothole at the time of his divorce. He immediately changed the subject. "Does the name James Mason Sanders ring a bell?"

"No."

"Are you aware that a second homicide victim was found in the same general location as Gemma Ralston?"

Beatrice nodded. "They said on the news that the second victim was an unidentified male."

Dave glanced in B.'s direction before answering, as though trying to decide how much he should say about the case with an interested bystander in the room. Ali understood Dave's concern, but she also knew that B. had enough security clearances to put Dave's to shame.

"One of the crime scene techs went up the road to have a smoke and found what he thought was an abandoned vehicle. Inside, he found the body of a man shot at close range through the driver's-side window. The second victim has been identified," the detective added. "That's the name I just gave you—James Mason Sanders. He was an ex-con who served time for counterfeiting years ago and dropped out of sight after completing his parole. Even though Mason's death preceded Gemma Ralston's by some period of time—twelve to fourteen hours, at least—due to his proximity to the Ralston crime scene, we're operating on the assumption that the two cases are related."

"He's not the one the newscaster called a person of interest—the one who called 911?" Beatrice asked.

"No," Dave said. "That call was made a matter of minutes before Ms. Ralston succumbed to her injuries. Mason died hours earlier than that, so he couldn't have made the call."

Beatrice thought before shaking her head. "I'm quite sure I've never heard that name. Do you think he was supposed to be a hit man or something?"

"That's one possibility we're pursuing."

Beatrice shook her head. "Lynn never mentioned knowing anyone like that. Maybe this Sanders guy was a friend of Chip's. Please, Detective Holman, I've answered all your questions, but you have yet to tell me where my daughter is being held or what's going to happen to her."

"She's in the Yavapai County Jail in Prescott."

"Can I see her? Will she be released on bond?"

"As I said earlier, she has yet to be officially charged," Dave answered. "If she ends up charged with homicide, there's not much possibility of her being released on bail. Nonetheless, I'd suggest you go see her as soon as possible. You might be able to convince her that her best bet will be to take the plea deal."

"What plea deal?" Beatrice asked.

Dave's eyes flicked briefly in Ali's direction before he answered. "The county attorney has made an offer to both your daughter's attorney and Dr. Ralston's. Whichever one agrees to testify against the other will walk away with a manslaughter conviction rather than standing trial on first-degree murder."

"My daughter has an attorney?"

"A court-appointed public defender," Dave replied. "Her name is Paula Urban, and she's fully aware of the situation. She also understands that the deal is only good for twenty-four hours. So if you have any influence with your daughter, I suggest you use it."

Beatrice stood up abruptly and collected her purse. "I most certainly will," she said. "I'll go see her immediately. I'll also use every bit of influence I have to convince my daughter to fight this tooth and nail. If Chip Ralston killed his ex-wife, I'm not going to stand still and let you lay that crime at Lynn's door. She would never do such a thing!"

With that, Beatrice stomped out of the house. Ali followed her. "Have you ever been to Prescott?" she asked.

"No, but I'm sure I can figure out how to get there. All I have to do is go back to Cordes Junction and turn right."

"If you take Exit 278 and turn right on High-way 169, you take several miles off the Cordes Junction route."

"Thanks," Beatrice said. "For the directions, the food, everything."

Ali reached into the cover of her iPhone and pulled out a business card. "Here's my name and number," she said. "Call me if you think I can be of any help."

"Thank you for that, too," Beatrice said. "I may just do that."

Back in the house, Ali discovered that B. and Dave had moseyed into the kitchen, where B. was ladling the last of the evening's stew into a bowl.

"For Dave," B. explained. "He missed dinner at home."

"Thanks for the help," Dave said, settling onto one of the kitchen chairs.

"It doesn't sound as though Beatrice is con-vinced her daughter had anything to do with what happened," Ali said.

Dave nodded. "Mothers are always the last ones to realize their little darlings have gone off the reservation."

"Lynn didn't strike me as the murderous type, either," Ali said.

"You've met her?"

Ali nodded. "Once. Last summer. We were at the same television station to tape a segment for a program based on Brenda's book. I told you about that."

"I don't know about types," Dave said grimly. "What I know is that when the CSI people sprayed her trunk and back bumper with BlueStar, they lit up like Christmas trees. And we found Lynn's supposedly missing phone at the crime scene. But all of that is strictly circumstantial. In all honesty, I think Cap Horning is jumping the gun here. I'm not sure what he's thinking. I've heard rumors that he may be gearing up to run for the state attorney general slot. If that's the case, a confession from Martinson or Ralston will sew this one up in a hurry and make his life so much simpler."

"So the plea deal is a way for Horning to keep from having to work so hard?" Ali asked.

Dave nodded, but Ali could tell he wasn't happy about it. "That's about the size of it. My take is that Horning is smart but lazy. He wants to get the job done with the least amount of effort."

"What about the 911 caller?" Ali asked.

"There's always a chance that the perp had a change of heart and came back in hopes of changing the outcome," Dave said. "Wouldn't be the first time that happened."

Placing a steaming bowl of stew on the table in front of Dave, B. sat down across from the detective as he dug in. "What's the ex-con's connection to all this?" B. asked.

"Remains to be seen," Dave said. "Once James Sanders finished his parole, he went off the grid. The car he was found in was licensed in Nevada. He bought it last week off Craigslist; paid cash. Not cash, actually. The guy who sold it said the victim paid for the car with two thousand-dollar gambling tokens from the MGM Grand, and once he drove off in it, he didn't bother changing the registration. No ID or driver's license was found on the body, and we're unable to locate a current driver's license for Sanders there or anywhere else.

No credit cards, although he does have a checking account. We found a blank check in his wallet."

"You're thinking Sanders may have been involved in some kind of criminal enterprise," B. suggested.

Dave nodded. "Something that's long on cash and short on credit cards. And it must have been working for him right up until someone blew out his brains at close range."

"So he was shot," Ali surmised. "What about Gemma Ralston?"

"Stabbed," Dave said, "but with no defensive wounds on her body and with nothing under her nails. There were no signs that she was restrained in any way. The ME is running a tox screen, which will take time, but he's operating under the theory that Gemma was incapacitated in some way before she was stabbed."

"Is it possible these are two entirely unrelated incidents?" Ali asked.

"Possible," Dave agreed. "Just not very likely."

He bolted his stew and took off for home while Ali and B. finished putting Leland's kitchen back to rights.

"If Leland was counting on serving stew for lunch tomorrow," B. said, "he's in for a surprise. Now, about that partner bonus? Jet lag just hit big-time."

10

Lynn Martinson lay in her jail cell with her head on her arm and tried to imagine how any of this could have happened to her. Her attorney, who was nice enough but very young, had outlined the terms of the county attorney's offer. All Lynn had to do was finger Chip for Gemma's murder, and Lynn herself would probably skate.

There was only one problem. Lynn couldn't bring herself to believe that any of it was true. She couldn't believe that a man who had dedicated his life to doing no harm would have taken anyone's life, including Gemma's. Yes, the woman had been a pain in the ass. Yes, paying her alimony and buying out her share of the medical practice and their joint real estate holdings was putting a crimp in Chip's bottom line. He had lost a bundle in real estate, and he'd turned over a big part of his pension, but Lynn refused to believe that money meant so much to him. After all, hadn't that been one of Gemma's major gripes about him? That he had backed away from the big-bucks medical practices in favor of shepherding the families of Alzheimer's patients? Was that the kind of man who would stoop to murder? Lynn didn't want to believe it. Wouldn't believe it. It just wasn't possible. Couldn't be. Could it?

Lynn had been on her way home from Chip's place early that morning when an unmarked patrol car had pulled her over on Shea Boulevard as she made her way toward the 101. Since she hadn't been speeding, she almost didn't stop. What if this was one of those times when the guy pulling her over turned out to be a bad guy masquerading as a cop?

"What seems to be the problem, Officer?" she had asked through the open window when she pulled over and Detective Holman walked up to the driver's window. "Was I doing something wrong?"

"Would you please step out of the vehicle, Ms. Martinson? I need to ask you a few questions."

It surprised her that he already knew her name, even though he hadn't asked to see her license or registration. It struck Lynn as odd, but she complied with her hands shaking and knees quaking. The badge and ID he showed her turned out to be from Yavapai County rather than one of the local jurisdictions.

"Where were you night before last?" he asked as she handed him back his ID.

"I was at my boyfriend's house," she said. "I spent the night."

"Your boyfriend would be Dr. Charles Ralston, right?"

"Yes," Lynn said hurriedly, "but what's this about? Does it have anything to do with my telephone?"

"What about your telephone?"

"I know my cell turned up at the scene of a homicide, but like I told the officer who came by the house yesterday, I evidently misplaced it sometime earlier. I have no idea how it could have made its way to a crime scene near Camp Verde. I've never even been there."

"Never?" he asked.

The way he looked at her when he said that was disquieting—as if he didn't believe her. Lynn's knees shook that much more. It was sounding much more serious than some kind of minor traffic violation. People going by on the street were rubbernecking, peering at her and trying to see what was going on. Fortunately, she was far enough from Surprise that it seemed unlikely any of the gawkers would know either her or her mother. Still it was embarrassing.

"Do we have to do this here?" she asked. "Couldn't we have our discussion somewhere more private?"

"Sure," Detective Holman agreed. "There's a Denny's just off Scottsdale Road. How about if we go there to talk? I can follow you."

It seemed like a reasonable enough request, so that was what they did. Lynn was grateful that he turned off the flashers on his light bar. When they pulled into the restaurant's parking lot, she was relieved to see that it was relatively full.

They went inside. Detective Holman ordered a Grand Slam. All Lynn wanted was coffee, and it was frustrating to see how much her hand shook as she raised the mug to her lips. She was nervous about talking to this guy. She couldn't help it.

"So let's go back to the night before last. What time did you arrive at Dr. Ralston's place?"

"Ten or so."

"You left there when?"

"About this time, maybe a little earlier."

"You come late and leave early," Holman said. "Why's that?"

She fudged a little on that one. "I leave early so Chip can get ready for work." The answer sounded lame, even to her.

"I understand you stopped by a car wash on your way home?"

How did he know that? Lynn wondered. Had she mentioned the car wash to the other cop when he came to the house asking about the phone? "Yes," she said.

"Why?"

That struck her as a stupid question. People went to car washes when their cars were dirty.

"When I went to get into the car in the morning, I noticed it was really dusty," she answered. "The wind must have come up overnight. Since I needed gas, I had it washed, too. There's a car wash on my way, and I usually stop there. I suspect that's where I lost my phone. I probably put it down on the counter when I was paying for my gas and forgot to put it back in my purse."

"What can you tell me about Dr. Ralston's former wife?"

Later, Lynn understood that was when she should have guessed what was really going on. If she had, she might have moderated her answer, but she didn't.

"Gemma Ralston is a money-grubbing bitch," Lynn replied. "She hired the best divorce lawyer money can buy, and she took Chip to the cleaners."

"Do you know her personally?"

"I don't really know her; I know of her," Lynn admitted.

"She stays in close contact with Dr. Ralston?"

"More with his mother and sister than with Chip. Chip's mother told him that just because he and Gemma were divorced didn't mean she was divorcing her daughter-in-law. As for Molly, Chip's sister? I understand that she and Gemma have been good friends since they met as college roommates years ago."

"That must make things awkward for you," Detective Holman surmised.

"A little," Lynn admitted, "but over time I expect Chip's family will come around. At least that's what I'm hoping. It's also one of the reasons we're not rushing into anything."

Another, Lynn thought to herself, *is that we can't afford it. I don't have a job, and he can't afford a house payment and alimony.*

"Have you ever heard Dr. Ralston voice any threats against his former wife?"

"Threats?" Lynn echoed. "Never. Not once."

"He never made any comments to you that maybe he'd be better off if Gemma were dead?"

"No!" Lynn said forcefully. "He never mentioned such a thing. Not to me, anyway, and I doubt he'd say it to anyone else, either. You need to understand, Chip Ralston is a good man—an honorable man."

"In your opinion," Detective Holman said.

The comment made Lynn flush, but she said nothing.

"Let's talk about the other night," Holman continued. "You spent the night."

"Yes," Lynn said. "I do most nights."

"You were there the whole night? Was Dr. Ralston there as well?"

"Yes, of course he was. We slept in the same bed."

"He didn't go out at any time? Was he on call?"

"We were both there all night," Lynn repeated.

"Is there a chance he might have slipped out of bed and been gone for a while without your noticing?"

Lynn paused before answering. For years she had struggled with sleep apnea. It was only with the arrival of a breathing aid, a CPAP machine, on the recommendation of a physician specializing in sleep disorders, that she had started sleeping well at night. When she and Chip started dating, she had been too embarrassed to bring it up. Who wants to think that a romantic partner is going to come to bed looking like a gas mask–wearing member of a hazmat team. But she also knew that the mask was the source of her ability to sleep well and safely.

So the first time she and Chip spent the night together—at a casino on the outskirts of Scottsdale—Lynn had brought her mask and machine along, tucked discreetly into her suitcase. She hadn't really intended to take it out or use it, but then a miracle happened. Chip opened his overnight bag, and Lynn caught sight of his machine, tucked in among his underwear and his shaving kit. Not only did they each have a CPAP machine, they had the same make and model.

Lynn had grabbed hers out of her suitcase, and they stood looking back and forth. "What," he said finally, grinning. "You, too? Looks like we're a matched set."

With that, the two of them had collapsed onto

the hotel bed, laughing hysterically. Months into the relationship, the masks and machines were an integral part of their lives. Chip bought Lynn an extra machine to leave at his house so she wouldn't have to carry hers back and forth. Over time they stopped being self-conscious about it. Donning their masks in the aftermath of lovemaking was as automatic as brushing their teeth after dinner. Lynn had adjusted to the comfort of the machine's white noise, and when she was at Chip's house, she slept in a welcome, dream-filled slumber that allowed her to awaken after only a few hours fully rested and alert. More than once, Chip had teased her, saying that when she was asleep with her mask on, the house could fall down around her and she wouldn't notice.

So he could have crept out without her knowledge, but she didn't mention that to Detective Holman. "No," she insisted instead. "That's just not possible."

"How long have you known Dr. Ralston?"

"I met him over a year ago."

"While he was still married to his wife?"

"Their marriage was over long before I came into the picture," Lynn said. "He was my father's doctor. That's how I met him. He does primary care for Alzheimer's patients and provides counseling for families dealing with Alzheimer's-related issues. You need to understand that Chip didn't make any inappropriate overtures to me while my father was alive and his patient. His behavior was entirely aboveboard."

"So you don't regard yourself as Gemma's rival?"

"Absolutely not. I told you. Their marriage was over before I came into Chip's life."

"When's the last time you remember using your phone?"

The abrupt change in direction caught Lynn momentarily off guard. "I'm pretty sure the last time I used the phone was when I called Chip that evening to let him know I was on my way to his house. The next time I tried to use it was in the morning after I got back to my mother's place in Surprise. That's when I discovered it was gone."

"What can you tell me about Dr. Ralston's demeanor the last time you saw him?"

"Nothing out of the ordinary. He was glad to see me. I was glad to see him."

"He didn't seem upset or preoccupied?"

"No. Not at all."

"He didn't seem angry?"

"No. Everything seemed normal."

"What if I told you that Gemma Ralston is dead?"

"She's dead?" Lynn repeated weakly.

And that was when he dropped the bomb—or at least what she thought was the bomb.

"And what if I told you that your phone was found at the scene of Gemma's murder?"

Stunned, Lynn said nothing.

The detective nodded. "Right next to her body, so here's the thing. How do you suppose your phone got there? Were you at the crime scene and left it behind without meaning to? Or was it left there by someone else in order to implicate you in the commission of that crime—to share the blame, as it were?"

Lynn's half-empty coffee mug clattered onto the tabletop, slopping coffee in every direction. "I didn't do it!" she said. She wanted to add, *And neither would he!*

"As you said earlier, Dr. Ralston has been under a good deal of financial pressure. People in those kinds of binds can do uncharacteristic things."

Lynn reached for her new phone. "I need to call him," she said. "I need to let him know what's going on."

"That's not necessary," Detective Holman said. "I'm quite sure Dr. Ralston is already aware of the situation."

"What can I do to help?"

"Just what you're doing," he answered. "Talk to me. Give me your take on what's going on. This has been a completely informal interview, and I really appreciate your help. But I'd like to have a more formal one. That would need to be done in Prescott—at the Sheriff's Department. That way I'll be able to record it; have it on the record."

"You're saying you want me to drive up to Prescott for an interview?"

"No. I'll be glad to give you a ride up and a ride back down."

"A ride. I'm not under arrest, am I?"

"Not at all."

"All right, then, but what about my car? Shouldn't I drive it home, and we can leave for Prescott from there?"

"It's just for a few hours," he said. "I'm sure it'll be fine here. Driving all the way out to Surprise and back will add two hours to the trip. I'll clear it with the restaurant manager before we leave."

That was how, a few minutes later, Lynn Martinson walked out of Denny's under her own power and waited patiently while Detective Holman unlocked his vehicle and opened the back door to let her inside. "There's too much stuff in the front seat," he explained.

It wasn't until after she was seated inside with the door locked from the outside that Lynn began to wonder if she'd been lied to again. By yet another man.

Her phone was in her pocket. Detective Holman had strongly suggested that she not try calling Chip; he hadn't said anything about Lynn not calling her mother. Still, Lynn left the phone where it was. If she hadn't told her mother about something as simple as losing her phone, how could she explain that she was somehow mixed up in a homicide?

No, Lynn thought as the big sedan eased out of the parking lot. *I'll tell her when this is all over. We'll laugh like crazy.*

Hours later and finding herself under arrest, Lynn Martinson wasn't laughing, and she had yet to call her mother. Beatrice would find out what had happened the same way Lynn had found out about Lucas's suicide. Someone else—a cop, most likely—would tell her. Having been on the receiving end of that kind of message, Lynn knew how much it hurt.

Sick at heart, Lynn turned over on her side until she was facing away from the barred door and the lit hallway outside her cell. She tried to be quiet about it, but she cried herself to sleep, wondering if any of it was true. Had Chip really crept out of bed without her knowing, murdered Gemma, and then come back to bed as though nothing at all had happened? Had he taken Lynn's phone with him and left it there in hopes of pin-

ning the blame on her? If so, that made Chip's betrayal far worse than anything Richard Lowensdale
had done.

It would have been easy to give up right then—
to fall asleep and, without the aid of her breathing machine, simply not wake up again. But that
wasn't what happened. The next morning, when
the lights came on at six-thirty and the jailers
rousted her out of bed, Lynn Martinson sat on the
edge of her narrow metal cot and realized for the
first time in her life that she was mad as hell and
she wasn't going to take it anymore.

Late in the afternoon, when they had finally
placed Lynn under arrest, they had told her that
Gemma's blood had been found in Lynn's Focus. If
that was true, if Gemma's blood had turned up in
Lynn's vehicle, she sure as hell hadn't put it there.
And if anybody thought they were going to get her
to plead guilty to something she hadn't done, then,
as her mother would say, they had another think
coming.

11

Long after B. was snoring up a storm, Ali lay awake thinking about Beatrice Hart and her daughter. When Dave brought up the possible plea bargain with Lynn Martinson's mother, he evidently assumed that Beatrice would do what she could to help get Lynn agree to the deal. In fact, she had headed out for Prescott determined to do the opposite.

Unable to sleep, Ali crept out of the bedroom and back to the library, where she relit the gas log and pulled her autographed copy of Brenda Riley's book, *Web of Lies: The Life and Death of a Cyberpath,* from its spot on the bookshelf.

Thumbing through the pages, Ali found herself reading the chapter that dealt with Lynn Martinson. It was easy to see how Lowensdale's phony claim of having a daughter with drug issues had given him an opening into Lynn's life. He had preyed on her vulnerabilities in the same way he played on the other women he had victimized. As the local superintendent of schools, she had been a public person with a troubled son, one who committed suicide while incarcerated on drug charges. Lucas's death had occurred after Lowensdale had ended his supposedly promising relationship with Lynn. Already brought low by her fiancé's unexplained abandonment, Lynn had fallen apart completely.

In the last passage in the chapter devoted to Lynn, she said that her experience with the cyberstalker had left her so emotionally depleted that she doubted she'd ever risk another romantic entanglement. It struck Ali as sad that she had become involved in yet another seemingly troubled relationship. This time she had a middle-aged boyfriend who lived at home with his mother and might or might not be involved in the murder of his former wife.

Yes, Ali thought, returning Brenda's book to the shelf. *Beatrice is right. Her daughter does have terrible taste in men.*

With that, Ali tiptoed back into the bedroom and snuggled up next to B. She drifted off to sleep grateful that she, unlike Lynn Martinson, was at home and lying in her own bed rather than locked up in a jail cell, awaiting possible homicide charges.

When Ali awakened hours later, she was alone in bed. B., whose interior time zone was perpetually half a world away, was seated on the bedroom love seat, engrossed in something on his iPad.

"Good morning, sleepyhead," he said.

"What time is it?"

"After eight. Want some coffee?"

"Please."

As he headed for the kitchen, Ali scrambled out of bed. She hadn't made it to the bathroom when her cell phone rang on its bedside charger. The 928 area code on the readout meant the call was coming from a Prescott-area telephone, though the number wasn't one Ali recognized.

"Is this Ali Reynolds?"

"Yes."

"My name is Paula Urban. I'm the public defender in Prescott—"

"And Lynn Martinson's attorney," Ali supplied.

"Exactly," Paula said. "Ms. Martinson's mother, Beatrice Hart, is in my office this morning. She suggested I call you. My client was offered a plea bargain that she has decided not to accept."

"Which means she may end up being charged with first-degree homicide," Ali suggested.

"That's correct. I was explaining that there may be some budget constraints in my office's ability to launch a full-scale investigation. Ms. Hart suggested that if I needed any investigative work done, you were a detective she would be glad to hire. We just Googled you, Ms. Reynolds. You appear to be extensively involved in a scholarship program of some kind, but I don't see anything that would lead me to believe you're a private investigator. Are you?"

"No," Ali said at once. "I've done some investigative work as a journalist on occasion, but I'm not a licensed private investigator. That takes years of law enforcement–based investigation experience that I don't happen to have."

"I was afraid that might be the case," Paula Urban replied, "but Ms. Hart may have come up with a work-around. Hang on for a moment. I'll let her explain."

While Ali waited on her end, B. returned to the bedroom with a mug of coffee gripped in each hand. "What's going on?" he asked. He passed one of the cups to Ali and then returned to the love seat.

"It's Lynn's attorney," Ali explained. Gratefully, she accepted her cup of coffee and perched on the edge of the bed.

A moment later, Paula Urban came back on the line. "Ms. Hart wants to discuss her proposal with you directly. If you don't mind, I'd like to put you on speaker."

A moment later, Beatrice's voice came on the line. "When I got to town last night, I was told I wouldn't be able to talk to Lynn until this morning, so I called her attorney to see if there was anything I could do to help. When she mentioned being worried about hiring an investigator, I immediately thought of you, but by then I felt it was too late to call. Instead, I called one of my friends in Surprise. She tells me the going rate for a private eye these days is eight hundred dollars a day plus expenses, and I'm fully prepared to pay that. Lynn may need the services of a court-appointed attorney, but she doesn't have to settle for a court-appointed detective, not if I have anything to do with it."

Ali more than half expected Paula Urban to take exception to Beatrice's dismissive remark about court-appointed attorneys, but she didn't.

"I'm sorry," Ali said, jumping into the uncomfortable silence. "Even though I'd like to help, I can't. As I just told Ms. Urban, I'm not a licensed detective."

"But you're a journalist, aren't you?" Beatrice Hart asked.

"Was," Ali said. "As in used to be. I'm not anymore."

"I want you to do what Brenda did for Lynn and

all those other poor women. I want to hire you to tell the story of what's going on in Lynn's life right now, and if you happen to pass along what you learn to Ms. Urban, so be it."

"Are you hearing this, Ms. Urban?" Ali asked, expecting the attorney to object.

"Works for me," Paula said.

"As I said before," Ali insisted, "I'm not a licensed private investigator. It's very generous for you to offer to pay me, but I can't take your money. It's out of the question."

"How about if I make a voluntary donation to your scholarship fund?" Beatrice offered. "Surely you couldn't object to that. And if you happen to report your findings to Ms. Urban before you get around to writing whatever it is you're going to write for me, then it would be all to the good, don't you think?"

Across the room, B. was saying nothing, but he was grinning into his cup.

"What kind of investigative help do you need, Ms. Urban?" Ali asked, saying yes without really meaning to.

"You're aware that another homicide victim was found near the first one?" Paula asked. "Near where Gemma Ralston was found?"

"Yes," Ali answered.

"So far, all I've been able to learn is the man's name," Paula said. "James Mason Sanders. I need to do a complete background check on him to see if we can find out whether he had any possible connections to Gemma Ralston or Dr. Ralston. Lynn claims she's never heard the name. I also need to know everything there is to know about Charles and Gemma Ralston. I've been told that they were involved in long, drawn-out, and very messy divorce proceedings, but I don't know any of the details. I need complete background information on them as well, individually and as a couple."

Ali glanced in B.'s direction. At the mention of background checks, he nodded. *Can do,* he mouthed silently.

"All right," Ali said into the phone. "Providing three sets of background checks sounds pretty doable. I'm assuming that whatever I find should be turned over to you?"

There was a pause during which Beatrice Hart was evidently considering Ali's question. "I'm not very computer-literate," she said. "I have a cell, but I hardly use it. Would it be all right if Ms. Reynolds interacted with you, Ms. Urban? Then you could collect the material and send it along to me."

"That would probably work," Paula Urban agreed.

The faux-journalist story gave all of them a thin veneer of cover; enough, Ali hoped, that should she be found operating as a private investigator without appropriate state licensing, she'd be able to dodge any resulting class-one misdemeanor charges.

"What's the situation with Chip Ralston?" Ali asked. "Any word on whether he intends to turn state's evidence?" Ali knew if that happened, it would be a game changer as far as Lynn's situation was concerned.

"No word so far," Paula said. "I'm not sure if that's good news or bad news."

Beatrice's voice came back on the line. "I don't know how to thank you enough," she said. "Should we draw up some kind of official contract for the article or story or whatever it is you're writing?"

"No," Ali said. "That's not necessary. We'll consider this a handshake agreement. If I end up doing anything helpful, I'll leave it up to you to decide if you're going to make a contribution to the fund and how much that should be. But I'll need complete contact information for both of you. And, as suggested, I'll send my progress reports to Ms. Urban, with the understanding that she'll forward them on to you."

When Paula Urban ended the call, Ali turned back to B., who was still grinning.

"What's so funny?"

"To quote George Bernard Shaw, 'We've established what you are, now we're merely haggling over the price.'"

"Right. What happens if I go to jail for operating without a license?"

"Then I guess I show up, checkbook in hand, to bail you out," B. said with a smile. "I'm also willing to put Stuart Ramey at your disposal."

"Really? You're sure you don't mind?"

"No, I don't mind," B. said. "He's gotten a real kick out of backstopping some of your escapades in the past, and I'm sure he'll be glad to do it again."

"But why—" Ali began.

"Because I heard you tell Beatrice Hart last night that I'm your partner. How about if I start acting like it?"

"Are you sure?" Ali asked.

"Yes," he replied. "I am. As your mother is so fond of saying, 'Sauce for the goose is sauce for the gander.' And speaking of sauce, Leland was close to putting breakfast on the table when I picked up the coffee. You'd better get a move on."

12

As soon as breakfast was over, Ali headed for High Noon's corporate offices in Cottonwood. Having been given a warning call by B., Stuart Ramey conducted her into a conference room and left her to read the mountain of material he had already accumulated, including the fact that for the past five years James Mason Sanders had lived and worked at a halfway house in North Las Vegas called the Mission, where people fresh out of jail could get three hots and a cot. According to the Mission's fund-raising newsletter, Sanders was the facility's on-site manager.

The back story on James Mason Sanders, as culled from newspaper articles, related the tragedy of a bright kid pulled into a college-age prank that went awry. A group of Arizona State University fraternity brothers had decided to see if it was possible to use their newly honed computer skills to print their own money. With Sanders doing most of the artwork and one of the other guys laying hands on a ready supply of the right kind of paper, they had printed up and spent a considerable amount of phony twenty-dollar bills. Had they been serious about the project, they probably would have moved on to printing hundreds.

Once the students were caught, the feds didn't see anything funny about it. The four perpetrators were tried separately. Two, Robert McDowell and Kevin Owens, were found innocent of all charges. It was clear from reading the articles that the two who got off came from families who had been able to pay for name-brand defense attorneys. The two who took the fall, James Sanders and Scott Ballentine, were represented by court-appointed attorneys. Scott, who procured the paper, got off with a five-thousand-dollar fine after agreeing to testify against James Sanders, who was considered the creative genius behind the project.

Sounds familiar, Ali thought, thinking about Lynn Martinson and Chip Ralston.

At the end of one article, Ali discovered a nugget of information:

> At the conclusion of the sentencing hearing, where Sanders was given a sentence of twelve to fifteen years, he was led stony-faced from Judge Mathison's courtroom without exchanging so much as a nod with his weeping wife and their infant child.

Ali picked up the phone and dialed Stuart Ramey. "What became of Sanders's wife and child?"

"What wife and child?" Stuart wanted to know.

Ali read him the passage.

"I missed that one completely," Stuart said, "but I'll look into it."

"How did you find out all the details about the Mission? When we were talking to Detective Holman last night, he claimed that Sanders had dropped off the grid after he got out of prison."

"I have my ways," Stuart said, "some of which you're probably better off not knowing. For as long as he's been at the Mission, he's maintained a checking account at a Wells Fargo branch in North Las Vegas, under the name Mason Sanders. I've studied the records for that account for the past three years. His paychecks come and go through that on an automatic deposit. Except for a blip two years ago, when the balance bumped up briefly to twenty grand and then went back down, it's stayed the same ever since."

"What about phone records?" Ali asked. "Wouldn't that be the easiest way to tell if he was in touch with either Chip Ralston or Lynn Martinson?"

"It would be if he had a phone listed in his name, but he didn't. No cell and no landline, either. What that probably means is that he used a phone at the Mission for making both business and personal calls. It'll take a while longer to locate those records and go through them. At first glance, I didn't spot any calls or texts to or from anyone in Las Vegas on Chip Ralston's phone records or Lynn Martinson's. That doesn't mean there isn't a connection. It just means I haven't found it yet."

"Have you spoken to anyone at the halfway house?" Ali asked.

"That's not my thing," Stuart said. "I'm great at backdoor data-mining, but I'm not much good at the direct approach of picking up the phone and asking questions."

"You're implying I'd be better at that than you are?" Ali asked.

"Aren't you?"

"Give me a name and number," Ali said with a laugh.

"The executive director is listed as Abigail Mattson." Stuart reeled off a phone number, and Ali jotted it down.

"What am I looking for in particular?"

"For whatever changed," Stuart said. "Sanders worked at the Mission for years without any record of his ever having a driver's license or owning a vehicle. Last week he evidently went out and bought a vehicle from a private party, paying for it with a handful of cash. The next thing we know, he's been found three hundred miles away, shot to death in that same vehicle, a ten-year-old Lumina, which is still registered to the original owner. How come he suddenly needed a car when he evidently hadn't needed one in years? And how did he suddenly have enough money to pay cash for the vehicle—seventeen hundred bucks—when there's no change in the balance of his bank account? The money had to come from somewhere."

"What's the going rate for knocking off a troublesome ex-wife these days?" Ali asked.

It was Stuart Ramey's turn to laugh. "Beats me," he said. "I've never had a current wife, to say nothing of a troublesome ex."

Once Ali was off the phone with Stuart, she sat for a moment, looking at the phone in her hand, while she considered what she would say and how she would say it. Straying too far from the truth probably wouldn't be a good idea. When she dialed and the phone rang, it was answered by a woman who sounded relatively young. "Ms. Mattson's office."

"My name's Alison Reynolds," Ali said. "I'm from Sedona, Arizona. I'm looking into the death of James Sanders. I believe Ms. Mattson was his supervisor. Is she in?"

There was a sharp intake of breath. "Are you a reporter?" the young woman asked.

Once Ali would have had to answer yes to that question. "No," she said. "I'm not a reporter. And you are?"

"I'm Regina, Ms. Mattson's secretary. Ms. Mattson isn't in today. She was so upset by what happened that she called in sick. She's taking the rest of the week off, but she gave me specific instructions that I'm not to discuss the situation with any reporters."

Without bothering to attempt a lame denial, Ali simply forged ahead. "Did you happen to know Mr. Sanders?"

Regina immediately burst into tears. "Of course I did," she sobbed. "Everybody here knew Mason and loved him. He's such a nice guy. Not like some of the other creeps who come through here."

"Through the Mission. You mean the clients?"

"I know we're here to help them, but some of them are such no-good losers," Regina declared. "They don't want any help. They don't want to make their lives better. Mason may have started out the same way years ago, but he wasn't like that at all, and what he did for me last week was just unbelievable."

"What was that?" Ali asked.

"I had fallen behind on my car payments," Regina said. "Way behind. One day while he was here in my office, sweeping and dusting, the finance company called me again. He heard the whole thing. Afterward he asked me about it. I told him how, every morning when I got up, I was afraid the repo guys might have come to get it overnight.

"The very next day he came into my office, stopped by my desk, and gave me what looked like a box of candy—See's peanut brittle, my favorite. When I looked inside there wasn't just peanut brittle in the box. There was also enough money to pay off my car loan—three thousand bucks. I told him he shouldn't have, but he just grinned at me. He said he'd had some good luck and he wanted to share the wealth. He asked me not to tell anyone, and I shouldn't have told you, either, but you can't imagine what a miracle that was in my life."

"He gave you that much money in cash?" Ali asked, wishing she weren't thinking about the counterfeit twenty-dollar bills that had landed James Sanders in prison in the first place.

"Not in cash," the woman answered. "In tokens. From the MGM Grand. Three thousand-dollar tokens. Over the weekend, I went to the casino and cashed them in. On Monday I was able to pay off my car loan. I could hardly wait to show the paperwork to Mason and to thank him, but he wasn't here on Monday, and he never came back to work. I sent him an e-mail thank-you note, but I don't know if he ever saw it."

"So he had an e-mail account?"

"Ms. Mattson let us use our Mission addresses for personal e-mail. I don't have a computer at home, you see," she added. "This was Mason's home, and he didn't have a computer of his own, either."

"So Friday was the last day you saw him?"

"Yes, like I said, he wasn't at work on Monday. Ms. Mattson reported him missing on Tuesday. Last night someone called and told her he'd been found murdered somewhere in Arizona. I can't believe he's dead. I just can't."

While Regina dissolved in tears once more, Ali was busy doing the math. In the week before he died, James Mason Sanders—a man whose checking account balance rarely made it over the thousand-dollar mark—had handed out close to five thousand dollars in cold cash without causing any appreciable movement in his bank balance.

"Did Mr. Sanders earn much money working at the Mission?" Ali asked.

"Minimum wage," the young woman answered. "That's what we all get, but he told me once that he didn't need much as long as he had a roof over his head and important work to do."

"What do you think he meant by that?"

"He believed in what the Mission does— helping people find their way, stay out of trouble, make something of themselves. I think he believed in it more than anyone else. He said that working here gave him a purpose in life."

"What about the three thousand dollars that he gave you? Did he mention where it came from? Was he a gambler, for instance?"

"Not that I know of." Regina paused. "Well, maybe he was, because how else would he get those tokens? I've heard of thousand-dollar tokens, but those are the first ones I ever saw. They're usually reserved for really high-stakes games."

"What exactly did Mr. Sanders do at the Mission?"

"He checked people in and out. Made sure the room and the bedding were clean when someone moved in. He swept the halls. Emptied the trash. Made sure people weren't smoking in their rooms. Replaced the batteries in the smoke alarms. Fixed leaky faucets. You know, stuff like that, but don't think he was just a glorified janitor. Ms. Mattson runs the place, but Mason was the glue that held it together. She was the one who was out in public, raising funds. He was the guy doing the hands-on work."

"So you're saying they were partners?"

"I guess," Regina said. "Not officially, maybe, but yes."

"Was he good friends with anyone else there?"

"Not really. Most people come and go in a matter of weeks. I've been here for about six months. I think Ms. Mattson is the only one who was here longer than Mason."

"How did you end up at the Mission?" Ali asked, changing the subject. She more than half expected a fudged response. Instead, Regina's answer was straightforward.

"I got six months for domestic violence. When I got out, my roommate hadn't paid the rent on our apartment. She had taken off with all my stuff. I was left with nothing and nowhere to live. The Mission was the last place I wanted to be, but it was also the only place I could go. While I was here, Ms. Mattson found out I could type, and gave me a job. I've worked here ever since, answering phones and doing whatever else Ms. Mattson needs."

"So the Mission takes both men and women?"

"Yes, but our rooms are on different floors. The men are on floors one and two; women are on floor three; and no staying-over privileges. You get caught on the wrong floor, and you are O-U-T! Ms. Mattson is very strict about that."

"Is there anything else you can tell me about Mr. Sanders?" Ali asked.

"He was smart. He read books. He could have worked anywhere. He stayed here because he liked it and because it gave him a sense of purpose. He liked helping people, and he made the Mission a better place. Oh, and he smoked, but always outside. There's a little picnic table out back for us smokers. That's where he smoked, too . . ." Regina's voice faded away momentarily. "Wait. I almost forgot. One day last week, I was outside having a smoke when a limo pulled up outside. A real live limo—a white stretch. We don't see many of those around this neighborhood. I thought maybe it was someone who had taken a wrong turn going to the wedding chapel up the street, but just then Mason came hotfooting it out the front door. The back door of the limo opened, he got in, and they drove away. I asked him about it the next day. He said it was a friend of his from a long time ago who had stopped by to say hello."

"Do you know what day this was?"

"Wednesday, maybe?"

"And what time?"

"In the afternoon. During my last break, so it must have been around four. I was surprised he was taking off early like that, but I'm sure Ms. Mattson knew about it. Not much gets past her." Another phone rang in the background. "I need to answer that," Regina said. "Do you want me to have Ms. Mattson call you when I hear from her? It may not be until sometime next week."

"Sure," Ali said. She read off her number. "She can call me, or I'll get back to her."

When Regina hung up, Ali felt as though she had caught wind of a tiny thread of James Sanders's story—gambling tokens from the MGM Grand, a limo, and a visit from an old friend. Maybe if she tugged on that thread hard enough, the whole thing would unravel.

With that, she left the conference room and went looking for Stuart Ramey.

13

What's wrong with you?" Sasha Miller wanted to know. "You've been like on the moon for days."

A.J., who had been dozing with his head on the Camry's headrest, opened his eyes and looked at his girlfriend of three months. After two mostly sleepless nights, the warmth of the sun-filled car had lulled him. His peanut-butter-and-jelly sandwich lay half eaten on the leg of his jeans.

He straightened up, grabbed the sandwich, and took another bite. "Sorry," he said. "It's nothing."

The presence of Sasha in his life was one of the unintended consequences of A.J.'s having his own set of wheels. Having his own car had greatly expanded his social milieu. Before the Camry, he'd been limited to places where he could walk or hitch a ride with one of his neighborhood pals. Back when he'd had to suffer the indignity of riding his bike home from work at Walgreens, the possibility of ever having a girlfriend had been nothing more than a pipe dream. Now the dream had come true, and Sasha Miller was a huge part of A.J.'s life—another part that his mother knew nothing about.

Sasha definitely hailed from outside his neighborhood. Her sprawling family home on Missouri was almost a mansion in comparison with the Sanderses' small but tidy bungalow. Sasha came from a privileged background, with an insurance-executive father, a stay-at-home mother, and three younger sisters. Sasha could have been a spoiled brat, but she wasn't. She was bright, funny, and fun. She was also black; well, partially black. That was something A.J. was prepared to tell his mother eventually, but not right now. Again, not an outright lie, but one of those sins of omission.

Although attending a private high school had been one of Sasha's options, she had elected to come to North High to take advantage of the Advanced Placement courses available through the International Baccalaureate program. She drove to and from school in a two-year-old BMW that had been given to her, fresh off a yearlong lease, for her sixteenth birthday.

The difference in their wheels—her shiny BMW versus A.J.'s less flashy Camry—testified to the disparity in family income and economic status. Yes, they had both gotten cars for their sixteenth birthdays, but A.J. had never mentioned to Sasha that his had been an unexpected gift from a mostly absent father who also happened to be an ex-con. And even though his father's treasure-hunt letter was the reason A.J. hadn't slept for the better part of two nights, he didn't mention his father to her now, either. Not that A.J. thought Sasha would care about his father one way or another, but he wasn't so sure about her family. The Millers attended church services two to three times a week, and A.J. had convinced himself that having an ex-con counterfeiter turn up in his family tree would be the ultimate deal-breaker.

A.J. and Sasha had met in Mr. Cotton's trigonometry class, where they were both star pupils, and they had been unofficially hanging out ever since the school year started. Because their classmates regarded them as something of an odd couple, they steered away from the cafeteria at lunchtime and ate their sack lunches in either his car or hers.

"It's not nothing," Sasha insisted, scanning his face with her penetrating brown-eyed stare. "Tell me."

He wanted to tell someone about his father's improbable letter and to find out whether other people thought it was for real. He wanted to tell someone about the horror of having that woman die right there in front of him. He wanted to, but he couldn't.

"Just some stuff with my mom," he said.

Sasha rolled her eyes at him and shook her head, making her beaded cornrows rattle.

"Come on," he added. "It's almost time for the bell."

Half an hour later, during trig, A.J.'s cover was blown when Mr. McArthur, the assistant principal, summoned him to the office. All the way there, A.J. was sure someone had figured out that his excuse was a forgery. When he walked into the principal's office and found his mother waiting for him, he was even more convinced that he was toast. One look at her face let him know she was beyond upset.

"Mom," he said, doing his best to play dumb. "What's the matter?"

"It's your father," Sylvia said, rising from her chair and coming to meet him. "James has been murdered. The police came by my office a little while ago to let me know."

A.J. felt his knees buckle. "Where?" he said, staggering to a nearby chair. "When? How?"

Somehow he suspected he knew the answer to his question even before she told him.

"Up near Camp Verde someplace," Sylvia answered. "Officers were investigating another homicide and found James's body nearby. At this point there's no way of knowing if he was involved in what went on with the other victim—a woman. They're still trying to sort that out. I wanted to come here to tell you so you wouldn't find out on your own."

A.J. nodded numbly, thinking about the dying woman and the light going out of those brilliant green eyes. Was this the time when he should admit that he had been there, too? Was this the time to say that he was the one who had sent the text to 911 to try to summon help for her? The problem was, A.J. knew that if he did so, his carefully constructed house of cards would crumble. His mother would know he had been in touch with his father behind her back. She would learn about the forged excuse; so would the school. At the very least, he'd probably receive a suspension. He'd end up having to tell the cops that lame story about his father's supposedly buried treasure. If his father was dead, chances are the pipe dream about his father's promised money easing his way through college was probably gone, too. More than that, if

A.J. admitted to having been at the crime scene, the cops might think he had something to do with the woman's death. As for Sasha? Having her find out the truth about any of this just wasn't an option. Looking at his mother's anxious face, A.J. made up his mind.

"What happened to him?"

"The cops told me he was shot at close range," Sylvia said.

"You said someone else was dead, a woman," A.J. managed. "Do the cops think he has something to do with what happened to her? Was my father a killer?" His voice cracked as he asked the last question.

"The officer I spoke to hinted that might be the case," Sylvia replied, "but I don't believe it. Not at all. James did plenty of questionable things in his time, but I can't believe he'd be involved in a homicide. I never once knew him to be violent."

A.J. was thinking about the shovel he had left behind at the crime scene. He was thinking about his damning fingerprints on the cell phone.

"I know you barely knew your father, but this has to come as a terrible shock," his mother began, studying his face. "If you want to go home—"

A.J. hopped up out of his chair. "No," he said quickly. "I should probably get back to class. We've got a big test tomorrow."

His mother looked a little surprised. "All right," she said. "But if you don't want to go to work this afternoon, I understand. I'll be glad to call Maddy to let her know you won't be in today."

"It's okay," he said. "I'll be fine, and I need to go to work."

The truth was, he dreaded being at home with

his mother. That would be far worse than going to work.

He made his way back to class. Sasha, seated two rows away, caught his eye as he returned to his desk.

A.J. sank into his chair and covered his face with one hand. He knew he would have to tell Sasha the truth sometime, and when he did, it would all be over.

Maybe that was just as well.

When the bell rang, she caught up with him before he made it to the corridor. "What's wrong? And don't try telling me it's nothing."

"It's my father," A.J. said softly after a long pause. "He's dead." Then, to his horror and as much as he tried to keep it from happening, he began to cry.

14

As soon as Ali located Stuart's office, tucked in the far corner of what was a former warehouse facility, she understood why he had sequestered her in the conference room. For one thing, he evidently lived in his office. Rumpled bedding on an army cot was half hidden behind a cloth-and-wood screen covered with Post-it notes and an impressive collection of pizza coupons. The room was in semi-darkness, and the air was thick with the perfume of pizza.

Stuart sat at one of a bank of computers in the middle of the room with a pizza box at his elbow. He looked up at her in surprise as she entered the room, then shoved the box in her direction. "Lunchtime," he said. "Want some?"

"No, thanks," she said. "I think I have a lead. I have reason to believe that James Sanders recently came into a sum of money, so maybe the idea of him being hired to make a hit isn't so far from the mark."

She went on to relate everything Regina had told her, including the fact that James had most likely used a work-based computer for both e-mail and telephone communications. Stuart listened, nodding absently while keeping one eye on the data flashing across the screen of the computer in front of him. It would have been easy for Ali to think that he wasn't paying attention, but she knew he was.

"There are a lot of stretch limos in Vegas," he said when Ali finished her recitation. "So that doesn't help us much, but knowing the token came from the MGM Grand might. Thousand-dollar tokens aren't handed over to every Tom, Dick, and Harry who wanders in off the Strip. And the casinos take their security arrangements very seriously. It's my understanding that they video everything—every hallway, every entrance, every table. And unlike the folks running the local traffic cams, casinos keep everything they video on a permanent basis. What day was that again?"

"Regina said she saw the limo on Wednesday a week ago. The limo picked Sanders up about four P.M. We don't know that they went directly to the hotel. That's just an educated guess."

"But the guy in the limo was evidently expected," Stuart said. "That means there must be some point of contact that we'll be able to find. Is it possible Dr. Ralston made a quick trip to Vegas last week? Let's say that's who the guy in the limo was—Charles Ralston. If that's the case, somewhere along the line, we're going to find some communications links between them. Let me work on this for a while. In the meantime, I've got something else that may interest you.

"James Mason Sanders married Sylvia Ruth Bixby on June sixteenth, 1996, a few days after she graduated from high school. The wedding was a little late, since their baby, Alexander James, who just turned seventeen himself, was born less than three months later. The wedding took place just before the whole counterfeiting mess started to come apart. I found records of the marriage but no sign of a divorce."

"So it was a shotgun wedding, but she stayed married to him the whole time he was in prison and even after he got out?" Ali asked.

Stuart nodded. "As far as I can tell, they stayed married then and were still married when he died."

"That's taking the words 'for better or worse' very seriously, with a lot more worse than better."

"I'll say," Stuart agreed. "I checked public records in Nevada, too, just in case Sanders instituted divorce proceedings there. No such luck. As for the kid? As far as I can tell, he's okay. Alexander is a senior honors student at North High School in Phoenix, where he's taking lots of Advanced Placement courses. His mother may have been on her own the whole time, but she's done something right in raising him."

Ali's phone rang. When she saw the number, she left Stuart's office and took the call in the corridor.

"You have got to be kidding me!" Dave Holman exclaimed. "Are you really working for the public defender?"

He spoke in a way that registered in Ali's ear as an audible sneer. He didn't utter the words "How could you?" aloud, but the message was there nonetheless.

"I'm actually doing a project for Lynn Martinson's mother," Ali said. That was the truth, if not the whole truth.

"Lynn Martinson is a suspect in a homicide in this jurisdiction," Dave pointed out, his voice flat with anger. "And you're a reserve officer. When I came by your place last night, I thought I was speaking to a fellow officer. It never occurred to me that I was talking to someone on the other side."

"When you were there last night, there was no other side—" Ali began, but Dave cut her off before she had a chance to finish.

"I've just been on the phone with Sheriff Maxwell. He'll be expecting your letter of resignation before the end of business today."

With that, Dave hung up. Ali was left with a dead phone in her hand and a puncture wound in her heart as well as her pride. Her primary responsibility as a reserve deputy had been to help transport prisoners from one jurisdiction or facility to another. The use of reserve deputies helped keep patrol officers where they needed to be—on patrol.

Ali hadn't intended to offend Dave, and so far she had done nothing to undermine his investigation. His reaction seemed over-the-top. She had seen the situation with Beatrice Hart and Paula Urban as a temporary arrangement. She hadn't expected it to be something that would undo years of established relationships, but it sounded as though irreparable damage had already been done. If Sheriff Maxwell was expecting her resignation, she would give it to him.

Ali called home to let Leland and B. know that she was on her way to Prescott. Before she headed out, she stuck her head back in Stuart's office and gave him the same information. "If you come up with anything," she said, "call me. I'll probably drop in on Paula Urban while I'm in Prescott and let her know what we have so far."

It should have taken an hour and fifteen minutes to get from Cottonwood to Prescott. She did it in just over an hour and considered herself lucky not to have a speeding ticket to show for her trouble. She pulled up in front of the Sheriff's Department and parked in a designated visitor's spot. After all, if she was being given her walking papers, that's what she was—a visitor.

During her brief stint as a media relations officer, her office had been temporarily shoehorned into a corner of the front lobby, which had done nothing to endear her to the front-office clerks who felt their territory had been invaded. That had all changed.

The revamped media relations department, with Ali's onetime intern Mike Sawyer in charge, was no longer housed in the lobby. All evidence of the previous arrangement had been eradicated. The cubicle where Ali's desk once sat was long gone. In its place was a long chest-high counter stocked with a supply of forms that could be filled out and passed to the clerks through a bank teller–like opening in their Plexiglas shield. Ali paused long enough to grab one of the forms. Using the back, she scrawled off a one-sentence note of resignation and then made her way to the service window.

Holly Mesina, the head clerk, greeted her with a knowing smirk. "The sheriff is expecting you," she said. "Do you need someone to show you the way?"

"No," Ali said. "I believe I can manage."

With that, Holly pressed the button unlocking

the door that accessed the department's interior offices. There was no one seated at the secretary's desk outside Sheriff Maxwell's open door, so Ali walked up to the door and tapped on the doorjamb. Gordon Maxwell sat leaning back in his desk chair while a Mozart piano concerto played through the speakers on his computer. The moment Ali knocked, he sat up and stifled the music.

"Come in and sit down, Ali," he said with a self-conscious grin. "I don't like people to know that I sit around in my office listening to Mozart. It's bad for my tough-guy image."

Ali had always liked Sheriff Maxwell and she still did. She sat.

"Understand old Dave's got his nose out of joint."

That was the thing about Sheriff Maxwell. Over the years Ali had discovered that conversations with him never went quite the way she had anticipated.

"You could say that," she agreed with a nod. "He said you wanted my letter of resignation today. Here it is." She placed the form on the desk and slid it over to him. Sheriff Maxwell picked it up, scanned it, put it down, and then slid it back to Ali.

"I'd prefer it if you reworded that," he said, "and turned it into a temporary leave of absence."

"But Dave said—"

"I know what Detective Holman said," Maxwell replied. "What really set him off was having Cap Horning jump into the middle of his homicide investigation with something Dave regards as a premature and half-cocked plea deal. The idea of your piling on was just the capper on the jug, if you'll pardon the expression."

"But . . ." Ali began again.

Sheriff Maxwell unfolded his long frame from the chair, rose, closed the door, and then returned to his desk. "Look," he said. "This is between you and me. I have some private concerns of my own about Cap Horning. Looks to me like he's out running roughshod over folks. If Dave comes up with some solid evidence to show that the people we have in custody are actually the responsible parties, that's one thing. If that happens, everybody comes out smelling like a rose, and good on 'em. But finding evidence takes time. It seems to me Horning is trying to streamline the process by making what Dave and I regard as premature plea deals. Paula Urban is good people—for a public defender—but we're in the justice business here. With Cap Horning pushing folks around, I'm worried about Paula Urban seeing to it that justice is done in this case."

Ali blinked. "You're saying you want me to help her?"

"I don't like seeing undue pressure applied. If the evidence is there, I trust that it'll carry the day with a judge and jury. The person or persons responsible for Gemma Ralston's murder will get what's coming to them because they're actually convicted of the crime rather than because Cap Horning's busy playing *Let's Make a Deal*. And if having you doing a research project for the suspect's mother ends up giving Paula some much needed help, I can't see that there's any harm done."

Which meant Sheriff Maxwell knew all about the writing-project cover. For all Ali knew, he might have suggested it.

Picking up Ali's scribbled note, Sheriff Maxwell handed it back to her. "As far as your letter is concerned," he added. "As I said before, if you'd be so kind as to rewrite it so it says 'leave of absence' rather than 'resignation,' I'll be happy to sign off on it. And you might want to stop by the jail before you leave town. It's my understanding that Paula Urban just went over there to have a meeting with her client. It might be a good idea if you turned up as well."

While Ali retrieved the paper and made the required changes, Sheriff Maxwell picked up his phone and dialed.

"Hey, Holly," he said. "Ali Reynolds is on her way over to the jail to meet with Paula Urban and her client. Could you write up a pass for her and let the jail commander know she's coming? She'll be out to pick it up in a couple of minutes."

That'll go over like a pregnant pole vaulter, Ali thought.

That was true. When Ali went out to the lobby minutes later, a sullen-faced Holly sailed the pass through the opening rather than handing it over.

"Thanks," Ali responded, retrieving the piece of paper from the floor halfway across the room. "You have a nice day, now."

With that, she headed for the jail, where she was shown to an interview room where Paula Urban and Lynn Martinson were already conferring. Pausing outside the window in the corridor, Ali gazed in at the two women seated at the scarred table. Though Ali had seen Paula before, she was still surprised. Paula's mop of springy red hair had been pulled back into a loose ponytail, but a halo of escaped curls made her look more

like a refugee from junior high than a thirtysomething legal beagle. As for Lynn Martinson? There
was very little resemblance between the somewhat
bedraggled woman in her orange jumpsuit and
the agitated woman who had joined Ali in the
television station greenroom months earlier. That
woman had been nervous but excited. This woman
looked completely devoid of hope.

Taking a deep breath, Ali let herself into the
interview room and cast a questioning glance in
the direction of the obvious video equipment in
the corner.

"Don't worry," Paula said reassuringly. "It's not
on. I believe you and Ms. Martinson have met?"

Lynn jumped up, grabbed Ali's hand, and
pumped it with heartbreakingly sincere enthusi-
asm that was at odds with the noisy rattle of the
shackles around her ankles. "Thank you for agreeing to help me," she said.

"Officially, I'm doing a project for your mother,
but you're welcome. As for how much good I'm
doing? I spent most of the morning looking into
the life of James Sanders, the guy whose body was
found just up the road from Gemma Ralston's."

"And?" Paula prompted.

"So far I haven't been able to find any connections."

"We haven't, either," Paula said. "I was just asking Lynn if she'd ever heard of the guy. She says
not. So who is he?"

"He's a small-time hood," Ali explained, "an
ex-con who got sent up on charges of counterfeiting in his early twenties. He was from the Phoenix
area originally, and his wife and son still live there.
He spent the years since he got out of prison living

and working at a halfway house in Vegas called the Mission, where he functioned as an assistant manager working for minimum wage plus room and board. In the last week or so, he suddenly came into a sum of money—over and above his regular paycheck. We're trying to uncover the source of same."

"You think he might have been a hired hit man?" Paula asked.

Ali nodded. "Could be."

Lynn Martinson was already shaking her head. "They're thinking I hired a hit man?" she asked. "How could I? I don't have that kind of money, and neither does Chip."

Paula gave her a sharp look. "You know what kind of money it takes to hire a hit man?"

Lynn looked startled. "Well, no. I don't. But truly. I would never do such a thing, and neither would Chip. You have to believe me," she pleaded, her eyes filling with tears. "He just wouldn't!"

Paula Urban gave the slightest shake of her head. Clearly, she wasn't persuaded by Lynn Martinson's opinions about what Chip Ralston would or wouldn't do.

"So about this other dead guy," Paula said. "Any chance that his wife and kid might know anything about what he was up to?"

"It's a possibility," Ali said.

"Would you mind driving down to Phoenix and talking to them about it?" Paula said.

Her question made it clear that she expected to make use of Ali's investigative skills. The defense attorney was going for more than limiting Ali's participation to doing routine background checks. That was the moment when Ali could have called a halt and kept to the original agreement. Instead, she pulled out her iPad and jotted the first of several notes.

"I'd also like you to interview Dr. Ralston's mother, Doris, and his sister, Molly Handraker."

"I doubt they'll talk to you," Lynn said. "Not if they know you're trying to help me."

"That's true," Paula agreed, "but since they were both at home that night, we need to know what, if anything, they're saying to the homicide investigators."

Ali turned to Lynn. "What do Chip's mother and sister have against you?"

"Mostly that I exist," Lynn answered, "and especially that I'm not Gemma. Look at me. No one is ever going to accuse me of being the kind of arm candy Gemma was. Doris thought the sun rose and set on her daughter-in-law. As for Chip's sister? I met her once in passing, but she was something less than cordial. Molly and Gemma have been good friends—best friends—for years. They were roommates at college, and they've maintained that friendship ever since."

"Even after Chip and Gemma divorced?"

"Yes, even after. It only happened a couple of times, but it was embarrassing to show up at Chip's place—his mother's place, really—to spend the night and find his ex-wife's car parked in the driveway."

"Did the two of you ever have words?" Ali asked.

"You mean did we have an argument?"

"Yes."

"I saw her once, but we were never properly introduced," Lynn admitted, "Even if we had been, why would we argue? I mean, it wasn't like she wanted him, so why make a scene? She regarded Chip as her own personal ATM, and that's all she wanted from him—his money. Other than that, she was done. The marriage was over, but he didn't do this."

"Did you?" Ali asked.

The direct question caused Paula Urban to raise one eyebrow, but she said nothing. Instead, she folded her hands on the table and waited for Lynn to answer.

"No, I didn't," Lynn declared. "Of course not."

"The victim's blood was found in your vehicle."

"That's what the detective said, but it can't be true."

"It is true," Ali said. "Dave Holman wouldn't lie about something like that. So if you didn't kill Gemma Ralston, how did her blood get in the trunk of your car and on the back bumper as well?"

Lynn shook her head wordlessly. "I don't know."

"If you didn't do it, then there's only one other possibility, isn't there? Chip did it, and he's trying to put the blame on you."

Lynn rose to her feet. "I don't want to talk about this anymore. Can I go back to my cell now, please?"

Paula picked up her phone and dialed a number. "She's ready to go back to her cell."

A moment later, the door opened. A uniformed guard entered, unfastened Lynn's shackles from the ring in the floor, and then led the prisoner away. Once she was gone, Paula turned to Ali. "Sooner or later, she's going to have to face facts," the attorney said. "What's the matter with her? Why on earth is she defending the guy? First he uses Lynn's vehicle to transport his dying victim's body, and then he leaves Lynn's phone at the crime scene in hopes of implicating her."

"You're convinced of her innocence?" Ali asked.

Paula nodded. "According to Lynn, they both use those CPAP breathing machines, and as long as she's using it, she's a deep sleeper who rarely wakes up before morning. Since he uses one, too, I suppose it could go either way but I'm wondering if maybe he waited until she was asleep and then used the breathing machine as cover to sneak out of the bedroom and out of the house without Lynn being any the wiser. For all his good-guy facade, I suspect Charles Ralston is really a manipulative creep. The sooner Lynn figures that out, the better off she'll be."

"Maybe we need to cut her a little slack on that score," Ali suggested. "Three times Lynn Martinson thought she landed Prince Charming. Now we're trying to tell her that prince number three is also a dud."

"Three strikes and you're out," Paula said. "In this case, the frogs are definitely winning. I don't know what the other two guys did to her, but this one is trying his damnedest to get her sent up for murder. Mark my words. Chip is going to jump at the prosecutor's deal and hang Lynn out to dry. Once he does that, there's enough physical evidence that there's a good chance Lynn Martinson will spend the rest of her life in the slammer."

"So what do we do?" Ali asked, abandoning all pretense about Beatrice's writing project.

"I want you to follow up on everything you learned this morning. I think the first way to attack this is to find out whatever we can about the other dead guy. Two bodies in the same place at the same time? There has to be a connection. I also want you to interview the Ralstons' neighbors. Regardless of what Chip's mother and sister may have seen or heard, they're not going to tell us anything that will make their son and brother look bad."

"Even if they know Chip's responsible, they'll try to put the blame on Lynn?"

"You bet," Paula replied. "The neighbors might not see Chip Ralston as quite the fair-haired boy his family seems to think he is. Meanwhile, the clock is ticking on that plea bargain."

Ali stood up. "All right, then," she said. "It looks like I'm headed for Phoenix."

15

Ali left the interview room while Paula was gathering her papers. She was on her way back to the jail entrance when she changed her mind. Pausing at the check-in desk, she asked to speak to the jail commander. Tex Higgins was someone Ali knew, and once the desk clerk handed her the in-house phone, she had no trouble getting through to him.

"So you're done with the interview room?" he asked.

"Not exactly," Ali said. "I'm wondering if Charles Ralston would agree to see me."

"You're working for the other side, aren't you?" Tex asked. "The girlfriend's side, I mean. I can't imagine that his attorney would agree to let you talk to him alone."

"I'm not asking his attorney," Ali said. "I'm asking him."

"Wait right there," Tex said. "I'll see what he says."

Much to her surprise, a few minutes later, a guard came to collect Ali. After she deposited her Taser and Glock in a locker, she was led to a standard jail visitation room, a grimly appointed place where shackled prisoners were led in and seated in separate cubicles with battle-scarred gray Formica countertops and walls. Inmates were separated from their visitors by the same kind of Plexiglas barrier that separated the departmental clerks from the general public. Here, however, all communications were conducted over handheld phone sets.

The man led to the spot opposite Ali was a long drink of water, probably once a high school basketball star, with graying curly locks that, in a different era, might have been worn in an Anglo approximation of an Afro. He didn't look like a Chip or a Charles. The long slim fingers that reached for the handset were delicate enough to belong to a piano player. The man looked to be somewhere in his late forties or early fifties, and what might have been a handsome face was puffy and gray with what was most likely a combination of worry and lack of sleep. The countenance he presented to Ali looked almost as defeated as Lynn Martinson's.

"You're the writer working for Lynn's mother?" he asked.

Ali nodded. "That means I have no official standing, and you're under no obligation to speak to me—" she began, but Chip Ralston cut her off.

"Have you seen Lynn?" he demanded with a distinct catch in his voice. "How is she? Is she all right? I'm so sorry to have dragged her into this mess."

Words of what sounded like genuine concern for Lynn weren't what Ali had expected to be the first thing out of the man's mouth. His undisguised anguish brought Ali down on the side of not pulling any punches.

"She's okay, considering the circumstances," Ali answered, "but I'm here to ask one question on her behalf: Are you going to take the deal?"

"The deal to point the finger at Lynn?" Ralston replied. "Absolutely not. Whatever Gemma's and my marital difficulties may have been, they weren't Lynn's fault. She'd have no earthly reason to kill Gemma. None. I just got off the phone with my attorney. I've instructed him to cut a different deal. I'll agree to plead guilty to first-degree manslaughter on the condition that he drops all charges against Lynn."

"That's not what the prosecutor proposed originally, and he probably won't be too happy about that," Ali said softly. "Your lawyer won't be, either."

"Of course my lawyer won't be," Chip Ralston agreed. "He's my mother's attorney, not mine, and he's looking to make a fortune because he thinks his fee will be coming out of her checking account. But I'm not going to be responsible for depleting my mother's economic resources. Truth be known, I'll probably end up qualifying for a public defender, too, but I'm not going to bother. This is exactly what Gemma wanted. She said she'd ruin me, and she has."

"Why?" Ali said.

"Why what?" Chip asked.

"Why did Gemma want to ruin you?"

"Because I was a disappointment to her," he said. "Because I never measured up to her lofty expectations. She thought she was getting a carbon copy of my dad—a world-renowned surgeon—not a 'do-gooder' general practitioner. I made reasonable money but not great money. She wanted the kind of prestige my father had and the kind of lifestyle my mother had, and if she had been just a little more patient, she could have had it regardless of how much money I make. My father died last year. My mother is eighty-eight, and she's not in the best of health. She's not going to last forever. I think Gemma got tired of waiting around for my parents to croak so she could grab half of my inheritance. She wanted to get out while she was young enough and attractive enough to find herself another meal ticket—not that she needed one after she took me to the cleaners. Now look where it got her."

"Who do you think killed her?" Ali asked.

"Probably her latest fling, whoever that guy is," Chip answered. There was no disguising the bitterness in his voice.

"Did you kill her?" Ali asked suddenly. "Or did you hire someone else to kill her?"

The phone in Chip Ralston's hand shook, but his voice was steady. He held Ali's eyes without blinking. "No," he said. "I did not."

"But you just told me you're going to plead guilty."

"To manslaughter," he agreed, "but only if I can get the prosecutor to drop all charges against Lynn. She's the one good thing that has happened to me in a very long time. I'm not going to let Gemma destroy her, too."

"Who is James Sanders?" Ali asked.

Chip blinked. "Who?"

"James Mason Sanders is a small-time crook whose body was found in the same general area as your former wife's body. I'm trying to figure out if there was any connection between them."

Chip Ralston shook his head. "It's not a name I recognize, but Gemma wasn't exactly forthcoming about her pals and her relationships. It's come to my attention that she engaged in a good deal of risky behavior, including signing up for any number of dating websites both before and after she filed for a divorce."

"You have reason to believe she was unfaithful?"

"Are you kidding? I don't believe she ever *was* faithful," he replied. "I just didn't know it at the time."

"What do you mean?"

"Look, I always wanted to have kids," he said. "I thought I'd make a great dad, and I wanted *us* to have kids. She claimed she did, too, at least at the beginning. Once I got through medical school, we tried for years to get pregnant, and it didn't work. We both went for tests. My sperm count was fine. She told me that her doctor said she was the one with the fertility problem, but she wasn't willing to do anything about it.

"I suggested in vitro. She said no dice. I said, 'Fine, let's adopt.' She said no, that if we were supposed to have kids, it would happen, but it didn't. Later, I found out that she was on the pill the whole time. I wasn't meant to find that out, you see. After she moved out of the house, someone in her doctor's office screwed up and mailed me a copy of her prescription renewal. After that, HIPAA be damned, I went looking for her prescription records. I found out she'd been taking the pill for years—for as long as we'd been married."

Ali looked at him and said nothing. She had suffered through a series of betrayals at the hands of her second husband, Paul Grayson. In Paul's case, his faithlessness had resulted in the out-of-wedlock birth of more than one child—something Ali had discovered only after the man's death. In Chip Ralston's case, he had no children at all to show for Gemma's betrayal. Ali understood, however, that the hurt was much the same.

"You might think I would have been pissed about that, but you know what?" Chip Ralston asked. "I ended up being grateful. It turns out Gemma was right not to have kids. She would have made a terrible mother."

"What about you?" Ali asked. "Did you have affairs?"

Chip shook his head. "Never. I didn't meet Lynn until long after Gemma had already flown the coop."

"Lynn said that even after the divorce, Gemma stayed friends with both your mother and your sister."

"Look," he said, "when it comes to families, I believe in live and let live. My mother always thought Gemma was terrific, and I never tried changing her mind. When Lynn showed up on the scene, I made it clear to my sister that I expected her to be civil. The one time she and Lynn met in public, Molly was polite, which is more than I can say for my mother."

"Did you object to your mother remaining on friendly terms with Gemma?"

"That was her business, not mine."

"Do you know of anyone who wished Gemma ill?" Ali asked.

"You mean other than yours truly?" Chip asked.

In spite of herself, Ali liked the guy. She was surprised to realize that, plea bargain or not, she more than half believed that he hadn't had anything to do with killing his wife. "Yes," she said. "Other than you."

"No," he said. "I'm sorry. I have no idea. If I did, I'd tell you."

"All right, then," she said, pushing back the molded plastic chair and standing up. "Thank you for agreeing to speak to me."

She watched him put down his handset. The county attorney had assumed that the plea bargain offer would cause the two suspects to start pointing accusing fingers at each other. Instead, Chip Ralston had thrown himself under the bus.

Unsure what to do about this unexpected turn of events, Ali left the visitation room, collected her weapons from the lockbox, and waited until a guard let her back outside. Determining guilt or innocence wasn't in Ali's job description.

Once on the street, Ali dialed B.'s number. "I'm on my way to Phoenix," she said. "I'll probably end up spending the night."

"Would you like me to join you?" B. asked.

Yes, that was what she wanted, but she hadn't wanted to say it in so many words.

"What about your work?" she asked. "Can you afford the interruption? Besides, you already spend so much time in hotels . . ."

"Not in hotels with you," he countered. "Besides, through the magic of telecommuting, I can work anywhere. It would give us a chance to revisit the Ritz," he added. "Return to the scene of the crime, as it were. With any kind of luck, maybe when you're finished working, we could grab a late dinner at Morton's."

The Ritz-Carlton at Twenty-fourth and Camelback was where B. and Ali had spent their first full night together, and Morton's, next door, was where they had shared a very romantic dinner.

"You're sure you don't mind?"

"If I minded, I wouldn't have offered," B. said. "Now, is there anything you need me to bring?"

It was close to four in the afternoon. The idea of driving directly to Phoenix without having to drive the eighty miles back to Sedona had some real appeal.

"Ask Leland to pack an overnight kit for me," she said. "Actually, ask him to make it for two nights, in case I have to stay longer."

Ali knew from experience that Leland would pack for her as well as or better than she would herself. The thought that at some point she would have to learn to get along without the faithful service of her aide-de-camp was one she quickly put aside.

"All right," she said. "You go straight to the hotel. I'll meet you there."

And I'll go track down James Sanders's grieving wife and son, she thought. Going to see them was the last thing she wanted to do, which was enough to move it to the top of the list. That was always one of Ali's mother's watchwords: Do the tough things first.

16

Not wanting to call undue attention to what they were doing, A.J. and Sasha decided that they wouldn't head north until after school got out. Ditching their afternoon classes wasn't the way to go unnoticed. A.J. called work and told them that he wouldn't be in due to a family emergency. Then, leaving the Camry in the school parking lot, they took off in Sasha's BMW. Unlike A.J., she had access to her father's credit card and didn't have to hoard every ounce of gas. When they stopped to fill up, she paid for fuel and for a pair of immense sodas. Later, when they stopped at Ace Hardware to buy a new shovel, she whipped out her credit card again.

"Don't worry," she said. "Daddy never checks, but if he asks me about it, I'll tell him it's for Christmas."

Nodding, A.J. went along with the program. He was too worried and conflicted to argue about any of it. He was worried about returning to the crime scene. He was worried that there would still be cops there. Most of all, now that he had told

Sasha everything, he was worried that the money wouldn't be there—that Sasha would see right through his father's lie and know that A.J. was stupid beyond words. Finding money under a rock was like the Tooth Fairy leaving money under a pillow—not gonna happen.

For a time, they drove north without speaking. It was only when Sasha spoke that A.J. realized that she, too, was chewing over what he had told her.

"So those are really the only times you remember seeing your father, at the store? That once and later when he bought you the car for your sixteenth birthday?"

A.J. nodded numbly.

"And he really did go to prison for counterfeiting?"

A.J. nodded again.

"Why didn't he come back home after he got out?"

"I have no idea," A.J. said. "That's one of the things I would have liked to ask him."

"I'm sorry you can't," Sasha said.

A.J.'s eyes filled with tears. "Me, too."

Traffic was slow leaving the city. It seemed to take forever to get to the turn-off, but at last they reached the General Crook Trail exit. As A.J. got out to open the gate, he scanned the horizon to see if there were any vehicles parked at or near the crime scene. He saw nothing. Sasha babied the BMW along the rutted road. When they reached the spot where the green-eyed woman had died, the place was marked with a series of streamers made up of bits of yellow crime scene tape blowing sideways in the wind.

"That's where I found the woman," he said, nodding toward the tape, "but keep going. When the mileage marker on the odometer hits six tenths of a mile, stop. You stay with the car and turn it around. That way, if I do find anything, we'll be able to take off in a hurry. I want to get out of here before someone sees us."

That was what A.J. told her, but the truth was, he had another reason for leaving Sasha in the car. He didn't want her to witness his humiliation when his shovel search came up empty. During the long slow drive from Phoenix, A.J. had convinced himself that the entire undertaking was beyond stupid. His father was a crook and a liar. There wasn't any hidden money and never had been. A.J. had spent much of the trip berating himself for telling Sasha about it in the first place. If only she hadn't insisted on coming along. If only he hadn't let her.

Sasha stopped the car next to another area that had been marked off with crime scene tape; here, most of it was intact. Feeling almost sick to his stomach, A.J. got out and stood looking at the spot where his father must have died. His mother had said his father had been shot. For a moment he stood there with his hand shading his eyes, peering around, more than half expecting to see a rough chalk outline of where James Sanders's body had been found. To his immense relief, there was no visible sign of bloodstains.

Glancing back over his shoulder, A.J. noticed that the place where the green-eyed woman had died wasn't visible from here. There was a slight rise between the two spots and a place where the road twisted sharply left and right, following a streambed. So although the two victims—his father and the green-eyed woman—hadn't died in exactly the same place, it had been close enough that even James Sanders's son had to confront the possibility that there was some terrible connection between them.

What if this money—the unexpected windfall from his father—had something to do with the murder of the green-eyed woman? What if his father was really a contract killer and the money he had promised A.J. was ill-gotten gains? A.J.'s mother had insisted that James would never be violent—that he'd never hurt someone—but how much did she know? As far as A.J. knew, his parents had never even lived together. Why was that? Had his mother understood what James was really like, and that was why she had avoided living with him once he got out of prison?

Turning away from both crime scenes—the one he could see and the one he couldn't—A.J. tried to shake off the dread-induced lethargy that had overtaken him. Only when Sasha pressed the trunk release and the lid flipped open did he snap out of it. Marching determinedly to the back of the BMW, he retrieved the shovel.

This area, like the spot where A.J. had found the dying woman, had been cleared of both scraggly vegetation and rocks and turned into an informal and illegal trash-dumping ground of long standing, with layers of general garbage along with abandoned mattresses and appliances littering the desert landscape. What rocks remained—boulders, really—were on the far perimeter of the clearing. With the shovel balanced on his shoulder, feeling like one of Snow White's dwarves, A.J. marched purposefully in what seemed to him to be the direction of due north, to the boulder where his father had claimed he had left a heart to mark the correct spot.

With every step he took, A.J. told himself that he shouldn't be disappointed when the designated heart wasn't there. But as soon as he came to the first boulder, there it was. The heart, tiny though it was, stood out because it was bright and recent and painted in what appeared to be nail polish. On either side of the glowing heart, scratched on the rock's rough surface and faded almost to invisibility, were two sets of barely legible initials. The first one was clearly J.S. The second one might have been an S and some other letter—a P or a B. A.J.'s mother's name was Sylvia. Her maiden name had been Bixby, so maybe the faded second letter was a B.

For a moment A.J. stood transfixed and staring at this artifact that testified to a time in Sylvia Sanders's far-distant past, back when carving their initials on a rock had been a way of declaring their love. A.J. was struck by the fact that his mother and James Sanders must have been about the same age then as he and Sasha were right now. If all that was true, if this had been a place of some teenage assignation, was that why James had summoned his son here, as a way of making amends for never having lived up to the demands of fatherhood? Was that what this was all about?

A.J. glanced back toward the idling BMW. Following his directions, Sasha had maneuvered the car into a deft U-turn and sat with the driver's window open, watching him with interest.

Forcing his limbs to move, A.J. walked all the

way around the boulder, studying the terrain. On the far side of the rock, he found evidence that the hard-packed dirt and smaller rocks had been disturbed. The ground nearby was all rock-hard caliche, but when he pushed the blade of the shovel into the earth at the base of the rock, it sank in easily. Four or five inches down, he hit something solid that sounded like metal.

He cleared out five or six heaping shovelfuls of dirt. Then, falling to his knees, A.J. dug with his hands alone, stripping away the dirt and sharp rocks from the surface and from around the sides of a rectangular metal box. As soon as he lifted it, A.J. realized that his mother had a metal box similar in size and shape to this one. She had told him that if anything ever happened to her, that was where he'd be able to find the important documents—things like birth certificates and insurance policies.

Once the box was out of the hole, A.J. hurriedly used the shovel to scrape the loose rocks and dirt back into it. Then, taking both the box and the shovel, he made a run for the car. Sasha opened the trunk as he approached. Dumping the shovel in, A.J. leaped into the passenger seat and slammed the door behind him. Once seated, he had to struggle to fasten his seat belt around the filthy box, which he held clutched to his chest.

When he looked at Sasha, she was grinning at him triumphantly. "See there?" she said. "You found it. What's in it?"

"I haven't had time to look," he said. "Let's get out of here first. Drive."

He carried the box with him when he got out of the car to open and close the gate to let them back onto the freeway entrance. Earlier, he had been awash in doubt. Now that he had found the box, he worried about what he'd find inside.

"Well," Sasha said impatiently, "are you just going to sit there, or are you going to open it?"

By then they were back on the freeway, speeding south at seventy miles an hour. With his fingers shaking, A.J. fumbled open the lock. Reaching inside, he pulled out a bright red clay disk and held it up so he could read what was printed on it. On one side were the words MGM GRAND. On the other, the printed number $1,000.

"What is it?" Sasha demanded.

"I think it's a gambling token," A.J. murmured. "It says it's worth a thousand bucks."

"A thousand bucks," Sasha repeated. "Are you kidding? How many of those are there?"

A.J. felt the inside of the box, sifting the tokens through his fingers. "I don't know," he said. "A lot."

"Don't be an idiot," Sasha said. "You need to count them."

A.J. did so, dumping the contents onto the floor and then counting them back into the box one at a time. The whole time, he was remembering what his mother had said about the gas and insurance money James had handed over along with the title to the Camry. "Is this even real?" If his father had gone to prison for counterfeiting U.S. currency, what were the chances he might try counterfeiting gambling tokens?

"Two hundred and fifty," he said at last.

"Whoa!" Sasha exclaimed. "Two hundred and fifty thousand dollars?"

A.J. nodded.

"That means you're rich," she said with a laugh.

Coming from Sasha, whose family really was rich, that seemed weird, and A.J. didn't bother mentioning his niggling worry that the tokens might be fake.

"He wanted me to use the money to go to school. He said this way I wouldn't have to get student loans or a job—I'd be able to concentrate on studying."

"How do you turn it into real money, so you can take it to a bank?" Sasha asked.

"I guess you have to take it back to the casino," A.J. said. "He told me in the note that I'd need someone of age to cash them in."

"Your mother?"

"No," A.J. said, shaking his head. He closed the box again and latched it. "I don't think my mother would be the one doing it."

"Are you going to tell her about this?"

A.J. thought about that. "No," he said finally. "You're the only one who knows. I don't want to tell anyone else, especially my mother."

There was an injury accident at the junction of I-17 and the 101. Both before and after the accident, traffic crawled along. By the time Sasha dropped A.J. back in the school parking lot, it was almost seven—far later than he should have been, even if he'd gone to work. He hoped his mother hadn't called Maddy to check on him.

Once Sasha left him, A.J. put the strongbox in the trunk of his Camry and covered it with a bag of discarded clothing that his mother had asked him to drop off at Goodwill two weeks earlier. After closing the trunk, he happened to look down at the clothing he was wearing. The jeans weren't bad, but his shirt was a grimy mess. The reddish-brown dirt from the strongbox had been ground into the material; and no amount of wiping would remove it.

A.J. reopened the trunk and dug through the bag of cast-off clothing. He found a shirt that he'd never liked much, even though it still fit him. He traded his dirty shirt for that one. Then, unsure what if anything he would say to his mother, A. J. Sanders headed home.

17

li's drive down I-17, from high desert to low desert, was uneventful, with light traffic in both directions, until she hit the exits to Anthem. That was also about the time Stuart Ramey called.

"Sorry to say, I don't have much for you. I'm making nice with people at the MGM Grand in order to get a copy of the tapes. I find that diplomacy generally takes more time than hacking, but B. prefers me to use up-front methods whenever possible."

Stuart's abilities to wander through complex computer systems as invisibly as a cyber ghost made him an invaluable asset to High Noon Security's anti-hacking initiative. Companies set up what they thought were foolproof cyber-security systems that Stuart routinely broke through. Although Ali had occasionally made use of Stuart's off-the-books hacking skills, she knew what he did, although expedient, was also skirting the law. She felt more comfortable when he used front-door rather than back-door methods.

"Right now I'm on my way to Phoenix to interview James Sanders's wife and son. I know you
gave me their address earlier, but could you send
it to my iPhone so I can program it into the GPS?"

"Done," Stuart said.

A moment later, an arriving message buzzed on
her phone. He rang her back. "Anything else?"

"I talked to Dr. Charles Ralston. He said his
wife was enrolled in several dating websites both
before and after the divorce. If we can find out
which ones, we might be able to find out if James
Sanders met up with her that way."

"Hearts Afire," Stuart said.

"I beg your pardon?" Ali asked.

"That's the name of the main dating website
Gemma Ralston was signed up with," Stuart answered. "I already know which one, because I
found her profile."

"I should have known you'd be one step ahead
of me," Ali said with a laugh.

"Gemma made no bones about looking for
someone with big bucks," Stuart continued, "and
she wasn't looking to get married. What she
wanted was a meaningless relationship—preferably
a high-end meaningless relationship. Since you
told me Sanders didn't have his own computer to
go online, I'll have to look through the browsing
history on the Mission's computers to find out if
there's a connection. Fortunately, almost nobody
thinks to clean their caches these days, which
makes my work child's play."

"All right," Ali said. "Thanks for the help. You
keep doing what you do, and I'll keep doing what
I do."

She pulled off at the next exit long enough to

program her GPS, then got back into the flow of traffic. The computerized voice in the dash told her to take the 101 to the 51 and then that down to Thomas. She had to jog around on surface streets in a modest working-class neighborhood until she found the correct address on East Cheery Lynn Road.

Ali stopped in front of a small white brick bungalow. The front yard was flat and unfenced. Once upon a time the yard might have boasted crops of lush green grass. Now, due to the escalating cost of water, the owners of that yard, as well as many of the near neighbors, had opted for xeriscaped patches of desert landscaping. Sylvia Sanders had moved one notch up on the scale of landscape severity by covering her entire front lawn with a layer of white gravel. Not so much as a single weed dared poke its head up through the thick blanket of tiny rocks.

In view of what had happened, Ali had expected that she would arrive to find a houseful of visiting friends and relatives. That didn't appear to be true. Other than Ali's Cayenne, the street in front of Sylvia Sanders's house was empty. A single aging Passat sat parked in the two-car carport.

Dreading the encounter and unsure of her reception, Ali walked up to the door and rang the bell. The woman who answered a few seconds later appeared to be somewhere in her mid-thirties. She came to the door in a well-worn jogging suit. She looked as though she had been crying.

"Ms. Sanders?" Ali asked, holding out a business card that contained nothing but her name and her cell phone number.

Nodding, the woman opened the door wide

enough to take the card. She glanced at it without appearing to take it in. "I'm Sylvia Sanders," she said.

"As it says there," Ali explained, "my name is Ali Reynolds. I'm very sorry for your loss, but I'm a journalist doing a story on the Camp Verde homicide—the other one," she added quickly. "I know this is a terribly challenging time for you, but would it be possible for me to ask a few questions?"

"I've already spoken to the cops, and the reporter from Las Vegas just left. I don't know how much more I can add."

"Please," Ali said. "Anything you can do to shed light on the situation for my client . . ."

"All right," Sylvia said with a sigh. She opened the door, stepped aside, and motioned Ali into the house, leading the way through a small entryway and into a combination living room/dining room. Sylvia directed Ali toward an old-fashioned sofa with brown and orange plaid upholstery and wide wooden arms. As Ali sat down, Sylvia resumed what was evidently her seat in a matching chair, where a coffee mug sat within arm's reach. She glanced at her watch before picking up the coffee mug. "My son's late getting home," she said. "He's usually here by now."

"That would be Alexander?" Ali asked, removing her iPad from her briefcase-size purse and opening the cover.

Sylvia nodded. "I call him A.J.," she said.

"This must be terribly difficult for both of you."

Two new tears squeezed out of Sylvia's eyes and coursed down her cheeks. "A.J. barely knew his father. I did my best to protect him from all that . . . notoriety. Now, though, all the details are bound to be back in the papers. In fact, that's what Betty Noonan was asking about."

"And she is?" Ali asked, deftly typing notes on the iPad's flat-screen keyboard.

"The reporter I told you about. From the *Las Vegas Examiner*. She left a few minutes ago, just before you got here. That's where James, my husband, had been living and working ever since he got out of prison—in a halfway house in Vegas called the Mission."

Ali had spent years as a television journalist. In this day of shrinking print newspapers and equally shrinking newspaper budgets, she wondered why the murder of a lowly halfway-house janitor would be important enough for a news editor to send a reporter on a three-hundred-mile one-way trip. Obviously, there was more to James Mason Sanders than anyone was letting on.

"You said James Sanders was your husband," Ali repeated. "Does that mean you never divorced?"

Sylvia nodded. "We're Catholic," she said simply. "If he had ever asked me for a divorce, I suppose I would have given it to him. After all, except for those first few months, we've lived apart the whole time. He never asked, and I never bothered. I thought the less said about that whole situation, the better off we'd be. Having all of this come to light now that A.J.'s a senior seems worse somehow. Maybe if I'd been more open about it when he was younger . . ."

"Open about what?" Ali asked. "About A.J.'s father going to prison for counterfeiting?"

She already knew the answer, but that was part

of the drill. If you knew what interviewees were supposed to say, it was a lot easier to see if they were telling the truth or lying.

"We started dating when we were in high school," Sylvia explained. "He went off to college while I was a junior. He got in to a fraternity at ASU. When he was a sophomore, one of his buddies came up with the stupid idea of trying to print money. It was just a lark. They wanted to see if they could get away with it. I don't think any of them thought of the long-term consequences. If they'd been serious about it, they would have made hundreds instead of twenties. When they got caught, two of them hired big-shot defense attorneys and got off completely, and the third one paid a fine. James was the one left holding the bag. He's the one who went to prison." Sylvia paused, her gaze far away. "We found out I was pregnant just before the whole thing blew up. We got married right away, but we ended up living with his grandparents in Tempe because we couldn't afford to rent a place on our own. James was willing to work, but no one would give him a job. A.J. was born while James was out on bail awaiting trial, and he was only three months old when his father was sent to prison."

"For what was essentially a first offense and a victimless crime," Ali said.

"The prosecutor didn't think it was victimless," Sylvia said.

"It must have been tough being left on your own with a baby."

"It wasn't easy," Sylvia agreed, "but we weren't completely adrift. My parents helped, and so did his. It was an inheritance from James's grandparents that made it possible for me to buy this house."

"Are you still in touch with his parents?"

"No," Sylvia said, shaking her head. "His father died a number of years ago. His mother remarried and moved to Sun River in Oregon. I called her earlier today to let her know what happened. She and her husband are leaving later today to drive down."

"Pardon me for saying this," Ali said, "but it's clear to see that you still cared about the man. When he got out of prison, why didn't he come to live with you?"

Sylvia bit her lip. "I asked him not to," she said finally. "I was trying to keep my son away from someone I thought would be a bad influence. Maybe it was wrong, but I thought A.J. would be better off with no father at all than with a father who'd spent years of his life in prison. Kids can be so mean about stuff like that, and I didn't want A.J. to be bullied."

Ali felt a rush of sympathy for this solitary woman who had damned herself to a life of loneliness in hopes of sparing her son. Ali had spent enough time as a single mother to know the drill—the unrelenting responsibility of having to make all the decisions on her own, all the while hoping against hope that those decisions were the right ones. And now that James Sanders's murder was in the public eye, all of Sylvia's efforts to dodge the unsavory past had gone for nothing.

"Since your husband's body was found in much the same location where the other victim, Gemma Ralston, was found, some people seem to be making the leap that he was somehow connected to what happened to her."

"I know about the other victim," Sylvia said. "The detective told me. I have no idea what James was doing there the night he was killed, but I do know he didn't go there to kill someone. For one thing, the James Sanders I knew wasn't a killer, but even if he was, he wouldn't have done something like that there! Never." Sylvia sounded like she was close to losing it.

Ali gave her a moment. "You sound certain of that."

There was a long pause before Sylvia answered. "I am certain," she replied, "because I know that place all too well. We were kids back then. We were horny. We went skiing up in Flagstaff with a bunch of our friends. On the way home, we stopped off at that very place—the turnoff to General Crook Trail. If we'd had more money, we might have gone to a motel. Instead, we found a likely place to pull off the road. Later on we figured out that's probably where it happened— where I got knocked up. So, no. Even if James turned out to be a cold-blooded killer—which he wasn't—I refuse to accept that he would have chosen that particular place to murder someone."

Just then a car door slammed shut outside the house. Several times during the conversation, Sylvia had glanced unobtrusively at her watch. She charged out of her chair and hurried toward the entryway as the front door banged open.

"Where have you been?" she demanded. "I've been worried sick. Maddy called to see how you were doing and was surprised to learn that I thought you had gone to work."

Sylvia returned to the living room accompanied by a rangy young man, a kid in his late teens who, at five-ten or so, was a good head and a half taller than she was. He was good-looking and carried what looked like a heavy book bag slung over one slender shoulder. Ali realized this had to be A.J. He reminded her of her own son back when Chris was a senior in high school.

"I needed some time to think, is all," he said. "It's a lot to take in."

"Were you with that girl?"

A.J. seemed to bristle. His ears turned red. "What girl?"

"Sasha something or other," Sylvia said. "A black girl. Maddy tells me she comes by the store when you're working. She always buys something, but she seems to like hanging out wherever you happen to be stocking shelves."

"Maddy Wurth needs to mind her own business," A.J. declared, "but like I said, I was by myself. I needed to think!" At that point, he caught sight of Ali and stopped short. "Who's this?" he demanded.

Sylvia leveled a look in her son's direction that, without saying a word aloud, let A.J. know that he needed to mind his manners.

Ali stood up and handed A.J. one of her cards. "My name's Ali Reynolds," she said.

A.J. glanced at the card, then back at Ali. For a fleeting moment, an odd look appeared on his face, something akin to panic. By then his mother had turned away from him, but Ali caught the expression before he managed to stifle it. By the time Sylvia sat back down, A.J. had recovered enough that the strange expression had been wiped clean.

"Are you a cop?" he asked.

"No, I'm a writer," Ali explained. "I'm working

on a story about the woman who died, but I'm also trying to piece together what happened to your father."

"You think he's the one who killed her?" A.J. asked.

"I've spoken to the lead investigator on the two cases. He seems to think that because of your father's somewhat dubious history, he might be involved in what happened."

"No," Sylvia declared, shaking her head. "That's not true. I told Ms. Reynolds here the same thing I told the detective earlier today, and it's the same thing I'm telling you right now. James Sanders didn't kill that woman. Whatever happened to her, your father was not involved."

"But if he was there at the same time—" A.J. began.

"From what I've been able to learn, your father was dead long before the other woman died," Ali said kindly. "So I'm not accusing your father of anything. I was simply hoping you and your mother might be able to shed some light on what happened. You two may be the only people in the world with a vested interest in proving that your father wasn't involved."

A.J. stood there, seemingly struggling with some kind of indecision. "I can't help you," he said finally. "I don't know anything about it. I've got homework," he added. "I'd better go do it."

"Do you want me to heat up that leftover *carne asada*?" Sylvia asked.

"Don't bother," he said. "I'm not hungry."

With that, A.J. disappeared down a hallway. Shortly thereafter, a door slammed hard behind him.

"I shouldn't have done that," Sylvia said, shaking her head. "That was a terrible blunder on my part. I've known about Sasha Miller for weeks now. I've been waiting for A.J. to come clean and tell me about her himself. I never should have mentioned her in front of company."

It occurred to Ali then that A.J. Sanders and his supposedly secret girlfriend might be following in his parents' footsteps. Perhaps he and Sasha had been off on their own somewhere and engaged in something far more interesting than solitary "thinking."

"That's what happens to boys when they grow up," Ali said. "Keeping secrets from their mothers is part of the deal. If you'll pardon my saying it, I'm under the impression that your son hardly knew his father. That's got to make things that much more difficult for both of you right now."

Sylvia nodded. "A.J. was a baby when James went to prison. From the time James walked out of the courtroom, A.J. saw him only once. That was a little over a year ago." For the first time, Ali heard real bitterness in Sylvia's response.

"James showed up here uninvited on A.J.'s sixteenth birthday, just in time to play the Great White Father. A.J. and I had agreed beforehand that he wasn't going to get a car because we couldn't afford it. Not only did James show up with the car, he gave me enough cold, hard cash to pay for insurance and gas for the next three years. Real money, by the way. I checked it *before* I took it to the bank. I didn't want to be caught passing out counterfeit bills that I didn't *know* were counterfeit."

"He gave A.J. a new car?" Ali asked.

"Not new, secondhand—a Camry. Even so, the

grand total came to over twenty thousand bucks. I convinced myself it was like having James pay back child support. That was the only reason I let A.J. keep it."

"I'm assuming there was no court-ordered child support, because you never went to court and asked for it," Ali said.

Sylvia nodded. "By the time James got out of prison, A.J. and I were settled in here and doing all right. I didn't want to be beholden to him, and I didn't want to get mixed up in some kind of visitation situation. I decided to just let sleeping dogs lie. When he showed up with the car, it was a big deal for A.J., and not such a good deal for me. My son had always taken me at my word that we were better off without his father in the picture. After the birthday adventure, I think A.J. started questioning that. I also think that's part of why this is and will be so hard for him. He was probably hoping that someday he'd have a chance to get to know his father. Now he never will."

"So they weren't in touch?" Ali asked. "They didn't exchange phone calls or e-mails?"

"Not as far as I know," Sylvia said with a sad smile, "but I could be wrong about that. Secrets, you know."

"And you don't know any of James's associates from Vegas—friends, girlfriends, that kind of thing?"

"No," Sylvia said. "I'm afraid we didn't have that kind of relationship. He came here briefly right after he got out of prison. When I sent him packing, that was the last we saw of him until the birthday car a year ago. I had no idea where he was living or how he ended up in Vegas. The detective who came here this morning told me that the dead woman is some kind of fancy-schmancy socialite from here in Phoenix. A doctor's wife or ex-wife. How would James Sanders have hooked up with someone like that? The detective told me he was working for minimum wage in a halfway house, for Pete's sake."

Ali busied herself writing a series of notes, remembering as she did so that Stuart Ramey had said James Sanders's checking account never went over the thousand-dollar mark. What came in went out again almost immediately. Having learned about the birthday gift, Ali realized that about a year earlier, there must have been another invisible influx of money, some or maybe even all of which James had squandered on a car for his son.

Ali made a show of closing her iPad and putting it away. "A.J. looks like a good kid. Where does he go to school?"

"North High," Sylvia answered. "You're right. He is a good kid, one who's never given me a moment's worth of trouble. He's in the Baccalaureate program at North High—the honors program. He also works two hours a day after school and a couple more on the weekends at a Walgreens where one of my good friends, Madeline Wurth, is the manager. He's saving money to go to college. We both are."

Ali stood up. "I'd better be going," she said. "I've taken up enough of your time."

"I'm sorry I wasn't more help," Sylvia said.

"Oh, you were a help, all right," Ali said. "The fact that you don't believe James Sanders would have been involved in any way in Gemma Ralston's murder doesn't mean it's one hundred percent certain. But in my book, let's say it seems a lot less likely."

Sylvia Sanders's hard-won composure took a hit. "Thank you," she said. "In spite of everything, I believe James was really a good man. Maybe not an honest man, but a good one."

A man who recently came into another unexplained batch of money, Ali thought, though she didn't say it aloud.

Ali stood up. "Don't bother getting up," she told Sylvia. "I can find my way out."

18

Ali's phone had buzzed twice while she was inside the house. Now she sat in the Cayenne and checked her phone. One call was a message from Stuart Ramey, giving her the exact address of Chip Ralston's Paradise Valley home, which she immediately fed into her GPS. The other call was from B., which Ali returned while the GPS was busy planning her route.

"I'm here," B. said. "Checked in to the hotel. How are you doing?"

"Busy trying to prove a negative," Ali said.

"How's that working out for you?"

"Not very well. So far I haven't found any obvious connections between Gemma Ralston and the other dead guy, but that doesn't mean they're not there."

Ali was about to put the Cayenne in gear when a sudden movement caught her eye. A.J. appeared in the front yard, emerging from the far side of the house. He paused furtively at the corner, as if checking the front door, then moved purposefully toward the second car, now parked in the carport.

Once again he was carrying the book bag slung over his shoulder. He quickly popped open the trunk and placed something inside. Then, removing the book bag, he closed the trunk and returned the way he had come, still moving with apparent caution. Whatever it was he had placed in the trunk, it was something A.J. hadn't wanted his mother to know about.

"Hey," B. said. "What happened? Are you still there?"

"Sorry," she said. "I wonder what that was all about."

"What was what all about?"

"Something odd," she said. "I was watching a teenager hiding something in a car that he doesn't want his mother to find."

"There's nothing odd about that at all," B. said with a laugh. "If it had been me, I would have been hiding my private hoard of *Penthouse* magazines. I always kept them in the car rather than under the bed. So what's next on your agenda?"

"Next scheduled stop is Chip Ralston's mother's place to talk to his mother and sister. I'm also hoping I'll be able to chat up a couple of their neighbors."

"Don't rush on my account," B. said. "I'll be here when you get here."

Ignoring the GPS's insistent directions that she retrace her path north on the 51, Ali made her way over to Twenty-fourth and up to Lincoln. Eventually, she found her way to Upper Glen Road, where she was disappointed to find that the Ralstons' place wasn't inside a gated community. One of those might have given her some security tapes to review or some rent-a-cops to question about vehicles coming and going on the night in question. When she finally located the right address, it was after dark. It was also clear there wouldn't be any neighbors to chat up. The Ralstons' house was at the far end of the road, with a yard that backed up to a looming wall of rocky desert cliffs.

The house seemed noticeably smaller than some of the sprawling mansions Ali had passed along the way, and its small fifties-era windows looked almost old-fashioned compared to some of the sharply angled, window-covered places she had seen on the way in. A series of lights showed off the towering palm trees and lush landscaping that made it clear the house had been there for decades longer than some of its more architecturally daring and starkly modern fellows.

As Ali drove up the front drive, she noticed a second, smaller driveway veering off to the right. Despite the lights gleaming in the windows, when Ali rang the bell, no one answered. Without leaving a note, she returned to her vehicle and headed down the driveway, intent on going straight to the hotel. When she reached the turnoff halfway down the drive, she changed her mind and turned up the side path. Driving past a four-car garage built at one end of the house, Ali discovered the casita tucked away at the far end of the driveway that she was sure was Chip's apartment.

The maid's quarters, Ali thought, looking at the house, a much smaller replica of the main house. *Not bad for an end-of-marriage bolt-hole.*

Ali had to admit that she didn't have much room to talk on that score. After all, what had she done after the collapse of her marriage to Paul Grayson? She had slunk home to Sedona and taken up residence in the double-wide she had inherited from Aunt Evie.

There were no lights on in the casita. Even so, Ali got out and tried knocking. As expected, no one answered. Ali returned to the Cayenne, pulled a U-turn at the back of the house, and started back toward the driveway. Before she got there, she found her path blocked by a pair of blazing headlights. A woman was standing directly in front of the vehicle. Her feet were spread apart in a shooting stance, while she used both hands to keep a weapon of some kind aimed on Ali. Slamming on the brakes, Ali stopped the Cayenne and buzzed down the window.

"Out of the vehicle," the woman ordered. "On your knees. Hands behind your head."

"I can explain," Ali said as she hurried to comply. Scrambling out of the Cayenne, she landed on her knees on the pavement while the open-door alarm chimed away behind her.

With the gun still trained on Ali, the woman spoke over her shoulder to her passenger. "Did you get through to 911, Mama?"

"Please," Ali said. "I can explain. Just put the gun down before someone gets hurt. My name is Ali Reynolds. I'm a freelancer working on an article about Gemma Ralston's murder. I came here hoping to speak to Chip Ralston's mother and sister—Doris Ralston and Molly Handraker."

As if on cue, the second woman—clearly the elderly mother in question—stepped out of the vehicle, an older-model Jaguar. For several long seconds, Doris Ralston stood swaying unsteadily beside the open passenger door while she used both hands in a vain attempt to operate a cell phone.

"Where are my reading glasses?" she grumbled. "Without them, I can't make this thing work. The numbers are too small."

"Oh, for pity's sake, Mama," Molly said. "Can't you do anything? Give me the phone and get back in the car." She lowered the weapon long enough to collect the phone. When the gun was no longer pointed in her direction, Ali, who wasn't wearing body armor, allowed herself a small sigh of relief.

"What are you doing prowling around in our backyard when nobody's home?"

"Please," Ali said. "You don't need to call the cops. If you're Molly Handraker, I just need to talk to you."

"What about?"

"Gemma Ralston's murder."

"Who are you again, and who are you working for?"

Even though the younger woman had yet to dial a number or press send, she still held the phone in one hand and the weapon in the other. Loose gravel from the driveway was biting into Ali's kneecaps. She needed to bring the confrontation to some kind of peaceful ending.

"My name is Alison Reynolds. As I said, I'm a freelancer. I've spoken to some of the investigators working the Gemma Ralston homicide. Some of them seem to be convinced that Lynn Martinson acted alone. Others seem to think your brother and she were in on it together. I wanted to get your take on it."

"You still haven't explained what you were doing prowling behind our house while we were out having dinner."

As she spoke, Molly walked over to the open

driver's door of Ali's Cayenne and peered inside. Ali suspected she was checking to see if the car was loaded with stolen goods. Meanwhile, the open-door alarm continued to ding away, filling the quiet night with its annoyingly tuneless racket.

"I rang the bell at the front door," Ali said. "When no one answered, I started to leave. On the way down the driveway, I decided to see if anyone was home at Chip's place."

"Chip doesn't live here anymore," Doris said, unexpectedly inserting herself into the conversation. "Not since he and Gemma got married."

"Mother!" Molly said warningly. "Stay out of this. Let me handle it. He does too live here. Remember?"

Ali didn't know why, but for some reason, the older woman's querulous comment seemed to have tipped the scales in Ali's favor. The young woman was wearing a loose-fitting denim jacket. The gun disappeared into one of the jacket pockets while the phone slipped into another.

"This isn't very convenient," the younger woman said, "but it's too cold to be standing around out here talking. Mother will catch her death. I need to get her inside. Come on."

With that, she walked over to Ali, held out one hand, and helped her to her feet. Close up, Ali noticed that the clear crisp air was alive with the sharp bite of booze. Molly had evidently enjoyed several cocktails along with dinner. That realization sent an additional surge of relief coursing through Ali's body. There was little doubt that she had just dodged a very real bullet. An angry woman with a handgun was dangerous enough. An angry drunk of either sex with a handgun was even more so.

"Do you have any ID?"

Ali fumbled in her own pocket, found a business card, and passed it over. Molly held it up to the headlights and examined it. "Something with a photo, maybe?"

"In my purse in the car," Ali said.

"Get it," Molly ordered. "I'm not letting you into our house until I know you are who you say you are."

Ali stumbled back to the car and grabbed her purse. In the process, she managed to pull the key from the ignition and shut off the door alarm. By the time she had her wallet open to her driver's license, Molly had stowed her mother back in the Jaguar's passenger seat. Molly examined the ID and then handed it back.

"As you can well imagine, it's been a tough day around here. You'll need to follow us back up to the front door. I take Mother in and out of the house that way. There are only a few steps from the garage up to the laundry room, but these days, even those are more than she can manage."

More than I could, too, Ali thought. Her knees and hands were still shaking as she made her way back to the Cayenne and managed to climb inside.

19

Molly backed the Jaguar onto the main driveway and then drove up to the front entrance while Ali followed in the Cayenne. Molly parked at the door before getting out of the vehicle and walking around it to assist her mother. Doris Ralston got out of the car, holding on to her daughter's arm with one hand while gripping a cane with the other.

Molly unlocked the oversize double doors and led the way into the house. Ali trailed behind them. She was surprised that no interior alarm sounded. What looked like a security control panel was right next to the door, but Molly and Doris bypassed it without stopping. They walked through a spacious entryway into a large, comfortably appointed living room—an old-money room—where the highly polished hardwood floor was dotted with aged but entirely authentic Navajo rugs. The chairs and tables were genuine Mission, and the lamps were equally genuine Tiffany. Above a massive and mostly unnecessary fireplace was a full-length oil painting of a much younger Doris Ralston clad in a sapphire evening gown.

As Molly eased her mother down onto a long leather sofa, Ali couldn't help noticing that although the two women resembled each other, mother and daughter were anything but a matched pair. Doris Ralston looked to be somewhere in her eighties, decidedly frail but utterly fashionable. She was dressed in a classic St. John's knit that was probably at least a decade old, as were her low-heeled pumps, but her thinning white hair was carefully combed, and her liver-spotted hands were beautifully manicured.

Molly, somewhere in her forties, with a mane of wavy auburn hair, was a younger image of her mother's good looks, but with a harder edge. Years of smoking were beginning to carve an indelible mark into the curve of her cheeks. In her choice of clothing, Molly Handraker diverged from her mother's in every way. The skimpy tank top she wore over possibly surgically enhanced breasts didn't quite meet the top of her low-rider jeans. The denim of the pencil-thin pants was suitably worn in all the right places, but Ali suspected that the wear in the denim came from that—actual wear—rather than the artificially preworn look available new at Old Navy. Her stiletto boots were far more of a fashion statement than they were practical. The outfit was topped by a short sequined denim jacket.

Once Doris was seated, Molly stripped off the jacket and dropped it on a nearby chair before joining her mother on the couch.

"Remind me," Doris said, nodding and frowning

in Ali's direction. "Who is this again, and what's she doing here?"

"She's a writer," Molly answered brusquely. "She's here to talk about Gemma."

"What about Gemma?" Doris asked, looking around the room with a puzzled expression, as though the object of her search might be hiding behind or under one of the room's massive pieces of furniture. "Did she call me today? Wasn't she supposed to come to dinner with us tonight? I do so enjoy her company."

Molly rolled her eyes. "Gemma couldn't come to dinner with us," she said shortly. "She's dead!"

Doris seemed remarkably unfazed by her daughter's blunt response. "Really?" she asked, frowning. "I didn't know that. Are you sure? When did that happen? Why didn't someone tell me about it?"

"Someone did tell you about it." Shaking her head in weary resignation, Molly turned from Doris to Ali. "As you can see, talking to my mother isn't going to do you much good, so I guess you'll need to talk to me. Go ahead and have a seat." She motioned Ali into a nearby chair, then returned to her mother. "Are you tired, Mama? Do you want to go to bed?"

"Oh, no," Doris Ralston said. "Not at all. I'll just sit here and wait for your father to come home. I can't imagine what's keeping him."

Ali remembered Beatrice Hart saying that Chip's father had died fairly recently of a stroke, but evidently not in Doris's rewritten version of reality. For the next half hour, Alzheimer's was the elephant in the living room while Ali conducted her interview. Doris's son, Chip, may have been the family expert in all things Alzheimer's, but if he was on his way to prison for murdering his ex-wife, then the responsibility for caring for their ailing mother would fall to Chip's sister, Molly.

"You're your mother's primary caregiver?" Ali asked.

Molly nodded. "Ironic, isn't it, considering Chip's line of work, but it turns out my perfect brother is far too busy taking care of other people's families to worry about his own. That's why our father wanted me to do it, and yes, it's pretty much up to me."

"I spoke to both Ms. Martinson and your brother. Neither one of them mentioned your mother's situation."

"There are a number of family scripts at work here, Ms. Reynolds. In our family, my brother was always destined to follow in our father's footsteps and become a surgeon. I was supposed to go to college long enough to find myself a suitable husband, so I could emulate my mother by staying home and being a wife and mother. All of that blew up for them when I dropped out of school and my brother ended up turning his back on surgery in favor of becoming a psychiatrist. I've never quite understood it, but for some strange reason, in my father's view, my sins were somehow more forgivable than Chip's.

"When our mother started going downhill, our father made it his business to keep everybody in the dark as much as possible."

"You're saying he concealed her symptoms?"

Molly nodded. "And made excuses for her. You have to give the man credit. He did an excellent job of running interference for a very long time. I suspect that the pressure involved in keeping up appearances and maintaining the pretense that she was okay may have contributed to his stroke. I know he and Chip had a big blow-up about Mother's situation the week before Daddy died. Chip dropped by the house unexpectedly and got a glimpse of what was really going on. When he tried to talk to our father about it, Daddy threw him out of the house.

"I'm sure the truth about Mama's condition would have come out eventually, but it was a shock to have it coming to the fore when we were dealing with Daddy's death."

"At the time of your father's death, your brother wasn't living in the casita?"

"No, the divorce proceedings were already under way, but I don't think anyone realized that Chip would end up being broke and in need of a place to live. Months earlier Daddy had drawn up the papers to give me a durable power of attorney. At the time I thought it was just a precaution. I didn't realize until I came home after Dad had his stroke how bad things really were with Mama.

"My husband and I were going through a rough patch right then, so it wasn't a big hardship for me to stay on and help out. I moved into my old room because it made looking after Mama that much easier than living anywhere else. Later on, when Chip needed a place to stay, he got around me by talking to our mother and asking to use the casita. Naturally, she said yes. I finally went along with the program, but only on the condition that Chip would agree to abide by my father's wishes."

"Which were?"

"That Chip have nothing to do with my mother's care."

"So he hasn't been backstopping you on that?"

"I don't need backstopping," Molly declared. "I'm fully capable of taking care of Mama on my own, and I don't need some self-proclaimed 'expert' telling me what I should or shouldn't be doing."

That last comment brought Molly's previous comment about what was forgivable and what was not into clear focus. In sorting out the care of frail and aging parents, what had once been a case of ordinary sibling rivalry between Molly and her brother had morphed into something more toxic. Out in the world, Dr. Charles Ralston may have been a well-respected Alzheimer's expert, but as far as his sister was concerned, that expertise counted as nothing but unwelcome interference. Ali was smart enough to recognize that as far as families went, this was probably not an isolated situation.

"Your mother's illness and your brother's divorce must have come to pass at the same time," Ali observed.

"Pretty much," Molly agreed, "and now we have this whole new crisis. I still can't believe Gem is dead."

"I understand you and she were friends?"

"And have been for years," Molly said with a nod. "We were roommates our freshman year in college, and we've been friends ever since, through good times and bad. I'm the one who introduced Gemma to Chip, so I guess you can lay the whole mess at my door."

"You and Gemma stayed friends even after she and Chip divorced?"

Molly nodded. "From my perspective, husbands tend to come and go with amazing regularity, but friends are friends forever. I couldn't just erase Gemma from my life on Chip's say-so, and neither could my mother. You adored Gemma, didn't you, Mama?"

"Gemma?" Doris asked vaguely. "Oh yes. Lovely girl. Just lovely. Did we talk today? On the phone, I mean. We usually do, you know. She calls me every morning, first thing."

Molly shook her head. "See there?" she said. "It's hopeless."

"Yes," Ali said. "I can see that. When did you last see Gemma?"

Ali's question was directed at Molly, but Doris was the one who answered. "It was tonight, wasn't it? I'm sure Gemma was here just a little while ago."

"No, Mama," Molly said patiently to Doris. "That's not right. She didn't come by today." To Ali, she added, "The last time I saw Gem was on Monday afternoon. We played tennis in the afternoon, and then we had a drink in the bar afterward."

Under the circumstances, Ali thought tennis sounded like an excellent idea. Considering the caregiving burden Molly Handraker was facing at home, the thought of being out in the sun and hitting something, or even just hitting *at* something, would be welcome.

"How was Gemma that day?" Ali asked. "Did she seem upset about anything? Worried? Out of sorts?"

"No, not at all. We played down at the club—the country club. She beat me in straight sets. She had a lot more time to play tennis recently than I did."

"Which country club?" Ali asked.

"Paradise Valley," Molly answered, as though any other choice were ludicrous. "I don't remember the exact time. Three-thirty or so, I think. They'll have the exact time at the reservation desk. We met there, played, stopped in the clubhouse for a drink or two, and then I came home. I had some help to look after Mama that night, so I didn't have to rush. But that was the last time I saw her. On Tuesday, she had a tennis date with another friend of ours—Valerie Sloan."

Ali held up a finger, pausing Molly's statement long enough to make a note of the name and contact information which Molly supplied from memory.

"When Gemma didn't show up for their match," Molly continued, "Val went by Gemma's place to check on her. Her car was in the garage. Her front door was unlocked and standing open. The alarm wasn't on. Gemma's purse and car keys were there, and so was her phone, but she wasn't. That seemed odd enough that Val called the cops to report her missing."

"No sign of a struggle at the apartment?"

"It's a town house, not an apartment," Molly corrected. "Just a couple of miles from here off Camelback. According to what Val told me, there was no sign of a struggle. Nothing was out of place, and there were no signs of forced entry, and apparently, nothing of value was taken. Her jewelry was in the box on the dresser in the bedroom; her computer and printer were in the office. Val said it was like Gemma simply walked out of her place and disappeared into thin air."

"It sounds like this makes you one of the last people to see her alive?" Ali asked.

"I suppose," Molly agreed. "I left her at the clubhouse about six-thirty or seven."

"Was she with anyone when you left?"

Molly shook her head. "Not that I noticed. We had been sitting at the bar. You could probably ask the bartender. His name is Luis."

"What was Gemma's home address?"

Molly recited it, and Ali jotted it down.

Doris, who had dozed off briefly, awakened with a start. "What's going on?" she wanted to know.

Molly heaved a heartfelt sigh. "Mama, please," she said patiently. "We're talking about Gemma."

"What about her?" Doris asked. "Where is she, and where's Chipper? Wherever Gemma is, he's probably there, too."

"She's not with Chip, Mama. Gemma's dead, and Chip's in jail in Prescott," Molly explained.

"In jail?" Doris was aghast. "Why on earth would he be in jail? This is serious. We have to do something about it."

"We already did do something about it, Mama, but you probably don't remember. I called Matt Greenburg earlier today and asked him to go up to Prescott to look into the situation. That's why this lady is here asking questions. She's working on an article about it."

"So things are under control?" Doris worried.

"As much as they can be," Molly said.

"Let's go back to Monday," Ali resumed. "You were aware that Lynn Martinson spent the night here on Monday?"

"She spends most nights here. I don't approve, but there's not much we can do about it," Molly said.

"She comes late, leaves early. For the time being, she and Chip have settled for sneaking around. Not very dignified, if you ask me."

"What's not dignified?" Doris asked.

"Chip and Lynn."

"Lynn?" Doris sounded genuinely puzzled. "Who's Lynn?"

"You know who Lynn Martinson is," Molly admonished. "You met her that one time after the concert. She's Chip's girlfriend."

"His girlfriend?" Doris echoed, visably shocked. "You're saying Chip has a girlfriend? How can he? He's married. Gemma won't tolerate such a thing, and neither will I. I'll disown him if I have to. I'll write him right out of my will."

Molly said nothing. Clearly, the woman's patience with her mother was stretched to the breaking point.

"Did you hear any vehicles come and go during the night?" Ali asked.

"No," Molly said, "but we wouldn't, anyway. Once Mama takes out her hearing aids, she turns her television set up so loud, it blasts you into the next county. She sleeps right through it. Besides, our bedrooms are over there." She pointed to the far side of the living room. "The driveway to the casita is at the other end of the house, so we didn't hear any cars coming and going, and we certainly didn't hear anyone coming into the kitchen for the knife."

"Knife?" Ali repeated. "What knife?"

"The murder weapon—a Henckels boning knife. I guess I'm supposed to say 'the alleged murder weapon.' They found it in Lynn Martinson's trunk, and the boning knife from Mama's Henckels set in the kitchen is currently missing from the knife block. As I told the detective earlier, for all we know, that knife could have been missing for months. When Chip moved into the casita, he came with the clothes on his back, and that was about it. Mama and I had Consuelo outfit him with whatever extras he needed from here."

"Who's Consuelo?"

"Mother's maid. Used to be full-time, but shortly after Chip came home, I had to let her go. Keeping her on was too expensive. At the time he was moving back in, I had her pack up some of Mama's extra linens, dishes, silverware, pots and pans, and take them over to the casita so he could use them. If it turns out it was our knife that the cops found in the back of the car, that's possibly where it came from—the stuff Consuelo sent over to his place, not from someone sneaking into the kitchen in the middle of the night to grab a knife."

Ali thought about how Molly and Doris had bypassed the alarm keypad on their way into the house. "What about your alarm system?" she asked. "If people were coming and going from the casita overnight, wouldn't your alarm have sounded?"

"There's no longer an active alarm system on the property," Molly said. "We used to have one, but it turned into too much of a hassle. Before I got Mother's sleep meds adjusted, she kept getting up during the night, wandering around the house, and punching buttons right and left. She'd be thinking she was turning the AC up or down or the heat on or off when she was really punching the keypad on the alarm. Finally, after several false alarms, we had to turn the system off."

"You keep your doors locked, don't you?" Ali asked.

"Of course," Molly snapped. "Without the alarm, we'd be stupid not to, but I have a master key, and so does Chip. I'm betting that's what she used."

"She?"

"Lynn Martinson," Molly said in exasperation. "Who do you think? The blood was found in her car. The knife was found in her car. I find that pretty compelling evidence."

"You're convinced that Lynn Martinson is the murderer, then?" Ali asked. "You don't believe your brother had anything to do with it?"

"No," Molly said. "Chip could never be a murderer. He doesn't have it in him."

"What's this about a murder?" Doris asked, once again rousing herself like a hopelessly broken record. Whatever information she gathered one minute was erased the next. "Who are you talking about?"

"We're talking about Gemma, Mama," Molly explained again. "About what happened to her."

"What's that?"

"Nothing, Mama. It's not important. I'll tell you about it later."

Ali was still focused on the knife. Dave hadn't mentioned anything about investigators finding a knife in Lynn's vehicle. Ali wondered if Paula Urban knew about it.

"Anyway," Molly continued, "when the detective showed up with his search warrant and a crime scene team this afternoon, I had to let them in, and they were dusting everything with that ugly fingerprint powder."

"That's when they told you about the knife?"

Molly nodded. "They didn't say much of anything to me. They were still here when Mama and I left for dinner, but they must have left before you got here."

Without putting up any crime scene tape, Ali thought. *Which means they found nothing.*

"If they're not treating the casita as a crime scene," Ali said, "that means that whatever happened to Gemma didn't happen in the casita and, according to what you said, apparently not in Gemma's town house, either. So where's the crime scene?"

"In the trunk, maybe?" Molly said. "Detective Holman seems to think Gemma was spirited away from her town house sometime in the middle of the night, after she got home from the bar. He thinks she may have left there voluntarily, most likely with someone she knew."

"She may have left her town house voluntarily," Ali observed, "but she didn't get in the trunk voluntarily. So does Lynn Martinson qualify as someone Gemma knew?"

"I suppose," Molly said, "and not necessarily in a good way. Chip and Gemma got into an argument out in the yard a couple of weeks ago. Lynn ended up being right in the middle of it."

"What kind of argument?"

"Over a real estate deal of some kind. Chip needed Gemma to sign a sales document, and she refused. Words were exchanged. When I went outside to check on what was going on, Lynn was saying something to the effect that if Gemma didn't stop tormenting Chip, she would figure out a way to put a stop to it. Gemma said the only way she'd be done messing with Chip was when she was dead."

"You told the detective about that?"

Molly nodded. "I did. It sounded too much like a direct threat to me. Given what's happened, I couldn't very well ignore it."

"From what you're saying, you think your brother isn't capable of doing something like this, but you think Lynn is?"

"Look," Molly said, "my brother is probably the best thing that ever happened to Lynn Martinson. With the divorce keeping him strapped for cash, I can see her thinking that if Gemma was out of the way, she'd have a clear shot at taking Chip to the altar."

"Could your mother have helped him with some of those money issues?"

"She could, but she didn't in the past, and she isn't going to in the future," Molly said determinedly. "Chip made his own mess, and I told him that he needs to clean it up on his own."

"I take it you're handling your mother's finances, then?"

"Yes," Molly said. "For right now, I'm the one writing the checks and paying the bills. I want to make sure her money doesn't run out before she does."

"What about the defense attorney you sent riding to your brother's rescue today?" Ali asked.

"I did do that," Molly agreed. "I wouldn't have been able to live with myself if I let him take the fall for something his girlfriend did. Besides, if Mother were in her right mind, I'm sure that's what she would have done, too. She would have regarded it as money well spent."

Doris sat up and blinked. "What money?" she asked.

"The money we spent on Matt Greenburg?"

"Matt Greenburg the lawyer?" Doris asked with a frown.

Molly nodded. "Yes, Mama."

"Matt was one of your father's good friends, but I never liked him much," Doris said. "He's one of those defense attorneys, isn't he? The kind who are always getting crooks out of jail and helping them get off on technicalities?"

"Maybe," Molly agreed. "About the technicalities."

Before Ali had time to ask another question, Doris Ralston levered her rail-thin frame off the sofa and headed out of the room.

"Where are you going, Mama?" Molly asked.

"I'm going to go check on Gemma and see if she's still sleeping in the car."

"She's not!" Molly insisted. "She's not sleeping anywhere, Mama! How many times do I have to tell you? Gemma is dead. Come on. Let's get you to bed."

Nodding, Doris reversed direction and started back across the room. "So where's my book?" she asked. "Have you seen where I put it?"

"It's right here where you left it, on the coffee table." Reaching over, Molly picked up what appeared to be a wedding album and handed it to her mother, who clutched it to her breast.

"Sorry," Molly apologized to Ali, getting to her feet. "When she gets too tired, things get worse. I'm going to have to get her to bed now. I'm sorry we got off to such a bad start earlier."

"That's all right," Ali said easily. "You had no idea who I was. Considering everything that's happened, I easily could have been someone who was up to no good."

"Do you have everything you need?"

"I think so," Ali answered.

"Well, if there's anything else, you're welcome to call." Molly reeled off a telephone number, which Ali jotted into her iPad.

After Molly and Doris left the room, Ali slipped her iPad into her purse and let herself out of the house. She had given Molly a card earlier, but she dropped another one on the entryway table on her way out.

After leaving Upper Glen Road, Ali drove back down to the hotel at Twenty-fourth and Camelback. Forty-five minutes later, showered and wearing her little black dress and a pair of suitable heels, Ali walked into Morton's on B.'s arm.

"Are we celebrating a special occasion tonight?" the hostess asked as she seated them and handed out menus.

"Yes, we are," B. said with a grin. "We're continuing to celebrate the launch of a brand-new partnership."

20

"Chip Ralston's mother has Alzheimer's?" B. asked thoughtfully as he sliced into his thick hunk of medium-rare prime rib. "I remember Beatrice Hart mentioning that Chip's father had died, but I don't think she said anything about his mother."

"She's suffering dementia issues of some kind, even if what she has isn't straight-out Alzheimer's," Ali answered. "The whole time I was talking to Molly, Doris would be asleep one minute and awake the next. And each time she woke up, she had no idea what was going on. It has to be driving her daughter nuts. And I have a feeling Beatrice didn't know about Doris Ralston's condition because I doubt her daughter knows about Doris's condition. I suspect Chip never told her."

"Why not?" B. sounded surprised. "After what happened to Lynn's father, why wouldn't he talk to her about that?"

Ali shook her head. "I don't know. I'm supposed to be in Lynn Martinson's corner, but all I've managed to do so far is turn up evidence of another whole level of betrayal. She finally worked up enough courage to fall in love again, but it looks like she's fallen for another dud. I like Chip, but apparently he's a liar from, let's just say, a troubled family. Doris Ralston's elevator doesn't go all the way to the top floor. She can't quite grasp that her former daughter-in-law is dead. Doris keeps talking about Gemma this and Gemma that. She seems far more enamored with Gemma than she is with either her own son or her daughter."

"She was talking like that in front of her daughter?"

Ali nodded.

"That's got to be tough on Molly," B. offered.

"You're right," Ali agreed, "especially since, if Chip ends up out of the picture, Molly's the one who'll be left shouldering most of Doris's care. I get the feeling that there's enough of a family fortune that she won't have to be pinching pennies and worrying about keeping a roof over her mother's head and food on the table, but dealing with a patient with dementia has to be incredibly challenging."

"Speaking of Chip being in or out of the picture, have you heard any word on the plea agreement?"

"I talked to Paula briefly. According to her, Chip Ralston and Cap Horning are back-and-forthing on Chip's proposed plea agreement. He's upped his offer to plead to second-degree homicide as long as Lynn walks. In that scenario, Chip goes to prison, Lynn gets off but she doesn't get her man, and Molly still ends up taking care of their mother."

"Lynn doesn't get her man *again*," B. added.

"In other words, no happily-ever-afters for anyone concerned."

"Not so much," Ali agreed.

"What's on your agenda for tomorrow?"

"I have one more lead to track down tomorrow morning. Molly gave me the name of another one of their gal pals—Valerie Sloan. She and Gemma were supposed to play tennis on Tuesday. When Gemma was a no-show, Valerie's the one who called in the missing persons report. I'm hoping that once I talk to her, Valerie may be able to fill in some of the blanks in Gemma's social history. I feel like I'm missing something."

"What?"

"Think about it. Chip Ralston's marriage goes on the rocks, and he runs home to his mother's place. He's a well-known—make that nationally known—expert on the subject of Alzheimer's, but he doesn't have the balls to tell Lynn that his mother is following in Lynn's father's footsteps. Does this sound like a cold-blooded killer to you?"

"I have to agree. More like a gutless wonder than a killer," B. agreed. "But if Chip Ralston didn't do it, why offer to take the plea?"

"To protect Lynn, maybe?" Ali asked. "But she doesn't strike me as much of a cold-blooded killer, either. She's someone who's been so traumatized by one bad relationship after another that she can't even find a job, to say nothing of hold one."

"Who's responsible, then?" B. asked. "The other dead guy? Maybe Sanders was a hired hit man who got cold feet and ended up being taken out by someone else."

"Which brings us back to square one, because hit men don't come cheap," Ali said.

"Okay, so who would be footing the bill for a hired hit?"

Ali shrugged. "According to what I've been able to find out, neither Chip Ralston nor Lynn Martinson is rolling in the dough. That's why I want to talk to Gemma's friend Valerie. There may be someone in her life that we don't know about so far, including something that leads back to James Sanders. He's the only one of the group who seemed to have plenty of cash to throw around at the moment. In the days before he died, he spent at least five thousand bucks with no clear indication of where it came from."

"In other words, for the time being, you keep looking for a possible connection."

Ali nodded. "Until either Paula Urban or Beatrice Hart tells me to back off. In the meantime, are we having dessert or another glass of wine?"

"I say we skip both in favor of going back to the hotel."

Which they did. Ali was sound asleep the next morning when her phone rang. Searching for it on her bedside table, she discovered that B.'s side of the bed was already empty. Through the glass doors between the bedroom and the sitting room, she could see him on the sofa, laptop on his lap and phone to his ear. There was a coffee service sitting on the coffee table in front of him. The fact that he could be up and working while she was asleep was one of the very real advantages of having a suite.

"I didn't wake you, did I?" Stuart Ramey said on the phone.

"You did," Ali admitted, "but I needed to get moving. What's up?"

"I never was able to get a line on that limo," Stuart said. "They must have gotten out of the vehicle before they got to the hotel entrance, but I sent their IT people a photo of James Sanders. They ran it through their facial recognition software, and voilà. They found both Sanders and the guy he was with."

"Who?"

"His name's Scott Ballentine. Turns out he's a whale."

"A what?"

"A whale. That's what casinos in Vegas call the big hitters, the regulars who come in a couple of times a month and can afford to drop a fortune at the baccarat tables."

"Wait a minute," Ali said. "Scott Ballentine. How come that name sounds so familiar?"

"Because he's one of James Sanders's counterfeiting pals from back in the old days. He's the guy who paid the fine and got off while Sanders went to prison. While James was in prison, Ballentine moved to California, where he invented some kind of medical device, made a fortune, and then went broke. A few months ago, he won a massive patent-infringement lawsuit, which means that he now has more money than God. At least that's what his website says, and his favorite outing is in Vegas, at the MGM Grand, playing baccarat. My new BFF—the casino's very capable IT lady, Laura Cameron—just sent me copies of the security tapes for the day in question, which I found most interesting," Stuart continued. "Want me to send them to you?"

"Please."

"Call me back after you take a look. I'll send them to you in short order."

Ali hustled out of bed, grabbed a robe from the bathroom, and then joined B. in the sitting room. "I'm on hold," he said, holding the phone away from his ear. "What's up?"

"Stuart's sending me some videos," she explained.

By the time Ali had poured her own cup of coffee, three different files had come through, each of them loaded with a film clip. Ali went through them one at a time. In the first one, two men walked through what appeared to be the front entrance to the casino. In the first clip, Ballentine—dressed in a sport coat and tie—appeared to be carrying a leather briefcase. Sanders, dressed in what looked like khaki work clothes, was carrying something as well. Ali paused the clip several times, trying to get a better look. The object Sanders was carrying appeared to be made of metal. It was smaller than a briefcase but wider. Blockier.

In the second clip, the two men were standing side by side at the counter of a cashier's cage with a lighted neon sign saying BACCARAT glowing in the background. There was some wordless chatting between Ballentine and the cashier in the cage. Eventually, Ballentine opened the briefcase and removed a long, narrow piece of paper. He pushed it through the opening at the bottom of the window. The cashier took it, held it up to the light, and studied it.

That's got to be a check, Ali thought.

After a little more talking, Ballentine pushed something that looked like an ID through the window. The cashier took the ID and the check and disappeared. Some time passed; Ali could see Ballentine chatting easily with Sanders. Ballentine seemed completely at ease, while Sanders looked the opposite—nervous and uneasy. Finally, the clerk returned and started pushing piles of gambling tokens out through the window and across the counter. Ballentine waited patiently, watching and probably counting, too.

Looking at the stacks of chips, Ali let out a whistle.

"What?" B. said.

"Look at those chips," she said, holding her iPad so B. could see it. "I'm betting every one of those chips is worth a thousand bucks."

Ballentine said something to the cashier, then nodded to Sanders, collapsed the stacks of chips into a mound, and pushed them in Sanders's direction. For a moment nothing happened. Ballentine said something and nodded again, as if encouraging Sanders. At that point, Sanders bent over, reached down, picked up the metal object, which had evidently been on the floor, and set it on the counter. That was when Ali realized what she was seeing was most likely a strongbox.

For a moment Sanders struggled with the latch. When he wrenched the box open, he held it along the edge of the counter and shoved the mound of chips inside. When he was done and the strongbox was latched, he waited while Ballentine finished loading his briefcase with the second pile of tokens. Once Ballentine's briefcase was closed, the two men shook hands briefly. After that, Ballentine turned and headed for the baccarat tables, while Sanders took his loaded strongbox and walked away.

The third and final clip showed Sanders alone, carrying the strongbox and exiting the casino. By the time it ended, Ali was already on the phone to Stuart Ramey. "Any idea how much money was there?" she asked.

"Five hundred thousand," Stuart said.

"Each chip is worth a thousand bucks?" Ali asked.

"That's right. My BFF was able to find out because special arrangements for cashing a cashier's check of that size had been made in advance. To prevent money laundering, transactions of that size are also reported to the IRS. The chips come out in stacks of ten each for ease of counting. Looks to me like Sanders got the lion's share—thirty stacks, as opposed to Ballentine's measly twenty."

"So we're talking about three hundred thousand dollars?"

"Yup," Stuart said. "And he walked out of the place carrying it in that little metal box."

Stuart may have said "metal," but Ali's mind immediately translated it into something else—"little tin box." One of the things Ali had inherited from her aunt Evie, along with the double-wide mobile home, was an extensive collection of musical comedy recordings, including the almost forgotten original cast recording of *Fiorello!* In it, the main character's poker-playing friends had accounted for their ill-gotten gains by claiming their riches came from money saved in "a little tin box that a little tin key unlocks."

Somehow Ali doubted James Mason Sanders had been humming a few bars of that as he walked through the casino with that box full of chips, but he should have been. "That's a big bundle of money to be carrying around, even in broad daylight," she said. "Did you check the tapes to see if anyone followed him out?"

"I already thought of that, and the answer is no," Stuart said. "Nobody followed him. Sanders walked out the main entrance, hailed a cab, and went straight back to the Mission. I got the cab's number from the security tapes. I already checked the cabbie's records."

"So he leaves the casino with three hundred thousand bucks, and in the next several days, he drops five thousand. Less than a week later, Sanders turns up dead. So where's the rest of the money? Did somebody search his room?"

"Yes," Stuart said. "He stayed in a one-bedroom unit at the Mission. Room and board were part of the paycheck. His unit was searched by the North Las Vegas police department, who executed a warrant at the request of investigators from Yavapai County. No money was found on the premises, and neither were any gambling chips."

"You know all this how?" Ali asked.

"A good buddy of mine works for them," Stuart answered.

In Ali's estimation, Stuart Ramey had "good buddies" almost everywhere.

"What about the strongbox?" Ali asked. "Did they find that?"

"Nope. *Nada*."

"We know he picked up the money," Ali mused. "He evidently preferred having chips rather than cash. How come?"

"He sure as hell didn't put it in the bank," Stuart said, "at least not into any of the accounts I've been able to find."

"So if James Sanders was still carrying the chips around, maybe his death was a straight-out armed robbery. That scenario makes it less likely that his case had anything to do with Gemma Ralston's death, even with the geographical proximity."

"Would you like me to keep following up on the money situation?" Stuart asked.

"Yes," Ali answered. "I'm guessing we're late to the party. We're probably not the first ones to learn about those gambling chips, and we're not the first ones who are asking what happened to them, either. A reporter from the *Las Vegas Examiner* was down here in Phoenix yesterday, asking questions about James Sanders. Her name is Betty Noonan. See what you can find out about her. It might be helpful if we knew what her angle is."

"I'll look into it," Stuart said. "Anything else?"

"Also see what else you can find out about Sanders's pal Ballentine," Ali said. "You said Gemma Ralston's Hearts Afire profile said she was looking for a high-end meaningless relationship. With a boatful of new money, Ballentine or even Sanders could be likely targets for someone like her."

"You're right," Stuart agreed. "Could be."

"Sorry, Stuart," Ali said. "I've got another call." She switched over to find Paula Urban on the line, in a state of high umbrage.

"Did anyone ever mention that Cap Horning is a complete jackass?"

It seemed to Ali that Sheriff Maxwell had come close, without using that exact word. "What's he done now?" she asked.

"I'd like him to quit waffling on the deal Chip Ralston proposed. Either Horning takes it and lets

Lynn Martinson walk, or else we go after her defense full-bore. The problem is, he has a while to go on that seventy-two-hour deadline, where he'll either have to charge them or let them go. Do you have anything for me?"

Ali brought Paula up to date with what she had learned from Stuart.

"All right, then," Paula said when Ali finished. "I think you're right. With that much money involved, robbery is far more likely. So let's step away from the Sanders situation and leave that one up to the cops while we concentrate on Gemma et al."

"Okay," Ali agreed. "I'll be tracking Valerie Sloan as soon as I get showered and dressed and have some breakfast."

"You stayed in Phoenix last night?"

"Yes."

"Where?"

"At the Ritz," Ali said.

"The Ritz! You're not expecting to bill Beatrice Hart for that hotel room, are you?" Paula asked.

"No," Ali said, grinning at B. "I'm pretty sure the hotel bill will be on someone else's nickel."

21

Valerie Baker Sloan lived in a condo development on the far side of Scottsdale Road that would have been considered a low-rent district by Paradise Valley standards. She was a blue-eyed blonde, but one in need of hair color. She had the nut-brown sun-damaged skin of a woman who spent much of her time in the great outdoors. In November, when visitors from the Midwest were all sporting shorts, she opened the door and showed her Arizona roots in her manner of dress—a jogging suit topped by a cardigan sweater knotted around her neck.

Ali had called ahead, so she was expected.

"You're the writer?"

Ali nodded.

"Come on in," Valerie said without bothering to ask for ID. "Please pardon the mess."

She led the way into a spacious living room dominated by an immense rear-projection television set and an equally huge treadmill, along with a gym-worthy collection of high-end weight-lifting equipment. She shifted a pile of grimy clothing onto the floor behind the couch. Moving the clothing uncovered a pair of football jerseys with two and a half pairs of dusty cleats. She pushed those onto the floor in front of the couch, where they bounced off an accumulation of empty soda cans and dirty paper plates, some with pizza crusts attached.

"Twins," Valerie explained, motioning Ali into a relatively clean easy chair. "Before the divorce, the boys had a separate room for all this junk and a housekeeper to pick up after them. Now we have this room, and I'm the unpaid housekeeper. I spend most of my time in the master, while I count the days until they leave for school next September. Once they do, they'll be fully qualified to live in any frat house on the planet. Then I'll be able to muck the place out and have a life again."

Ali looked around what could best be categorized as an upscale pigsty and compared it to Sylvia Sanders's far more humble but compulsively neat living room. Ali suspected the same would be true for Valerie's twins—that they wouldn't compare very favorably with Sylvia's son, A.J.

"You're here to talk about Gemma?" Valerie asked. She had perched herself on one arm of the sofa in a none too subtle hint that she didn't expect Ali to stay long.

"Yes," Ali said. "I'm a freelancer doing a research project on the investigation into Gemma's homicide." That little white lie was getting easier to say every time she repeated it.

"I've already told the cops everything I know," Valerie said. "Couldn't you talk to them?"

"I'm sorry for the loss of your friend, but I'd rather talk to you," Ali said placatingly.

"All right," Valerie said, giving in. "What do you want to know?"

"Tell me about Tuesday. I understand you're the person who reported Gemma Ralston missing."

Valerie nodded. Her eyes misted over briefly, then she shrugged off the sadness in the same determined way she had shifted the stack of clothing from the couch to the floor, as though she didn't have either the time or energy to give way to an overly emotional response. "When Gemma didn't show up for our tennis date and didn't answer my calls, I went to her place to check on her. She wasn't there, but her stuff was—her purse, keys, and car. The front door was unlocked and open. I called the cops. They took over from there. End of story."

"You've been friends a long time?"

"Since college," Valerie replied. "Gemma, Molly, and I ended up as roommates our freshman year at ASU. I was dirt-poor. Gemma's parents were gone; she had been raised by her grandparents. They had a fair amount of money. Molly's family was absolutely loaded but judgmental. In spades. Since Molly was at odds with her family most of the time, she dragged Gemma and me along to family get-togethers and used us as human shields to keep her parents off her back. That's how we ended up at a Christmas party at their house our freshman year, when Chip came home for the holidays.

"Gemma had told us at the beginning of the year that she was going to find a good-looking guy who was going to be a doctor, preferably a surgeon, to marry. We thought she was kidding. Molly had told Gemma that her brother was doing premed at USC, but she didn't pay much attention. That changed as soon as Gemma saw Chip in the flesh. Once that happened, it was like she flipped a switch and turned into a heat-seeking missile. After that, no matter how long it took to land him, Chip Ralston was the only guy she was interested in. She never dated anyone else."

"Until after her divorce," Ali offered.

Valerie waggled her hand up and down as if to say maybe not quite until after. "Their marriage lasted for fifteen years," she said. "Mine, too."

"What happened?" Ali asked.

"To my marriage?" Valerie asked. "My husband—now ex—had a midlife crisis and an affair. Brad and his new wife have a two-year-old now. You can imagine how thrilled my twins are about that!"

"What about Chip and Gemma's marriage?"

"Chip had his midlife crisis early on, while he was in the last year of his residency. From the time Chip and Gemma started dating, she told everyone who would listen that Chip was going to be a world-famous surgeon someday, just like his dad. Gemma believed it. Chip's mother believed it. I think his father believed it, too. The only problem was Chip didn't believe it, and it never happened.

"During his residency, one of the patients under Chip's care died. I don't know all the gory details. It's one of those things people don't talk about, and it's not polite to ask. Gemma told me it was some kind of routine surgery that went terribly wrong, where the guy shouldn't have died but did, and it was held to be Chip's fault. After that, Chip walked away from surgery and never looked back. Pissed Gemma off, too, I can tell you." Warming to the conversation, Valerie had dropped from the arm of the sofa and settled on the seat. "What else do you want to know?"

"How long were they married?"

"Like I said," Valerie answered, "fifteen years, give or take."

"Do you know why it ended?"

"A bad case of terminal boredom, I suppose," Valerie said. "At least on Gemma's part. She told me that being married to Chip was like being married to an Eagle Scout. From my point of view, the big advantage of being married to an Eagle Scout is maybe you don't have to worry about picking up an STD."

That rueful remark told Ali way too much about the end of Valerie Sloan's own marriage.

"Gemma spent years waiting for him to get through medical school. Because the surgeon thing turned out so badly, I think she always felt like she'd been sold a bill of goods—as though Chip never lived up to his end of the bargain. I think Chip's parents were disappointed, too. The thing is, disgruntled parents don't get to divorce their kids the way disgruntled wives get to shed husbands and vice versa. When Chip got into financial trouble, Gemma didn't see any point in hanging around. She bailed."

"What kind of financial trouble?" Ali asked.

"Chip made some bad investments along the way. Bought more houses than he could afford, and just before the bubble burst. Bought high and had to sell low. He's still trying to sell some of them. When the downturn came, his retirement accounts dropped like rocks, too. Gemma could see that she needed to get out while there was something left to take. Once she was gone, Chip had to go back home to live. Doris was already sick by then, but I don't think anyone knew how bad it was, and her condition has worsened since then."

"Given Chip Ralston's expertise, I don't understand why the full burden of their mother's care falls on Molly."

"Because that's the way Dr. Ralston—the elder Dr. Ralston—wanted it," Valerie answered. "Turns out it's the way Molly wants it, too. Given her history with her parents, I was a little surprised that her father gave her a durable medical power of attorney, but he did. And that's why, once he was gone, Molly took over as Doris's caregiver on a twenty-four/seven basis."

"From what you've said, I take it Molly has a history of troubled relations with her parents?"

Valerie nodded. "Chip wasn't the only kid who disappointed the Ralstons, although Molly went off the rails a lot earlier than Chip did. She was the wild one in the family—the rebel, the one who got bad grades and partied way too much."

"What do you mean, partied?" Ali asked.

"What do you think I mean? Booze and drugs. She managed to get accepted to ASU, but by the end of our freshman year, she was on academic probation. She dropped out after the first semester of our sophomore year and eloped with her then-boyfriend, who by that time was a senior at NAU up in Flagstaff. For years after that, Molly was completely estranged from her parents. They didn't see her for several years and probably wouldn't have for a lot longer than that if Gemma hadn't insisted that she come home and be in the wedding.

"Molly's first marriage lasted five years. Number two less than that. She's still married to number three, a guy named Barry Handraker. He's currently an out-of-work pharmacist in Minneapolis. Their marriage was on the rocks when she came home for her father's funeral, and she didn't bother going back. She stayed on to help with her mother."

"So during the time Molly was off living her life and running through less than wonderful husbands, Doris was busy turning all her motherly focus on Gemma."

Valerie nodded. "Gemma and Doris were always birds of a feather, almost from day one. I'm sure all of Doris's constant harping about Gemma is tough on Molly; hurts her feelings. I know I'd probably resent the hell out of it if my mother decided she liked my brother's wife better than she liked me. But what can Molly do? I can understand why she's resigned to her fate. She's dead broke. If she weren't staying with Doris Ralston and looking after her, she wouldn't even have a roof over her head."

"She and her husband lost their house?" Ali asked.

Valerie nodded. "Foreclosure."

"They're not divorced?" Ali asked.

"Molly's emotionally stuck," Valerie said. "That's one of the things Gemma and I were trying to encourage her to do—cut her losses and dump the guy while she still has her looks and a chance of hooking up with somebody decent."

Ali glanced around Valerie's cluttered living room, and the words "the blind leading the blind" came to mind. It occurred to Ali that Molly Handraker wasn't the only one who was stuck.

"Tell me about Molly and her brother," Ali said. "How do they get along?"

"Not well," Valerie said. "Think fire and water. When they were growing up, Chip was definitely the favorite, the apple of his mother's eye and his father's pride and joy. He was the true-blue honor student, the one who could do no wrong. I think they rubbed Molly's nose in that a lot. Later on, though, the worm turned. By the time anybody knew Doris was sick, James Ralston was at war with his beloved son. I think giving Molly the power of attorney and making sure she'd be the one calling the shots was their father's way of getting back at Chip once and for all."

"This doesn't sound like a warm-and-fuzzy family. So how did Chip end up going back home to live?"

"He went around Molly and asked his mother," Valerie said. "Doris may have said yes, but Molly is the one who dictated the terms, and she had him over a barrel. She agreed that he could live in the casita, but only on one condition—that he stay out of her way."

"He has no say in his mother's care?"

"None. If it were up to me, I'd be going around looking for help from whoever was available, but Molly's not me. So Chip lives in the casita, and his new girlfriend stays over more nights than not."

"I got the feeling Doris doesn't approve," Ali offered.

Valerie laughed. "Yes," she said, "and never the twain should meet. Well, they did once, sort of. Lynn came up the driveway just as Molly and Doris were coming home from a concert. Chip came out and tried to introduce Lynn to his mother, but

Doris went completely nuts. She may not remember much of anything else, but she's still all Gemma, all the time. Doris went into a screaming fit and tried to go after Lynn with her cane. She ended up having to be physically restrained. I don't think they've crossed paths since. Chip's made sure of it."

"And what about Lynn and Gemma? Did they ever meet?"

"Oh, yes," Valerie said. "There was a big stink just last week. Something about the divorce settlement that was still hanging. Gemma had stopped by to see Doris. As she was leaving, Chip tried to talk to her about some documents he needed her to sign—something to do with a purchase offer on a piece of property they're trying to sell.

"Gemma said forget it, that she wasn't signing anything without talking to her attorney and maybe not even then. Lynn was with Chip at the time, and the three of them got into a huge shouting match out in the yard. According to Molly, Lynn was screaming at Gemma that she had no right to destroy Chip and why couldn't she just let the poor guy be. To which Gemma replied that as far as she was concerned, the only way she would be done tormenting Chip Ralston was when he was dead or else when she was. To which Lynn said something to the effect of maybe that could be arranged. I think that's when it happened, when Lynn decided to take Gemma out of the equation."

"How is it that you know about this quarrel?"

"Gemma told me all about it first, but so did Molly. Gemma thought the whole thing was a big joke. Once she went missing, I didn't think it was funny. The first time I talked to the cops at Gemma's house, I told them they needed to take a close look at Chip and Lynn; that if there had been some kind of foul play, one of them would be behind it."

"All right, then," Ali said, changing the subject. "Let's talk about Gemma's personal life for a moment. Can you tell me anything about her current romantic entanglements?"

"Not much," Valerie allowed. "I know she had dipped her toe back in the dating game, but I also know she had no intention of getting married again. She just wanted to have fun—nothing too serious. You know, the old friends-with-benefits kind of thing."

"And nothing that would risk turning off her alimony checks from Chip Ralston."

Valerie smiled. "That, too."

"Did she have any beaus in particular?"

"None that I can think of," Valerie answered. "She was mostly just playing the field."

"Did she tell you about her boyfriends?"

"Not really," Valerie said, shaking her head. "We played tennis, but between Gemma and me, talking about our love lives was off limits—sisterly rivalry and all that. Gemma wasn't much good when it came to that kind of competition."

There had been a slight lull in the conversation while Ali considered her next question, but her train of thought was interrupted by a question from Valerie. "Did she do it?"

For a moment Ali was stumped. "Did who do what?"

Valerie shook her head in exasperation. "Did Chip's girlfriend murder Gemma? That's what Molly seems to think, regardless of who pulled the trigger—not that there was a trigger," she corrected quickly. "I'm sure you know what I mean, there's only one person who's ultimately responsible for what happened."

"Who would that be?" Ali asked.

"Chip Ralston, of course. That's his modus operandi. Sooner or later, he lets everybody down—his parents, his wife, his sister. Mark my words, he'll do the same thing to Lynn Martinson."

There didn't seem to be anything more to be gained by continuing to ask questions. Ali closed her iPad and stood up. "Thanks for your help," she said, walking toward the door.

"Isn't that what friends are for?" Valerie asked.

As Ali headed for her car, she found herself feeling incredibly sad. Supposedly, Gemma and Molly and Valerie had been the best of friends, but there seemed to be very little genuine grief coming from the two survivors. The only person who seemed to be truly mourning Gemma Ralston's death was the woman's former mother-in-law, someone whose current mental condition left her unlikely to remember much of anything, including the fact that Gemma was no longer among the living.

Ali walked away from Valerie Sloan's house feeling sorry for everyone involved but for Gemma Ralston most of all.

22

Ali's cell phone rang as she climbed into the Cayenne. She put the Porsche in gear and got on the road toward Phoenix before she answered.

"What the hell do you think you're doing?" Dave Holman demanded. "I want you to get out of my case and stay out."

"Good morning to you, too," Ali said.

"I mean it, Ali. I've got two homicides on my hands, and I don't need someone like you running interference with potential witnesses."

"Why?" Ali asked. "Has someone complained?"

"Yes, as a matter of fact, they have. I'll give you three guesses."

"Molly Handraker?"

"She says she caught you prowling around her mother's place last night. She said she almost called the cops."

"Did she also happen to mention that she pulled a gun on me?"

"She did, but it turns out she has a concealed-carry permit. It's a miracle the two of you didn't plug each other. Not only that, from what she said, it sounds as though you're passing yourself off as a private detective, which, according to the laws of Arizona, you can't possibly be."

"I've accepted a writing assignment," Ali said.

"I don't care what you say you're doing. I want you to get out of my case and stay out."

Ali was messing around in two of his cases, but remembering the old saw about the best defense, Ali turned the tables. "I must have missed the memo," she said.

Dave paused in midrant. "What memo?"

"Either we got married without my noticing, or you've been elected sheriff and I'm one of your hapless deputies, because I don't see any other possibilities for your deciding you can order me around. Just because we're friends doesn't give you the right to meddle in what jobs I take or how I do them."

Before Dave had time to respond, call waiting buzzed. Ali glanced at her phone. The 602 area code meant it was a Phoenix call. By then she was sailing along, westbound on Camelback, in light midmorning traffic.

"Phone call, Dave," Ali said, dismissing him. "Gotta go."

"Ms. Reynolds?" a young male voice said when she switched over to the other call.

Ali glanced again at the phone number to see if it would give her a clue about the caller's identity. "Yes, this is Ali Reynolds. Who is this?"

"It's A.J.," he said. "A. J. Sanders. I'm calling to ask you a question. Is it true what you said last night—that my father was dead a long time before that woman died?"

"Yes, that's my understanding. Why?"

"And you're not a cop."

"No. What's going on?"

"I need to talk to someone who knows something about the case, but someone who isn't a cop and someone who isn't my mother. I can't talk to her about this. I don't know what to do."

"I'll see what I can do," Ali said. "What's up?"

A.J.'s words came out in a rush. "I found a gun in our trash this morning when I took the garbage out. Not in the big can in the alley, but in the smaller one we keep on the back porch. I found it when I dumped the little one into the big one."

Ali envisaged some kind of gangbanger running through the neighborhood and dropping a weapon into the first trash can that presented itself. What she didn't understand was why A.J. would seek advice from a complete stranger as opposed to his own mother. Still, she didn't blow him off.

"I noticed yesterday there's no fence around your yard," she said. "If someone from the neighborhood was trying to ditch a weapon, it would be easy to sneak through your yard and dump it in the trash. What kind of gun are we talking about?"

"I don't know much about guns," A.J. admitted. "It's a revolver, I think, and not very big."

"A snub-nose, maybe?"

"I guess," A.J. said. "Whoever put the gun there did it because they're trying to frame me for my father's death. Mom told me last night that the cops said my dad was carrying a large amount of money at the time he died, and now it's gone. She also said he was shot at close range. I'll bet the gun I found this morning is the murder weapon. As for the money?" He paused and didn't continue.

"What about the money?" Ali urged.

A.J. took a deep breath. "I have it," he croaked.

"You have it?"

"Yeah, but I didn't take it. All two hundred and fifty thousand dollars' worth. My father gave it to me."

"He gave it to you in person? You mean you saw him, met with him? What?"

"No. He left it for me and sent me directions so I could find it. Sent them through the mail. He wanted me to have the money, Ms. Reynolds. He wanted me to use it to go to school. I didn't kill him to get it. Honest."

A.J. seemed like a nice enough kid, and Ali wanted to believe him, but how many times on *COPS* had she heard dim-bulb crooks swear that the drugs or drug paraphernalia found in a purse or backpack didn't belong to them and that they had no idea how the illicit goods might have gotten there. This sounded a little too close to the same thing. Before she could respond, A.J. plunged on.

"The problem is, as soon as they check my fingerprints, they'll know I was there—at the crime scene."

"What fingerprints?" Ali asked.

"The ones on the woman's phone and on the shovel."

"What shovel and what phone are we talking about?"

"I brought the shovel from home, and the phone is one I found near that woman, the one who died. I used it to call 911. At least I *tried* to call 911, but there wasn't enough signal. A regular call wouldn't go through. I had to text them instead."

"Wait, wait, wait," Ali said. "You're saying you're the one who called in the report about Gemma Ralston?"

"Right. The green-eyed woman. I went to the place my dad told me to, expecting to find the money, but I found her instead. As soon as I saw her, I knew she was hurt pretty bad, but I didn't know she was dying. That's why I tried to call 911."

"So Gemma Ralston was alive when you got there."

"She was for a little while, but not very long. I went back to the car to get some water for her, and when I came back, she was almost gone."

"Did she say anything to you?"

"A couple of words is all. It was hard for her to talk. I think she was talking about her boyfriend, or maybe a husband. Someone named Dennis. That's all. It was awful, and I didn't know what to do. There were ants and bugs and blood. It was like she was paralyzed or something. I mean, the phone was right there beside her, but she must not have been able to reach it.

"Anyway, when I came back from the car with the water, she was almost gone. A few minutes later she stopped breathing, and her eyes just glazed over. I've never been around someone dead like that. I panicked, I guess, and that's when I took off. I was ditching school, and all I could think of was that I didn't want to get caught."

A.J. stopped talking as if he suddenly realized he had said too much. Ali realized that A. J. Sanders was the person of interest Dave Holman had been looking for in relation to Gemma Ralston's death. Now, with the revelation about having his father's missing money, A.J. would move into the prime-suspect column.

"Where was the money?" Ali asked.

"He hid it behind a boulder. Buried it. I dug it up."

"And how did you know exactly where to dig?"

"He gave me directions. Six tenths of a mile from the turnoff; walk due north; find the rock with the heart on it," A.J. recited. "So that's where it was, just like he said, but I didn't find it the same day I found the woman. That day I just got the hell out of there. Sasha and I went back yesterday after school and dug it up."

"You're going to need an attorney," Ali said.

"Why?"

"Think about it. You were at the crime scene—twice—and investigators will be able to prove it. You have your father's missing money. That looks bad. Now the gun thing. If there's the slightest chance this is the murder weapon, you have to turn it in. You're not allowed to withhold evidence. If the gun you found turns out to be the murder weapon, it's going to be that much worse. Believe me, you will need an attorney."

"How do we pay for an attorney? My mom can't afford to hire one. I suppose I could use some of the money my father gave me."

"No," Ali said. "As soon as the homicide cops hear about that money, they're going to consider it evidence. You won't be able to touch it, but the court will appoint an attorney for you."

"Am I going to end up in jail? If that happens, I probably won't even graduate." The poor kid sounded close to tears.

"Okay, okay," Ali told him soothingly. "I can tell you're upset. Where are you?"

"At school. I'm sitting in my car in the parking lot at North High on East Thomas."

"Where's the money?"

"It's in the trunk. I took it into the house yesterday evening, but I was afraid my mom would be suspicious, so I smuggled it back out to the car. I barely slept all night, worrying that someone might steal it. We don't have a garage, only a carport, and Camrys get stolen all the time. I have one of those steering-wheel locks, the Club, but I don't know how well they work."

"What about the gun you found? Where's that?"

"It's in the trunk, too."

"Is it loaded or not?"

"I'll go check. How do I tell?"

"Wait, wait," Ali cautioned. "Whatever you do, do not open the trunk. Do not touch the gun."

Shades of the terrible massacre at Columbine High flashed through Ali's head. She knew that if she called for assistance and reported the presence of a gun at a high school, there would be an emergency response out of all proportion to the actual danger.

"Listen to me, A.J.," Ali said. "I'm on my way there right now, coming from Scottsdale. At this time of day, it shouldn't take long for me to get there. Tell me exactly where you are."

"Like I said, I'm at school. In the student parking lot."

"I'm from out of town," Ali told him. "I need to know where the school is."

"On Thomas, ten blocks east of Central, on the south side of the street."

"Whereabouts in the parking lot?"

"The row closest to the street, three cars in. Why?"

"Because I want to know where to look for you. Once I get there, we'll figure out what to do."

By then Ali had already turned off Camelback and was headed south on Twenty-fourth. Just as she pulled into traffic, not one but five police cars—lights flashing and sirens screaming—came bearing down on her. She pulled over to the curb to let them roar past. There was a chance they might be going someplace else, but as she watched them race by, her intuition told her otherwise. She guessed they were headed the same place she was—the student parking lot at North High School. Last row. Third car in.

"Listen to me, A.J.," she commanded urgently. "This is very important! Did you tell anyone at school that you had the gun?"

"Only my girlfriend, Sasha. Why?"

"A bunch of cops just went rolling past me, and I believe they're headed your way. If they don't come there, fine, we're good. But if they're coming for you, do not do anything to provoke them, do you understand? Step out of the car, put your phone on the ground, spread your feet, and stand with both hands on your car. Do not make any sudden moves, and whatever you do, don't try to run!"

Ali pulled back into traffic in time to see the parade of speeding police cars slow down enough to turn right on Thomas, convincing her that she had made the right call.

"Are they going to arrest me?" A.J. asked. He sounded scared, and she didn't blame him.

"I can't tell for sure," Ali said, "but probably."

She heard a choking sound like a stifled sob before A.J. managed to speak again. "What am I going to tell my mom?"

"I'll tell her for you," Ali offered. "Where is she? At home?"

"No. She went to work. Dr. Westmoreland's office. He's a dentist. His office is in Tempe, in the shopping center at the corner of Baseline and Rural roads."

"Okay," Ali said. "Now remember. If you're taken into custody, all you say is 'I want my lawyer.' That's it! After that, they can't ask you anything else, and don't tell them anything else. Nothing. Do not talk while you're in the car, even with uniformed officers. Keep your mouth shut. Do you understand?"

"Yes, but—"

In the background, Ali could already hear the wail of multiple police sirens. There could be no doubt. That was where they were going.

"No buts, A.J.," Ali warned him. "Close your phone now. Get out of the car, put the phone on the ground, and then stand with both hands on the hood or the trunk of your car. If you make any sudden moves, you're liable to end up dead."

Afraid he would keep talking rather than following her directions, Ali punched the button to end the call in time to make her own right-hand turn onto Thomas. As soon as she did so, she could see a flock of emergency vehicles lined up across the street in front of her, creating a roadblock that diverted all westbound traffic off Thomas and either north or south on Sixteenth Street.

For A.J.'s sake, all Ali could hope was that he

had heard what she'd said and done what she'd told him to do. If not, chances were, armed or not, in the next few minutes, a very promising young man might well be dead.

As for Dave Holman? Even though Ali knew what she had to do, she didn't like it. When he found out about her phone call from A. J. Sanders, he was going to be even more bent out of shape. The problem was, A.J. had handed her a clue in Dave Holman's homicide investigation, and as much as she might have wanted to, withholding that information wasn't an option.

23

With westbound traffic already backing up, Ali executed a U-turn and made her way to the 51. While at a stop sign, she programmed Dr. Westmoreland's Tempe address into her GPS. It would take a matter of minutes for the news of an armed confrontation at North High to spread through the city, and Ali felt compelled to make good on her promise to A.J. that she would be the one to let Sylvia Sanders know what was going on.

Once on the 51 and speeding southbound, she found Dave's last call and punched send. "I wondered if you'd call me back and apologize," he said.

"Look, Mr. Grumbly Bear," she said, "I'm calling with some information for you. Do you want to hear it, or do you want to keep on hassling?"

"I'll hear it," he said grudgingly. "What information?"

"I believe someone you're looking for is about to be taken into custody by Phoenix PD, at the North High School campus in Phoenix."

"Who?"

"The person of interest in the Gemma Ralston case," Ali answered. "The kid who summoned 911."

"Who?" Dave repeated.

"His name is A. J. Sanders. You interviewed his mother, Sylvia, yesterday."

"James Sanders's son was at the crime scene? Why is he being taken into custody, and why don't I know anything about it?"

"The answer to the first question would be because he showed up at school with a trunkful of gambling tokens and a weapon—most likely a revolver. And the reason you don't know about it is that it's happening as we speak."

"We're talking an armed standoff?"

"It's no standoff. The gun is in the trunk of his Camry. I told him to turn himself in." *And to keep his mouth shut,* Ali thought.

"You know all this how?" Dave demanded.

"Because he called me and told me," Ali replied. "The uniformed response was happening as I ended the call. I dialed you next."

"But I don't understand how—"

"Look," Ali interrupted, "do you want to argue about this, or do you want me to tell you what I think you're going to want to know?"

"Tell me."

"Assuming A.J. is taken into custody and gets booked, you'll most likely find his fingerprints on the cell phone that was used to send the 911 text from the Ralston homicide scene. A.J. also said something about a shovel that may have been left at the scene. He claims Gemma Ralston was alive when he got there, and he said that before she died, she mentioned someone's name. Dennis."

"Last name?" Dave asked.

"First name only. A.J. said he went back to his car to get her some water, and shortly after that, she was dead."

"All right," Dave said. "Thanks. It happens that I'm at Anthem, heading south, so I'll be able to go to work on this right away. I have a feeling it's going to be a jurisdictional nightmare, but thanks, Ali. I owe you one."

This time Dave was the one who ended the call.

The Baseline exit came up fast. Before Ali made it onto the arterial, her phone rang again. Stuart Ramey was on the line. Ali quickly brought him up to date on the morning's events.

"Okay," Stuart said. "I'll go looking for somebody named Dennis in Gemma's e-mail correspondence. He'll turn up either there or in her contacts list."

"Which you have somehow accessed," Ali said.

"Exactly," Stuart returned. "Do you need anything else?"

"Yes, I want to know how somebody bringing home minimum wage can afford to give away most of a three-hundred-thousand-dollar payday. Why so generous? And did you come up with anything on that reporter, Betty Noonan?"

"Nothing," Stuart replied. "As far as I can tell, there's no such animal, unless you want to count the Elizabeth Louise Noonan, aka Betty, who is eighty-six years old and living in Rapid City, South Dakota. I've checked with the *Examiner*. They don't have anyone by that name working for them and never have."

"But someone claiming to be Betty Noonan stopped by to see Sylvia Sanders yesterday."

"I believe 'claiming' is the operant word," Stuart said. "Did Sylvia see what kind of vehicle the faux reporter was driving? Did she give you any kind of description?"

"I didn't ask for one," Ali said. "It didn't seem all that important at the time, but I'm on my way to see Sylvia right now. I can ask for more details when I see her, and I'll check with the folks at the Mission in Vegas as well. Since our intrepid reporter claimed to be from the *Las Vegas Examiner,* maybe she's been in touch with the folks there, too. If you have time, you might give the Mission a call. If you can't reach Abigail Mattson, check with her assistant. Her name's Regina."

By then Ali was pulling into the parking lot at the corner of Baseline and Rural. The shopping center was on one side of the parking lot, with a string of professional offices on the other. Ali pulled into a parking place just in time to see Sylvia Sanders come racing into the lot. Ali knew from the panicked expression on her face that she was too late. The breaking-news alert about the situation at North High School must have landed. Ali scrambled out of the Cayenne and ran to head the woman off.

"Sylvia," Ali called, chasing after her. "Stop, please. I need to speak to you."

Sylvia didn't pause until she reached her car. "I've got to go," she said desperately. "There's a problem at A.J.'s high school. They're reporting a possible shooter on campus. I tried calling his cell, but he isn't picking up. I've got to make sure he's all right."

"That's what I need to talk to you about," Ali insisted. "A.J. wanted me to be the one to tell you. That's why I'm here."

Sylvia froze with her hand on the door handle. "Tell me what?"

"About what's really going on. This is important, Sylvia. Is there somewhere we can talk in private?"

Sylvia looked back at the door to her office. Then, without a word, she walked away from her Passat, leading the way to a small taqueria at the far end of the development.

"What?" she said once they were seated. "Tell me what's going on."

In answer, Ali pulled out her iPad and hit a local news feed, playing it for Sylvia to hear. "Phoenix PD authorities are telling us that the situation at North High School has been resolved and that the alleged shooter has been taken into custody without incident."

"He may not be answering his phone, but that probably also means he's okay," Ali said.

"Wait," Sylvia said, looking aghast. "Are you saying A.J. was the shooter?"

"He's not a shooter," Ali said, "because there was no shooter, but he did take a gun to school. It was in the trunk of his car."

"That's impossible," Sylvia Sanders insisted, shaking her head. "You don't know what you're talking about. My son doesn't own a gun. I don't own a gun. I don't allow guns in my house. And if A.J. is the one who's been arrested, I need to go there—to the jail or the police department or wherever he is—to see what I can do to help."

She started to get up out of the booth, but Ali took hold of Sylvia's arm and bodily pulled her back down. "Right now the best thing you can do to help your son is sit here and talk to me. I told A.J. that the first thing he needs to do once he's taken into custody is to ask for an attorney. Appointing attorneys takes time, especially since two different jurisdictions are involved—Phoenix PD, where the alleged gun incident happened, and the Yavapai County Sheriff's Department, where your son is a possible suspect in one homicide and a person of interest in another."

"This can't be happening!" Sylvia exclaimed. "A.J. is a suspect in a homicide?"

"Are you going to listen or not?" Ali asked.

"I'll listen."

For the next ten minutes, Ali related everything she had learned, both from her phone call with A.J. and from her own investigations.

"From what you're telling me, it's like he's been living a double life. We've always been so close. I don't understand why he didn't talk to me about any of this. And why did he call you instead of me?"

"I think he was ashamed about betraying you," Ali said. "Now tell me what you know about the girlfriend, Sasha. A.J. said she was the only one who knew about the gun at school. She probably mentioned it to someone without realizing that other people would be upset about it and report it to the authorities."

"Maddy told me Sasha's last name is Miller."

"Any idea where she lives?"

Sylvia shook her head. "Somewhere inside the school boundaries, I suppose."

"No matter. I'll be able to find her."

Sylvia fell quiet, then nodded as if having come to an understanding. "I know why A.J. didn't tell me about the money."

"Why?"

"Being given that much money must have seemed like a miracle to him, but he knew that when I found out about it, I'd probably insist that he give the money back. For one thing, who knows how James got it? If Scott Ballentine is involved, it's probably some crooked deal or another. I'd rather A.J. take six years to work his way through school than use ill-gotten gains for some kind of free ride."

"Tell me about Scott Ballentine," Ali said.

"Scott and James were good pals at one time. Best friends, even. He was one of the four guys involved in that counterfeiting scheme from years ago. He paid a fine. James went to prison. Some friend!"

"Did you stay in touch with any of those guys afterward?"

"Are you kidding?" Sylvia replied. "Why would I? After my husband went to prison, I barely stayed in touch with him. The other three of them all walked away and hung James out to dry. I wouldn't cross the road to see any of them, not ever."

"I watched the security tape from the casino," Ali said. "Ballentine turned over three hundred thousand in gambling chips to James Sanders, who loaded them into a strongbox and walked away. Four days later, James was dead. Your son admitted to being in possession of two hundred and fifty grand of that money. We've accounted for another five thousand. So where's the other forty-five thousand? Do you know?"

"Wait," Sylvia said, her cheeks reddening. "You're asking me if I have it?"

"Do you?" Ali asked. "If James slipped money to his son without your knowledge, the reverse might also be true. Maybe he gave you some of it, too."

"No," Sylvia declared. "He didn't, and even if he had, I wouldn't have accepted it."

"Tell me about the reporter," Ali said. "The one who came to see you yesterday."

"Betty Noonan?"

Ali nodded. "What did she look like?"

"Tall," Sylvia said at once. "About your height. Light reddish-brown hair. Curly."

"Did you see what kind of vehicle she was driving?"

"An SUV, I think—a little white SUV—but I can't tell you which kind," Sylvia said. "I've never been particularly interested in cars, and I'm not very good at telling one make and model from another."

"Did anything she said strike you as odd?"

Sylvia frowned. "Not then," she said, "but now I realize she seemed to be under the impression that we had seen James sometime very recently. I told her that wasn't true. That the last time we'd seen him was when he gave A.J. the car on his sixteenth birthday, but that was over a year ago."

Looking out the window beyond Sylvia's shoulder, Ali watched as a pair of unmarked Phoenix PD patrol cars nosed into the parking lot. One stopped directly behind Sylvia's Passat and stayed there, making it impossible for the vehicle to drive away. Two plainclothes detectives got out of the first vehicle and walked into the office building.

"Oops," Ali said. "It looks to me like you've got company. A pair of cops just went into your office."

Sylvia turned around and stared out the window. "They blocked my car," she said.

"Yes," Ali agreed. "I'm pretty sure they want to talk to you in person."

"What should I tell them?"

"The truth," Ali answered. "You don't know where A.J. got the gun. You may be tempted to give him an alibi by claiming he was home the whole time, but save your breath. Pretending it's impossible for A.J. to sneak out of the house at night without your knowledge is a joke. I know for a fact that he did it at least once yesterday."

"How do you know that?"

"I saw him. He came out of the house after my interview with you. He was carrying a backpack loaded with the strongbox containing all those gambling tokens. He put it in the trunk of the car and went back inside without your ever being the wiser."

Sylvia said nothing. "He's been playing me," she said finally, making no effort to hide her disappointment.

"It certainly sounds like it," Ali agreed, "but that makes him a kid, not a killer. You need to go talk to the cops now. Don't make them come into the restaurant looking for you. It'll be better if you show up voluntarily. You'll look less like you've got something to hide."

"What's going to happen to A.J.?"

"I'm not sure," Ali answered. "For the next little while, he's going to be a jurisdictional football. Phoenix PD will want to charge him on the unlawful possession of a firearm. Right now he's a person of interest in Yavapai County. If the weapon they found on him turns out to be the murder weapon, the county prosecutor will be the one lodging possible homicide charges against him. My best guess is that Yavapai will ultimately win the toss. The chief detective there, Dave Holman, is a friend of mine.

He can be a jerk on occasion, especially when he's shorthanded and dealing with two separate homicides, but he's also a straight shooter. I'm not sure the same can be said for Cap Horning, the Yavapai County prosecutor. Make sure A.J. gets a court-appointed attorney before he talks to anyone."

"What about you?" Sylvia asked, giving Ali an appraising look. "Are you a straight shooter?"

"Yes," Ali said. "I am, but I don't have any way of proving it. You'll just have to take my word for it."

"What's your part in all of this?" Sylvia asked. "Why are you helping us? Why are you helping A.J.?"

"I have a son whom I raised on my own a lot of the time. A.J. reminds me of him. They're both good kids. From what I can tell, A.J. was an unwitting pawn in whatever was going on between you and his father. I'm sure he picked up on the idea that the only way he'd be able to accept this very generous gift from his father—a life-changing gift—was to try to keep it a secret from you. That might have worked for him if you hadn't raised him to be a responsible kind of guy who, when the chips were down, would pick up a phone and try to help a dying woman by calling 911."

"That's true," Sylvia said. "He is a good kid."

"From what I've learned about James Sanders, he got sold down the river by his friends and by the criminal justice system for something that was very likely an ill-informed teenage prank. I'd like to see that his son gets a better deal. Wouldn't you?"

Sylvia nodded. "Thank you," she said.

"Now get going," Ali said, dismissing her. "And remember, when you talk to the cops, tell the truth, but the less you say, the better."

Sylvia sat for a moment longer, studying Ali. Then she seemed to pull herself together. "All right, then," she said, standing up. "I guess I'd better go do this."

Watching her go, Ali couldn't help but be astounded by the remarkable transformation between the panicked woman who had come into the restaurant and the resolute one leaving. Striding determinedly across the parking lot, Sylvia Sanders reminded Ali of a mama bear on the way to rescue her endangered cub.

She would either succeed, or she'd die trying.

24

While Sylvia marched across the parking lot and into the office building, Ali's phone rang.

"Hey," B. said. "Busy morning?"

"Very," Ali said without going into detail. "How about you?"

"Checkout time is fast approaching. I'm on my way to the first of two meetings scheduled for this afternoon, then I need to head back to Sedona. Do you want me to pack up your stuff and check you out of the hotel, or do you want to keep the room for another night?"

Ali had expected to be back from her meeting with Valerie Sloan in plenty of time to do her own packing. "Sorry," she said. "I got held up, and I'm all the way out in Tempe. If you don't mind grabbing my stuff, I'd appreciate it."

"Don't mind at all," B. said. "See you at home."

For the next ten minutes, Ali sat in the booth, sipping her drink, and watching the building into which Sylvia Sanders had disappeared. At last the glass doors opened. Sylvia emerged first, accompanied by one of the plainclothes detectives and followed by the second. The first one helped her into the back of one of the waiting unmarked patrol cars. Then he and his partner got into the car and drove out of the parking lot, followed closely by the vehicle with a uniformed officer that had been keeping Sylvia's Passat blocked in its parking place.

Still unsure what to do next, Ali was gathering her things to leave when Stuart Ramey called. "Any luck on the Dennis front?" she asked, subsiding back into the booth.

"Nada," Stuart said. "I'm unable to find any mention of someone named Dennis in Gemma's e-mail history or in her contacts list. I checked both."

"Who was he, then?" Ali asked.

"You're sure the witness got the name right?"

"Relatively," Ali said. "I already checked with Gemma's one tennis partner earlier today. She claimed they never discussed romantic entanglements. Maybe I should have another chat with the other one." Ali stopped talking abruptly when she realized what she'd said. "Maybe that's it," she said.

"Maybe what?" Stuart sounded genuinely puzzled.

"Maybe Gemma said the word 'tennis,' not Dennis," Ali explained excitedly. "Molly Handraker told me that she and Gemma played tennis on Monday afternoon. Maybe Gemma was talking about something that happened while they were playing or after they finished." Calling up her notes, Ali read through them until she found what she was looking for. "Last night's interview with

Molly ended a little abruptly. I think I'll go back to Paradise Valley and ask her about Dennis. And I'm going to need an address and phone number for a student at North High School in Phoenix. Sasha Miller."

"Will do," Stuart said.

Minutes later, feeling more like a commuter than anything else, Ali headed north on the 51. Whatever Gemma's dying word had been, it was the best clue Ali had, and she was sure that everyone else involved in the case—especially Dave Holman—was currently too busy with other things to follow up on it. The jurisdictional wrangling over what to do about A.J. was going to keep any number of people completely occupied for the next several hours. Right that moment, Ali had a clear field, and she intended to use it.

Her first plan was to drive back to the Ralston place on Upper Glen Road, but as she turned off on Lincoln and saw the sign to the Paradise Valley Country Club, she changed her mind. The last time Molly Handraker had seen Gemma Ralston, she was sitting at the bar in the country club. With any luck, someone—the bartender, maybe?—had noticed Gemma leaving with someone else, maybe even the mysterious Dennis.

The country club was for members only, but Ali had a way around that. Pulling over on a side road, she found the number, called it, and asked to be connected to the dining room.

"This is Doris Ralston's new PA," she said. "She needs a reservation for lunch at twelve-thirty today, and she's expecting a guest—Ali Reynolds. Got that?"

"Of course," the hostess said. "I'm assuming she'd like her usual table? And Ms. Handraker will be there as well?"

"Yes, a reservation for three," Ali said with a smile. "That will be perfect." *As long as Doris and Molly don't show up on their own,* Ali thought.

A glance at her watch told her she had a few minutes to kill. Since she was only a mile or so away from Gemma's condo, Ali headed there. She spent the time canvassing Gemma's near neighbors. It was late morning on a weekday. Mostly, no one was home, but as Ali walked through the neighborhood, she noted the addresses of any houses with obvious security cameras. They might be worth having Stuart Ramey check into later.

At exactly twelve-fifteen, she presented herself at the gatehouse for the Paradise Valley Country Club. She nodded at the guard as he waved her through. Parking in the clubhouse lot, she scanned through her iPad notes until she located the name of the bartender. Luis, with no last name. Armed with nothing but the name Luis, Ali made her way into the clubhouse. The dining room was busy, and the harried hostess cast a worried glance first at her list and then in the direction of an occupied table by the far window.

"The rest of your party isn't here yet," she said. "Would you mind waiting in the bar?"

"Not at all," Ali said graciously. *And please don't throw me in the briar patch.* She turned back to the hostess. "Is Luis working today?"

"Luis Cruz?" The hostess nodded. "He came on at eleven."

Better and better, Ali thought.

She made her way into the bar. There were a

number of people there, some of them watching CNN and the others glued to a golf tournament being played in some cold clime where the players and the few fans braving the edges of the fairways and the grandstands at the greens were bundled up to ward off wind and rain.

Ali took a seat and waited for the bartender—a guy in his thirties with a buzz cut, a pencil-thin mustache, and a bull neck—to turn in her direction. "What can I get you?" he asked.

"Just water," she said. "I'm meeting Doris Ralston and her daughter, and they're not here yet."

"Ice?" he asked.

"Yes, please."

The bartender brought the water and set it in front of her. "Not a good time for the Ralstons," he said.

"So you've heard?"

"Everybody's talking about it," Luis said with a shrug. "First Molly's father died a few months back; the mother is having health issues of some kind; and now her brother is accused of murder. From where I'm standing, Molly Handraker has her hands full."

"You know her then? Molly, I mean."

He shrugged. "Not well. I've only known her since she got back to town, but I've heard stories about her family. You know the type—the sons are the fair-haired boys and can do no wrong, and the girls are second-class citizens who are supposed to grow up and be wives and mothers and join the Junior League. When you're playing that game, being beautiful helps. Molly's not bad-looking, but taking care of her mother is wearing her down. I feel sorry for her."

"What can you tell me about Gemma Ralston?"

Luis gave Ali a searching look, then shook his head. "Gemma's another story," he said, "and this would probably be an excellent time for me to keep my mouth shut. How about those Cardinals?"

Turning his back, Luis walked away from Ali's end of the bar. For the next few minutes, he made dutiful rounds of all the other customers, mixing cocktails and pouring drinks for them and for waitresses from the dining room, and providing another pitcher of beer for the guys watching the golf tournament. Finally, he returned to Ali.

"I take it you didn't like Gemma Ralston?" she asked.

He gave her a baleful look. "What's your deal in all this?"

"I'm a freelancer," Ali said, producing a business card and handing it over. "My name is Ali Reynolds, and I'm doing a writing project on early-onset Alzheimer's."

She had noticed that the word "freelancer" prompted far fewer negative reactions than the word "reporter." Maybe freelancing put people in mind less of out-of-control journalists and more of men out in armor, tilting at windmills and slaying the occasional dragon. What could be a more understandable dragon to slay than a dread disease that scared the hell out of everyone?

"Luis Cruz," he said, accepting both the card and the explanation. "I've never had a problem with any of the other Ralstons, but Gemma is another story. Let's just say whoever took that woman out did the whole world a favor. And in case you're interested, I told the cops the same thing."

"They talked to you?"

"Sure. Why wouldn't they? Gemma Ralston was here on Monday night, the same night she went missing. As a matter of fact, she and Molly Handraker were here together. I overheard them talking about a diamond necklace, Mrs. Ralston's most likely. It had disappeared, and Gemma mentioned dropping by the next day to help look for it. Molly said something like 'You don't need to bother—she won't even remember,' and Gemma says, 'I told your mother I'd come help, and I will.' Molly stayed around a while longer after that, but when she left, I got the feeling that she was upset about something."

"Did Gemma leave then, too?" Ali asked.

"It would have been great if she had, but she didn't," Luis continued. "As usual, she stayed on, drinking and throwing her weight around. As soon as Molly's back was turned, Gemma started bad-mouthing the woman who was supposed to be her best friend. That didn't sit too well with me. Snobs don't bother me—there are plenty of those around here—but I don't like two-faced snobs."

"Did she leave with anyone?"

Luis shook his head. "The cops asked the same question. She left by herself around nine or so. Not quite drunk but getting there. She raised hell when I cut her off and suggested she call a taxi. She threw a fit and went screaming to my manager about it. She wanted him to fire me on the spot."

"I guess that didn't work," Ali observed with a smile.

"No, it didn't, but no thanks to her," Luis replied. "Even though I was in the right for cutting her off, I still ended up getting a write-up. Customer complaints are a big deal around here, so pardon me if I say good riddance. By the way, she evidently disregarded my advice and drove herself home after all. So don't bother asking where I was on Monday night, because I was here working until two A.M. You can check the time clock. I'm sure the cops already did. And after I left work, I went straight home. There's a security camera on the parking garage of my building. It'll show that I was home safe and sound at two-thirty. They're welcome to check that for themselves, and so are you."

Two more golfers, one of them in an ordinary polo shirt and chinos and the other in vivid yellow-and-orange-checked pants with a matching orange shirt, bellied up to the bar and ordered Bloody Marys. While Luis mixed their drinks, Ali considered her next move.

"When Gemma left, did she say where she was going?"

"It was hard to tell. She was so busy screeching at me and telling me to go to hell for eighty-sixing her that I don't believe she mentioned any destination in particular. And let me tell you, as long as she wasn't in my bar, I didn't care where she was going."

"So if you were going to make a wild guess about who might have wanted her dead . . ."

"Besides me, you mean."

"Right," Ali said with a smile. "Who else besides you?"

"My money's on the guy in jail," Luis replied. "Doris Ralston's son, the ex-husband. I, for one, don't blame him a bit."

"Was Chip Ralston here on Monday?"

"Hardly," Luis said. "He's not a member anymore. From what I can tell, when he and Gemma divorced, he got the shaft, and she got the membership."

"Did you ever hear Gemma talking with or about someone named Dennis?" Ali asked.

"Dennis who?"

"I have no idea," she replied. "All I have is the first name."

"Doesn't ring a bell," Luis said.

Ali glanced at her watch. It was twelve-forty-five.

"Let me guess," Luis said. "The old lady stood you up?"

"Looks like."

Luis nodded sagely. "I'm not surprised. She does that a lot. Makes a reservation and then doesn't show."

Ali pulled a five-dollar bill out of her purse and slapped it on the bar. "Thanks for the water," she said. "Turns out it was just what I needed."

Dodging the hostess in the dining room, Ali made for her car. Once she reached it, she sat inside for several long moments, thinking. It was one thing for Gemma Ralston to be vilified by her ex-husband or the ex-husband's new girlfriend. They were bound to have their own kind of biases. Hearing the same thing from the bartender, however, gave Ali pause.

The professional bartenders she had known over the years, especially ones who worked in high-end clubs and bars, generally maintained a certain client confidentiality as far as their regular customers were concerned. The fact that Luis had blurted out derogatory comments about Gemma Ralston to a complete stranger came as something of a surprise. If someone like Luis had no trouble wishing Gemma ill, there might be a few others out there as well, and who more likely to know where some of those bodies were buried than Gemma's ex-sister-in-law and maybe not such a great friend Molly Handraker?

And what about that missing diamond necklace? Molly hadn't mentioned it. Was that a deliberate oversight on her part or an accidental one? Maybe in a household like theirs, where someone was operating with severe mental deficits, misplaced pieces of jewelry were so commonplace that they weren't worth discussing, to say nothing of bringing in someone else to help with the search.

Luis had said that Molly had seemed upset when she left. That was something else that had gone unsaid in Molly's version.

Dave Holman had obviously already gotten Luis's take on the situation and probably had come to similar conclusions. Therefore, the Yavapai County homicide cop could hardly complain if Ali wound up following the same trail of leads.

Dave was investigating, and so was she. With that in mind, her next stop would be Upper Glen Road, but before she went there, she needed answers to a few more questions. To that end, she got out her phone and dialed the number for the Yavapai County sheriff, Gordon Maxwell.

"Hey," the sheriff said with an easy chuckle when he heard her voice on the phone. "Dave Holman tells me you've been running circles around him this morning, but now that he's busy duking it out with the Phoenix PD over the custody of a possible suspect, I believe he's a lot happier with you at the moment than he was a little earlier. His exact words to me were 'We owe her one.'"

"That's good to know," Ali said, "because it turns out, I'm here to collect."

"Why? What do you need?"

"To talk to Chip Ralston on the phone, and I'm wondering if you can make that happen."

Her request was followed by a long period of silence that Ali didn't take as a good omen, especially since her main goal was to ask Chip if he knew anything about the mysterious Dennis who evidently was a presence in his ex-wife's life.

"I have some questions about his mother," Ali added quickly. "She's an Alzheimer's patient, and Dr. Ralston is a nationally recognized Alzheimer's expert."

"I suppose I could give it a try," Maxwell said. "Give me your number and five minutes. I'll see if I can arrange to get him to a phone, but even if I do, that doesn't guarantee he'll be interested in calling you back. He's under no obligation to talk to anyone."

"Tell him it's about his mother," Ali suggested. "That should do the trick."

Ali stayed parked where she was in the country club lot, scrolling through her notes while she waited. Five minutes later, her phone rang, and Chip Ralston was on the line.

"What's this about my mother?" he asked. "Is something wrong?"

"How long have you known she has Alzheimer's?"

Chip hesitated before he answered. "The better part of two years," he said finally. "Given my training and experience, I was the first one to notice and suspect what was going on. What my dad was willing to write off as simple forgetfulness, I saw as something else. When I tried to discuss it with him, my father went into total denial, at least at first. Then he did everything he could to cover it up and keep anyone else from knowing what was really going on."

"How did that work out?"

"Okay for a while. I think for a long time he managed to pull the wool over almost everyone's eyes. Then he had a stroke and died. All of a sudden Mom's condition was out in the open, because she was clearly losing ground. I never quite figured out how it happened, but I ended up being the bad guy in that scenario. People who knew my parents came to the conclusion that I should have done something to help sooner—as though I should have been able to fix it. The problem is, Alzheimer's isn't fixable. Besides, given my father's attitude toward my specialty, he would have eaten ground glass before accepting my help."

"Did Molly know about your mother's condition for a long time?"

"I doubt it. She came home when Dad ended up in a hospital with a stroke, but she showed up armed with the trump card. The folks had given Molly a medical power of attorney for both of them. As soon as she got here, she used it to post the DNR in Dad's room. And ever since, she's used it to keep me out of the loop as far as Mom's treatment is concerned."

"How do you feel about that?" Ali asked.

"How do you think I feel?" he asked with an edge of bitterness. "At the time, Molly went ballistic right along with everyone else, and blamed me for Mom's deteriorating condition, although I wasn't allowed to do anything about it then and haven't been able to since then, either."

"So you have no say in decisions about your mother's care?"

"None whatsoever. I probably could have fought that in the beginning, but I was up to my eyeballs in fighting with Gemma and her attorneys. I didn't have the energy to wage another war on a whole different front with Molly, especially since Molly, Gemma, and Mom were thick as thieves. My financial life was already spinning out of control. A few months later, it went over a cliff. When I saw I would need a place to stay while I got on my feet, I ended up having to go to Molly, practically on bended knee, for help. She made it clear that I could live in the casita but only so long as I promised not to interfere in any way with how she was caring for our mother."

"As long as she had the durable power of attorney, she had you over a barrel."

"In spades," Chip agreed. "Did then and still does."

"From what you're saying, I take it you and your sister aren't on the best of terms?"

"Molly and I were never on good terms," Chip replied. "I know there are families where brothers and sisters get along like gangbusters and chum around together. Our family has never been like that. We're likely to show up for compulsory photo ops on major holidays, but that's about it. More for show than go."

"Did you ever tell Lynn what was going on with your mother?"

Chip paused. "No," he said finally.

"Why not?"

"Because I was ashamed, I guess," he admitted. "Because I didn't want her to think I was a hypocrite.

Here I am, out at the support group meetings, telling my patients that Alzheimer's is something that has to be handled as a family, while as far as my own family is concerned, I'm completely shut out from practicing what I preach. So that's one part of my reluctance to have Lynn involved in my mother's life. The other part is my mother's total focus on Gemma. It doesn't matter if Gemma is dead or alive. As long as Mom maintains that powerful connection to my ex-wife, she's never going to accept Lynn's presence in my life. On the one occasion I did try to introduce them—"

"I know. Your mother went ballistic."

"That's putting it mildly."

"How would you characterize your sister's care of your mother?"

"I'm not privy to everything that goes on, but she seems to be doing a good enough job. For a while there were problems with Mom setting off the alarm system overnight, but I believe they adjusted her meds so she's sleeping better. At least she was. There's a chance that the shock of Gemma's death might spark another crisis. In that case, Molly might end up needing extra help. She might even call Consuelo back.".

"That's the maid your sister fired?"

"Yes," Chip said. "I'm sure she could use the work. She was really loyal to my mom. It's a shame she had to be let go. Molly always claimed it was a matter of saving money."

"Might the maid have stolen something?"

"Consuelo? Never," Chip declared. "Why?"

"Your mother said something to Gemma about losing a necklace, a diamond necklace. With your mother's condition, it's hard to tell if it's something that happened recently or a long time ago."

"Yes," Chip agreed. "The time lines do tend to get muddled, but I can't imagine Consuelo ever stealing something from anyone at all, much less from Mother. I think it's more likely that whatever it is simply got misplaced."

"Okay," Ali said. "One last question. Did your ex-wife have a friend or acquaintance named Dennis?"

"What I don't know about my ex's affairs, romantic or otherwise, would fill volumes—for all I know, there could have been a dozen Dennises in her life, but I don't remember hearing that name mentioned. Ever."

"I take it there's still no word from Cap Horning?"

"Not so far. Anything else?"

Ali's phone buzzed. Stuart Ramey's name and number appeared on the screen. "Thanks for your help, Chip. I have to run. I've got another call."

25

"Hey," Stuart said when she switched over. "How are things?"

"It's been an interesting morning." While she put the Cayenne in gear and eased out of the parking lot, she gave Stu a quick summary of her day so far. She finished by saying, "Now I'm on my way to Doris Ralston's house to have another chat with her daughter about Monday night. Our interview last night ended abruptly. I know a little more about their situation now, and I have a few more questions. What about you?"

"After you told me about Sanders giving that chunk of change to his son, I went digging in the Mission's finances and picked up an interesting tidbit. Contributions are down across the board, and so is fund-raising. As a result, the Mission coffers have been running on empty. Until this week, they were three months behind on their lease and behind on payments to suppliers. They've evidently been using rent money to make payroll and pay their food vendors. As of Wednesday of this week, their lease is current. It looks like an anonymous forty-five-thousand-dollar cash donation came in at the end of last week. I'm guessing they used some of that to bring their rent up to date and get caught up with their suppliers."

"Let me guess where this sudden windfall came from," Ali said. "Would this anonymous benefactor happen to be James Sanders, aka Mason?"

"That's what I'm thinking," Stuart replied. "According to my math, we've accounted for all the money Scott Ballentine handed over to Sanders in gambling chips."

"But why would he give the whole sum away?" Ali asked. "Why not keep it?"

"I don't know," Stuart said. "I'll keep digging on that. As for what you asked me earlier? I'll keep looking, but so far, I've come up empty on the Dennis situation. Anything else?"

"Just for argument's sake, I'd like you to take a look at Molly Handraker."

"Why? What am I looking for?"

"Just background material," Ali said. "There's something about Gemma, Valerie, and Molly that doesn't ring true. So far, I've discovered that at least two of these so-called best friends are underhanded backstabbers who maintain a wonderfully goody-goody public persona. As far as the world is concerned, Molly is the downtrodden younger sister bravely assuming the entire burden of caring for an aging mother."

"You're thinking appearances might be deceiving?"

"Maybe. Just let me know what you find. Molly's been married three times. She's still married to a guy named Barry Handraker. They used to live in Minneapolis, and I'm assuming he still does. Gemma and Valerie Sloan have a very low opinion of the guy and were counseling Molly to dump him."

"Okay," Stuart said. "Will do. Call me back when you get out of your interview."

By then Ali had arrived at the Ralston residence and parked in the driveway just outside the front entrance. It was much easier to find the second time, in bright November daylight, rather than in the dark. Everything about the place was impressive, from the red-tiled roof to the lush green lawn edged with beds of newly planted petunias and pansies. Ali knew that maintaining that kind of landscape didn't come cheap in terms of water or labor. In fact, as she watched, a yard guy wearing an immense white Stetson and pushing a lawn mower emerged from the side of the house. Seeing her, he tipped his hat in her direction. Then he turned on the mower and went to work as Ali rang the bell.

No one answered on the first ring or the second, but the house was large enough that Ali waited a minute and then tried a third time. That was when she heard Molly's voice from somewhere inside.

"I'm coming. I'm coming." There was a pause and the sound of something being slammed shut in the entryway. "Where's the damned deadbolt key?" Molly muttered. "Somebody must have moved it. Wait just a minute. I'll be back."

Long seconds passed. Eventually, Ali heard the sound of a key scraping in the lock, and the door was flung open. An angry Molly Handraker stood in the doorway. Though it was early afternoon, she had clearly just stepped out of the shower. Barefoot and wearing nothing but a terry-cloth robe, she had a damp towel wrapped around her head.

"You again?" she demanded irritably, peering first at Ali and then glancing around the rest of the yard. "Couldn't you at least have called first?"

"I'm sorry if it's inconvenient," Ali said placatingly. "I was in the neighborhood. I just have a few more questions."

"All right, all right," Molly said impatiently. "Come in."

As Ali stepped into the entryway, she saw a stack of luggage sitting near the front door as if waiting to be loaded into a vehicle. She waited while Molly slammed the door shut, then stomped around the luggage and through the entryway, leading the way into the living room.

"Is someone taking a trip?" Ali asked, pulling out her iPad and opening the lid.

"Not that it's any of your business," Molly replied, "but I'm going to drop Mother off in Palm Springs and let her spend a couple of days with Jack and Gloria Manning, some friends of my father's. All the emotional turmoil with Gemma and Chip is too much for her. As you saw last night, she can't remember from one moment to another if Gemma's alive or dead, and it's too hard on both of us for me to keep telling her what's what over and over. I've decided it'll be easier if she's out of town, at least until after the funeral."

"Wouldn't participating in a funeral help her?" Ali asked, talking as she typed "Jack and Gloria Manning" and "Palm Springs" into her iPad. "I mean, maybe the formal mourning rituals would help clarify the situation for her."

"I'll take care of my mother," Molly said. "Now what do you want?"

The night before, Ali had come away with the impression that Molly Handraker was close to saintliness as far as her dealings with her ailing mother were concerned. This morning the saintly mask had slipped a little, and Molly's mean-girl tone and manner were more in line with what Ali might have expected from one of Gemma Ralston's and Valerie Sloan's "best friends."

"I just wanted to clarify one or two things. I understand that you and Gemma had a disagreement of some kind the other night—the night she went missing. I wondered if it might be important."

Molly seemed to consider her answer before she spoke. "You know that old saw about people who live in glass houses not throwing stones?"

Ali nodded. "What about it?"

"I got tired of being the target of all that stone throwing," Molly said. "I mean, here's Gemma busily telling me 'What you need to do is this' and 'What you need to do is that,' when her own life isn't exactly a model of perfect relationships. I figured she didn't have much room to talk, and I told her so. Then I left, came home, and went to bed. That's all there was to it."

"Then there was that odd moment when your mother said something about Gemma being asleep in the car."

"You may have noticed, my mother gets confused on occasion," Molly said. "Things that happened months ago seem like yesterday to her. You have to know that Gemma was known to have a few too many now and then. A couple of months ago, when she was in no condition to drive, we brought her home from the club and left her in Mother's car long enough to sleep it off. Once she sobered up, I took her back down to the club to pick up her car so she could drive herself home.

"The whole episode offended Mother's tender sensibilities and, like everything else to do with Gemma, it's stuck in her very random access memory. At the time, she thought I should have brought Gemma into the house and put her to bed properly, in one of the guest rooms. Of course, Mama didn't bother considering the physical impossibility of my being able to get a sleeping drunk up the stairs and through the house single-handed. That was all my problem, not hers. So periodically, Mama goes off on one of those 'Gemma's sleeping' rants, just like she did last night. When that happens, I try to consider the source and ignore it."

Having heard what Luis had to say about Gemma's drinking habits, Ali was tempted to accept Molly's explanation at face value. Still, something about the supposedly plausible answer jarred. It was a little too smooth, too pat—as though it had been rehearsed or delivered before, verbatim.

"What about your mother's missing necklace?" Ali asked.

That one caught Molly off guard. Her cheeks paled. "What missing necklace?" she asked.

"You know," Ali said with a careless shrug. "The one Gemma offered to come help find."

There was a momentary silence. Gradually, color seeped back into Molly's face. Ali knew something important had just happened, though she wasn't sure what.

Shaking her head, Molly regrouped. "Oh, that," she said offhandedly. "Same thing. As I said before,

Mother gets confused from time to time. She had told Gemma that morning on the phone that she had lost her favorite necklace, one Daddy gave her for their fiftieth wedding anniversary. Turns out Mama had it put away in an old jewelry box instead of the one she usually uses, so the necklace was never lost in the first place."

"Where is she, by the way?" Ali asked.

"Mama? I asked her to stay out of the way while we were packing. She's probably in her room, mooning over that damned photo album from Gemma and Chip's wedding. She barely lets it out of her sight. Drags it with her everywhere she goes. It drives me nuts."

The night before, when Ali had seen Doris cradling the wedding album, she had assumed Doris was reliving her own or her daughter's wedding. Apparently, that assumption had been wrong.

"Your mother's unrelenting focus on Gemma must be overwhelming at times."

"You think?" Molly asked with more than a trace of rancor. "Yes, in the wedding sweepstakes, I always come in second best. Actually, I'm so far behind the field that no one even knows I'm there. It's especially helpful that my mother's condition makes it possible for her to forget everything about everyone else, but she doesn't forget a single thing about Gemma. That's still all there, every bit of it, and Mama never hesitates to rub it in."

Ali's iPad dinged, letting her know there was an arriving message, but she had no time to look at it. Somewhere in the back of the house, a door slammed shut, and heavy footsteps came rushing toward the living room. A heavyset man with a fleshy face and coal-black slicked-back hair appeared in the doorway between the dining room and living room.

"If you're here," he demanded, "where's the Jag?"

"What do you mean, where's the Jag?" Molly returned. "It's in the garage, where it's supposed to be."

"No, it's not. It was there a few minutes ago, and you were in the shower when I took the Mercedes down to fill up with gas. Now it's gone."

Molly looked at him, then wordlessly, she got up and left the room. Moments later, she was back. Once again her face had gone ashen. "She's gone," she said.

"Did you give her the medicine?"

Molly nodded.

"Are you sure she took it?"

"It's gone."

"Did you up the dose?"

"I gave her the usual amount."

"Crap," the man muttered. "How could you be so dumb? I've been trying to tell you all along that she might end up developing a tolerance for the stuff. But did you listen? Of course not."

"I'm sorry," Molly murmured.

"And today of all days!" he continued to rage. "We're on a very tight schedule here. We've got a plane to catch. Losing track of your mother right now is the last thing we need!"

"I'm sorry," Molly said again.

"Sorry doesn't cut it," he said, ignoring the apology. "How the hell did this happen?"

"I don't know. When I got out of the shower, I noticed that the dead-bolt key was missing from the entryway table. As far as I knew, Mama was in her room. I thought maybe you had taken the key."

"What makes you think I'd use the front door to get to the garage?" the man said. "Do I look stupid? We've got to find her. Where do you think she went?"

"I don't know. The last thing we talked about was going to Palm Springs."

"Would she try driving there on her own? How could she? Does she have keys to the Jaguar? Where are those?"

"In my purse?"

"Are you sure?"

With Molly and the stranger embroiled in their heated argument, and with Molly searching her purse for keys, Ali stole a moment to tap her iPad over to the message page, where she was startled to see two photos—mug shots—of the very man who was standing in the doorway.

The message from Stuart was short and to the point: "Barry Handraker is VERY bad news. Armed and dangerous. If he's involved in any way, get the hell out. Now!"

Unfortunately, the warning had arrived a few seconds too late, and getting out wasn't an option. Ali sent the message away so no one else would be able to see it.

"What the hell are we going to do now?"

"I have no idea," Molly said, crossing the room. She sat down hard on the sofa and buried her face in her hands. "There's no telling where she's gone. She might have gone down to the club. That would be my first guess. Do you want me to call and check?"

It seemed possible to Ali that both Molly and her husband, locked in their furious blame game, had forgotten her presence in the room. Cautiously, she leaned over, slipped the iPad into her purse, and pulled out her iPhone, intent on dialing 911. Before she could slide the phone to the on position, however, Barry crossed the room in two gigantic strides and knocked the device out of her hands. The phone sailed across the room, whacked into a wall, and then tumbled to the floor.

"Who the hell is this broad?" he demanded, grasping Ali's wrist and holding it in a numbing grip that twisted her arm and half lifted her out of the chair. "What's she doing here? Is she a cop?"

"She's a writer," Molly answered. "She told me she's working on a piece about Gemma."

"Like hell she is. I'm betting she's undercover and that she's really after me. Check her purse. If she's a cop of some kind, there'll be ID."

"I'm not a cop—" Ali began.

"Shut up!"

Molly dutifully retrieved the purse and emptied it onto the coffee table. The Taser came out first and landed with a hard thump. Next came the wallet and the iPad, followed by a compact, several tubes of lipstick, a random collection of pens, and some loose change.

Barry recognized the Taser at once. "That's a civilian Taser, not a law enforcement one, but I don't know many writers walking around armed with Tasers, do you?" He turned his full attention on Ali, giving her a hard shake. "Who are you working for?" When she didn't answer, he looked at Molly, who was still thumbing through Ali's wallet. "How much does she know?"

Molly stopped and chewed her lower lip before she answered, as though reluctant to do so. It occurred to Ali that Molly was also scared of Barry

Handraker. What was it Stuart had said about him in that last text message? "VERY bad news."

"She knows about Mother's necklace," Molly whispered.

"The one Gemma went off about?" Barry asked.

Molly nodded. Ali wasn't sure what she supposedly knew about the necklace that maybe was or wasn't missing, but whatever it was, Barry Handraker didn't like it. The viselike hold on her wrist tightened. He leaned down and snarled directly in Ali's ear, his breath hot on her cheek. "Tell me who you're working for. Are you some kind of bounty hunter? Or did some of my former pals and business associates send you looking for me?"

"I have no idea what you're talking about," Ali told him. "None."

"Okay," he said to Molly, straightening up. "That settles it. We need to get out of here now. With your mother on the loose, we can't afford to hang around any longer."

"What are we going to do, leave her here?" Molly gestured to Ali.

"No, she's going with us," he said. "One way or another, she's going to tell me who she's working for. Then we'll get rid of her. Bring me the DB."

"What's DB?" Ali asked as Molly hurried out of the room.

"You ever heard of devil's breath?"

Ali shook her head. "Never."

"You will."

Ali's mind was reeling. When Barry Handraker said "get rid of," she knew exactly what he meant—that she was dead meat. When she had come here alone with her few unanswered questions, it hadn't occurred to her that she was walking into any kind of serious danger. As she'd rung the doorbell and stepped into the entryway, she hadn't even begun to formulate the idea that Molly might have been involved in Gemma's murder. Obviously, she was, and Ali had blundered into a potentially deadly situation.

Where could she look for backup? Stuart Ramey, her virtual partner, was the only person on earth who had any idea where she was. Unfortunately, he was completely out of reach. Her phone was lying probably broken on the far side of the room. Her Taser and iPad lay in a jumble on the coffee table, inches away but totally out of reach. Her Glock, however, was in the holster at the small of her back. There was a chance she might be able to get it out. No one here knew she had a second weapon. The problem with that, of course, was that she was right-handed, and that was the hand still trapped in Barry Handraker's murderous grip.

Molly returned from the kitchen. In one hand, she carried a saucer with a tablespoon of white powder on it. In her other hand, she held a single straw.

"She's not your mother. You don't need that much," Barry said when Molly set the saucer on the table. "About half should do it. Otherwise, she'll be out all night."

There was an empty ashtray on an end table. Molly dumped half the powder into that and then turned back to Ali.

"Be careful not to breathe it in when you do this," Barry warned Molly. "I'll stay with her until she goes under. You get the luggage loaded. We need a diversion that will give us a chance to get out of Dodge, and I've got just the ticket."

Ali stared as the white powder–laden saucer came nearer. With a shock, she realized that whatever they were about to give her was the same thing Molly must have been routinely administering to Doris Ralston.

"Please let me go," Ali said, struggling. "Please."

"Shut the hell up," Barry snarled, twisting Ali's arm even more painfully behind her.

Whatever poison was coming, Ali understood they expected her to inhale it, so she did the only thing she could think of to do. Waiting until Molly was two steps away, Ali took a deep breath, quietly pulling air deep into her chest and holding it as long as she could. That was when Barry let go of her wrist long enough to punch her in the gut, pounding the air out of her lungs. She was bent over gasping for breath when Molly leaned down and blew the powder out of the saucer and into the air.

Coughing and choking, Ali was conscious of a bitter taste in her mouth as whatever was in the air crossed her tongue. She attempted to get to her feet, but by then Barry had her wrist imprisoned again, and he forced her back into the chair.

She was still coughing as the blackness settled over her. After that, she knew nothing.

26

Stuart Ramey was no prima donna. One of the reasons he liked working for B. Simpson was that his services were always acknowledged and appreciated. Up to now, the same thing had been true whenever he worked with Ali. In the past, when he contacted her with some piece of needed information, she got back to him promptly.

This time it didn't happen. He had regarded the warning message about Barry Handraker as nothing short of critical. He didn't know whether Molly's husband was in town or involved, but Stuart couldn't afford to ignore the possibility that he might be. Stuart had texted his warning to Ali at ten past two and had expected her to reply in a matter of minutes.

To keep himself occupied while he waited, he turned to his computer and busied himself studying all things Handraker.

The original information on Barry Handraker's criminal past, including the mug shots Stuart shot over to Ali in the message, had come through reliable but not entirely legal channels. Had Stuart

Ramey been a police officer, having that information wouldn't have been a problem. Since he wasn't, it was. So rather than chasing more information that had the potential of landing him in hot water, he shopped the Net looking for whatever was readily accessible. Newspapers in the Minneapolis area proved especially helpful.

Barry Handraker, a pharmacist with ten years of experience in the field, had been fired from his job a year earlier when it had come to light that he was systematically skimming from the store's inventory of over-the-counter medications and using them in the manufacture of drugs that were far more lucrative out on the street. Even though money shouldn't have been a huge problem, he nonetheless stopped paying his mortgage. As a result, the bank had foreclosed, but when the house came back as a bank-held property, it was essentially worthless, since it had been used as a meth lab.

Handraker's venture into the illicit drug field had included manufacturing and distribution, and he had gained a reputation for being smart and ruthless. Tipped off by persons unknown, he had disappeared two months earlier, days before the DEA could carry out a planned raid to shut down his operation. Some of the petty criminals Handraker used as hired help had been caught in the raid, but the big cheese himself was long gone when the cops moved in. After his disappearance, he had been declared the prime suspect in two drug-related homicides and featured more than once on *Minnesota's Most Wanted*. There were numerous warrants out for Barry Handraker's arrest, and he was said to be armed and dangerous.

Stuart found it interesting that Molly Handraker's name was mostly missing from those newspaper accounts. The one time she was mentioned, she was referred to as "Handraker's estranged wife, now living in Arizona." The other references to her showed up in relation to her work with various battered-women's shelters in the area. She was never mentioned as being a suspect in her husband's crimes. The people writing the newspaper accounts seemed to assume that Molly Handraker was a good guy and Barry was a bad one.

Pulling away from his screen and keyboard, Stuart rubbed his eyes and looked at his watch. It was now three-fifteen. Over an hour had passed since he sent the warning to Ali. She had told him that she would be doing an interview. In B. Simpson's world, meetings with outsiders were sacrosanct and not to be interrupted. Stuart's dealings with Ali were an extension of that, and as a consequence, her meetings were accorded the same courtesy. Still, Ali had said she had a "few more questions" for Molly Handraker. How long could that take? Stuart didn't want to push panic buttons, but if Ali was in some kind of trouble, he didn't want to be sitting around doing nothing, either.

Finally, at three-forty, an hour and a half after the original message, Stuart determined that he had waited long enough. Sacrosanct interview or not, he sent Ali another message. "I'm worrying here. Where are you? Call me. Or text. I need to hear from you." Just to be sure, he dialed Ali's cell phone. The call went to voice mail. He tried to keep the steam out of his voice as he left a voice message to the same effect.

When the clock on his computer showed four-ten, two full hours into Ali's uncharacteristic silence, Stuart ran up the flag to B. Simpson. Stuart may have been doing a freebie for Ali Reynolds, but B. was the one who signed his check. If Ali was in trouble, B. needed to know about it.

"Hey, Stu," B. said easily when he heard Stuart's voice. "What gives?"

"We may have a problem," Stuart said.

"What kind of problem?"

"I sent Ali an important message two hours ago, more than that now. I wanted to warn her that the husband of the woman she was interviewing was a player—a possibly dangerous drug dealer from Minnesota who may be involved in whatever's going on. I expected her to get back to me right away. So far she hasn't, and I'm worried. Has she been in touch with you?"

"The last I heard from her was this morning before I left the hotel," B. said, "but I agree. Her not getting back to you is worrisome. That's not the Ali Reynolds I know. Maybe she's been in a traffic accident of some kind. Maybe she's had some kind of medical emergency. Have you called the cops?"

"I was afraid that if I did that and it turned out that there's nothing wrong—"

"—there'd be hell to pay," B. said with a chuckle, finishing Stu's sentence for him. "Have you tried tracking her phone or her iPad?"

"Not yet. I'm about to, but before I sign in to her iCloud account, I wanted you to know."

"You're not fooling me," B. said. "You want someone to share the blame."

"That, too," Stuart admitted, "but I was really hoping you could give me her current password. I can get in without one, but it'll go a lot faster if I have it."

For years B. had teased Ali about her obdurate resistance to changing her password. Now he was glad she hadn't. "Sugarloaf#1 should do it."

"She's still using that?" Stuart asked.

"Still," B. said.

"All right. Where are you?"

"I got out of my meeting an hour ago, and I'm heading back to Sedona on I-17, but if Ali is in Phoenix and in some kind of difficulty, I'll turn around at the next exit and head back south. You do what you need to do. Call me when you have her current location."

Other people might have considered summoning some kind of police presence at that point, but Stuart Ramey wasn't surprised that he and B. were on the same page. From his office perch in Cottonwood, Stu logged in to Ali's iCloud and activated her Find My iPhone app. Within seconds he had a location. As soon as he had done a little further research into the location, Stuart called B. back.

"Her phone's in the parking lot at a place called the Franciscan Renewal Center on East Lincoln Drive in Phoenix. I'm looking at some info on the center. It's a place that specializes in family counseling. Maybe there's a legitimate reason for her being there and not mentioning it to me. I don't want to step on any toes here, boss, but is there a chance she's having some kind of emotional difficulty? Are you?"

"Nobody's having a 'difficulty' of any kind," B. declared forcefully. "If Ali's there, it has to be for some good reason. I'm on my way now. Give me the address so I can program it into my GPS."

"While you're in a moving vehicle?" Stuart replied with a disapproving click of his tongue. "Perish the thought."

"It says I'm fifty-seven minutes out," B. said a moment later. "I'll see if I can shave some off that."

"I can hear the radar detector coming online as we speak."

27

At three minutes past five, almost three hours after Stuart sent the warning message to Ali, B. Simpson pulled into the parking lot at the Franciscan Renewal Center. He was on the phone with Stuart seconds later.

"I found the car," B. said hurriedly. "It's parked in a far corner of the lot, well away from the other cars here. It's unlocked, with the key in the ignition."

"I'm surprised somebody didn't steal it," Stuart observed. "What about her purse?"

"No sign of it, but her phone is here. The screen is a mess—looks like it's been run over by a Mack truck. The miracle is, the phone stayed on. That's why you were able to find it."

"What about the iPad?" Stuart asked. He waited, listening to the rustling of B.'s cursory search of the car.

"Not here," B. said at last. "What next?"

Stuart turned to the computer he had dedicated to accessing Ali's iCloud account and stared

at the screen for Find My Device. "There's no sign
of her iPad anywhere, boss," he said. "It looks like
the damned thing's off."

"Have you tried calling the Ralston house?"

"I have. Several times. No answer."

"That's my next stop," B. said. "Give me the
address."

Stuart wasn't one to sit on his hands in the
meantime. He went to Ali's mail app and began to
scroll through the individual messages and notes
synced from her iPad, which was like following
a trail of virtual bread crumbs recounting Ali's
travels over the past two days. He found names,
numbers, and addresses for Sylvia Sanders, Molly
Handraker, Valerie Stone, and Gemma Ralston.
Among them he found Molly's listing along with a
series of phone numbers.

Stuart paused long enough to try all of them,
including another attempt at Doris Ralston's landline. No one answered any of them. Going through
the saved notes, Stu found a listing for Manning,
Jack and Gloria. The notation for them said only
Palm Springs. There was no accompanying address
or phone number.

Still waiting for B. to call back, Stuart scratched
his head. Then he realized that, in processing messages from Gemma's e-mail account, he might
have passed over Molly Handraker's e-mail address. Within seconds, he was working on accessing her account when a shaken B. Simpson called
him back ten minutes later.

"Bad news," he said, his voice breaking.
"There's been a fire."

"What kind of fire? Where?"

"At the Ralston house. They've put up a police

perimeter, and I'm on the wrong side of it. People are telling me the house is a complete loss."

"What house?" Stu asked, not quite believing what he was hearing.

"Doris Ralston's house!" B. said, his voice thick with despair. "What if Ali's dead, Stu? What if I've lost her?"

"That can't be," Stuart said. "How did it start?"

"I have no idea. Firefighters are still actively involved in fighting it. According to the one guy I did talk to, the roof collapsed. That's only hearsay, because I can't get close enough to see for myself."

"I'm sure she's okay," Stuart said hurriedly. "Just because the house burned down doesn't mean she was inside."

That last bit of reassurance was as much for his own benefit as it was for B.'s. Stuart couldn't handle the idea that Ali Reynolds might have been in mortal danger while he had done nothing but focus on his growing annoyance about her not returning his message.

"Thanks for saying that," B. replied, taking a ragged breath, "but it doesn't look good, does it? If Ali was okay, she would have been in touch with one of us by now." He paused and then added, "What the hell am I going to tell her parents?" There was uncharacteristic panic in B.'s voice.

"Let's not jump to conclusions," Stuart advised, trying to sound calm. "When did the fire start?"

"A neighbor reported seeing smoke and called in the alarm sometime shortly after three. By the time the first engines arrived, the place was fully engulfed. What do we do now, Stu? I'm at a loss. If Ali is dead and this turns out to be arson, whoever set it is guilty of murder."

"When will they know if it's arson or not?" Stuart asked.

"It'll be a while," B. said. "The fire's still too hot and the structure too unstable to send investigators inside, and until they do, we won't know about possible victims. In the meantime, I'm going to call Dave Holman. He may be able to pull some strings to get me inside the perimeter."

"You do that," Stuart said. "I'll see what I can do on this end."

"Wait," B. said. "Something else just occurred to me. When I went to check on the Cayenne, I'm sure I saw security cameras in the parking lot at the Renewal Center. Just because they have cameras doesn't mean they were running at the time, but why don't you see if you can access them. Somebody went to the trouble of dropping Ali's car off there. I'd like to know who did it and when."

"I'm on it," Stuart said.

Because it was the thing most likely to give them a concrete lead, he did that first. Stuart was an old hand at getting inside other people's secure surveillance systems, and this one was no exception. In fact, the system was so ridiculously simple to hack in to that it occurred to Stuart that someone from High Noon should probably talk to them about upgrading. Once he had access to the videos, he used the timing of the fire as a marker and looked at recordings that were time-stamped between two-thirty and three P.M. He soon found what he expected to find.

At 2:46:35 he spotted a vehicle that looked like Ali's Cayenne nosing into the parking lot. It drove past innumerable empty spots before pulling into one that was as distant as possible from the camera's stationary location. The Cayenne was followed by a large black Mercedes, an S550 sedan, with a solo male driver. While Stuart watched, a woman who was clearly not Ali got out of the Cayenne, walked over to the second vehicle, and climbed into the passenger seat. Moments later, the Mercedes exited the parking lot and sped westbound on Lincoln.

Stuart tried enhancing the image enough to read the vehicle license, but it didn't work. He sat there, staring blindly at the computer screen and wondering what to do next. He couldn't dodge the gut feeling that told him Barry Handraker was an important part of whatever was going on. If so, where was the point of contact? The wife? Yes, but did that mean Molly Handraker was an active participant, or was she a victim? Remembering that Molly had worked for battered-women's shelters prior to leaving Minnesota, Stuart suspected he knew the answer. Once the fire department made it into the burned-out house, they would find the charred remains of three victims—Molly; her mother, Doris Ralston; and Ali Reynolds, while Barry Handraker would once again disappear into the ethers.

"Not if I can help it," Stuart muttered under his breath.

That was when he decided to come at the problem from a different angle. He went straight back to Ali's notes and looked up Molly's phone numbers. What he did next was entirely illegal and completely necessary. Within a matter of moments, he was examining not only Molly Handraker's phone records but her mother's. Once the numbers were laid out in front of him, what struck him as odd was the sheer volume of phone calls from Doris Ralston's landline to an unlisted number in Las Vegas. A little more sleuthing disclosed that the landline was located in a unit in Turnberry Towers and bills for that number were being sent to Doris Ralston's Phoenix address.

Stuart was puzzling over what to do with that information when a sudden movement on the iCloud-dedicated computer caught his eye. He watched as a map gradually filled in the blanks on the Find My Device screen. As soon as it finished, he verified the location and then grabbed his phone to call B.

"Guess what," he announced breathlessly. "Ali's iPad just phoned home. It's at the Love's Travel Stop, a truck stop just east of Kingman."

"Kingman," B. echoed. He sounded enormously relieved but puzzled. "What would Ali be doing there?"

"I thought maybe you could tell me."

"No idea," B. replied, "but I've got Dave Holman on the other line. I'm still at the fire. He was trying to get them to let me past the perimeter, but it's not working. Let me call you back."

"Wait," Stuart said. "If Dave's on the line, where is he?"

"At the Sheriff's Department in Prescott. Why?"

"Doris Ralston's son, Chip, is still in the lockup there, isn't he?"

"Yes, he is. Dave told me that once he's off the phone, he's going over to the jail to let Chip know about the fire."

"While he's there, have him ask Chip if he knows who would be staying in his mother's condo in Vegas."

"Anything else?" B. asked.

Still accessing the information from Ali's iPad, Stu switched over to her notes file and scrolled through the most recent items, focusing on the last one—the note containing the information on Jack and Gloria Manning. The time stamp on that note, which Ali had written bare minutes before the arrival of Stu's message about Barry Handraker, meant that the information had to be something she had gleaned from her interview with Molly Handraker.

"Ask Dave to mention the names Jack and Gloria Manning to Chip Ralston. See if he has any idea why those names might have come up this morning when Ali was questioning Molly."

"Will do," B. answered. "What's happening to the iPad?"

"Nothing," Stu answered. "It's in the same spot. But here's one more possible assignment for Dave. I can do it if I have to, but it'll be easier and faster if Dave makes the call for us. Have him check with the DMV to see what vehicles are licensed to Doris Ralston's address on Upper Glen Road. I'm betting one of them will turn out to be that same S550 that followed Ali's Cayenne into the Renewal Center's parking lot. Tell him I need the VIN."

"I'll get back to you," B. said. He sounded more like himself, energized and determined. "Thank you, Stu. At least I have a tiny thread of hope that Ali is alive."

"Just because the iPad's there doesn't mean she is," Stu cautioned.

"It doesn't mean that she isn't, either. But thinking she's still alive and in a vehicle in King-man is better than thinking she's up the street in the charred remains of that house. If she's in King-man, I'm going there, too."

"That's got to be close to two hundred miles from where you are right now," Stu objected.

"Yes, it is, and that's why, while I'm on the phone with Dave, I need you to call a charter company for me," B. said urgently. "Heli-Pros is a helicopter charter outfit based at the FBO at Scottsdale Airport. I've worked with them before. Tell them I'm going to need one of their aircraft fueled and ready to go in forty-five minutes to an hour. Wherever that signal is going, that's where I'm going."

Once B. hung up, Stuart did as he was asked and soon discovered that as far as Heli-Pros was concerned, B. Simpson's name was nothing short of a magic wand. With assurances that a pilot and fully fueled helicopter would be awaiting B.'s ar-rival at the airport, Stuart focused again on the Find My Device screen. Unfortunately, Ali's iPad was no longer visible.

Staring at a stationary picture on the screen was useless. Instead, Stuart returned to his favorite pastime—data mining. He had already succeeded in getting Molly Handraker's telephone billing in-formation. What Stuart needed now was a lot more complicated. He was fully engaged in the project when B. called him back.

"Anything more from Find My Device?" he asked.

"Not so far. I've looked on the cell tower maps, though, and on the far side of Kingman, coverage is spotty. So don't worry. If they're going that way, it may just be that the iPad has moved out of range."

"On Ali's list of devices, there's a phone called Extra. Where's that one?"

"Probably at home in Sedona," B. said. "It's not even turned on."

"Any chance you could stop by Sedona on your way to Kingman and pick it up?"

"I suppose," B. agreed reluctantly. "Are you sure we need another phone? Can't we use mine?"

"No," Stuart insisted. "We need that phone. Tell Leland Brooks to bring it to the airport, and no matter what, don't turn it on. By the way, are you packing?"

"You mean as in carrying a weapon? Not me. Ali's the one with a CWP."

"You'd best be prepared," Stuart warned. "See if Leland Brooks can pick up a sidearm or at least some kind of weapon for you to have on hand. Barry Handraker is evil. If you end up in some kind of confrontation with the guy, it's better to be prepared."

"All right. When I meet up with the pilot, I'll check with him, too. I know from flying with them in the past that some of their guys are ex–Special Forces. In the meantime, here's the rest of the information you wanted. Chip Ralston's mother does own an S550. Here's the VIN." As B. read off the number, Stuart jotted it down. "She also owns a seafrost-green 2006 Jaguar XJ8 L. According to Chip, Jack and Gloria Manning were once good friends with the Ralstons. Gloria died two years ago, and Chip thinks Jack may have remarried. He has no idea why someone would have mentioned them to Ali. He also has no idea who might be living in his mother's condo in Turnberry Towers.

As far as he knew, the unit was unoccupied. His father bought it as an estate tax dodge and didn't live long enough to use it."

Stuart jotted a note, giving himself yet another security surveillance system to target.

"Dave put in a call to the Mohave County Sheriff's Office," B. went on, "but they weren't the least bit helpful. All we have for sure is an iPad that's somewhere it shouldn't be, and the department's official position is that they don't have the personnel to go chasing after someone's stolen electronic equipment, especially since the iPad disappeared from one jurisdiction, Dave is from a second, and the iPad is in a third. Dave tried to get them to put out a BOLO on the S550. They nixed that, too. Until we get something solid on the fire—until somebody from Phoenix PD says for sure it's arson or fatality arson—nobody's lifting a finger. So Dave's going to stay on that problem. Right now they're talking warrants. Dave's our best bet for getting a statewide APB out on that S550."

"How long will that take?"

"Who knows?" B. growled. "Could as well be forever. Whoever's running the show there right now doesn't want to risk the possibility of one of those high-speed chases. We all know how dangerous *those* can be."

Stu heard the sarcasm in B.'s voice. "Those sound a lot like weasel words to me," he observed.

"Of course they're weasel words," B. agreed. "But just because Phoenix PD is standing around with their politically correct thumbs up their butts doesn't mean you and I have to."

Stu got the unspoken message loud and clear. B. was telling him that it was time for him to unleash his considerable hacking skills, knowing full well that most of what he found would never hold up in a court of law.

"In other words, when it comes to saving Ali's bacon, we're it," Stu said.

"For the time being," B. said. "At least until Dave jars loose that APB. My hope is that once he does, we'll be able to point responding officers in the right direction."

"With any kind of luck, we'll be able to do far more than point. We'll be able to give them an exact location. That's where the phone comes in."

"We'll have the phone with us. How's that going to help us?"

"I'll be using someone else's phone to find them. Once we locate Ali, that phone will need to be turned on and on her person. I don't care where you put it. It can be in her bra or her panties, for all I care. But she's got to have it with her so we can claim that's how we found her."

"Which gives us plausible deniability," B. concluded.

"Exactly," Stuart said, suppressing a grin. "That's the name of the game."

"Mr. Ramey," B. said, "you are a gem, and I'm on my way to collect that phone."

28

Ali awakened in the dark. She was cold and lying on her side in a moving vehicle. She could feel rough carpeting under her cheek and against her nose. She was crammed into a space that was far too small for her five-ten frame. One arm was locked under her body; her legs were drawn up into a fetal position. When she tried to straighten them, she couldn't. There was no room to stretch out or even move from her side to a more comfortable position. Something behind her—luggage or boxes or both—made it impossible for her to move so much as an inch, even though her whole body was screaming for relief.

Ali had no idea how she had come to be there. She tried to remember where she had been and what she had been doing. She could assemble only a few broken pieces of memory. It played in an endless loop like an old newsreel, jagged and jerky. She made one futile effort to yell for help, but that came to nothing. The roar of passing freeway traffic, mostly trucks, drowned out everything. Knowing no one could have heard her, she didn't bother expending the energy to shout again.

She shut her eyes to close out the artificial darkness, hoping that would help focus her mind and take her back to what had happened before she landed in this trunk. Someone in a trunk. Those words lodged in her brain; it seemed as though they were important and should mean something to her. Had this happened to her before, or had it happened to someone else? No matter how she tried, soon everything but the crammed trunk and the feel of scratchy carpet on her face was shrouded in a wad of thick, cottony mental fog.

She lay there for a long time, drifting between waking and sleeping and trying to put the odd fragments of memory into some kind of reasonable order. She remembered a house—a big house with wooden floors. She remembered seeing a huge fireplace with a painting over it. The woman in the picture had been wearing a bright blue evening dress—an old-fashioned evening dress, something from the fifties or maybe the sixties. Who was she? Where was she? Was she someone Ali knew? Did she have something to do with a woman in a trunk?

The more Ali tried to force order out of chaos, the more the images slipped away from her. It was like grasping at straws.

Straws. That word caught in her head and spun there like a piece of dried grass whirling in an eddy in a rocky mountain stream. What kind of straw was it? One of those that folded over, like in a hospital room? A tall thick one, like from a DQ milk shake? A tiny thin one that might show up in a cocktail from a bar? Or was it maybe the other kind of straw, like in *The Three Little Pigs:* I'll huff and I'll puff and I'll blow your house in!

Then, as suddenly as the word had landed in her brain, the whole idea of straw drifted away into nothingness. A little later, she realized dimly that the car had stopped. It occurred to her that perhaps she should try to do something about that—pound on the trunk lid or scream her head off—but she couldn't bring herself to do either one. Lulled by a strange listlessness that was more hopelessness than anything, she fell back into a sleep that offered some blessed relief from the waking nightmare of being locked in a trunk.

29

Lucy Ramirez noticed the old woman in the far corner of the restaurant as soon as she came on duty at three o'clock for her four-hour afternoon shift at the Burger King in Gila Bend, where she worked as head cashier. The old woman, who looked to be years younger than Nana, Lucy's grandmother, sat quietly in the booth, thumbing through a photo album. She seemed to be waiting for someone to bring her an order from the serving line. The problem was, no customers were waiting in the serving line.

"What about the woman in the corner?" Lucy asked Rosemary, who was closing out her register.

"No idea," Rosemary replied. "She showed up about an hour ago. An Indian guy from the reservation dropped her off. She got out of his pickup and came inside alone. I guess she's waiting for someone."

Lucy settled in to work. As a single mother with three kids to support, she was grateful to have any job at all in a place like Gila Bend, where jobs were scarce. She had come back home after her divorce because she and her kids were able to live rent-free in her grandmother's single-wide mobile home. Lucy was also grateful that Nana was willing to look after the kids once they got out of school in the afternoon. If she'd had to pay for a babysitter out of her paltry weekly paychecks, there wouldn't have been any point in working.

Lucy had given up fighting to get money from Sam, her deadbeat ex, who had never paid so much as a single dime of court-ordered child support. The state had tried to go after him, but when Sam did bother to work, it was usually for cash under the table, so there was no paycheck to garnish. Since he didn't mess around with bank accounts, either, the state couldn't collect.

That was the bad news, but things were beginning to change for the better. Lucy had a new boyfriend. Tommy Grayson was a really nice guy who swore he loved her and seemed to love her kids as well. He made decent money working as a guard in the prison just up the road. He had a house that was way better than Nana's single-wide. If she moved in with Tommy, not only would the kids be able to go to the same school, they'd be only a few miles from Nana.

In the two years since Lucy's divorce, Tommy Grayson was her first serious relationship. And where had she met him? In the order line, of course. A Whopper Full Meal Deal, hold the mayo, and a Diet Coke. Tommy was another reason Lucy was grateful for her job. It even seemed possible that someday he would get around to popping the question. There was no doubt in Lucy's mind that she would say yes.

When Lucy finished working through her

first batch of arriving customers, the old lady was still there, sitting and studying the photo album with intense concentration. She was there later, after the minor afternoon rush of kids once school got out. When things slowed down and Lucy went out to bus tables and pick up trash, the woman was still sitting there, paging through the book. Approaching the table, Lucy could see it was a wedding album. One glimpse of the beautiful bride and the handsome tux-clad groom was enough to make Lucy's mouth water. It looked like a fairy-tale wedding, the kind Lucy had always wanted.

"Your daughter's wedding?" Lucy asked when the old woman looked up and noticed her.

"Oh, no, not my daughter's," she said. "My son's."

Lucy was about to leave the woman to her book when she spotted the colorful metal cane propped next to the woman on the bench seat. "Are you all right?" Lucy asked.

The woman seemed momentarily mystified. "Oh, yes," she said finally. "I'm just fine. I'm waiting for my husband, James. I think he went into the restroom. I'm sure he'll be out in a minute."

It didn't seem possible that someone could have been in the men's restroom that long, but maybe something had happened to the old guy. If he was as old as the woman, maybe he was frail and sick and had passed out in one of the stalls. Once Lucy got back to the counter, she asked one of the cooks to check the men's restroom, just in case.

"Nobody's in there," he reported. "No one at all."

Lucy went back over to the woman in the booth. "Can I get you something?"

"A cup of coffee would be very nice," the woman said. Then she looked around the booth anxiously. "But I don't see my purse. Do you?"

Lucy looked. There was no purse. "I don't see it," she said. "Did you maybe leave it in your car?"

The woman frowned. "I might have."

"What kind of car?" Lucy asked. "What color?"

"The Jag," the woman said. "It's green."

Lucy went outside and checked the parking lot. There were two white pickup trucks and a ratty old Jeep Cherokee. There were no Jaguars in sight, and no green cars, either.

Back inside, Lucy poured a cup of coffee from the machine behind the counter, then delivered it to the woman in the corner booth. "Cream and sugar?" she asked, setting it down in front of the woman.

"No, black is fine, but I can't possibly take this. I don't have any money. James could pay—I'm sure he will pay—but I don't know where he went."

"Don't worry about it," Lucy said. "Are you hungry? Can I bring you something?"

"A hamburger would be nice," the woman said. "One of the small ones."

Nodding, Lucy went back to the counter and ordered a Whopper Junior.

"What do you think you're doing?" Lucy's manager asked when he saw her taking money from her own pocket and putting it into the till, enough to cover the burger and the senior coffee. In Lucy's opinion, Richard Marino was a jerk, but she didn't dare cross him if she wanted to keep her job.

"That poor lady's hungry," Lucy told him. "She lost her purse, and she's got no money."

"Likely story," Richard said sarcastically. "So what are you, friggin' Mother Teresa?"

"She reminds me of my grandmother," Lucy said. "If Nana was here, broke and hungry, I hope someone would help her." With that and a toss of her heavy black braids, she went out to the woman's booth to deliver the food.

"I'm Lucy," she announced, setting the tray down on the table in front of the old woman. "Lucy Ramirez."

"Glad to meet you, Lucy," the woman said with a smile. She moved the book aside to make room for the tray. "I'm Doris," she said. "Doris Ralston. James and I are on our way to see some friends in Palm Springs."

Lucy nodded and started to walk away.

"Wait," Doris said. "I need to pay you for that." Once again she searched the booth, frantically looking for a purse Lucy already knew was no-where to be found. Obviously, Doris had already forgotten it was missing.

"Don't worry about it," Lucy said gently. "This is on me. You've been here for quite a while, and I haven't seen anyone else sitting here. Are you sure your husband came to the restaurant with you? Someone told me a man in a pickup dropped you off."

"Oh, no. I wouldn't be riding around in a pickup. I've never been in one of those in my life. And of course James is here," Doris declared. "Where else would he be?"

A new set of customers—three separate couples of gray-haired retirees, traveling in a caravan of RVs—came in, talking and laughing. With a glance at Richard's disapproving scowl, Lucy left Doris to eat her Whopper Junior in peace and hurried back to the register. At some point in the course of the next hour, Doris got up and limped to the bathroom. When she came out, she stood at the end of the corridor and looked around the restaurant as if unsure where to go.

"You're over there, Doris," Lucy said, pointing. "In the corner booth."

Doris smiled at her. "Thank you."

Richard sidled up behind Lucy as Doris returned to her booth. "What's the matter with her?" he asked. "Is she nuts? We should call the cops."

"Leave her be," Lucy said. "She's not bothering anyone."

When Richard went outside for a cigarette break during the next lull, Lucy went to fill the ice machine, then back over to Doris's booth. "Where do you live?" she asked.

"Phoenix," Doris said at once. "You'd like it. It's a lovely place, right next to the mountains."

"If you're from Phoenix and you're going to Palm Springs, what are you doing here?" Lucy asked. "Why didn't you stay on I-10?"

Doris frowned. "You'll have to ask James about that," she said. "He's the one who was driving. But where is he? It seems like he's been gone a long time."

"Don't worry," Lucy assured her. "You stay right here. I get off work in another hour, then we'll see about getting you a ride back home."

Doris's expression darkened. "I'm not sure I want to go back. Not if he's there."

"He who? Your husband?"

"Oh, no, not James. He's fine," Doris said. "Barry's

the one I don't like. I don't trust him. I think he stole my necklace."

"Don't worry about any of that right now," Lucy said. "You just sit here and wait for me. Once I get off work, we'll sort it all out."

"What does that mean?" Richard asked when Lucy returned to her register. He had evidently been listening. "Are you planning on taking her home with you like she's some kind of stray dog?"

"No," Lucy said. "I called Tommy and Nana on my break. Nana will look after the kids while Tommy and I figure out a way to take Doris home."

"Doris," Richard sneered. "So now you're on a first-name basis?"

You could be, too, Lucy thought, *but it's never gonna happen.*

Five minutes before Lucy's shift ended, Tommy showed up and ordered his usual. "Where is she?" he asked.

"Over in the corner," Lucy said, swiping his card. "Her name is Doris. Her husband's name is James."

"Yes," he said, "and she lives on Upper Glen Road in Phoenix. At least she used to."

"How do you know where she lives?" Lucy demanded.

"Where she used to live," Tommy corrected. "I know about it because I've got a friend who's a dispatcher for the Arizona Highway Patrol. About an hour ago, a light green Jaguar was reported abandoned near a rest area on I-8. It was out of gas, and Doris Ralston's purse was found inside. They're sending a patrol officer here to pick her up. He should be here any minute."

"Wait," Lucy said, outraged. "You mean they're going to arrest her? The poor woman hasn't done anything wrong. She's just confused."

"She may be confused," Tommy said, "but she's also really, really lucky."

"Why?"

"Because she's still alive. Somebody burned her house down earlier this afternoon," Tommy said. "Until I called in the report about your lost friend being at the Burger King in Gila Bend, everybody thought she was dead."

"Oh my God!" Lucy exclaimed. "That's what she said!"

"What did she say?"

"She told me she was afraid of someone. That he scared her. That he had stolen something that belonged to her. She also mentioned that her husband, James, was supposedly driving the car. Where's he?"

"Maybe he's the guy who set the fire," Tommy suggested.

"No," Lucy said. "I don't think so. It's the other guy she's scared of. She's not afraid of James."

"If somebody burned down her house," Tommy said, "it sounds to me like she had good reason to be afraid."

Nodding, Lucy turned back to the window, where she picked up Tommy's order and set it on a tray. Then she caught the backup cashier's eye. "Hey," she said. "Take over for me for a minute, would you?"

Ignoring Richard Marino's looming objection, Lucy took the tray and led Tommy to the corner booth, where Doris was once again paging through photographs.

"Hey, Doris," she said, "this is my boyfriend, Tommy. If you don't mind, he'd like to sit with you for a little while. Maybe you could tell him about your day."

"I suppose that would be all right," Doris said, "but if James comes back . . ."

"Tommy will move, of course," Lucy said, "but right now he has some good news. The Arizona Highway Patrol found your car. It was on the freeway, out of gas."

Doris looked devastated. "You mean James wasn't there?"

"Just talk to the officer when he gets here," Lucy said reassuringly. "Tommy will look after you until he does. Don't worry. We'll be able to help find your husband. I'm sure he can't have gone far."

30

Stuart had already launched into the hard part of the job. When B. called, Stu was well into the process of hacking into Molly's cell phone provider. Once B. gave him the S550's VIN, Stu set aside his triangulation effort and concentrated on the Mercedes.

Computerized records being what they were, he was easily able to track down the original bill of sale for Doris Ralston's S550. As Stu hoped, at the time James Ralston purchased the vehicle, he also signed a yearlong contract with Prestige Auto Concierge Service, which had long since lapsed.

Stuart refrained from high-fiving himself. He had dealt with the company before. In fact, he had designed some of their anti-hacking security measures, so it was easy for him to find an untraceable back-door entry into their servers and backup servers, and he did so with no concern that they'd be able to detect his unauthorized entry.

Within minutes, he had updated the records of the S550's service account, bringing the billing up to current status. For good measure, he changed the name of the account from James Ralston to Doris Ralston, backdating the order to two months ago, citing the receipt of James Ralston's actual death certificate as the reason for the billing change.

Stuart was tempted to give the updated account a new password. He favored something like MMWRUS, which would have been short for "Minnesota's Most Wanted Are Us." Instead, he left James Ralston's original password. As far as Stu was concerned, Jimmyjim wasn't a particularly secure password, but that wasn't his problem. What made him smile was his newly acquired ability to see that Doris Ralston's S550 was moving steadily west on Arizona Highway 68 west.

With his silver bullet properly locked and loaded, Stuart exited Prestige's system and returned to the task at hand, infiltrating Molly Handraker's cell phone provider. Within minutes, he succeeded. Once he had the first cell triangulation ping, Stuart Ramey also had his answer. Molly Handraker's cell phone, and most likely Ali's iPad, were in the S550.

"Okay," Stu said, watching the cell phone screen. "I've just located Doris Ralston's vehicle and Molly's cell phone. They just turned off Arizona Highway 68 west, northbound on Davis Dam Road."

"All right." B. was off the line for a moment while he conferred with someone else. "Okay," he said, speaking to Stuart. "The pilot says we're still about twenty minutes out. What's the program?"

"I'll keep monitoring their movements. Call me again when you're at Davis Dam Road. Above Cabin Site Road, there's a tangle of unnamed dirt roads that lead to boat launches; I'll probably need to help guide you in. When I believe you're close

enough, I'm going to use Prestige's auto theft recovery system to shut down that Mercedes. Once
they're stopped dead, it's up to you. Do you want
me to call in law enforcement?"

"We'll get back to you on that," B. said.

Stuart sat back, closed his eyes, and uttered a
silent but fervent prayer—that Ali would be there,
that she'd be alive, that they'd be able to save
her. If none of those things turned out to be true,
Stuart didn't think he'd ever be able to face himself
in the mirror again. He wouldn't be able to face
B. Simpson, either.

To keep himself occupied, he put himself back
to work. Within minutes he had hacked his way in
to the surveillance cameras at Turnberry Towers.
There were dozens of them, but he focused on
the ones that opened from the elevators into the
various parking garage levels. Once he had those
cameras isolated, he called up the related recordings. After inserting Barry Handraker's mug shots
into a beta facial recognition program that High
Noon Enterprises had been testing, he turned the
program loose on the tapes.

Scanning the tapes manually would have taken
days. The new program accomplished the goal
within minutes. In a section of tape dated Sunday
evening at 06:28:31, Stuart found Barry Handraker
exiting the elevator on level three of the parking
garage. He was pulling a single piece of roll-aboard
luggage. Two minutes later, another camera located at the parking garage entrance showed him
driving an S550 with Arizona plates.

"I've got you, you scumbag," Stuart said aloud
to the monitor. Not only had Barry Handraker

been living in Doris Ralston's condo, he had evidently been using her vehicle.

Stuart had every expectation that his silver bullet was going to work, but just in case it didn't, he wanted to make sure he had backup. To that end, he used an untraceable VOIP connection to send a copy of the Turnberry Towers tape to the *Minnesota's Most Wanted* website. If Barry managed to slip through the first trap, he probably wouldn't be as lucky with the professionals from the Las Vegas Police Department. They had plenty of practice in taking down fugitives.

31

When Ali's eyes blinked open again, more time had passed, although she couldn't guess how much. She noticed that the darkness wasn't as complete as it had seemed before. Her moving prison was suffused in a strange green glow. Did that mean it was night? She didn't know. Some time ago, long before she found herself locked in this prison, it had been morning. She had been somewhere—Phoenix, maybe?—and on her way to see someone, driving under a clear blue sky. She remembered being somewhere that had seemed like a bar, and a guy with a mustache who had been angry about something. Maybe he was the one who had locked her in here. Maybe he was the one who was driving her God knows where.

She remembered someone else—had that been earlier than the bar or later? She didn't know. A woman who seemed to be walking away from Ali, striding off across a parking lot. Concentrating, Ali could almost sort out the woman's features but not her name. What was it? Susan, maybe, or Sally or Cynthia? Whatever her name was, part of the time she had been scared and part of the time angry, but she was worried about someone else. Her child, a son. The kid was in some kind of trouble—trouble that had something to do with a box. Suddenly, for no reason Ali could imagine, the lyrics to a song from *Fiorello!* were running unchecked through her head:

> *A little tin box*
> *A little tin box*
> *That a little tin key unlocks.*

What was that all about? As the song went back out of her head, Ali realized she was no longer hearing the roar of traffic from outside. Yes, there were occasional vehicles coming and going, but they sounded more like cars than trucks. There was pavement under the tires, but they were no longer traveling on a freeway. They were on a less traveled road.

As Ali attempted to assemble the pieces, her heart filled with dread: They were on a less traveled road to some deserted corner of the desert. It might be night. She was being driven there by someone evil who, for reasons she didn't understand, had locked her in a trunk. When they got wherever they were going, she was going to die, because she remembered that much. That was what had happened to the other woman, the one in the trunk, and this was the same thing. The person driving the car had killed that other woman—what was her name? Jan. Gina. Jill. No matter how hard she tried, she couldn't dredge it up.

This time, much as she wanted to, Ali didn't allow herself to fall back asleep. She willed herself to fight through the mental fog—to remember whatever it was that she didn't want to forget. She twisted her cramping body and managed to free the arm that had been trapped. As circulation returned to her aching limb, Ali used the painful waves of needles and pins as a reminder that she was alive.

The car turned sharply to the right, thumping off the pavement and onto something much rougher. A dirt track, maybe? If that was the case, they were probably getting closer to stopping, getting closer to the end—of everything she held dear.

Her mind was filled with an endless parade of folks she'd never see again if she were dead. These were the beloved people she had left behind that day, or even the day before, without holding them close and saying a proper goodbye. B., of course, and then her parents; Chris and Athena; Colin and Colleen. It pained her to think that her grandchildren most likely wouldn't remember anything at all about her except that she had been hauled off in a trunk and murdered. And then there was Leland Brooks. What would happen to him?

It was remembering all those people that did the trick, that made her want to go on living. That made her refuse to give up.

"I may die," Ali Reynolds said aloud in the moving darkness, "but I sure as hell won't go out without a fight!"

32

When the car lurched to a hard stop, the load of luggage behind Ali shifted, slamming her forward and mashing her face into the carpet-covered wall in front of her. The abrupt change of position sent a whole new agony of needles and pins powering through her legs and feet and a new awareness through her brain.

She had been at Doris Ralston's house. A man had come into the room unannounced, a man who had to be Molly Handraker's husband. Those were the only connections she had managed to make when she heard shouting from somewhere outside the vehicle—two voices, a man and a woman's, screaming.

"What's wrong?"

"The damned thing just stopped!"

"Can't you start it again?" Ali recognized Molly's voice.

"No, I can't start it again. Since when am I a damned mechanic?"

"What are we going to do?" Molly sounded desperate and close to tears.

"We're going to finish this thing once and for all."

"Why did we have to bring her all the way out here? Why couldn't we just—"

"Because I said so," he told her. "Now shut up."

For all the bluster in the man's voice, Ali detected what she hoped was a hint of panic. The car's breakdown wasn't part of his plan, whatever that plan might be. While they figured out how to cope with the crisis, there was a chance they'd make a mistake of some kind, one that might give Ali an opportunity to escape.

Waiting for the trunk to open, she tried to steel herself for whatever would come. She had a pretty good idea what it would be. As her brain cleared, she remembered more of what had gone on. That other woman had been stabbed before she was dumped out in the desert and left to die.

If that was what was going on here, what was Ali's best tactic? Would the element of surprise help if she shot up and out the moment the trunk lid opened, like some kind of enraged jack-in-the-box? Even though that idea was initially appealing, she concluded that there were far too many unknowns. The worst of those was whether she would be able to trust her own body. Yes, circulation had returned to her trapped extremities, but they had been held immobile for so long, would they work as she commanded them? Ali had some faith in her ability as a sprinter, but what if her legs didn't respond and she fell to the ground and flopped there, helpless as a landed fish?

By the time the trunk lid thumped open and the greenish glow disappeared, Ali had made a decision: She would lie perfectly still and wait. Staring at the carpet directly in front of her, she was amazed to see that she could make out individual fibers. She had spent hours confined in the blackness of her moving prison. Over time her eyes had adjusted to the almost total darkness. Now the mere presence of starlight seemed close to daylight for her light-starved vision. If her opponent's eyes were coping with the loss of the car's headlights, that might give Ali a small advantage.

Maybe.

"While you get your crap out of the car, I'll check on the plane," the man continued. "With the car broken down, I'll have to see if they can send someone out to pick us up."

"Are you kidding? Out here in the middle of nowhere?"

"Depends on how much we're willing to pay," the man muttered. "So like I said, get that junk out of the trunk. We need to get rid of her."

Ali had known all along that would be the most likely endgame. Still, hearing the words said aloud almost took her breath away. She listened as his heavy footsteps crunched away from the vehicle. When he stopped moving, she heard the indistinct mumbling of him talking on the phone. Moments later, the pressure on Ali's back eased a little as Molly began unpacking the trunk, as she'd been ordered to do, and removing the obstacles that had kept Ali confined to the front of the trunk.

When the last item was removed, it took an act of will on Ali's part to keep her hand from straying to the holster in search of her Glock. She didn't dare risk it. Instead, with her heart pounding in her chest, Ali forced herself to remain utterly still, playing possum in hopes of convincing Molly that she was helpless and lost in a drug-induced fog. Ali needed the element of surprise on her side. When she mounted her attack, it would work only if Molly hadn't seen it coming.

Finished unloading, Molly stood at the back of the car. The task had taken its toll. Ali listened to Molly's labored breathing, all the while keeping her own eyes shut and her breathing slow and even.

"Okay," Molly called. "Everything's out but her. What now?"

"Get her out, too," Barry said. "I'll be there to help in a minute."

Ali knew this was it. If she were to have any chance of getting away, she had to do it now, while she was dealing with Molly alone. Once Barry finished with his lengthy telephone negotiation, he would come to help. Then it would be two against one and too late.

Molly hesitated for another few moments. In the silence, Ali heard the distant rumble of the man's voice and maybe something else, too, but before she could identify the new sound, Molly reached into the trunk and used both hands to grasp Ali's shoulders. Grunting with effort, Molly flipped Ali over and dragged her a few short inches toward her. Ali concentrated on being unresisting deadweight. She kept her eyes shut, kept her limbs limp and pliable. She had no doubt that her life depended on the subterfuge. Barry Handraker might be armed and dangerous, but he wasn't the only one. Molly hadn't hesitated to draw a weapon the other night, and Ali suspected she would do so again with the smallest amount of provocation.

Grunting and pulling, Molly managed to shift

Ali's body a few inches, then she stopped. "Barry, she's too heavy," she called over her shoulder. "I need some help here."

Ali could tell from the sound of Molly's voice that she had turned in Barry's direction to call to him. Taking full advantage of the momentary distraction, Ali quietly straightened her legs. The cramping in her calves nearly took her breath away, but even if her legs weren't ready to function properly, Ali knew now was the time. She had to make her move while Molly was alone.

"What the hell's that noise?" Molly demanded. "It sounds like a helicopter."

Ali heard it, too, the distant thwack of rotating helicopter blades. Suspecting Molly was searching the surrounding sky for the aircraft, Ali opened her eyes. Molly's back was turned. She was staring off into the distance. "Barry, do you hear that?"

Holding her breath, Ali turned back onto her belly. Raising herself into a half crouch, she waited for Molly to turn toward her once more. When it happened, Ali was ready. Throwing all her weight behind a karate chop, Ali caught Molly in the side of the neck. Ali had hoped to catch her full in the throat, but the blow had enough force to send the other woman sprawling.

The moment Molly fell, Ali leaped out of the trunk. She had been right to worry about her legs. She hit the ground hard, landing on a bed of sharp rocks that bit into the soles of her bare feet. She paused in midflight, looking left and right. The car was parked in a rough clearing that fell sharply downhill, where the ground appeared to end in utter blackness that Ali took to be water. To the right, the same clearing ran uphill until it gave way to scattered brush and what looked like a series of low-lying hills.

Stripped of shoes in that rugged terrain, outgunned and alone, Ali could have given up, but she didn't. Instead, realizing she needed to give her legs some time before they would work, she dove for cover, scrambling under the car and wriggling forward under it commando-style.

"Barry!" Molly screamed. "Come quick. She's getting away."

"My God, woman," he demanded. "What's the matter with you?"

Ali thought she might get away clean, but when she shot out from under the front end of the car, Barry was waiting for her, holding a weapon Ali suspected was her own Glock.

"Not so fast, bitch!" he growled. "You're not going anywhere."

With the weapon in one hand, he grabbed the collar of Ali's jacket with the other and began hauling her to her feet. Ali realized she might have one more chance. She waited until both of her feet were firmly on the ground, then she straightened up, butting him under the chin so hard that she saw stars. She heard his teeth slam together as she knocked him off balance. When he let go of her and staggered backward, Ali darted away, running uphill, away from the water and toward the desert.

Her feet screamed in agony as she raced through the rock-strewn, eerily starlit landscape. Dreading the sound of bullets whistling past, Ali spotted a low-lying ridge of rock and dirt that looked to have been bladed away to clear a space that was evidently some kind of boat launch. She dove for that, throwing herself over the ridge and rolling down the other side. She was airborne when she saw her mistake.

The ditch on the other side of the ridge glittered with the debris of a thousand broken beer bottles. As she rolled, pieces of jagged glass sliced into her body. When she came to rest, she could hear someone running toward her on the other side of the ridge. Desperate for a weapon, she looked for a suitable rock. She found something far better. Inches from her hand lay the remains of a broken beer bottle. The neck was intact. The body was a ring of jagged glass.

A broken bottle isn't much, Ali thought as her fingers closed around what she hoped would be a lethal weapon, *but it's more than I had before.*

She lay waiting, and Molly didn't disappoint. She topped the ridge of dirt, drawn weapon in hand. Convinced that Ali was still running, Molly made the mistake of looking off into the distance. Misjudging her footing, she tumbled into the ditch. As she landed, the gun flew out of her hands while she came to rest just beyond Ali.

This was hand-to-hand combat, and Ali didn't hesitate. Closing her fingers around the glass, she jammed the bottle with everything she had into the top of Molly's thigh, then grabbed up the fallen gun and took off into the desert while Molly writhed on the ground and shrieked in pain.

A bullet that was far too close ricocheted off a rock three feet away from Ali as she dove for cover again, this time behind a scraggly bush. Once she was behind it, she slithered away on the ground until she settled behind a nearby boulder, coming to rest a good ten yards to the right from where Barry would have seen her last. Crouching there, bruised and bleeding, she was grateful to have Molly's weapon in her hand. It was a lightweight Kahr PM9. The nine-millimeter semi-automatic wasn't a handgun Ali had ever used, but it would do, and she was a good marksman.

She could see Barry coming toward her, easing his way up over the ridge. Ali held her fire. Ali judged him to be too far away to risk a shot. She'd have to wait. Breathing deeply, she concentrated on stilling her mind and calming herself.

He came up on the far side of the ridge, crossing it at almost the same place where Molly lay in the ditch. She had given up screaming in favor of whimpering. "Help me," she begged. "Please. You've got to, or I'll end up bleeding to death."

He paused and looked down at her. What happened next shocked Ali Reynolds beyond anything she had ever seen in her life. He simply aimed his weapon full at his wife's face and pulled the trigger.

Ali had already known this was life or death, but she hadn't understood the depth of Barry Handraker's cold-blooded ruthlessness. Now she did, and she realized with a chill that he was coming after her next. She felt a momentary temptation to flee again, to try to put some distance between herself and the murderous thug, but she knew that running offered only the illusion of safety. She was barefoot. He was not. If she ran, he would pursue her to the bitter end. With this boulder as her protection, Ali knew she was far better off standing her ground.

Barry walked forward, leaving Molly dead in the ditch without so much as a backward glance. He came after Ali with the same kind of single-minded concentration. In the end, it was that total focus that did him in, along with the sound of that fatal gunshot reverberating in his ears.

When Ali saw the ghostly figure rise up out of the ditch behind him, she was puzzled at first. Who was this person? Where had he come from? Or was it Molly? Had she somehow survived and followed him?

Gradually, the second figure closed the distance, moving with a careful stealth that allowed him to go both unnoticed and unheard. His right hand held an upraised weapon, a club of some kind. The pursuer was only a few feet away when something must have warned Barry. He half turned. As he did so, the club in the other man's hand swung around and caught him in the back of the head. Barry stumbled forward half a step and then crumpled to the ground.

Without knowing the identity of her rescuer, Ali stayed where she was. Perhaps it wasn't a rescuer at all but another member of a gang of crooks, bad guys who were busy turning on one another. Far in the background, Ali heard another sound or, rather, two other sounds—the distant wail of an approaching siren, and again the heavy thwack of a helicopter rotor. With those sounds filling up her ears, it took her a moment to recognize the familiar voice calling to her.

"Madame Reynolds, where are you?" There was no mistaking Leland Brooks's distinctive voice. Leaning down, he appeared to pick up Barry's weapon and pocket it; then he called to her again. "Please show yourself, Madame, and let me know you're all right."

Dumbfounded, Ali rose up from behind her boulder and stumbled toward him. This time, if rocks cut into her feet as she sprinted across the clearing, she didn't notice. Moments later, she had her arms wrapped around the old man, hugging him close and weeping unashamedly into his shoulder.

"Are you hurt?"

"No, no," she blubbered. "Well, maybe a little, but how did you find us? How did you get here? And how did you do that? Is he dead?"

Leland held her at arm's length as if not trusting her words and needing the reassurance of seeing for himself that she wasn't injured. "He's not dead," Leland said at last, "but I fear he's going to wish he were."

"Did you see what he did? He killed her," Ali said. "He shot her right in the face!"

Leland nodded. "I know," he said, "and I did see it."

By then, he was reaching into the pocket of his pants. Pulling something out, he handed it to her. "Here," he said. "Wipe this down to remove my prints, then turn it on and put it somewhere on your person."

Ali looked down. She was holding an iPhone. Even in the starlight, she could make out the bright red nail-polish E she had written in the upper corner of the glass face. It was the phone she had given her mother to use during the campaign. She had designated it EXTRA.

"Why?" she asked.

"Because we need a way of having found you that won't reflect badly on Mr. Ramey and Mr. Simpson. I'm afraid some of their methods may have been slightly beyond the pale."

Without further argument, Ali did as she'd been

told. Once the phone was wiped clean and turned on, she stuck it safely in her bra.

Leland nodded in satisfaction. "Good," he said.

"You still haven't told me how you managed to take him down like that," Ali said.

"I had to hit him," he said with a shrug. "With you out there hiding in the dark, I couldn't risk taking a shot."

"I saw you sneak up on him. It was impressive," Ali said wonderingly. "He never saw you coming."

"I should think not," Leland said. "They may have used me as a cook, but I was trained to be a Royal Marine. You know what they say. Once a Marine, always a Marine."

On the ground beside them, Barry Handraker groaned.

"Oh, dear," Leland said. "He seems to be coming around. Fortunately, I happen to have just the thing."

Reaching into his pocket, he pulled out a roll of duct tape. "This is almost empty," he said, "but I believe there's enough there to do the trick. If you don't mind, I'll keep the gun on him while you do the honors."

Before Barry managed to come all the way around, Ali knelt down and secured his hands behind his back. Intent on her task, she was aware that a helicopter was circling overhead, blowing clouds of dust everywhere. She was relieved when it rose up and flew off in another direction, heading back toward the road, where it landed on the far side of the crippled Mercedes.

Seconds later, B. was running toward her, a phone pressed to his ear as he ran. "Yes, yes, Stuart!" he was saying into the phone. "I can see her now. We've got her. She's alive. She's okay, and so is Leland!"

The next thing Ali knew, she was in B.'s arms, and they were both crying like babies. "They gave me something," she sobbed, "some drug that knocked me out completely. Then they locked me in the trunk."

"Sounds like the same thing that happened to Gemma."

Ali nodded. "It was the same thing, done by the same people, and in the same way, and I believe I know why. Doris noticed that one of her necklaces went missing. Gemma was supposed to go to the house on Tuesday morning to help look for it. Since she was murdered before she had a chance, I'm guessing that necklace isn't the only thing missing from Doris Ralston's house."

"It's far worse than that," B. said quietly. "The whole house is missing. It burned to the ground earlier this afternoon."

Ali's jaw dropped. "No!" she said in horror. "It's completely gone?"

"Completely."

"What about Doris?"

B. bit his lip before he answered. "I'm afraid she's missing, too," he said. "Given what we've seen here tonight, I'd say missing and presumed dead."

33

When the first Mohave County deputy showed up at the crime scene, it was immediately clear to everyone that they were in for a very long night. An ambulance was summoned to take Barry Handraker to the hospital in Bullhead City to be checked out for a possible concussion; he went in handcuffs and under a police guard.

While homicide detectives were being summoned to the scene from Kingman, some forty miles away, yet another ambulance was sent on Ali's behalf. The EMT who examined the cuts and scratches on her bloody feet urged a trip to the ER for her, too. Ali tried to object, but she was overruled by B. and Leland acting in accord.

"You're going, and I'm going," B. said in a tone that brooked no objection. "Leland can stay here and talk to the cops. I've already talked to the helicopter pilot. I'm sending him back to pick up Dave Holman. It would take him three hours to drive. This is his case. We need him here sooner than three hours."

Once they reached the ER, they were in for

an almost two-hour wait before they could see the doctor. Ali used the time to call home. First she told the story—as much of it as she could remember—to Chris and Athena. Then she had to turn around and repeat the whole thing to her parents. Chris and Athena generally told her, "Way to go!" Her parents fussed and fumed and said they wished she wouldn't keep putting herself in danger.

When the ER doctor finally showed up, she examined and disinfected the cuts on Ali's feet and arms. X-rays revealed several slivers of glass that had to be removed before the wounds could be covered with a liquid bandage and then wrapped with gauze. Once Ali's feet were swathed in an outside layer of elastic bandage, it was time for the obligatory tetanus shot.

"I want a blood draw," Ali insisted. "They gave me something—blew a powder of some kind into my face—and I want to know what it was. I'll bet if they send a CSI team back to Gemma's house, they'll find traces of the same thing."

The doctor looked askance at the request but nodded. "Okay," she said. "You're the boss."

While Ali was hanging around in the ER, B. had arranged to rent a car, which was waiting outside when Ali, barefoot except for the bandages, was wheeled out of the building. She was grateful when B., seemingly effortlessly, picked her up and deposited her in the passenger seat.

"I also rented a hotel room at the Lake Mohave Resort," he explained. "I tried Laughlin, but they didn't have any rooms available. We can't go to the hotel just yet. First we need to visit the sheriff substation so you can talk to the detectives and answer some questions. By the way, about the phone Leland gave you, the one we supposedly used to find you?"

"You mean the phone that's currently in my bra?" Ali asked with a smile. "I'm pretty sure Barry and Molly Handraker thought I was only a one-phone girl. They missed that one completely."

"Thanks," B. said. "Stuart pulled out all the stops to find you, most of which could land all of us in very hot water. We're saying we found you using your device location from iCloud. If the phone's in your pocket when the detective asks about it, they probably won't give it a second thought. They'll assume it was with you the whole time."

"This sounds like a variation on 'Don't ask, don't tell,'" Ali observed.

B. nodded. "With the added advantage that none of us gets caught lying to a police officer."

34

As far as Lucy was concerned, it felt like a date. With the prospect of a whole free evening, she was carefree and lighthearted. Nana had the kids. She and Tommy were on their own with her new friend Doris safely stowed in the backseat of Tommy's Ford Explorer. The old woman sat dozing, her head resting against the closed window and her treasured photo album clutched tightly to her breast.

Tommy's friend in the state patrol had given him Doris's home phone number, but when they tried calling, no one answered. The original plan had been for Tommy and Lucy to retrieve Doris's car from the impound lot and tag-team it back to the house. The hitch in that program came along when the towing company required full payment and an impound fee before releasing the vehicle. Yes, a purse had been found in the abandoned Jaguar; yes, the photo ID clearly belonged to Doris Ralston. Unfortunately, of the several credit cards stashed in the old woman's wallet, there wasn't one that was valid. They had all been canceled.

"Okay, then," Tommy said. "We're not paying it.

Somebody who's driving around in a Jaguar can cough up towing charges a lot easier than we can. We'll just take her home and drop her off. After that, I'll take you to Applebee's for dinner."

Dinner together without the kids? Lucy thought. *What could be better?*

Seemingly worn out by her adventure at Burger King, Doris slept the whole way home.

"I still don't understand how she wound up on I-8," Tommy said. "If she was going to Palm Springs, like she said, why wasn't she on I-10?"

"She probably got confused at one of the freeway interchanges," Lucy said. "When they stack one road over another, it's easy to get mixed up."

The guy at the towing company had been kind enough to give them printed MapQuest directions to follow back to Doris's house. As they were going up the hill from Lincoln Drive, Doris sat up in the backseat. "Almost home," she said, looking around. "It's just a few more blocks."

Except when Tommy tried to turn off Upper Glen Road, they found the driveway blocked by a fire truck and an officer who told them they couldn't proceed.

"What is it?" Doris asked, alarm in her voice.

"There's been a fire, ma'am," the officer said. "No one's allowed on the property until after the fire investigators finish their work on the scene."

"But that's my house," Doris insisted. "I live there."

"I'm sorry to have to tell you this, ma'am. I'm afraid nobody lives there anymore. What was your name again?"

"Doris," she said firmly. "I'm Doris Ralston."

"Well, I'll be!" the officer exclaimed as a smile spread across his face. "If you're Doris, I need to call the detective right away. Everybody thought you were dead!"

Doris bristled at that. "As you can see, I'm not at all dead. Now, if you'll just get in touch with my daughter, we can straighten all this out."

Except it turned out that wasn't the least bit true. It was another hour before Tommy and Lucy were able to divest themselves of Doris and her problems.

"She told me she was scared of someone," Lucy told the detective who came to collect her. "She said she didn't want to go home. And she said something had been stolen."

"Yes, ma'am," the detective said. "We'll look into it."

It was almost ten o'clock by the time Lucy and Tommy stopped at Applebee's on their way out of town.

"Thank you for helping me with Doris," Lucy said. "A lot of guys wouldn't have bothered with a poor old woman like that."

"Yes," Tommy said with a grin. "I don't think your pal Richard from work would have lifted a finger."

"Are you kidding? That jerk was ready to call the cops on her for sitting in the booth and not buying food, like she was trespassing or something. But what's going to happen to her now?" Lucy worried. "With her house gone and her daughter missing, who's going to take care of her?"

"I don't know," Tommy said. "We did what we could. Now we need to look after us. What would you like to eat?"

"Anything at all," Lucy Ramirez told him with a smile, "just so long as it isn't a Whopper."

35

Dave came hurrying to meet them as Ali and B. limped into the substation's conference room. "How are you doing?" he asked.

"A lot better than I could have been," Ali said with a laugh.

"I've got a piece of good news for you," he said. "Several pieces, as a matter of fact. I just heard from Detective Carson at Phoenix PD. Doris Ralston has been found alive."

"Where?" Ali demanded.

"It seems she went AWOL in her own Jag. She was trying to drive to Palm Springs but ended up on I-8 instead of I-10. She ran out of gas. After walking away from her vehicle, she was given a ride into Gila Bend, where she spent the afternoon at a Burger King. One of the people there took pity on her and gave her a ride back home, where they discovered her house had been burned down."

"Does Chip Ralston know?"

"Yes," Dave said. "He does now, because I told him. Based on what we've learned tonight, I've notified Cap Horning that Dr. Ralston and

Lynn Martinson need to be released immediately. Shortly after you left the crime scene, a woman showed up looking for Barry Handraker. She had photo ID, including a passport, that said she was Molly Handraker. Only, as you already know, Molly Handraker is dead."

"He was two-timing Molly?" Ali asked.

"I'm sure she had no idea. Fortunately for us, the faux Molly has been in here talking her head off. She says she's been living with Barry in Vegas the whole time Molly has been in Phoenix looking after her mother. It sounds like they've been systematically stripping everything of value out of the house and pawning what they could. They've also moved most of Doris Ralston's considerable funds to a bank in Belize. That's one of the few countries where you can still open an offshore bank account without showing up."

"With Molly gone, Barry and Faux Molly go to Belize and live off the fat of the land while Chip rots in jail charged for a homicide that Barry and the real Molly Handraker committed."

"I'm guessing Chip had no idea that they were systematically stripping everything of value out of his mother's life."

Dave nodded. "True," he said. "I already asked him."

"Why bother to drag me halfway across the state to kill me?" Ali asked.

"Doris was supposed to die in the fire," Dave said. "That was the plan from the beginning. It was going to be a grease fire caused by her cooking something on the stove. I'm not sure how a fire could have gotten that far without an alarm going off . . ."

"The alarms had all been disconnected," Ali

said. "Molly told me so. She said they'd had to shut them off due to too many false alarms."

"So the first fly in the ointment was Doris taking off on her own. The second one was you showing up and asking questions about some missing necklace."

Ali nodded. "The same necklace that got Gemma killed."

"Barry couldn't afford to leave you behind," Dave explained. "He decided to bring you along. Faux Molly said that Barry told her their car, Doris's S550, had broken down and that if she'd come pick him up, he'd fix it so it looked like you and the real Molly got into a gun fight and shot each other. Fortunately for all of us, that didn't happen, either."

Ali thought about what she'd been told. "If they've been stripping out the valuables and assets, that means they've been working this gig for a long time. Months. Probably since Doris's husband died."

"Most likely since before James Ralston died," Dave corrected grimly. "Faux Molly tells us that the elder Dr. Ralston was given a bit of a chemical boost on his way out. Barry is a former pharmacist. He'd know how to pull something like that off without arousing suspicion, and since James Ralston was in a hospital and under a doctor's care, they could be relatively certain no postmortem would be done, especially in view of the fact that a proper DNR was posted in James Ralston's room."

"Contemptible people," Ali muttered. "Truly contemptible."

"Yes," Dave agreed. "Scary people. Greedy people, and picking on someone who's mentally deficient like that . . ." He shook his head.

"She may not be," Ali said.

"What do you mean?"

"I think they've been dosing her with low levels of the same drug they gave me and most likely Gemma Ralston as well."

"If they've been dosing her all along, that's probably one reason why Molly was so adamant about keeping Chip away from their mother."

Ali nodded. "He might have recognized that her confusion was something other than what they were pretending it was, namely Alzheimer's."

"I'll let him know," Dave said. "Tell him that he should probably have his mother checked out."

"Earlier, you said you had several pieces of good news," Ali pointed out. "What else?"

"Oh, that kid you were worried about—the one with the strongbox full of gambling chips."

"A. J. Sanders? What about him?"

"He's in the clear. A woman walked into the North Las Vegas Police Department this afternoon and turned herself in. Said she was the one who killed James Sanders."

"What woman?"

"Abigail Mattson."

"The executive director of the Mission?"

"That's the one. She claimed that she and James Sanders had a thing going, and he knew what a struggle she was having keeping the place afloat. Recently, when he came into a bunch of money, he gave her a chunk of it to help out. It pissed her off that, instead of using his windfall to grubstake her pet project, he decided to give the lion's share of it to his kid.

"That was when the whole thing went deadly. Abigail admitted to putting a GPS device—an illegal one—on his car, in hopes of grabbing the money before he dropped it off. Fortunately for Sanders's son, James beat her to the punch. She also said she planted the murder weapon at A.J.'s house to implicate him, but when one of the cops in Las Vegas started asking too many questions, she crumbled. A.J. said Gemma Ralston mentioned someone named Dennis just before she died. We're trying to sort out if he's an associate of Barry and Molly's."

"I'll bet he isn't," Ali said. "I'll bet he doesn't exist. Gemma was drunk out of her head the night she died. Between the booze and whatever drug they gave her, I'll bet playing tennis with Molly is the last thing she remembered. Tennis/Dennis."

"Makes sense," Dave said. "But for the time being, we'll keep looking for him, just in case."

Ali leaned back in her chair and closed her eyes. The doctor had given her something for the pain, and she was starting to feel drowsy. "You're right," Ali said at last. "That's all good news."

"It's good for me, too." Dave grinned. "The county attorney has been going after Sheriff Maxwell in a big way. One of his metrics is our closure rate, which has taken a big step up today. I think you could say the Yavapai County Sheriff's Department is currently batting a thousand."

"Does A.J. get to keep the money?"

"As far as I can tell. There's one more thing you probably haven't heard. I finally got James Sanders's autopsy results today. The official one. Two weeks ago he got a cancer diagnosis—pancreatic, stage four. Scott Ballentine had stayed in touch with him. Said he owed James a huge debt for taking the fall on that counterfeiting rap years ago. Ballentine said he had told James over the years that he had more money than sense, and if there was ever anything he could do for him, to let him know."

"Let me guess," Ali said. "He took him up on it exactly twice—once a year ago, so he could get A.J. a car for his sixteenth birthday, and again last week, so the kid could have money to go to school."

"You're pretty smart for a girl," Dave said. They were both laughing when the door to the interview room swung open. A plainclothes cop came out, escorting a lush blonde who looked to be fifteen years younger than the real Molly Handraker.

"We've got a name on this one now," the cop said, speaking mostly to Dave. "Candace Kestral. We've got a car outside that's going to transport her to the jail in Kingman. If you have questions for Ms. Kestral, that's where she'll be. We've been in touch with Las Vegas PD. Turns out that earlier this evening, someone contacted an outfit called *Minnesota's Most Wanted* with an anonymous tip, letting them know that Barry Handraker, one of their top fugitives, was living it up in a unit at Turnberry Towers. It turns out Ms. Kestral lives there, too. Las Vegas PD was in the process of obtaining a search warrant when all hell broke loose over here. Turns out Handraker has been on the lam for months, but they got the tip and we got Handraker at almost the same time. Odd how it all came together, isn't it?"

Dave Holman glanced in B.'s direction and then turned back to the other detective. "It's odd, all right," he agreed.

The Mohave County detective examined Ali,

taking in her torn and bloodied clothing as well as the bandages on her feet. "Today's kidnapping victim, I assume?" he asked.

"One and the same," Dave said. "Her name's Alison Reynolds."

"Very good," the detective said to Ali. "Just let me get this one sent off to the slammer, Ms. Reynolds. I'll be right back to take statements—Mr. Brooks's statement first and then yours. Do you need anything while you're waiting? Something to eat or drink? It's not too late to order pizza."

Until he said that, Ali hadn't thought about being either hungry or thirsty, but she realized she was famished. "Pizza sounds good."

"What kind?" the detective asked.

Now it was B.'s turn to interject. "When it comes to pizza and the lady, there's only one kind, and that's pepperoni."

There was a considerable delay before the detective reappeared. While he was out of the room and they waited for the pizza delivery, Ali went over to the couch, where Leland Brooks was sitting apart from the others.

"While we were in the ER, B. told me what you did," she said. "That he had asked you to bring him the phone, but you insisted on coming along. To hear him tell it, you practically hijacked the helicopter to be allowed on board."

"I wasn't about to be left out of all the excitement," Leland said. "When we saw the situation on the ground, I told Mr. Simpson that it made sense for me to be the one dropped off to make contact with the enemy. After all, I've had some actual training in hand-to-hand combat. I'm afraid

Mr. Simpson's experience is more of the video-game variety, which is good as far as it goes, but when it comes time for cracking heads, I say go for someone who understands how to get the job done."

Pizza and sodas came and disappeared. It was almost two o'clock in the morning before Ali finished giving her statement. B. had asked the helicopter to hang around long enough to give Leland Brooks and Dave Holman a lift back to Sedona. Only after they flew away did Ali and B. head for the barn.

The room in the Lake Mohave Resort was far humbler than the one in the suite in the Ritz-Carlton in Phoenix, but the king-size bed was spacious, the sheets were clean, and the nonsmoking room smelled fresh. Even had the room not been comfortable, it was unlikely Ali Reynolds would have noticed.

She was far too intent on cuddling up to the warmth of B. Simpson's long bare back and falling fast asleep.

36

When Ali awakened the next morning, her body felt like it had taken a beating.

"It did," B. said when she complained to him about it over breakfast in the resort's dining room. "After a day spent throwing yourself into ditches, dragging yourself through piles of broken glass, and spending hours crammed in a trunk? I'm surprised you can walk."

"You know what was nice about that whole thing?" Ali asked.

"What?"

"Bullhead City is the end of the known universe as far as the media is concerned. No reporters."

"You're right," B. agreed. "Considering High Noon's somewhat illicit involvement, I think it's advantageous."

They drove B.'s Enterprise rental back home to Sedona, taking their time. When they got as far as Williams, B. turned off and headed for the Grand Canyon.

"Why?" Ali wanted to know.

"Because I want to," B. said. "Because yesterday, while you were out risking life and limb, I was figuring out what was important. I almost lost you, Ali. It's one way of getting a guy's undivided attention. So now I've got some debts to repay, except they're mostly not repayable."

"Stuart Ramey, for one?" Ali asked.

"Yup," B. said. "You've got it. He went way out on a limb yesterday, and if it hadn't been for his working like crazy in the background, there's no way we would have found you in time for Leland Brooks to knock Barry Handraker senseless before he managed to finish you off."

"What are you going to do about it?"

"You mean what are *we* going to do about it?" B. asked. "Stu's already earning top dollar. I'll no doubt give him another raise, but what's he going to do to enjoy it? The man spends his whole life—morning, noon, and night—sitting in front of a computer screen. I asked him, if he could go anywhere on the planet, where would it be? And guess what? He said he's always wanted to go to Paris, to the Louvre. So I'm sending him on a compulsory vacation. Three weeks. First class. All expenses paid."

"Does Stuart speak French?" Ali asked.

"Not a word, so I'll be making arrangements for him to have his own personal guide."

There was another short pause. "Let me guess," Ali said. "The next debt is to Leland Brooks."

"Yup. Big-time."

"What's your idea there?"

"You told me about his invitation to that family reunion. I can understand after so many years of being separated from his family, his reluctance for the initial contact to be at a huge cattle-call family event that has the potential for turning into an over-the-top circus. So how about if, sometime between now and Christmas, you use my frequent-flier miles and take him across the pond? That way he'll have you there to rent a car and do the driving. I have it on good authority that UK car-rental companies won't rent to anyone his age, so he'll have a nonfamily member there to run interference for him. If his relatives turn out to be a bunch of homophobic bigots, you can drag him out of the fray and bring him home."

Ali nodded. "And making contact now will put him in a lot better place to decide whether he's going to the family reunion come next summer."

"Exactly," B. said.

They fell quiet after that, lost in their own thoughts. Ali was thinking about how, the previous day, B. and Stuart Ramey had risked everything they had worked for over the years in order to save her from what was, essentially, a bit of her own foolishness. She never should have gone to see a homicide suspect on her own. But B. and Stuart had stepped up. Together they had put everything on the line. Yes, Stuart had been the one with his fingers on the keyboard, but he had done it with B.'s full knowledge and encouragement.

Given all of that, her previous objections to marrying B. Simpson seemed downright petty. *Maybe,* she thought, *after turning him down so many times, I'll have to do the proposing.*

Those were the thoughts running through her head as they headed north toward the Grand Canyon, but she didn't say any of them aloud. When they got to Bright Angel Lodge, Ali was surprised to learn that on this supposedly spur-of-the-moment side trip, they had a luncheon reservation. As B. helped her from the car to the door, Ali worried that her bandaged bare feet would consign them to the "no shoes no service" side of the universe. It didn't happen. Their reserved table next to the restaurant's massive windows gave them a spectacular and unobstructed view of the canyon.

When it came time for dessert, Ali tried to turn it down, but B. insisted on sharing a slice of pumpkin cheesecake. Halfway through, Ali's fork ran into something surprisingly solid. When she pulled out the offending item, it turned out to be an amazing diamond solitaire.

"How did you manage this?" she asked, dipping the ring in her water glass and rubbing it clean with her napkin.

"I already had the ring picked out," B. admitted. "I called the jeweler in Flagstaff first thing this morning and asked him to drive it over. I was going to give it to you for Christmas, but that's too far away. Yesterday I almost lost you. I couldn't believe how much it hurt. If you had ended up in a hospital somewhere, badly hurt or dying, I wouldn't even have had the right to see you. Please marry me, Ali. It's time."

For a moment she didn't answer him. She was too busy fussing with the ring. When it was properly dried, she slipped it on her finger.

"You're right," she said. "It is time."

"So that's a yes?"

"Yes," she said with a smile, leaning over to give him a light peck on the cheek. "That's definitely a yes."

Afterword

By the time they got home that evening, they had decided on and arranged for a Christmas Eve wedding in Las Vegas. Stuart Ramey would be the best man. Sister Anselm would be the matron of honor. The twins, Colin and Colleen, would be ring bearer and flower girl, respectively.

Back at home, still feeling more than a little stiff, Ali put her Googling skills to work and located Scott Ballentine at his office in Newport Beach, California. She used the old freelancer ruse to get past the corporate gatekeepers.

"You've heard what happened?" she asked once Ballentine knew who she was and why she was calling.

"Yes," he said. "I heard he was murdered, and most likely over the money. Jimmy told me he was ill and that he didn't have much time, but I feel sick about it. I don't know what I should do. I thought about sending Sylvia and A.J. a sympathy card, but I'm not sure how it would be received."

"Let me make a suggestion," Ali said. "Sylvia called late last night. They're going to have a private service at a funeral home in Phoenix on Monday of next week. She invited me to come, and I'm inviting you."

"You don't think she'll throw me out?"

"No," Ali said. "I think she'll be glad to see you, and I think A.J. will be delighted to meet one of his father's friends."

"I'm willing," Scott Ballentine said. "But do me a favor. Check with Sylvia first. Make sure it's okay with her. I'd rather not be an unwelcome surprise."

Which was how, on Monday of the following week, Ali and B. accompanied Scott Ballentine to James Sanders's very small and very private funeral. Among the twenty or so people in attendance, Ali was introduced to several, including A.J.'s vivacious girlfriend, Sasha, her parents, and her three sisters; Maddy Worth, Sylvia's lifelong friend and A.J.'s boss; two of A.J.'s teachers from school; and a number of people from Sylvia's workplace. When Ali introduced Scott Ballentine to Sylvia, she didn't hesitate. She grabbed the man, hugged him, and said, "Thank you. I thought all of James's friends deserted him. I'm so glad you didn't."

In those few words, Ali heard a world of forgiveness.

Beatrice Hart had sent Ali a message asking her to stop by, and after the funeral was the first opportunity to make that visit.

When Ali rang the bell, Lynn Martinson was the one who answered. She smiled broadly as soon as she saw Ali and B. standing there. "Hey, Mom," she called over her shoulder. "I believe the woman of the hour has arrived. Come on in. Mom's making spaghetti. You'll never guess who's coming to dinner."

"Who?"

"Chip and his mother."

"How is Doris?"

"Amazingly better," Lynn said. "I know about the Alzheimer's now. But it turns out you were right. Molly had been dosing her with scopolamine for months, so her Alzheimer's hasn't progressed nearly as far as Chip feared. Her big problem right now is dealing with her husband's death. Now that she's detoxed, she's having to deal with the grief of losing him. She's also grieving for Molly and Gemma and her beloved house. It's tough. My heart goes out to her."

"Chip's helping her with all that?" Ali asked.

Lynn nodded. "He's got an attorney working on dragging the money back from Belize. He's also made some progress on retrieving some of Doris's keepsakes, things that were stolen and pawned."

"The missing necklace, for instance?"

"Yes," Lynn said. "That was one of the first items he found. He isn't as focused on getting back things like oil paintings and china, because there won't be any place to put them. He's taking the insurance settlement on the house and using some of that to move Doris into an upscale assisted-living place that specializes in the care of Alzheimer's patients. There are gradually increasing levels of assistance, so as Doris's symptoms worsen, she won't have to move on to some other place."

Beatrice came into the living room, wiping her hands on an apron and beaming. "There's going to be plenty of food," she said. "Would you like to stay for dinner?"

"No, thank you," Ali said. "We told people we'd be back home for dinner. We're having company."

That's a white lie, Ali thought. *Leland is only expecting us, and he's grilling lamb chops for two.* "Let's get the official business out of the way," she added, holding out a file folder.

"Your written report?" Beatrice asked.

Ali nodded.

"Excellent," Beatrice said. "The check is written and waiting."

She bustled over to a nearby table and retrieved a personal check. It was made out to the Amelia Dougherty Scholarship Fund in the amount of ten thousand dollars.

Ali looked at it and attempted to hand it back. "Thank you, but this is far too generous."

"No, it's not," Beatrice Hart said with a smile. "You gave me back my daughter. You also gave Lynn back her shot at happiness. As far as I can see, I'm still in your debt, and I'll probably be making another contribution next year."

"Thank you, then," Ali said. "I thank you, and lots of deserving students will be thanking you as well."

Ali and B. left soon after that. "Yes," B. said as he buckled up and put his new Audi R8 4.2 in gear. "Dave Holman got it right the other night."

"Dave got what right?"

"When he said you're not bad for a girl."

Ali reached over and gave B. a playful whack on the shoulder. "And you're not bad for a boy," she said. "So I guess that makes us even."

Turn the page
for a sneak peek
at the next novel from
New York Times bestselling author
J.A. JANCE

MOVING TARGET

Coming soon from Touchstone

PROLOGUE

Lance Tucker had always hated ladders, but between climbing up and down a ladder in the recreation hall and sitting through another one of Mrs. Stone's endless GED classes, there was no contest. Climbing the rickety ladder to decorate the nine-foot Christmas tree was definitely the lesser of two evils.

Lance was five months into a six-month sentence at the San Leandro County Juvenile Detention Facility in the hill country some fifty miles northwest of Austin. All his life he had hated having a December birthday—hated having whatever he was getting for his birthday and for Christmas lumped into a single gift that never measured up to what other kids got. This year, though, his December 18 birthday meant that he'd be out in time for Christmas—out and able to go home. The problem with that, of course, was that he might not have a home to go to.

The last time he'd seen his mother, on visiting day two weeks ago, she had told him that she was probably going to lose the house. She'd finally admitted to him that she'd had to take out a second mortgage in order to pay the king's ransom in court-ordered restitution. Now that her hours had been cut back at work, she wasn't able to keep up the payments on both mortgages, which meant that most likely the house would go into foreclosure.

That was all his fault, too. Ears reddening with shame, Lance climbed down the ladder, moved it a few inches toward the next undecorated section of branches, picked up another tray of decorations, and clambered back up.

Don't think about it, he told himself firmly. What was it the counselor kept saying? Don't waste your time worrying about things you can't change.

This definitely fell into the category of stuff that couldn't be changed. What's done was done.

He heard a burst of laughter from the classroom. It was just off the dining room. The kids were probably giving Mrs. Stone hell again. He felt sorry for her. She seemed like a nice enough person, and he knew she was genuinely trying to help them. But what she was offering—course work leading up to earning a GED—wasn't at all what Lance wanted. It had never been part of what he had envisioned as his own future.

Less than a year ago—just last spring—he'd had a promising future. As a high school junior honor student at San Leandro High, Lance had been enrolled in three Advanced Placement classes and had done well on his SATs, coming in with a respectable 1540. With the help of his beloved math teacher, Mr. Jackson, Lance had also been preparing to lead his computer science club team to their third championship in a row for that year's Longhorn Computer Science Competition.

Now his life had changed, and not for the better. Mr. Jackson was dead. Lance's mother had told him that San Leandro High had won the Longhorn trophy after all, but they had done so without Lance's help because someone else was now the team captain. As for doing his senior year in the top 10 percent of his class and wearing whatever he wanted to school? Instead, Lance found himself locked up twenty-four hours a day and wearing an orange jumpsuit. Rather than being able to take advantage of the college scholarship the state of Texas routinely offers to kids in the top 10 percent of their respective classes, Lance was now considered to be a high school dropout with an institution-earned GED as his best possible educational outcome. No matter what his SAT score said, getting into Texas A&M or any college anywhere else with only a lowly GED to his credit wasn't going to work.

The problem was that the GED class was the only one offered inside the facility. Some of the other kids were able to take online classes, but since Lance's sentence stipulated no computer and no Internet access, those classes weren't accessible to him. His court-mandated restrictions made the GED route the only one available. It was also boring as hell.

Lance had looked at the questions on the sample test. He already knew he could ace the thing in a heartbeat without having to sit though another dreary minute of class. Mrs. Stone probably understood that as well as he did. That was why she had let him out of class yesterday and today. That way he got to deal with the Christmas tree issue, and she got to look after the dummies. Not that his classmates were really dumb, at least not all of them. Several of the guys spoke no English. He suspected that several of them probably had issues with dyslexia. One of those, a fifteen-year-old kid named Jason who couldn't read at all, filled his books with caricatures of Mrs. Stone. The pencil drawings were realistic enough that you could tell who it was. They were also unrealistic in that Mrs. Stone was usually pictured nude, and not in a nice way.

All of which left Lance dealing with the Christmas tree. It was big and came in four separate pieces. It was also at least ten years old, according to Mr. Dunn, the grizzled old black man who was in charge of maintenance at the facility. He was the one who had enlisted Lance's help to drag the tree as well as the boxes of decorations out of storage.

"No money for a new tree," Mr. Dunn said. "Not in the budget, but at least I got us some new lights. By the time we took the tree down last year, half the lights had quit working. We'll have to restring it before we put it up."

That part of the project had taken the better part of a day. First they removed the old strings of lights. Then they took the new ones out of their boxes and wound them into the branches, carefully positioning the plug ends of each string close enough to the metal tree trunk so that all of the lights could easily be fastened together once the pieces were dropped into place. It was time-consuming, tedious work, but Lance liked the careful way Mr. Dunn went about it—his methodical system of testing each new string of lights before letting Lance take them out of the box.

"No sense in putting on a defective string of lights that won't light up the first time you plug it in," Mr. Dunn muttered under his breath.

The way Mr. Dunn talked as he worked, more to himself than to anyone else, reminded Lance of Grandpa Frank, his father's father back in Arizona. Lance missed Grandpa Frank, but his grandfather along with his entire collection of aunts, uncles, and cousins had all disappeared when his parents got a divorce. It wasn't fair. Just because parents couldn't get along shouldn't mean that the poor kids involved had to lose everybody.

Lance's favorite memory of Grandpa Frank was going with him to the state fair in Phoenix where he ate so much cotton candy that he ended up getting sick on the Ferris wheel. The attendant had given him hell while cleaning up the mess. At the time, Lance had been beyond embarrassed, but Grandpa Frank had just laughed it off.

"Look," he said. "Crap happens. You just clean up your own mess, tell the world to piss off, and get on with your life. You want some more cotton candy?"

Lance had not wanted any more cotton candy. Ever. And he wished he'd been able to talk to

Grandpa Frank after he got into trouble. His advice probably would have been a lot like some of the things the counselor said, only a lot more colorful. Unfortunately, sometime between the divorce and now, Grandpa Frank had dropped dead of a heart attack or maybe a stroke. Lance didn't know for sure. If his parents had been able to talk to each other, Lance might have had more information—might even have been able to go back to Phoenix for the funeral. But that hadn't happened. Grandpa Frank was gone without Lance even being able to say goodbye.

"You gonna hand me another string of them lights?" Mr. Dunn asked. "Or are you just gonna stand there all day staring into space?"

Jarred out of his Grandpa Frank reverie, Lance fumbled another string of lights out of a box and plugged it into the outlet. The new one lit right up, just as they all had, but as Mr. Dunn said, "Better safe than sorry."

"I didn't know artificial trees could be so much trouble," Lance remarked.

"They are if you think you can keep 'em forever," Mr. Dunn replied, "but with budgets as tight as they are, we were lucky to get the new lights."

When the tree was finally upright and glowing with hundreds of brand-new multicolored lights, Mr. Dunn studied it for a moment and then shook his head.

"Tomorrow's my day off. Ms. Stone tells me you're gonna be the one putting on the decorations."

Lance shrugged. "Fine with me," he said.

"Before I go tonight, I'll leave everything you

need in the closet next to my office, and I'll make sure the guy who comes in tomorrow knows what's what. The flocking's looking pretty sorry these days. I got us some glitter and some glue. Before you put on the decorations, spray some glue on the tree and toss some glitter on it. It's supposed to make it look a little better."

"Okay," Lance said. "Will do."

Mr. Dunn turned to him then. "You seem like a good kid," he said. "Not like some of them other ornery ones. What the hell are you doing here?"

Lance bit his lip. That was the whole problem—he was a good kid. He should never have been locked up here in the first place, but he didn't want to go into it, not with this old man.

"Long story," Lance said.

Mr. Dunn shook his head sadly. "Aren't they all!" he said.

Which brought Lance to the next day when he was working on his own. Marvin Cotton, one of the guards, had opened the door to the closet next to Mr. Dunn's office. Had Mr. Dunn been there, he for sure would have helped him carry all the stuff into the rec room. Marvin was only a couple of years older than Lance. The guy was thick-necked, stupid, and surly, and probably didn't have a college degree, either. He wandered in and out of the rec room from time to time to check on things without saying a word or even nodding in Lance's direction. But then there were plenty of guards who acted like that—who treated the prisoners as something less than human.

Rather than worry about Marvin, Lance concentrated on the tree. For as long as he could remember, decorating Christmas trees had been high on his list of favorite things to do. Not this time. At home, they always had live trees, although his mother usually bought them late on Christmas Eve, when they were already marked down and cheap. That meant that the trees they had were the rejects—scrawny, uneven, and downright ugly. But his mom made sure all four of them always did the decorating together—Lance, his mom, and his two younger brothers, Connor and Thad. Connor was only six and he still believed in Santa Claus. Lance and Thad no longer had that option. Still, at home, decorating the tree was a joyous occasion with laughter and joking around and plenty of popcorn and homemade cookies. Here, although it was a solitary chore, it was still preferable to suffering through the agonies of Mrs. Stone's class.

A few people besides Marvin had come and gone while Lance worked, so he didn't turn to look when the metal door clicked open behind him. Instead, intent on having lost the wire hanger to one of the Christmas balls, he was staring into the tree branch trying to find it when he heard an unexpected hissing from the glue can he had left on the table with the other decorations. Just as quickly, he felt the cold on his legs as the aerosol spray landed on them. He glanced down then.

"Hey!" he demanded. "What the hell do you think you're doing?"

All he could see below him was a hand holding one of the spray cans of glue. Then a second hand came into his line of vision. It took a moment for it to register in his brain that what he was seeing in the second hand was a cigarette lighter. Lance had time enough to register the flash of flame from the lighter, then the air around him seemed to catch fire. Writhing in pain, he attempted to pat out the flames on his legs. That was enough to tip the shaky ladder. The next thing Lance knew, he was falling and burning.

Mercifully, for a long time after that, he remembered nothing.